THE QUEEN'S GAMBIT

IRINA SHAPIRO

Storm

PUBLISHING

Ebook ISBN: 978-1-80508-152-4
Paperback ISBN: 978-1-80508-153-1

Previously published in 2016 by Merlin Press LLC.

Cover design: Debbie Clement
Cover images: Shutterstock

Published by Storm Publishing.
For further information, visit:
www.stormpublishing.co

ALSO BY IRINA SHAPIRO

Wonderland Series

The Passage

Wonderland

Sins of Omission

The Queen's Gambit

Comes the Dawn

ONE

Rouen, France

"I want Mama," came the desperate wail from downstairs. "I want Mama now!"

It was well past midnight, but Valentine was wide awake, sensing, as children often do, that something wasn't quite right. Her piercing voice shook with desperation and fear, a sure sign that tears weren't far behind. I couldn't hear what Hugo said to her, but the sound of his baritone carried up the stairs and gave me momentary comfort before another contraction rolled over me and I forgot about everything but the pain that had me in its grip.

Despite the cold temperature outside, the room was stifling, with a fire burning high and all the windows tightly shut and shuttered against the night. My forehead was beaded with sweat, and my shift stuck to my overheated skin, the thin fabric damp and clingy. I tried to breathe through the contraction, but the air in the room was stale and overly warm.

"Open the window," I panted. "I can't breathe."

"The night air is bad for your health," Madame Duvall answered patiently.

The local midwife was in her sixties, like Sister Angela who'd delivered Frances's baby, but the similarities ended there. She was rail-thin, with wide gray eyes, and dark-brown hair which was scraped off her face and covered by a plain linen cap. She still had most of her teeth, and her face was surprisingly unlined for a woman of her years, possibly from lack of smiling. She was utterly devoid of the motherly touch that Sister Angela exuded, but she was competent. Village lore had it that most women survived childbirth under Madame Duvall's care, unlike the staggering fifty percent who died, which was the statistic of the day.

"You are almost there, milady," Madame Duvall informed me coolly.

Her stern presence was balanced out by Frances, who insisted on staying with me despite the objections of Madame Duvall, who felt that there should be no distractions during the birth. Frances talked to me softly and reassured me when I needed it, and just sat quietly and held my hand when I couldn't summon the strength to utter another word.

She wrung out a cloth and wiped my face, making me feel momentarily cooler. "You heard Madame Duvall; you are almost there," Frances said soothingly as she held the damp cloth to my forehead. She was wearing an old smock, and her hair was tied back with a kerchief, but she still looked as angelic as ever, her eyes full of warmth and compassion.

But almost there wasn't good enough. I was so tired—so very tired. I'd been in labor for more than twenty-four hours now and had used up my last reserve of energy a few hours ago, but the baby still hadn't come. I hadn't eaten anything, and had been given very little to drink, since Madame Duvall felt that digestion would interfere with birth and require the use of the chamber pot, which was unseemly during labor. She allowed me half a cup of water every hour—just enough to keep me hydrated. My body felt depleted and battered from pain and lack of nourishment.

According to the midwife, who used her fingers to check for dilation, I was progressing very slowly, about a centimeter every few hours. This labor was vastly different from the first one. Valentine had been born within a few hours and slid out with the minimum of fuss. I thought I was dying at the time, and only had Archie for a midwife, but compared to what I had endured since the previous evening, it had been a walk in the park.

My body seemed to have changed since Valentine was born, and whereas my cycle used to be like clockwork, it was now erratic, and there had been a few false alarms before I finally became pregnant. I thought I'd been prepared for it—physically and mentally—but I was wrong. I am not sure why, but I thought that the second pregnancy was meant to be easier, but it had been quite the reverse. I'd suffered from severe morning sickness, which had lasted well into my second trimester, and could barely keep anything down other than broth, bread, and the occasional cup of milk.

I no longer had any prenatal vitamins, nor was I consuming enough of a variety of foods to guarantee that my baby was getting proper nutrition, which was something that worried me constantly. I was always tired, the fatigue sometimes so crippling that I needed to stay in bed for days at a time. When out of bed, my back ached, my ankles were swollen, and I waddled breathlessly around the house since the baby seemed to be pushing against my diaphragm and preventing me from taking deep breaths. I was suffering, but the baby seemed to be thriving. My belly was much larger than it had been with Valentine. It was always heaving, as if the child within was frustrated by the confines of my womb and wanted to get out before its time. And now that it was time, it refused to leave.

I briefly worried that the child was too large because I might be suffering from gestational diabetes, but there was no way to know, and anyway, a modern doctor would have most likely told me to augment my diet. I was barely eating anything as it was, so there wasn't too much I could do.

"It's time to push, milady," the midwife said as she positioned herself between my legs, ready to receive the baby. She gave Frances a dirty look as the girl got into position behind me to offer support, but Frances completely ignored her and wrapped her arms around me.

I took a deep breath and gathered whatever shreds of strength I had left and bore down. Nothing happened.

"Again."

I pushed for what seemed like hours before the baby finally slithered out of my body, its furious cry filling the house. I slumped back against the pillows as soon as Frances carefully got off the bed, unable to keep my eyes open a moment longer. It was alive; that was all I needed to know. I only needed a few moments to rest, I told myself as I drifted off.

I vaguely heard the pounding of boots on the stairs, Valentine's shrill voice, and the opening of a door, but I couldn't force myself to open my eyes.

"Is Mama sick?" Valentine asked, her voice shaking with fear.

"No, darling; Mama is just tired," Frances replied soothingly. "Come with me and let your papa visit Mama. It will make her feel better."

"Noooo, I want to stay here," Valentine wailed, but I heard her giggle a moment later as Archie scooped her up and twirled her around. She loved that. I heard his deep voice singing to her as he carried her away.

The bed sagged as Hugo sat down next to me, his cool hand on my cheek.

"Is my wife all right?" he asked the midwife. He sounded frightened, poor man.

I wanted to tell him that all was well but couldn't bring myself out of my stupor. I seemed to be floating somewhere above the bed, completely disconnected from my body, which felt as heavy and unwieldy as a sack of potatoes.

"She's fine, milord, just very tired. It was a difficult labor, and a long one." Madame Duvall's voice sounded deferential as she addressed Hugo. He was nobility; someone Madame Duvall considered to be one of her betters. She didn't seem to feel the same way about me since she'd learned through local gossip that I was only a noblewoman by marriage and not through distinguished lineage. "Would you like to see your daughter?"

The word brought me to my senses. I pried open my eyes to see Hugo opening his arms to receive the squirming bundle from the midwife. A tiny hand freed itself from the blanket and grabbed his finger.

"I'm sorry, Hugo," I mumbled. "I know how much you wanted a boy."

"I couldn't be happier," he replied as he bent down to kiss the baby's fuzzy head. "She's perfect."

I smiled inwardly. A little girl. A healthy little girl.

I began to shake violently, my body suddenly releasing the tension of the past hours. I hadn't realized how scared I was, thinking that the baby had died inside me. She was alive and healthy. That was all that mattered. We had both survived, which in this day and age was a miracle in itself.

Hugo handed the baby back to Madame Duvall and pulled me to him very carefully. "You did so well," he whispered as he kissed the top of my head. "You've earned your rest. Go to sleep and don't worry about a thing."

"It hurts," I moaned, suddenly aware of the pain building in my belly and spreading to my back.

"Is something wrong?" Hugo asked Madame Duvall as she rushed over to the bed.

"No, milord, it's only the afterbirth. Quite normal."

"Ooooh," I moaned as the pain grew stronger. "It really hurts."

I could hear Hugo's sharp intake of breath as he wiped my brow with a cool towel.

"I think you should leave now, milord," the midwife advised respectfully as she deposited the baby into a waiting cradle and turned to examine me. "A gentleman shouldn't have to see this."

"I'm not going anywhere. Do what you must."

I gasped as Madame Duvall slid her fingers inside me, the battered flesh screaming in protest at this unwelcome intrusion. She sucked in her breath as my body clamped down around her hand, an unbearable pain gripping me once again. What was happening? Why was my body still contracting? I was so exhausted, I couldn't take any more.

"*Mon Dieu*, there's one more," Madame Duvall exclaimed, her stern face transformed by surprise.

"What?" Hugo and I asked in unison.

"And it's coming fast. Push, milady."

I grabbed Hugo's hand and squeezed until he gasped with pain. I was crushing his fingers as I bore down, desperate for something to hold on to. My complacency of only a moment ago was replaced with a determination born out of fear. I had to get this baby out. An irrational fear gripped me, whispering into my ear that the baby was dead, and that was the reason no one had realized I'd been carrying twins. Of course, without a sonogram, no one would have been able to tell for sure, but an experienced midwife would have heard the second heartbeat through her wooden stethoscope and would have felt the additional limbs when palpating my stomach.

"Sorry," I grunted as I slumped back against the pillows for a moment's respite.

"Squeeze as hard as you need to," Hugo replied as he

gripped my hand and put his other arm around my shoulders for support.

"Push, milady," the midwife insisted, having regained her composure. She didn't seem like the type of woman who was often caught off guard. "Now!"

I gathered what was left of my strength and gave one final push as the baby slid out right into the waiting hands of Madame Duvall. My lips were dry and sweat stung my eyes. I tried to speak, but my throat was raw from hours of screaming, and my voice seemed to have deserted me.

"Is it alive?" I whispered. The baby wasn't crying, confirming my worst suspicions. A jolt of adrenaline shot through me, giving me the strength to sit up. "Is it alive?" I cried hoarsely.

I could only see Madame Duvall's narrow back as she bent over the child.

Hugo sat frozen beside me, his eyes fixed on the midwife, his hand still gripping mine.

It seemed like an eternity, but it must have been less than a minute before the baby let out a squeal.

"Very much alive," the midwife said as she cleaned the baby and wrapped it in a towel, since there'd only been one blanket ready. "And very much a boy."

"A boy," Hugo whispered, his voice full of awe. "A son."

Madame Duvall didn't even bother to spare me a glance as she handed Hugo the child. Her face beamed with pride, as if she were the one who had just given birth to a son and heir, but I wasn't bothered by her attitude. Silent tears of relief and joy coursed down my face. He was alive; that was all I cared about. And a boy.

Hugo gazed in wonder at the little face which looked red and furious among the folds of the towel. The baby scrunched up his face, but seemed to change his mind about crying and opened his eyes instead. Father and son stared at each other silently as they sowed the seeds of their bond.

I slumped against the pillows and closed my eyes. I was still exhausted, and very thirsty, but a warm glow seemed to spread through me, making me feel almost euphoric. I had delivered two healthy children this night, and lived. No woman felt more blessed.

TWO

By the time I finally woke up, the sun was streaming through the leaded windows, casting a golden haze onto the polished surfaces of the furniture and dispelling the gloom of the long night. My limbs felt heavy, and there was a painful soreness between my legs, rivaled only by the ache in my swollen breasts. Blue veins showed under the skin like rivers on a map, and damp patches appeared on the front of my not-so-fresh shift.

I wanted to wash, but Madame Duvall shook her head in disapproval as she pulled aside the bed hangings. The stern look of last night was gone, replaced by one of relief. Perhaps she wasn't as unfeeling as I first thought, her demeanor caused by anxiety for the mother in her charge and her child.

"It's time to feed your babies, milady," she said. "But, first, you must eat something."

I wolfed down several slices of buttered bread with cheese and drank a large cup of milky tea. I could have eaten more, but sounds of discontent were coming from the cradle, so I'd have to wait.

The midwife lifted a baby from the cradle and gave it to me

as she returned for the second one. Feeding them both at the same time would take some getting used to, and I hoped that I would have enough milk for them to thrive, otherwise we would have to find a wet nurse, and I hoped to avoid that at all cost. The idea of some woman, who was probably none too clean and consumed alcohol on a daily basis, feeding my babies gave me a momentary feeling of panic, but I pushed it aside.

I pulled down my shift and put both babies to my breasts. I looked like some strange Renaissance painting with two infants at my bare breasts, but they were gumming my nipples happily; their eyes closed in contentment. My breasts were tender and swollen, the milk still in the process of coming in, and I winced with discomfort as the babies sucked harder.

"What if I don't have enough milk for them both?" I asked Madame Duvall, who was looking on with approval.

"Don't worry, milady. The more they suckle, the more milk you will produce. Nature has a way of providing. If it gave you twins, it will give you the nourishment they need."

I had my doubts about this theory, but I knew that the milk usually took at least twenty-four hours to come in. Hopefully, by tomorrow, I would be lactating like a cow.

"May we come in?" Hugo asked as he poked his head through the door. He was holding Valentine, whose eyes grew as round as saucers when she saw the babies at my breast. The look of astonishment was instantly replaced by an outburst of jealousy. Her lip quivered and her eyes filled with tears as she realized that she would now have to share me with other children. She was fairly independent for her age and hated to be mollycoddled, but she'd never been anything but the center of attention in our household. We made a valiant effort not to spoil her, but it was hard to resist an adorable toddler, especially one with golden curls and big brown eyes fringed by thick lashes. She was the carbon copy of me at that age if old photographs I'd seen were anything to go by. "Come now, darling," Hugo said, "don't you want to meet your brother and sister?"

"No," Valentine wailed. "Make them go away. My Mama."

"You will now be a big sister, and you can order them about," Hugo suggested with a sly smile.

Valentine gave this some thought as she looked speculatively at the babies. The thought of bossing them about clearly appealed. "I can?"

"As soon as they are a little older."

Valentine glared at Hugo as if he'd just tricked her. At almost two, she was already showing us what it meant to have a toddler. I had no idea that a child that small could be so opinionated, but Valentine reminded me every day that she had her own ideas and wouldn't be easily fooled. Surprisingly, only one person had the magic touch, and it wasn't either myself or Hugo.

"I think Buttercup is feeling a little hungry," Archie said as he stopped in the doorway and glanced away in embarrassment when he saw the babies at my breasts. "I have an apple for her, but if you're not interested, I'll give it to her myself. I was on my way to the stables anyhow." Archie shrugged his shoulders as if it were all the same to him, but Valentine went rigid in Hugo's arms, her attention suddenly focused on Archie.

Buttercup was Valentine's pony, a sweet-tempered, cream-colored creature whose large brown eyes practically lit up when the pony beheld an apple.

"Down," Valentine ordered. Hugo put her down and she grabbed Archie's hand as if it were a life preserver. "Want to feed Buttercup."

"All right, if you insist. Perhaps we should stop by the kitchen and get an extra apple, just in case."

"Can I ride?" Valentine asked as she gazed into Archie's eyes imploringly.

"If you are good," Archie replied noncommittally as he led Valentine away.

"How does he always do that?" Hugo asked with a grin as he watched the two of them make their way down the stairs and out the door.

Valentine was as docile as a lamb with Archie, knowing that he wouldn't take any lip from her. And the promise of feeding the pony or riding for a few minutes was like catnip. Hugo was concerned that Valentine was too young to ride, but Archie just harrumphed in that way he did, dismissing the idea. He was probably born in the saddle and thought a child could be put astride before they even learned to walk. His theory seemed to apply to Valentine, who had no fear of riding and sat with her back straight and her feet planted in the stirrups as she rode around the small area Archie had designated for a paddock.

Hugo sat down next to me and watched, enraptured, as I finished feeding the babies and pulled up my shift. The babies seemed to be asleep, breathing evenly as their sparse eyelashes fanned out against their still-puffy faces. I passed the boy to Hugo and held on to the girl, studying her with interest. They looked very much alike when wrapped up, their faces almost a mirror image of each other, but the girl's hair was darker, and her lips a little plumper, while the boy had a slightly higher forehead and rounder cheeks. I suppose a stranger would think them identical, but I could already tell the difference, highly aware of each child's individuality.

Had I been pregnant in the twenty-first century, Hugo and I would have had names already picked out, but few people chose names in this time before a child was born, for fear of tempting fate. So many children died in utero and during the birth that the parents did as little as possible to forge a bond with the baby until they were sure it had a chance of survival.

"What shall we name them?" Hugo asked, as if reading my mind.

Naming children in the seventeenth century was vastly different than in the future. Only a handful of names were popular, and they were either the names of saints or monarchs. People often named their children after whoever sat on the throne, so once Mary and William were crowned, those would be the top names in the realm. Giving a child a name that was unique or cutesy was bound to cause suspicion and set the child apart. But I had never been partial to Mary, and although I liked James, given what was about to happen, James wasn't a wise choice for a boy. William didn't seem to fit either.

Hugo glanced over at my bundle. "What about Elena?" he asked. "I quite like that. We can give Mary as a second name," he added, knowing that naming after a queen might help the child should she ever come to Court or become a lady-in-waiting.

"Elena Mary," I mused. "What do you think?" I asked the baby, but she was sound asleep, her lips pursed as if she were displeased with the idea.

"Would you like to name him?" I asked, knowing how happy Hugo was to finally have a son. I was sure that he already had a name secretly written on his heart.

"Michael," Hugo responded immediately. "I'd like to call him Michael. Michael Joseph."

"Any special reason?"

"I was always fond of St. Michael," Hugo replied. "He was a natural leader, a warrior of God, and a symbol of courage. And Joseph after my father. He was called Joss by those who knew him, but Joseph was his full name."

"I thought you didn't get on with your father," I remarked carefully, surprised that Hugo would wish to name his son after the man who'd been so harsh and unfeeling toward him, especially when he was a small child who'd recently lost his mother.

"My father and I had a difficult relationship, but he is responsible for the man I am today, and although some lessons were harsh ones, they were necessary. I can't say that I loved the man, but I did respect him," Hugo explained. "I think it's only right that Michael bear his name since Valentine bears my mother's name, Elise." Hugo suddenly looked contrite. "Did you perhaps wish to name the children after your own parents?"

That question gave me pause. Did I? I suppose I had finally forgiven my mother for her neglect of me after my father had left, but I didn't feel magnanimous enough to name my daughter after the woman who had caused me so much pain. My father had turned his back on me, never so much as bothering to see me or even ring after he'd left. No, he didn't deserve the honor either. I'd never met Hugo's parents, but his mother had been a kind, gentle woman, and his father, although stern and at times unforgiving, had taught Hugo how to take responsibility for his actions and to do his duty by those who depended on him—not something I could ever say of my own father, who wouldn't know responsibility and duty if he tripped over them on the way to the nearest pub.

"All right then, Elena Mary and Michael Joseph," I agreed, gazing down at the sleeping children. I rested my head against Hugo's shoulder, and we just sat peacefully for a few moments, enjoying a moment of quiet bliss before Valentine's voice shattered the silence.

"I want Mama," she roared as her little feet pounded up the stairs.

My first responsibility as a mother of three was to make sure that Valentine didn't feel neglected.

"Come here," I whispered to her as I held my finger to my lips. "Be very quiet and you can take a look at the babies."

Valentine didn't seem impressed by this promise, but she obediently quieted down and allowed Hugo to help her onto the high bed. She squeezed between the two of us and gazed from one baby to another.

"What do you think?" Hugo asked her as he held up Michael for her inspection.

Valentine didn't answer. She just huddled between us as silent tears of hurt slid down her cheeks.

Being a mother of three was going to be a challenge.

THREE

DECEMBER 1688

Surrey, England

I tried to ignore the manic racing of my heart as the hired carriage drew closer to Cranley. The sky was the deep lilac of a winter twilight, tinged in places with streaks of fuchsia and gold. It must have snowed a few days ago, because the country-side was blanketed in a thin layer of white, which shimmered in the remaining light and glittered on trees and bushes. A few shy stars and a pale moon had already appeared in the sky, ready to take up reign from the sun that had abdicated for the night. I could see the outline of Everly Manor rising in the distance, its bulk a shadowy blight on the countryside. I stared more intently, willing light to appear in the windows. Hugo had written to Brad, advising him of our arrival, and asking him to see to some basic domestic arrangements that would make it easier for us to settle in once we returned, but I saw no evidence of life in the darkened windows or smokeless chimneys.

When we docked in Portsmouth that morning, we'd decided to go directly to Everly Manor without stopping for the night en route. It would be a long ride for the children, but we were so eager to come home at last that delaying our arrival by even a day seemed like an eternity. We'd been traveling for weeks, and my secret little fantasy had been to have a good meal that wasn't tack and stringy stew, and then soak in a hot bath before going to sleep in a real bed that wasn't a hard wooden berth on a boat rolling from side to side as it crossed the heaving Channel in late autumn. I'd have to settle for the no-rolling part since there would obviously be no home-cooked meal or a hot bath. Perhaps Brad had never got the letter. Hugo had sent more than one, knowing that mail was unreliable, and letters often went astray, but judging by the dark, silent house, none of them had reached their destination. Another day or two of discomfort wouldn't kill us, and life at the manor would be humming in no time, but although I was slightly disappointed, nothing could mar the happiness of this day.

I'd envisioned this moment a thousand times over the past few years, but now that it was finally here, I felt like I would burst with impatience. It had been a difficult journey, partially because we had made it so late in the year, and partially because of the children. I'd never imagined how trying it would be to travel with three children under the age of three without the benefit of running water, electricity, disposable nappies, and, most importantly, television and video games to keep them occupied during the long hours of the voyage. Modern-day mothers thought they had it hard, but they'd never traveled by carriage or been confined to a tiny windowless cabin on a ship in the seventeenth century.

We had to remain vigilant every moment of the day, making sure that the children never went near the steep steps down to the hold; stayed out of the way of the sailors, who weren't accustomed to having small children underfoot; and never climbed on anything that might elevate them high enough to allow them to tumble over the side. By the time the children were finally rocked to sleep at night by the movement of the ship, we were all exhausted and fell asleep within moments, ready to wake up and do it all again the next day.

The children in question were now sound asleep, lulled by the motion of the carriage. Valentine was curled up in Archie's lap; Michael was wedged between myself and Hugo, a little wooden horse that Archie had carved for him still in his hand, and Elena was snoring softly in Hugo's lap, sleeping deeply at last. She was easily overexcited and had slept fitfully ever since we'd left our house outside Rouen, which often left her cranky and tired.

The twins had turned one the day before we left Rouen, but, although they had been born less than half an hour apart, couldn't be more different in personality or development. Michael was a serious child who enjoyed playing quietly and being read to. He was slightly taller than Elena, but weaker of constitution and more easily upset and frightened. Elena, on the other hand, was a little daredevil who had no fear of anything, and never cried even when she fell and hurt herself. She was a natural leader and held her own when Valentine tried to boss her around.

Elena was currently going through a "daddy phase," and wanted little to do with me. She hardly gave poor Hugo a moment of peace on the voyage, climbing up him the way the sailors climbed the rigging. Michael was more content to stay with me where it was safe, and chose Frances as a substitute if I weren't available. He seemed to be intimidated by Archie, who was a favorite with the girls.

Valentine, being nearly three, was still nursing her infatuation for Archie. He seemed to be the only one who could talk her round, and despite his often-taciturn exterior, he seemed to enjoy the attention. The two of them were practically inseparable, which left Frances feeling a bit left out. She willingly helped out with the children, but they tired her, and she often sought a quiet corner in which to read or just sit and think.

She'd been unusually quiet since leaving France, the memories of her life in England weighing her down, as was her fear of some sort of retaliation from her father-in-law.

Frances had complied with Hugo's request and waited to marry Archie, but I could understand her fear. As Archie's wife, she would be his by law to support and protect. As the widow of Lionel Finch, she was still vulnerable and beholden to his family. Gideon Warburton had assured Hugo that he would pursue all legal avenues regarding Frances's share of the estate, but there had been no word from him in over a year, and Hugo was beginning to question the wisdom of leaving Frances so exposed.

I was in favor of having Frances and Archie wait, but for reasons of my own. Frances had been severely emotionally and physically traumatized, which, in my opinion, had led her straight into the arms of the first man who had showed her any affection and kindness. Had Archie responded to her advances, perhaps things would have been different, but Frances had nearly died as a result of her vulnerability and misplaced trust, and she needed time to heal.

Now, nearly three years after her near-fatal abortion attempt, Frances was finally in a good place. She had matured, gained confidence, and lost some of the fear that had shaped her decisions in the past. Receiving financial compensation from the Finches might benefit her in some ways, but it would also complicate her relationship with Archie, which was something Hugo chose not to acknowledge from his practical, masculine perspective. I knew that Frances was anxious about our home-coming and would have happily remained in France as long as the rest of us remained there with her.

I felt a jolt of tension roll over Hugo as he spotted the manor house in the distance. He'd dreamed of this moment, had longed for home, and had taken the risk of sailing to England at the end of November when events leading up to the fall of

James II were about to unfold. The prudent thing would have been to wait until spring and allow the political dust to settle, if such a thing were possible in England, but Hugo simply couldn't wait any longer. He was desperate to go home and reclaim his life.

I put my hand in his as an array of emotions raced across Hugo's features. This was uncharted territory, and neither one of us had any inkling of what this homecoming would bring.

FOUR

The house was as cold as a tomb and just as dark when everyone finally trooped into the foyer. Archie had to break one of the high windows in the cellar kitchen and come around to open the front door since there was no other way in. Hugo had never needed a key to his own house; there had always been servants to let him in. Now, he stood in the darkened foyer, listening to the deafening silence of the empty house. All he heard was the howling of the wind outside and the creaking of the wood as the house settled for the night.

Archie had grabbed a few candles on the way from the kitchen and now lit one, casting the travelers into a golden pool of light. It reflected off the breastplate of Bruce's armor which had guarded the foyer since the house had been built during the reign of Henry VIII.

"Mama, I'm hungry," Valentine whined as the younger children rubbed their eyes. After a day of traveling, they were ready for bed despite having slept in the coach.

Neve looked bemused, the fatigue clearly showing on her face. She needed to warm up, have something to eat, and rest. The past weeks had been hard on her, and although one more night wouldn't make all that much of a difference, Hugo felt as if he'd let everyone down. They all huddled together, like a band of refugees, and it was time to get matters under control. Tomorrow, he would figure out what had gone wrong, but for tonight, he had to get them all fed and settled.

Hugo herded everyone into the front parlor and lit a few candles, dispelling the gloom of the winter evening. Opening the shutters was pointless since it was already pitch dark outside. The furniture was covered in dust sheets, and according to Archie there wasn't a scrap of food in the larder, nor was there much firewood. The house had been deserted for years.

"Archie," Hugo began, "go to the tavern and get some food, enough to last through tomorrow. Don't forget milk for the children."

He then turned to the coachman who came with the rented coach. The man would wish to return to Portsmouth come morning, but for tonight he was Hugo's responsibility.

"Master Harvey, please see to the coach and horses and fetch some water from the well," Hugo requested of the man, who looked none too pleased at arriving at a house that hadn't been inhabited in years. After a day of driving through the cold, barren countryside, he'd no doubt been looking forward to a hot meal and a comfortable bed.

"I'll stay at the inn tonight, if it's all the same to you, Your Lordship," he replied, jamming the hat back on his head. He'd already been paid for his services, so there was nothing to keep him from leaving.

"As you wish, Master Harvey. Perhaps you can give Archie a ride then, since we have no horses of our own," Hugo responded without missing a beat.

"It would be my pleasure," the coachman replied sarcastically, clearly annoyed at having to spend his hard-earned money on lodging and food.

Hugo reached into his purse and passed the man several coins, having correctly deduced the reason for his surliness.

"Thank you kindly, sir, and a goodnight to you all."

Hugo waited for the man to leave before continuing with his instructions. "Neve, please prepare two bedchambers for tonight. The children can go in with us, and Archie and Frances can share for one night. I doubt anyone will be particularly shocked," he added, seeing the look of astonishment on Frances's face. Frances, mind the children while Neve is upstairs. I will lay the fires in the rooms and kitchen and put on some water to heat. There'll be no hot baths tonight, but at least we'll have some hot water for washing."

Hugo left the women to it and went out to get firewood. He hoped it was dry or it would be a very cold night indeed.

His mind buzzed with questions as he chose the driest logs from the sorry pile behind the house. Why was the house empty? Where the devil was everyone, and where were the horses? The stable was dark and empty, as was the kennel which normally housed a few dogs. Where was Brad?

Bradford Nash was not the type of person to just ignore a request, or to forget. Hugo felt a twinge of unease as he thought of his friend, but there was nothing he could do until tomorrow.

Hugo gathered as much firewood as he could and went back into the kitchen. It took him some time to get the fire going, but the damp wood finally caught, illuminating the large room which seemingly hadn't been used in years. There was no water, so he found a bucket and went to the well. The water was frozen solid, and throwing the bucket against the ice did little to crack the crust of ice. Hugo went out to the shed, where he found a long stick resembling a pike. That would do it, or so he hoped.

* * *

The church clock struck ten, the distant chime reverberating through the silent house. There had always been plenty of empty rooms, but for some reason, the house had never felt as forlorn as it did tonight.

Hugo gazed at the children who were fast asleep in the big bed. They'd been overwrought and tearful, but Archie had brought some fresh bread and cheese, hot stew and meat pies, as well as bottles of ale and milk, and they'd had a feast in the kitchen, seated around the long table and warmed by the roaring fire. The food and cozy atmosphere had lifted everyone's sagging spirits. The children were washed and put to bed after supper, leaving Hugo alone with Neve. They hadn't been alone since they'd left their house in Rouen, and it had felt wonderfully peaceful just to sit by the fire and talk awhile before joining the children in bed.

Archie and Frances had also retired after cleaning up the remains of their meal. Archie had insisted on making a pallet on the floor and allowing Frances to take the bed, which had confirmed Hugo's suspicion that their relationship had never been consummated despite their betrothal. He wouldn't have blamed them if it had been but was glad that Archie chose to wait. Hugo never asked Archie any personal questions, but he was sure that Archie had been as celibate as a monk since declaring his love for Frances. Who would have thought that Archie would last that long? Hugo mused with an inward smile, but love did amazing things to people, as he knew only too well.

"Do you think the letter went astray?" Neve asked as she turned her back to allow Hugo to unlace her gown. It was travel-stained and smelled of Neve's particular scent, which Hugo loved, but Neve wrinkled her nose in disgust and threw the gown into the basket of items to be laundered at the first opportunity. The basket was already overflowing with children's clothes, dirty clouts, and the damp and yellowed linen that Neve had pulled off the beds.

"I can only assume that it did," Hugo replied thoughtfully. He didn't want to worry Neve unnecessarily but couldn't hide his unease from her shrewd gaze. Neve knew Brad well enough to know that had he received the letter, their reception would have been a very different one, but there could be other reasons why Brad had been unable to comply with Hugo's request, such as illness or death. Hugo hadn't had a letter from Brad since September; a letter which had been penned in July. A lot could happen in five months.

"You think something is wrong," Neve stated as she turned around to face him. "Tell me."

"I don't know; I really don't," Hugo replied as he pulled Neve onto his lap and wrapped his arms around her to keep her warm. "Archie said that there was much talk at the tavern. James II tried to flee London three days ago. He threw his royal seal into the Thames before he was apprehended and turned back by forces loyal to William. I knew this would happen, but somehow it still shocks me to hear it. How could he not stay and fight, and defend his kingdom and God-given right to the throne?"

"Reading about history is never the same as being a part of it, is it?" Neve acknowledged as she snuggled closer to Hugo. "I should know," she added with a smile, "I used to consider myself quite the expert."

"No, things never appear as frightening or real as they do from a safe distance of four hundred years."

"James will be gone in less than ten days," Neve reminded Hugo. "William will allow him to leave unharmed. I think that's a generous gesture on his part."

"It has little to do with generosity," Hugo replied as he stared at the leaping flames of the fire. "William is no fool. He realizes that throwing his father-in-law, who also happens to be his uncle, into the Tower as one of his first acts as future king will make him look petty in the eyes of the people, and the last thing he wants to do is turn James into a martyr for Catholics. Allowing James and his family to live in exile is a savvy political decision, since he will be seen as being magnanimous by both the Catholics and the Protestants."

"But it will also give the Catholics hope, which will lead to decades of failed rebellions and countless deaths," Neve countered hotly.

"Yes, but William and Mary don't know what you do, and besides, executing James wouldn't put an end to the problem. William would also have to kill the child—his own wife's little brother—which would be seen as unnecessarily cruel and incite rebellion anyway."

"You know," Neve said as she yawned, covering her mouth daintily. "There was a time at school when I thought British history was boring," she remarked with a smile as she slid off Hugo's lap.

"Really?" Hugo asked, stunned.

"Yes. It was such a chore trying to remember who was related to whom, who'd been executed, crowned, or exiled. I never imagined I'd get to live it."

"There are days when I would give a lot to be bored," Hugo replied as he pulled back the covers and got into bed next to Valentine, who was snoring lightly. Michael was between the two girls, his fair head resting on Elena's pillow and her arm protectively placed around his middle.

"Me too," Neve replied. She got in on the other side to make sure that no one rolled off the high bed during the night.

Hugo reached out and took Neve's hand, holding it for a moment while they bracketed their children. His whole world was in this bed, and he meant to keep them safe, no matter what it took.

FIVE

The next day dawned bright and sunny, but very cold. Frost sparkled on the windows, the crystals arranged in fanciful patterns, and the bare trees made a lacework quilt against the nearly colorless sky. Getting out of bed was a daring feat, but Hugo finally forced himself to throw off the covers and leave the warmth and comfort of the bed. The floorboards were ice-cold, and his breath came out in gossamer spheres of vapor as he hastily pulled on his clothes. The water left over in the basin from last night had a thin crust of ice, and the fire had long since died out, leaving behind a heap of ash.

"Stay in bed," Hugo whispered to Neve. "I'll get the fire going here and in the parlor and then you can wake the children. I don't want them catching a chill."

"Don't mind if I do," Neve replied sheepishly. She hated being cold.

Hugo cleaned out the ashes and laid a fire in the hearth, waiting around for a few minutes to make sure that the logs were burning brightly. The room began to fill with a pleasant warmth, although it would take at least a half-hour for the fire to drive out the arctic chill. Neve seemed to have fallen back to sleep, so Hugo let himself out of the room and made his way downstairs to the parlor. The room was shrouded in darkness; the dust sheets looking like lumpy ghosts in the half-light. Hugo threw open the shutters and began pulling off the sheets. The parlor was the heart of the house, and it was time to bring it back to life.

The fireplace was clean, not having seen a fire in several years, and the mantel covered with a thick layer of dust. The house needed a good cleaning, but that would have to wait. There were more pressing matters, such as food and firewood. The rhythmic thwack of an axe could be heard from outside, where Archie was already chopping wood. There was hardly enough left in the dwindling pile to last through the day.

"You are up early," Hugo remarked as he loaded up with wood.

"Don't enjoy sleeping on the cold floor as much as I used to," Archie replied sarcastically. "Besides, there's work to be done. I think it's actually colder inside than it is out here. I'll get the fire going in the kitchen momentarily," he said as he swung the axe again. "We have enough food left for this morning, but then we'll need supplies."

"I'll see to that," Hugo replied grimly.

Brad had mentioned in his letters that the estate was being well looked after, but after having seen the state of the house, Hugo wasn't so sure. His first stop would be the home of Godfrey Bowden, the estate manager. He would be up at such an early hour—or at least he should be, Hugo reasoned, if he hoped to keep his position. After a meeting with Bowden, Hugo would head over to see Brad. Hugo didn't relish having to walk to Bowden's cottage and then make his way to Nash House on foot, but there were no horses in the stable.

Hugo turned his head suspiciously as he heard a faint neighing coming from the stable. Was he hearing things?

"I hired a horse from the inn's livery," Archie informed him with a wry smile. "How do you think I brought all that food back last night? I've only got the two hands, you know. Besides, I knew you'd need to see to business this morning."

Hugo just nodded in gratitude. "Archie, you are the most practical man I've ever met, and I love you for it," he said with an impish smile.

"Oh, go on with you," Archie replied, his attention already back on his chopping.

* * *

There was much to do, so Hugo made sure the family was up and having breakfast before setting off. The horse from the livery wasn't a shining example of fine horseflesh, but it had four legs and it moved, saving Hugo time and the misery of having to trudge through frozen snow for miles.

Master Bowden lived alone in a cottage on the estate and kept only one servant, a middle-aged widow named Abigail, who Hugo strongly suspected did more than wash the master's hose. He was of middle years, bald as an egg, and shaped like one as well. Neve had met him only once but secretly referred to him as Humpty Dumpty. The man was utterly lacking in any personal charm, but he was fastidious, intelligent, and extremely practical; all excellent qualities in a manager. Godfrey's father had managed the estate for Joss Everly, and Godfrey had actually been born in the cottage where he now lived, having seen no desire to travel farther afield in search of his own future.

Hugo was surprised when a new servant answered the door, a girl of no more than twelve, and invited him in. Master Bowden had just sat down to break his fast when Hugo arrived, an attractive young woman sitting across from him. Had Hugo not been so annoyed, he might have been amused by the reaction of the manager. The man nearly fell out of his chair at the sight of his master, and the young woman became flustered, unsure of whether she should remain seated, or follow Godfrey's suit and jump to her feet.

"Your Lordship," Godfrey Bowden stammered, bowing to Hugo as if he were the king himself. "What a surprise. Welcome home. I do hope you had a pleasant journey. May I present my wife, Mistress Bowden."

The young woman began to rise, but Hugo forestalled her by walking over and bowing over her hand. "Mistress Bowden, a pleasure. Many felicitations on your marriage." *Poor Abigail*, Hugo thought as he looked into the peachy oval of Godfrey's wife's face. He'd done well for himself, and had no doubt gotten rid of Abigail before the new mistress arrived. Gazing into the hazel depths of her eyes, Hugo had no doubt that the young girl who answered the door had been hand-picked by her—the child being too young and skinny to be of any interest to her new husband for a good few years yet, not that Godfrey Bowden had a reputation for lechery.

"Welcome home, Your Lordship," the woman said, blushing prettily.

"Thank you, it's good to be home," Hugo replied truthfully. Despite the cold and the lack of staff and provisions, he was deeply happy to be home at last.

"Will you excuse us for a few minutes, my dear?" Godfrey asked his wife as he escorted Hugo into his study. He waited to sit down until Hugo made himself comfortable.

"Master Bowden," Hugo began, "I was surprised to find the house locked up with nary a scrap of food or any firewood prepared for the winter months. Has Master Nash not informed you of my arrival?"

"No, Your Lordship. I haven't seen Master Nash in some months, but he did take a very keen interest in the running of the estate and had audited the accounts himself every quarter. I think you will find everything to be in good order." The man had lost some of his nervousness as he made his speech, which Hugo took as a good sign. Had things gone to seed, he'd be a lot more apprehensive at the master's unexpected arrival.

"Master Bowden, I will expect to see the books and go over the accounts with you directly after Boxing Day, but right now I'm more concerned with the welfare of my family. I shall require a minimum of fifty cords of wood to be delivered to the manor, as well as foodstuffs that will last for two weeks at the very least. You may requisition the necessary provisions from the farmers on the estate and offset their quarterly taxes as payment."

Hugo waited for Bowden to process this before addressing the next issue.

"I will also need a cook and at least three maids. I'm sure there are girls on the estate who are old enough to go into service and would like an opportunity to get away from farm work. Two grooms and a boot boy will be needed as well, but that's not as urgent. I noticed that the stables are empty. Where are all my horses? Have they been properly looked after?"

"Of course, Your Lordship. Master Nash had the horses removed to his own estate where he could exercise them regularly," Bowden replied with a noticeable look of resentment.

Having Brad take all the horses would seem like an insult to the manager, but Hugo was grateful that he had. He was very fond of his horses and expected them to be properly looked after, not simply fed and watered.

"I'm afraid Aamir is long gone," Bowden stammered. "Mistress Hiddleston sold him some years ago."

Hugo belatedly realized that Bowden had not seen him since his near arrest in May of 1685, and had to answer to Jane while she was alive. Bowden knew how much Hugo had loved his Arabian stallion, but the sale hadn't been his fault.

"Not to worry, Master Bowden. What's done is done. Please

see to the other matters this afternoon. My wife and children are cold and hungry."

"Yes, sir. Right away, sir." Bowden bowed stiffly, his eyes already doing the calculations of what could be obtained where. "My regards to your good lady," Bowden stammered as Hugo turned to leave.

Hugo mounted his horse and rode toward the Nash estate. He tried to tell himself that all was well and he was worrying for nothing, but the seed of doubt that had been planted last night had now taken root. Bowden hadn't seen Brad in months, and had no inkling of Hugo's imminent arrival. Even if Brad never received Hugo's letter, he would have been by to check on things, especially with Christmas just two weeks away, and Boxing Day to prepare for. Hugo tried to nudge the old nag to go faster, suddenly fearing the worst.

SIX

Hugo felt a lump in his throat as the pitched roof of Nash House came into view above the shaggy line of bare trees. He hadn't seen Brad since leaving London in November of 1685, and he missed his friend terribly. Brad had been a permanent fixture in Hugo's life since he'd been a child, and there hadn't been a secret or a thought that he hadn't shared with him. Brad was the one person whom Hugo had always counted on for understanding and support, especially when his own father offered neither. Brad's wife, Beth, had been a childhood friend as well, and Hugo looked forward to seeing her and their children, the youngest of whom had been born while he was abroad. The years had flown by, and so much had changed in his absence.

Hugo tossed the reins to a surprised groom and strode up the steps, glancing briefly at the ugly face of the gargoyle knocker that Brad's father had been so proud of. He was eager to be ushered into the warmth of the house, but apprehensive about what he'd find. He prayed there was a simple explanation, one him and Brad could laugh about over breakfast. Hugo was cold and hungry, since he'd left whatever food was available for

Neve and the children. He tried to contain his impatience as he heard the footsteps approaching the door. They seemed rather hurried.

Hugo was taken aback when the door flew open, revealing not a servant, but Beth, who looked haunted and pale, her dark eyes huge in her face. She was somberly dressed, which was totally out of character since Beth loved color and light, and her wardrobe reflected her sprightly personality. The charcoal gray of her gown drained all color from her face and added years to her appearance.

Beth's expression went from hope to disappointment, and back to hope again as she absorbed the fact that Hugo Everly was standing on her doorstep.

"Beth, what is it? What's happened?" Hugo asked as she grabbed his arm and dragged him inside. The warmth enveloped him at once, but he wasn't able to enjoy it when Beth was so clearly distressed.

"Where is he, Hugo?" she cried, still clutching his arm and staring up into his eyes as if he had all the answers. "Please, tell me. I can't take not knowing. That's why you are here, isn't it? To break the news to me gently?" Beth maneuvered him into the parlor and slammed the door shut behind them, facing Hugo and devouring him with those imploring eyes. "Where is Brad?" she whispered now, suddenly realizing that Hugo had no idea.

"When was the last time you saw him? Where had he gone?" Hugo asked. "We've only just arrived last night. Had Brad not received my letter?"

"I don't know," Beth replied vaguely. "He left in October. I've heard nothing since."

"Beth, please calm down and tell me everything from the beginning," Hugo suggested as he pulled Beth toward a settle. He wished it was later in the day so that Beth might have a medicinal brandy, but it was scarcely past ten, and she had never been one for the drink anyway.

Beth took a seat and began nervously plucking at the lace at her wrist, searching for the best way to tell her story. Hugo felt a knot in his stomach as he watched his childhood friend; she was much changed, and not for the better. He'd suspected something was wrong, but this exceeded his worst expectations. Brad had been gone for two months; this was serious.

"I don't know how much you know, having been away for so long," Beth began, the look in her eyes suggesting that she knew exactly how much he knew, given his involvement in politics in the past. "It all started to unravel when Her Majesty gave birth in June. There were all these vicious rumors that the baby was stillborn, and a male child had been smuggled into the bedchamber by a maid carrying a bed warmer, but, of course, it was all just malicious gossip. As if it were even possible!" Beth exclaimed, outraged. "The child would have to have been no bigger than a kitten and would probably tumble straight out. But, of course, there were many who refused to believe that after years of infertility, the queen had been blessed with a son. Brad was so happy. With the birth of a son, a Catholic monarchy was assured, and he dared to hope that, in time, the discrimination and prejudice against Catholics would diminish, and perhaps, in our own lifetime, we might be able to worship openly and not fear persecution."

Beth pulled out a handkerchief and delicately wiped at her eyes before continuing.

"Now that His Majesty had a son, his daughter Mary was no longer first in the line of succession, assuring a Protestant monarchy, and fear began to spread."

Beth looked so defeated that Hugo decided to spare her the pain of telling the rest of it.

"Beth, I know what happened, but where is Brad? Where had he gone?"

"Brad couldn't reconcile himself to just hiding in the country while the rightful king was being forced out by a foreign prince. He joined His Majesty's forces on Salisbury Plain, determined to do his bit in fighting for his king. I haven't heard from him since, nor do I know what's happening." Beth sniffled, her eyes turning to Hugo again. "I've heard rumors, terrible rumors, that the king's forces were defeated, and he fled to London, leaving his men behind, but that couldn't be true. Could it? Only yesterday I heard that James had tried to flee the country, having thrown his seal in the Thames. The fight is lost, but where is my husband? He should have returned by now, unless he was wounded—or killed," Beth wailed, finally losing control.

"Beth, I don't know exactly what happened on Salisbury Plain, but I do know that it wasn't a bloody battle. There were hardly any casualties." Of course, Hugo knew this from having done research on the Glorious Revolution while in the twenty-first century, but he could hardly tell that to Beth. There was another battle that was fought only a week ago at Reading, but it had also been a defeat for the Royalists, although not a terribly bloody one.

"I hear that the queen has escaped with the child," Beth sighed. "They are running like rats from a sinking ship."

Hugo smiled at the comparison. Beth's father had been a sea captain, one who liked to use naval metaphors around his children.

"Beth, I fear it's over," Hugo said gently, knowing for a fact that it was. James would make one more attempt at recapturing his throne, but it would fail miserably, and he would live out his life in exile at the palace of Saint-Germain-en-Laye, just west of Paris, where he would die—defiant and fanatically pious till the end.

"Find him, Hugo," Beth pleaded as she grabbed his arms and stared into his eyes. "Please."

"Beth, I can't." At any other time, Hugo wouldn't have thought twice before rushing to the rescue, but he simply couldn't leave, not now. "Beth, I can't leave Neve and the children alone. I need a few days at the very least to make sure that they are settled and provided for. There isn't even enough firewood to last the week, and there's no food and no staff. I must see to my family."

"Before you see to mine," Beth replied bitterly, releasing Hugo. "Thank you for calling, Lord Everly. Mary will see you out."

"Beth, please," Hugo replied, feeling a crushing guilt settling over him. "Just give me three days. If Brad is not back by then, you have my word that I will go and look for him. Please," he repeated, needing her understanding and forgiveness.

"All right, Hugo; I understand. Of course you must see to your family. I'm just distraught; that's all. Please give my regards to your wife." Beth looked deflated, but she managed to give Hugo a weak smile as he got up to leave.

"He will be back, Beth. I know it."

She just nodded and left the room.

SEVEN

I gazed out the window, judging it to be past noon based on the position of the sun. The sky was that particular shade of winter blue, a pale, but bright expanse with not a cloud in sight. Frost shimmered on the diamond panes of the windows, and the world outside looked like a winter wonderland; the snow covering all the imperfections and blanketing the ground in a sparkling quilt. But, in less than four hours, it would start to grow dark, and we would be faced with spending another night in a cold, gloomy house. We had no food, barely any firewood, and were running short on candles.

The children were huddled in the parlor with Frances, looking at an illuminated text which she'd found in the library. It was one of the few books that had any illustrations, and the children seemed mesmerized by the brilliant colors and gold leaf used as the background for the images. Frances and I had tried to clean some of the rooms, but it was impossible with the children underfoot. They were restless, agitated, and bored. Michael had his wooden horse, but the girls had little to occupy them and weren't the type to play quietly at the best of times. Not for the first time, I reflected on how much the world had changed in its treatment of children.

In the seventeenth century, no one paid much heed to the needs of children. They were to be had, raised, and married off. There were no toys, no books, no educational tools, and certainly no entertainment geared toward children. The offspring of nobility had tutors, but the rest of the children were put to work as soon as they were old enough to help. The boys assisted their fathers, while the girls were taught to sew, embroider, cook, and care for younger children. Childhood was short and joyless, since the parents were either too indifferent or too poor to indulge their offspring and see them as anything more than an heir or another mouth to feed. I hoped that my children would be the exception, since I planned to be involved in every aspect of their lives. I would not be passing them on to nursemaids and tutors and see them for an hour a day as a matter of duty.

I threw down the dusting rag and wedged myself next to Elena, smiling as she leaned into me in that trusting way of children. Michael immediately forgot about the pictures and climbed into my lap, making Valentine glare at him in disgust before she moved closer to Frances for a better look.

Soon, we would have to figure out what to feed the children for supper and get the fires going in the bedrooms, but for the moment, we were content, although I was starting to worry about Hugo. He'd been gone for hours. I hoped that he was enjoying a glass of brandy with Bradford before returning home, but deep down I knew that even if everything was well and Bradford was at home, Hugo would not linger while we were trapped in a cold house with no supplies or food. And Archie had gone out on some mysterious errand, leaving Frances and myself to hold down the fort.

"Where's Archie?" Valentine demanded petulantly. "He promised me a pony."

"Pony," the twins repeated in awe as they looked at their sister. They were just beginning to talk, so every new word was like a gem, to be admired and fought over, to see who could say it better.

"If Archie promised you a pony, then I am sure he'll get you one, but perhaps when it gets warmer. It's too cold to ride just now," I answered, aware of the impatience in my voice. Knowing Valentine, this was the first inquiry in a series of hundreds. She wasn't one to just take no for an answer. If Archie had promised her a pony, he'd have to deliver, and soon.

"I think someone is coming," Frances said as she set aside the book and walked over to the window.

The children instantly jumped up and ran after her but couldn't see anything since they weren't tall enough. Frances picked up Valentine and I grabbed the twins. They pressed their noses against the glass, eager to see what was happening outside.

"Pony," Michael breathed, enraptured.

I thought Frances had spotted Hugo or Archie coming up the drive, but what I saw was a wagon train. There were three of them; two piled with firewood, and another with its contents covered with some sort of cloth. The third wagon was driven by Humpty Dumpty himself. He looked around nervously as he helped a woman down from the bench. A young girl sat in the back of the wagon, a cloth bundle clutched to her chest. She looked awfully young, and I felt a wave of pity for her as I saw her gaping at the house, her mouth open.

"You mustn't let them see that you pity them," Frances suddenly said as she stepped away from the window and set Valentine down.

"What do you mean?"

"You are no longer the mistress or the wife of an exiled traitor. You are now the lady of the house, and you must act accordingly," Frances instructed me.

I was surprised by her advice but realized that she was probably right. I'd never had to run a household, not on this scale, and I'd had some trouble with the servants in France who hadn't treated me with the respect or deference they should have shown. I didn't really care as long as they got the work done, but this was different. This was Everly Manor, Hugo's home, and I had to learn to act like Lady Everly.

"They must respect you—and fear you a little, otherwise you will not be able to run a household effectively. You are not their friend; you are their mistress," Frances reminded me. She'd never actually asked me about my background, but she knew that I didn't come from either nobility or landed gentry, and wasn't raised to run a nobleman's home. I would need some help, and although Frances had little say in household matters when she was married to Lionel Finch, in some ways, she knew more than I did.

"You are right, Frances. How should I approach this?" I asked, hoping she'd have some good advice.

"You are desperate for staff, but that doesn't mean that you should hire anyone who comes to your door. Interview them, ask them questions about their background and work experience; show them that you want nothing but the best for your family."

"That might be a stretch given the circumstances," I mumbled, but, of course, Frances had a point.

"I'll mind the children. Go on," Frances said with a small smile.

"I want to come too," Valentine demanded, but Frances was already beckoning to her.

"I don't think you've seen this beautiful picture," Frances observed shrewdly. "Is that a fairy?"

Of course it wasn't a fairy, since it was a religious text, but Valentine was sufficiently intrigued, so I seized the moment and made my escape.

Godfrey Bowden was already in the kitchen, having entered through the back door. The two women stood in the middle of the cavernous room, grasping their bundles as if someone were about to set the dogs on them. The older woman looked familiar, but I'd never seen the girl.

"My lady," Bowden said as he bowed to me from the neck. "Welcome home. I do apologize for not anticipating your arrival." This was total rot, of course, since he clearly had no idea we were coming home, but to insinuate that Hugo was somehow at fault for not informing him just wouldn't do. "Lord Everly indicated that you are in urgent need of staff and provisions. My men are unloading the wood and will bring in the foodstuffs shortly. There's enough to last for at least a few weeks. It was rather difficult to get more on such short notice," he added reproachfully.

"Thank you for your efforts on our behalf, Master Bowden," I answered politely. There was something about the man's blunt features that set my teeth on edge. Perhaps it was his utter lack of humor or the cold judgment in his eyes. He didn't think I belonged here, and having to treat me as a lady gave him a turn. The old me would have felt inadequate and uncomfortable, but I'd been with Hugo long enough to have learned something: people always looked for a chink in your armor, so it was best not to have one. I stared at Bowden imperiously, finally forcing him to lower his gaze.

"My lady, this is Abigail Fowler," he began, eager to fill the awkward silence.

Now I knew where I'd seen her. I'd visited Bowden with Hugo once and had seen Abigail in his home. She used to be his housekeeper, and, according to Hugo, his lover. I wondered what had happened there, but couldn't come out and ask.

"Mistress Fowler has never worked in a great house such as this, but she's an excellent cook," Bowden rushed to reassure me.

Judging by Bowden's round shape, Abigail Fowler must be at least a decent cook. I was about to agree when I remembered Frances's advice. I had no idea what to ask a seventeenth-century cook, but I had to pretend that I knew what I was talking about. Simply taking her on without any kind of interview would mark me as gullible.

"Mistress Fowler," I began, "what type of culinary experience do you have?"

The woman looked nervous, but Bowden gave her a barely perceptible shove.

"Before working for Master Bowden, I worked for Master Garwood for ten years; you might have heard of him. He wasn't a titled gentleman, but did entertain frequently, and liked to dazzle his friends with the finest dishes. He'd spent some years in France, seeing to his, eh... importing interests, and had developed quite a taste for the exotic," she added lamely.

"And why did Master Garwood dismiss you?" I asked, trying not to feel sorry for this plain, simple woman.

"He died, my lady. Quite unexpectedly," she added, the color drenching from her face as her eyes slid downward in the general direction of the floor.

I had heard of Master Garwood from Hugo. He was a colorful character whose father had nearly brought the family to ruin with his gambling. Thankfully, he'd died before losing everything, leaving his son to rebuild the family fortune through some less than honorable channels. The younger Garwood had amassed a fortune through smuggling, and, according to Hugo, mixed with some dangerous types. He had been a fervent supporter of the Duke of Monmouth, since a Catholic monarchy would, in time, ruin his profitable business by means of increased trade with France and the lowering of taxes on French imports. I wasn't sure if I was reading correctly between the lines, but it seemed that Master Garwood had met with a sorry end when he'd stepped on someone's toes. Abigail Fowler wouldn't be so distressed if the man had died of an illness. Death at a young age was common enough, so her reaction would have been one of acceptance rather than fear. However, if Abigail knew something of French cuisine, I was happy to overlook her association with hardened criminals.

"And who is this?" I asked, glancing at the young girl who kept backing up until she was practically in the hearth.

"This is Ruby Henshall, my lady," Bowden made the introduction.

"How old are you, Ruby?"

"Seventeen, me lady," the girl mumbled as she clutched her bundle to her chest even harder.

"And what type of domestic experience do you have?" I asked, already knowing that I was going to hire her no matter what she said. She looked so desperate that I couldn't bear to send her away.

"I've never been in service, me lady, but I'm the oldest o' eleven, so I've had to help me mam with me siblings and do everything 'round the house, from cooking and cleaning, to laundry. I'm not afraid o' hard work, me lady," she added.

I figured that, at seventeen, Ruby was already a drain on her parents. With so many mouths to feed, Ruby's wage would help them tremendously, and save them from providing for an extra child. Ruby was a pretty girl with dark wavy hair and large dark eyes, but her hands were red and raw, and her clothes were threadbare and way too large for her nearly emaciated frame. This girl's only chance of escaping her hard life was to either marry or find employment in a house where food and lodging would be provided. This poor girl must have been worked as hard as a slave, as her mother birthed one child after another and relied on her eldest to pick up the slack in running a household.

"Very well," I said, trying to sound like a mistress. "I will show you to your rooms, and then you can start on supper if you will. Whatever you see fit to make, Mistress Fowler. Ruby, please help Cook with whatever she needs, and we will work out your exact duties once we have more staff. I daresay this house needs to be cleaned from top to bottom, and there's laundry to be done, but that can certainly wait a few days."

"My lady, Harriet Pilcher—you might remember her from before—would like to come back to work, if that's all right. She's been ill these past few days, but should be able to start tomorrow or the day after. What shall I tell her?"

I did remember Harriet from before. She was a docile girl who got her work done. Not the sharpest knife in the box, but much better than Liza, who was entirely too sharp for her own good, and had sold Hugo out to Lionel Finch for a few coins.

"Yes, you may tell Harriet that she can return. And what happened to Liza?" I asked carefully.

"Liza hasn't been seen in these parts since she followed her captain to London," Bowden answered, clearly uncomfortable with gossip. "I hear she took to the streets."

I had a sneaking suspicion that Bowden knew more than he was letting on, but decided not to press him. As long as Liza wasn't in Cranley, we had nothing to worry about.

I wished Master Bowden a good afternoon and led the two women up to the top floor where their rooms would be. They both looked relieved at having been hired, and I was tempted to reassure them and tell them that everything would work out well, but decided not to get too friendly.

The attic rooms were colder than the inside of a refrigerator, and I was shocked to see that they had no fireplaces. Servants froze in the winter and sweated in the summer.

"I wonder if we might share a room, Your Ladyship?" Abigail asked timidly.

"Why?" I asked, not immediately grasping the problem. Who wouldn't want the privacy of their own room, especially when coming from a family of thirteen like Ruby?

"It's just that it's warmer to sleep with another body in the bed," Abigail explained.

"I will have Master Hicks bring a brazier up here," I promised as I left them to get settled. I didn't want them to see the compassion in my eyes, but I did feel sorry for them, and at that moment didn't particularly relish my position as lady of the house.

* * *

"We have a cook and a maid," I announced to Hugo as he finally came in, dusting the snow off his cloak and tossing his hat onto a table in the foyer. He looked tired and hungry, and I suddenly realized that he probably hadn't eaten anything since yesterday.

I followed him into the parlor where a merry fire was burning bright.

Hugo held his hands out to the fire and just stared into the flames as he allowed himself to thaw.

"Would you like something to eat? I can organize some bread and cheese; that should tide you over till supper, which I hope will be edible. Abigail Fowler claims to have cooked for Master Garwood, who was something of a gourmet."

"Abigail is to be our cook?" Hugo asked, the corner of his mouth twitching.

"Yes, why?"

"It seems that Humpty Dumpty threw her over for a younger woman, whom he's married. Abigail must not have had an easy time of it these past few months. I suppose it's decent of him to try to find her a new place."

"Yes, let's pat him on the back for being such a good bloke," I replied sarcastically. I really didn't like the man.

Hugo just shrugged, no longer interested in Bowden. "I'd dined at Garwood's house a few times before he died. He contributed lavishly to Monmouth's cause. Garwood kept a fine cellar and a good table. Abigail will do nicely."

"Was he murdered?" I asked, curious about the man's untimely end.

"Horace Garwood was an entrepreneur who enjoyed the finer things in life," Hugo said as he finally felt warm enough to take a seat. "He was, however, a ruthless businessman, from what I've heard. I believe he drowned in a barrel of brandy, which could hardly have been an accident. An execution, perhaps."

"An execution?" I gasped. "What are you talking about?"

Hugo just shrugged, as if being drowned in brandy was the most common of occurrences. "At one time, drowning someone in a vat of malmsey wine was a form of execution. George Plantagenet, the 1st Duke of Clarence, was executed in that manner. I suppose someone with a sense of humor would see drowning Garwood in brandy as a just punishment for swindling them."

"Ah, nothing can rival the justice administered in the Middle Ages," I said sarcastically as I poured Hugo a brandy and sat across from him, ready to tackle the subject that stood between us like a two-thousand-pound elephant. "What happened to Bradford?" I asked, knowing that whatever Hugo had learned wasn't good since he'd been back for nearly twenty minutes and hadn't said a word about Brad.

"I don't know. He left in October to join James's army and hasn't been heard from since. James is in London plotting his escape. Her Majesty and their son are already out of the country. The army has disbursed, so unless Brad has been wounded, he should have come home by now."

"And Gideon Warburton?" We hadn't heard from Gideon in over a year, which was strange since he was one of the most meticulous people I'd ever met. Gideon Warburton was not a man to let a letter go unanswered, or a request go unfulfilled.

"I didn't have an opportunity to ask after Gideon Warbur-

ton; Beth was too distraught. She's asked me to go after Brad."
Hugo shifted uncomfortably in his seat, knowing that I wouldn't
take this piece of news well—and he was right.

"Hugo, we have been at home for less than twenty-four
hours. You can't leave us," I protested, knowing that it was
futile.

"Neve, I have no choice. I will be back as soon as I can; I
promise."

"Hugo, things are still very uncertain. You haven't received
an official pardon, and James is technically still the king. I know
that apprehending you is not anyone's priority at the moment,
but you are not entirely out of danger."

"I know, and you are absolutely right, but I cannot abandon
a friend in need. Bradford came to my aid when I needed him,
as he did to yours. He placed himself in danger to help us
without a second thought. How can I refuse to help him simply
because the timing happens to be inconvenient?"

"Well, when you put it that way," I replied, knowing that I'd
lost this one. Hugo wouldn't be Hugo if he didn't follow his
conscience, and even though I frequently wanted to strangle
him, I respected him for his devotion to causes and people who
mattered to him.

"Say you understand," Hugo urged as he pulled me onto his
lap and nuzzled my ear.

"I understand," I replied obediently. And I did. "When will
you leave?"

"Tomorrow. Archie will remain here with you."

That made me feel a little better.

EIGHT

I gazed about the parlor with a modicum of satisfaction, noting the gleaming windows, polished floor, and dustless mantel. I've never been a control freak, but cleanliness was important to me, and seeing the room restored to its proper state gave me some small measure of control over my surroundings.

Ruby had been up since dawn, cleaning and scrubbing, while Cook had set about putting the kitchen to rights and taking an inventory of the supplies. The two women seemed eager to please me, and I thanked them for their efforts; genuinely grateful for their help. There was still much to do, but at least we were making a start. The next order of business was attacking the growing pile of laundry. I would have gladly helped Ruby on laundry day, but remembered Frances's warning and kept quiet. The lady of the house did not launder.

I had to admit that now that we had help, I found myself feeling rather useless. The household would be running properly in no time, so it was up to me to discover what a lady did while at home. There were the children, of course, but a nursemaid would be engaged in due course to look after their daily needs, while I would see to their rearing and education. In the meantime, they needed to be kept busy.

Despite living in the seventeenth century, I still believed that children needed to have fun, and not remain confined indoors for fear of getting ill. Most children of noble families boasted pale complexions and fragile heath. Children needed fresh air and exercise, which was not something that was prescribed by the physicians of the day, and so did I. I'd barely left the house since we'd arrived.

I stepped closer to the window when I saw Archie disappearing into the shed with something resembling a door beneath his arm. What was he up to? Archie was another one who couldn't stay cooped up for long. Frances liked to sleep in, but Archie was usually up at dawn, seeing to the horses, chopping wood, and fixing whatever he thought needed his urgent attention. He needed to keep busy, something I understood only too well.

Hugo had mentioned that there might be visits from tenants over the next few days, and I would have to receive them in his place. They might be coming by to welcome us home, or to bring a grievance of some sort, one they felt hadn't been properly handled by Godfrey Bowden. But, for the moment, all was quiet since it was still fairly early in the morning.

The children were still asleep, so I threw on my cloak and stepped into the chilly morning, suddenly desperate for a breath of fresh air. I crossed the yard and headed for the shed, curious to see what Archie was doing with the door. I found him hard at work, his hair tied back and his coat hanging from a nail. His sleeves were rolled up as he filed a piece of wood and regularly checked the surface for smoothness with his thumb.

"What are you doing?" I asked as I took in the heavy carved door from an old armoire lying on the worktable. Archie had already attached a sturdy rectangle of wood to one side, and it stuck up from the door at a ninety-degree angle.

He glanced at me over his shoulder, a happy smile on his face. "I'm making a surprise for the children," he replied, clearly expecting me to share in his delight. I would have, had I known what I was looking at.

I gave Archie a guilty smile and shrugged my shoulders in ignorance.

Archie shook his head in dismay, amazed by my puzzlement, and a little hurt by the lack of enthusiasm. "It's going to be a sled. This is the back," Archie explained as he pointed to the piece of wood which protruded from the door, "and I am now making the sides. I'm going to attach this old leather strap, like so," he showed me where the strap would go, "and pull them along, or let them slide down the hillock."

"Oh, Archie, that's genius," I exclaimed, now embarrassed by my lack of imagination. "They'll love it."

"Some village lads made a sled every winter when I was a boy. We had such fun, we forgot all about the cold. We'd take turns going down the ridge or pulling each other along. We'd run faster and faster, until the boy on the sled could no longer hold on and tumbled off. Of course, all we needed was a flat piece of wood, but with the children being so young, they need something to keep them from sliding off," he explained.

"I wouldn't mind taking a ride myself," I said wistfully, my statement greeted by a look of reproach from Archie. The wife of Lord Everly would not be seen sliding down a hill with her skirts kirtled up and her cheeks red from the cold. I lowered my eyes in embarrassment and admired the sled some more. "How soon will it be ready?"

"Oh, by the time they finish with their breakfast, I reckon," Archie replied, his attention already back on the wood. "I'll need an old blanket or two to wrap them up, or they'll catch their death."

"I'll see what I can find," I replied as I turned to leave.

I now understood why Jane always had her work basket

nearby. She needed something to do, and sewing or embroidering gave her a sense of purpose. I wasn't very good at sewing, and embroidery was completely beyond me, so I would have to find something to occupy the hours since I wasn't supposed to do anything around the house. There was a fine library at Everly Manor, but as much I liked to read, I needed to be physically active.

I wonder what the official position on a woman walking alone is, I thought stubbornly as I returned to the house and heard Elena's voice coming from upstairs.

"Mama, where are you?" The sound of her little voice instantly dispelled my displeasure, and I raced up the stairs in a most unladylike way, eager to give her a hug while she was still warm and sleepy.

The three of them were already sitting up in bed, bright-eyed and eager to get up. They were always hungry in the mornings, especially Michael, who was fidgeting in a way that suggested that he needed to use the chamber pot urgently, so I snatched him up first and thrust the pot in front of him after pulling off his clout. Valentine was already toilet-trained, but the twins still needed a nappy when they went to bed. Unlike the future, where parents could afford to hold off potty training until the children were older, in the seventeenth century, most children were toilet-trained well before the age of two. Not only did it drastically reduce the amount of laundry, but keeping the children dry also prevented them from getting sick in cold, drafty houses and when outdoors.

"You two stay in the warm bed while I get Michael dressed," I instructed the girls, who were already hiding under the covers and giggling.

"Horse," Michael said, looking around in desperation. "Horse," he wailed.

"It's right here next to your pillow, darling," I replied soothingly.

Michael held out his chubby hands for his toy while I pulled on his hose and breeches. Most boys walked around in gowns until they were breeched, but I preferred Michael not to look as if he were wearing a nightgown all day long. I helped him on with his coat to keep him from getting cold and set him down on the floor to play while I helped the girls.

Little girls dressed much as older women, so it took some time in the morning to don all the layers of clothing and do up the laces. They looked like little women once they were fully dressed, especially with their hair brushed out and piled on top of their heads.

"There, all done. Ready for breakfast? I believe Archie has a wonderful surprise for you," I said, smiling at their eager faces.

"What surprise?" Valentine demanded.

"You'll just have to wait and see."

I scooped up the twins and allowed Valentine to hold on to my skirt as we slowly descended the stairs and headed for the warm kitchen where the children would break their fast.

NINE

Frances opened her eyes and stretched luxuriously. Cold winter sunshine filtered through the not-so-clean windows and bathed the room in golden light. The room was chilly, but it was warm and comfortable beneath the down quilt, and there was really no reason to rush. The wonderful smell of fresh bread and fried bacon wafted from downstairs, and although she wouldn't be getting her morning chocolate in England, it was still good to be home, especially on this day. Today she turned eighteen, and it was time to take control of her life as a grown woman should.

The past two years had been the happiest she'd ever known. For the first time in her life, Frances had a loving family, a sense of safety and peace, and a man who genuinely loved her. She no longer had to deal with an indifferent father who couldn't wait to get her off his hands; a mean-spirited brother, or a cruel husband who derived pleasure from her pain. She was free to choose for herself, and she had chosen Archie.

She would have married Archie years ago, but Archie had realized something which Frances had failed to see, being young and deeply traumatized by her experiences. She needed time to heal, physically and emotionally, and he had given her that time, and in his quiet way aided in the healing. Archie was like a balm for the soul, a steady and faithful presence in her life who never made any demands on her, just made her feel protected and loved. He was like a guardian angel who picked her up when she was in a free fall and never let go.

Frances had been physically unwell and emotionally unstable after leaving Paris for Rouen. She'd wanted to be a grown-up, but instead she'd nearly ruined her life, first by dallying with Luke Marsden, and then by trusting Sabine to put things right. But the wily maid had lied to her, and given her a remedy she herself had never tried. Frances still had nightmares of nearly bleeding to death while trying to self-abort Luke's baby. No one had seen Sabine after the night she'd given Frances the oil of rue; she'd vanished into the labyrinth of Paris's streets, never to be heard from again, fearful of what she had done. She hadn't even remained in the house long enough to see if Frances would survive. Well, Frances had learned her lesson there. She'd given her trust too easily and had paid the price.

Another man might have forsaken her after what she'd done, but not Archie. He never uttered a word of reproach and had taken it upon himself to heal her spirit. They went for long walks, galloped through the countryside, and, at times, just sat companionably side by side as Archie sharpened his dagger and Frances read her favorite book of poems. Sitting in silence was never awkward, just joyful, especially when Archie looked away from his task and smiled into her eyes, a smile that was reserved for her alone, before planting a sweet kiss on her lips.

Frances would have lain with him, but Archie wouldn't have it. He held her when she needed it, and kissed her tenderly, but that was as far as it went. He would wait until they were married, and thanks to Hugo, their wedding had been indefinitely postponed. Well, there had been no word from Gideon Warburton, and she wasn't willing to wait any longer.

She didn't wish for her life with Archie to be financed by the money she got from Finch. Besides, Archie would feel emasculated if his wife was wealthier than him, and she didn't want that. Frances had learned in Rouen that she was perfectly happy when living modestly; she didn't need a big house or servants. She just wanted a place where they could finally be alone, and start their life together in earnest. Of course, she still wanted to remain close to the Everlys; they were her family, and she would never abandon them.

Frances finally gave up the warmth of the bed and put her foot experimentally onto the freezing floorboards. She yanked it right back, but then sighed with resignation and firmly planted her feet on the floor. Her stomach was growling with hunger, so it was time to go down. Last night's supper had been quite good, so she had high hopes for breakfast.

She peeked out the window as she heard shrieks coming from outside. She instantly tensed, expecting to see something unpleasant, but was greeted by the sight of the children, bundled into what looked like a three-sided wooden box, and pulled along by Archie through the snow. Archie's face was ruddy with cold, but he was laughing—not a sight one often saw. The children were howling with laughter, their little faces alight with joy. Frances spotted Neve standing off to the side, her cheeks pink with cold. She was huddled in her cloak for warmth, and was stomping her feet on the ground, but refused to go inside. She looked a little envious, truth be told, as Archie did another circle around the yard.

Frances finally tore her gaze away from the window and spotted a surprise of her own. A square box stood on the dressing table where she couldn't fail to spot it. It hadn't been there when she went to bed, so someone must have been in her room. Frances grabbed the box and dove back under the covers to warm her feet. She opened the box slowly, savoring the delight of receiving a birthday present, to find a pink and blue enamel box wrapped in tissue paper. The box had a golden clasp, and there was a miniature picture of two cherubs frolicking among the clouds. It was absolutely charming, and perfect for safekeeping small bits of jewelry. Frances hugged the box to herself and smiled. Archie must have bought it before they'd left France to have it ready for her birthday.

Setting the box in pride of place on the dressing table, Frances dressed as quickly as she could, wrapped a woolen shawl around her shoulders for added warmth, and made her way downstairs. She took Archie's present as an omen that today was the day she'd make a change.

* * *

Frances was just sipping some hot broth after finishing her bread and bacon when Archie strode into the kitchen. He smelled of winter and pine, and his face was rosy from the cold. His eyes lit up when he saw bread and a bowl of drippings on the table.

He stripped off his gloves and threw them aside. "I'm starving," he growled. "Haven't had my breakfast yet. Is there any bacon left?"

Frances buttered a slice of bread for Archie and pushed the plate toward him as he took a seat at the table. She was already finished with her breakfast, so she got up and planted a kiss on top of Archie's head. "Thank you for my present," she whispered in his ear.

"Do you like it?" he asked carefully. Archie never looked nervous, but Frances knew him well enough to see the need for approval in his eyes. He wanted her to like his present; it meant the world to him.

"I love it," she replied honestly. "It's exquisite."

Archie lit up from the inside from her praise, his lips stretching into a happy smile. "I'm glad."

The cook gave Frances a look of disapproval from beneath her lashes. As Lord Everly's ward, she had no business in the kitchen, but she hated eating alone, and she wanted to be with Archie, especially today.

Frances stared down the cook, poured herself more broth, and sat down across from Archie, happy to keep him company while he ate.

"I thought I heard hoofbeats in my sleep," Frances said as she took a sip.

"Hugo left at dawn," Archie replied, but didn't elaborate. He gave her a meaningful look across the table, silencing the next question. Whatever Hugo was doing, was not for the ears of the cook.

"Will you walk to the church with me this morning?" Frances asked as she smiled at Archie sweetly.

"Of course. You wish to pray?"

"Not exactly," Frances replied as she gave him her own look, warning him not to ask anything more.

"I'll bring in some firewood and fetch water for Ruby; then I'm free to go, but I must be back by noon. Master Bowden is sending over two grooms for me to interview. If they suit, I'll ride over to Nash House with them to collect the rest of Lord Everly's horses," Archie informed her as he reached for another slice of bread. "Just give me a quarter of an hour."

"I'll be waiting," Frances answered with a wicked grin before leaving the kitchen.

* * *

Frances slid wooden pattens over her shoes, fastened her cloak, and pulled on her hood. It was terribly cold outside, but she didn't mind. The walk to the church wasn't that long, and if things went as she planned, she'd have her joy to keep her warm.

She watched as Archie finally emerged from the house. He was wearing a warm cape that bulged slightly over the hilt of his sword, and a wide-brimmed hat, which made him look like a dashing highwayman.

"So, why do you really want to go to church?" Archie asked as they set off. Normally, Archie wouldn't hold her hand when walking in public view, but the frosty grass was slippery, making her glide in her pattens rather than walk. It was the gentlemanly thing to do.

"Because I want to advise the vicar of our intention to marry. He can call the banns this coming Sunday, and after calling them again for three consecutive Sundays, we'll be free to marry."

Archie stopped short and stared at Frances as if he were seeing her for the first time. "And when did you decide this?"

Frances wasn't sure if Archie was angry or amused. Sometimes it was hard to tell. His expression was very serious, but his eyes were twinkling beneath the brim of his hat, and his lips twitched as if he were trying not to smile.

"This morning. I am now eighteen, and there's no reason for us to wait any longer."

"But Lord Everly..." Archie began.

"Archie, I know that you have great admiration for Lord Everly and want to honor his wishes, but this should be our decision. I don't want Lionel's money. Do you?"

"Never did," Archie replied as he smiled widely at Frances. "But I thought you wanted to be a June bride with a bouquet of wildflowers and blooms in your hair," he teased.

"At this point, I don't mind carrying a bouquet of bare twigs and wearing an extra petticoat for warmth. I just don't want to wait any longer. I want us to be man and wife at last."

"Let's go talk to the vicar then."

Archie pulled her close and planted a solid kiss on her lips, in full view of the woman who was walking down the lane. The woman gaped at them just as Frances lost her footing on the slippery slope and grabbed Archie's arm to keep from falling. Archie wrapped an arm around her and pulled her against him, nearly falling himself. They burst out laughing, making the woman walk faster as if she might catch whatever they had.

TEN

DECEMBER 2014

Surrey, England

The graveyard was bathed in abundant sunshine, making the snow on the ancient tombstones sparkle in a festive way not at all appropriate to a cemetery. The squat church tower with its familiar blue clock rose toward the cloudless sky, reminding Simon of the time. It was nearly eleven—time for the appointment with Reverend Lambert.

"Oh, come on, Simon," Heather called impatiently from the church porch. "We'll be late." She had no desire to loiter in the cemetery; instead, she marched directly to the church, eager to begin.

Simon threw one last look at the headstone of Roland Everly, the man who'd fathered him and watched him grow, but never once acknowledged him as his own son, or even so much as attempted to forge any kind of relationship with him. Roland had paid for Simon's education, which was the extent of his involvement in Simon's life, and he wouldn't even have done that much had Stella Harding not threatened him with exposure. Roland would not have relished a divorce from his frosty wife, so he had just whipped out his checkbook and wrote out a check, relieved to have gotten off so easily.

Roland was a man who liked ease. His friends referred to him as Rolly—a pet name worthy of the playboy. He hadn't worked a day in his life, instead devoting his time to numerous affairs, jaunts to Scotland for grouse shooting and rounds of golf on the world's finest courses, and a devotion to his wine cellar, which was probably the finest in Surrey.

Simon never did understand what drew his practical, logical mother to a man like Roland Everly. She'd given over twenty years of her life to that pillock, and he hadn't so much as mentioned her in his will for fear of alerting his wife to his relationship with the housekeeper. It was a blessing of sorts that Simon never knew Roland was his father until after his death, or he would have had a few choice words for his "devoted" sire. The only good thing that came out of all this was Simon's relationship with Max, who was his older half-brother.

If only they had known. And now it was too late.

In time, Max's stone would take its place next to his father's, Simon remaining the only Everly left of the line. Heather was forever on him to change his surname, but Simon was hesitant. Max had been gone for just over three years now, but despite Simon's discovery of the blog post stating that Maximillian Everly had died in Barbados in 1686, he was still considered alive in 2014. It would take years to have Max declared legally dead, and, truth be told, Simon still held out hope that Max would one day just saunter into the village and say it was all a great big misunderstanding. They would go have a pint or two and have a laugh at Simon's overactive imagination and the impossibility of time travel.

For a few months, Simon had harbored fantasies of following Max to the seventeenth century, but had finally given up on the idea. It seemed plausible in the middle of the night when the shifting shadows looked like faces of the dead and the memories of Max flooded his mind, but in the cold light of day, it was ludicrous. Even if the passage really existed, and even if traveling back in time were possible, there seemed no way to navigate it all, and once there, Simon had no idea how he would even go about looking for Max. Max could be long dead by the time Simon finally showed up, or possibly not even there yet, because, for all he knew, Simon could end up in the realm of Elizabeth I, or, better yet, her famous father. No, rescuing Max was just a pipe dream; a younger brother's longing to help the only flesh and blood he had left besides his mother.

"Simon," Heather bellowed from the porch. She was stomping from foot to foot, freezing in her stylish high-heeled boots and short leather jacket trimmed with fox fur. For some unfathomable reason, she felt the need to look sexy for the vicar, God bless her soul. Simon supposed he had no cause to complain about his girlfriend—no—fiancée now, looking beautiful, but her choice of attire just annoyed him. Heather was all about appearances, and although in this day and age there was nothing unusual about that, he sometimes wished there was a little more substance to his fiancée.

Simon obediently turned away from the gravestone and began walking toward the church when something caught his eye. He knew this graveyard like the back of his hand, had played hide-and-go-seek here as a boy, and then spent Halloween night here on a dare when he was sixteen. He'd nearly soiled himself when he'd heard someone prowling around in the darkness, an eerie howl splitting the night just as the moon was obscured by the clouds and it grew pitch dark. Of course, it had been his friends playing a dirty trick on him, but it had scared him shitless.

The two graves looked weathered and old, the larger stone leaning a bit to the side, and the smaller one practically swallowed by weeds. These graves weren't there before, Simon was sure of that. He brushed aside the snow-covered weeds to read the barely legible inscription.

Elena Mary Everly
Beloved daughter

Simon stared at the grave, confused. He knew every Everly in this cemetery thanks to Max, and he'd never seen this child's grave. And it had to be a child since the stone was much smaller than the rest. The date of death had been swallowed by the earth long ago, and despite his curiosity, Simon had no time to start digging up the stone.

He brushed the snow from the larger stone.

Hugo Everly
Born 1650—Died 1689

Simon took an involuntary step back, his skin prickling with gooseflesh. What did this mean? He'd seen Hugo Everly's portrait every day of his life; had heard the story of his disappearance and had even speculated with Max as to what could have befallen him. The seventeenth-century lord had vanished without a trace one day, never to return—much like Max. There was no record of when he'd died or where he was buried, all his correspondence gone and his personal possessions much as he left them. To Max, who was fascinated with family history, it was a tantalizing mystery, but to Simon, who only participated in order to please his idol, it was all rubbish. He never much cared for the overbearing, scowling man in the portrait. But now, Hugo Everly was suddenly buried in the graveyard with the year of his death there for all to see. He'd vanished in 1685, but died in 1689. Where had he been for four years, and how did he die? Where had the gravestone suddenly come from? Simon shivered, unable to tear his gaze away.

"Simon, don't make me come and get you," Heather screeched, now really annoyed.

Simon tore his attention away from the two stones and jogged to the church. He would come back tomorrow without Heather and see if the stones were still there.

* * *

Reverend Lambert was waiting for them in his office, his round face wreathed in a smile of welcome. "Simon, how good to see you. It's been a while," he added as he poured tea for them and added a splash of milk to his own mug. Translation: I haven't seen you at Sunday service since you were a teenager and your mother dragged you here by force, but nice of you to show up now that you need someone to marry you. God forgives all sinners, even you.

"Reverend Lambert, it's such a pleasure to finally meet you," Heather interjected smoothly. "Simon was saying just the other day that we should just get married in London, but I think it's important to stick to tradition. So many generations of Everlys married in this very church, and Simon, being the last of the line, should be married here as well, don't you agree?" She had removed her jacket, revealing the blood-red cashmere jersey with a deep V-neck that left the good reverend nearly speechless with awe.

"Well, yes," the reverend agreed, his eyes finally leaving Heather's ample cleavage, "but Simon is technically not an Everly—at least not in the eyes of the church. His parents were never married, my dear."

"Yes, I know, but it's just a formality these days, isn't it? No such a thing as 'bastard' anymore," Heather reminded the reverend cheerfully. "Once Max is declared legally dead, Simon will be the new Lord Everly and will officially change his name from Harding to Everly, won't you, darling?" she prattled on.

"If it means that much to you," Simon muttered. He was more than happy to keep his mother's name. Stella Harding had raised him, loved him, and supported him all his life. Her name meant more to him than the surname of the pompous liar and cheat who had impregnated his mother. The man was more interested in stuffing dead animals at that hideaway of his than spending time with either of his sons. Roland had brought other women there too, because having a wife and a long-term mistress living under the same roof just wasn't enough for that pathetic letch.

"Simon," Heather nudged him. "You are a million miles away. I was just telling the reverend how eager we are to be married."

"I rather like summer weddings," Simon offered, but Heather completely ignored him.

"End of January, I think. It's taken me this long to finally get Simon to propose, so I see no reason to wait another six months to marry. Do you have an open Saturday?"

"Let me just check the calendar," Reverend Lambert suggested as he threw Simon a sympathetic look. "Ah yes, here. The last Saturday in January is available, so we have much to discuss."

"I'll just leave all the planning to you two," Simon said as he edged toward the door. Weddings normally took months to arrange, but Heather, being a photographer, had numerous contacts in the wedding industry, and could plan a lavish affair in a matter of weeks by calling in some favors. Simon was sure that she already had a dress picked out, and a caterer she wanted to use. Her business partner would take care of the wedding photos, and the invitations could be printed by the end of the week and in the mail by Friday. Heather's father would finance the whole enterprise, so all Simon had to do was show up on the appointed day and remember to say "I do" when asked a question by the reverend.

"But, Simon," Heather called after him as he escaped from the overheated office.

"I know you'll have it all in hand, darling," Simon replied as he sped past the altar and toward the steps to the crypt. He hadn't been in the church in years, and having read Henry's diary was curious to see if he could spot the six-petaled flower which supposedly opened the passage to the past. Let Heather make her plans and weave her wicked web; he had more interesting things to do.

ELEVEN
DECEMBER 1688

Paris, France

Max leaned against the stone parapet of Pont Neuf and gazed at the city spread before him, the winding ribbon of the Seine splitting it in half. Today, the water was a pewter-gray, reflecting the leaden sky liberally dotted with thick, stormy clouds. Max often crossed the bridge on his way to Notre Dame Cathedral. At first, he'd gone there simply as a tourist, to enjoy the architecture and the stunning windows, but, as time passed, he found himself drawn to the great cathedral for other reasons.

Max had been raised in the Church of England, but his religious life consisted of going to church on Christmas and Easter, and attending the weddings, christenings, and funerals of various acquaintances. Religion meant nothing to him, and Max secretly subscribed to the sentiments of Karl Marx, who called it "the opium of the masses."

But Notre Dame stirred something inside of Max, a desire for something higher than himself perhaps. He enjoyed finding a seat in an out-of-the-way pew and studying the breathtaking beauty of the Gothic cathedral. On fine days, the sun shone through the magnificent stained-glass windows, turning the nave into a rainbow of color as each bit of colored glass took on a life of its own, and added its tiny voice to the harmony that was the music of the heavens. Sometimes, Max got lucky enough to come upon choir practice, and he remained still for the duration, sitting with his eyes closed as the notes soared to the vaulted ceiling above, the voices of the children as pure as the souls of angels.

Max wasn't really sure when he began praying. It was a need he'd often suppressed, especially while healing from his injury, but in the anonymity of Notre Dame, he was finally able to pour his heart out to the God he'd never believed in, and found solace he'd never sought. But what he also found was an unwanted truth. He was alive only by the grace of God, he knew that, and perhaps by the grace of Vivienne Benoit as well.

Vivienne had taken it upon herself to get Max back on his feet, and she had succeeded. Max had been told that he likely wouldn't survive for very long. The hole in his intestine would leak gastric fluids into his abdominal cavity, and he would die of infection—sooner rather than later. One physician had offered to operate, but Max had refused. If he didn't die of infection, he'd die of whatever botched procedure the seventeenth-century quack would try to perform. With no sterilization, antibiotics, or anesthesia, it would be easier to simply slit his wrists and be done with it.

It had been Vivienne who'd hit upon a solution after Max's prolonged suffering. She'd noticed that Max felt better until he ingested solid foods, and had put him on a regime of liquids for a month, having reasonably deduced that if his gut was leaking, he'd be long dead, therefore, the damage couldn't be so drastic that it couldn't be healed. The liquid diet had left Max feeling weak and permanently hungry, but the pain in his abdomen had decreased dramatically, since there was no strain on the affected area. Vivienne had gradually introduced some milk-soaked bread, mashed vegetables, and bits of fish, monitoring Max's reaction to the food.

Miraculously, he felt better. The hole must have had an opportunity to heal on its own, allowing Max to slowly return to a somewhat normal diet. He still avoided eating foods that were hard to digest, but at least he was thriving, so much so that he had eventually renewed his visits to Juliette. Max supposed he should have been saving every penny for his return voyage instead of spending his money on a whore, but he needed to feel that he was living rather than just existing. He visited Juliette once a fortnight, spending his precious wages on a few hours of sexual oblivion in the arms of a woman who was grateful for his patronage, and devoted herself to pleasing him rather than judging him as a mistress would.

And now, his long-dormant conscience was speaking, or perhaps it was the voice of God taking him to task, but over the past two years, Max had come to realize some harsh truths about himself and the world he'd left behind. It had taken him a long time to admit to himself that perhaps he was purposely delaying his return to England, not because he didn't have enough money saved to pay for a passage, but because he'd come to realize that, after all this time, there was very little left for him to return to.

He was sure that his unexplained absence made for a great story and put Cranleigh on the map, until another more interesting headline overtook the news agencies. But once the reporters had gone and the cameras stopped clicking, who actually cared that he was gone? His mother and Stella, of course, and Simon, but no one else. His school friends probably added Max's disappearance to their party anecdotes, eager to point out that they knew firsthand someone who'd been in the news and increasing their perceived social value. And his supporters and potential sponsors probably wrote him off as either a victim of a crime or some flake who had just decided to shirk his responsibilities and fall off the grid. There was no wife, no children, not even a loving girlfriend. And now, after three years, even his mother—if she were still alive—Stella and Simon would have moved on with their lives.

Max wondered if Neve ever spared him a thought. He'd come to realize that perhaps what he had felt for her was a sort of transference. He wanted to be loved, and had convinced himself that Hugo had cheated him out of a budding romance, when, in fact, Neve might not have even been interested in him. She'd been vulnerable after the breakup of her last relationship, and Max had thought that he could step in and fix her, make her dependent on him and turn that dependence into love. Perhaps Neve saw him for the man he really was: selfish, self-centered, vain, and manipulative. No wonder she fell in love with Hugo. Who wouldn't be swept off their feet by someone charismatic and selfless, someone willing to lay down his life for a cause, or his family?

Hugo would have died to protect Neve and their daughter, of that Max was sure, and he admired the man for it. However, what he admired even more was Hugo's cunning. The man was the ultimate survivor. Contrary to the family stories he'd heard all his life, about a hapless ancestor who'd gone and died somewhere without leaving so much as a headstone, Hugo was anything but. Hugo was clever, resourceful, and brave; qualities that Max utterly lacked until finding himself thrust into the churning waters of seventeenth-century politics. He was stronger now, more ruthless, but bravery was still something that eluded him. His number-one concern had always been with saving his own skin, and although he was still very much alive, he had very little to show for his efforts.

And now, his employment with Captain Benoit was drawing to a close, and there were decisions to be made; not a pleasant prospect. Max had rather enjoyed living with the Benoits. He adored Vivienne and had grown close to the children, whose enthusiasm and easy trust brought out the best in him. He'd never realized how much he enjoyed the company of children until he'd met Banjo and the Benoit boys. With children, there was no need to pretend, no need to impress or deceive. They were so pure, so eager to learn and to please that Max found himself responding to their excitement and curiosity. And now, he would be parted from Lucien and Edouard as well. Another loss—another end.

Max pushed away from the parapet and turned his steps toward home, or what would be home for a few more months, until the captain sailed away in the spring, taking his sons with him on their first journey. Max had been invited to leave at that time, and he would. He supposed it was time to go home and try to rebuild what was left of his life, but, sadly, the prospect of home no longer appealed. Max lay awake at night, trying to picture his return to the future, and his welcome at Everly Manor, but all he saw in his mind's eye were the shocked faces of people, awkward pauses in conversation, and a barrage of questions he'd have no way of answering. His political career would be dead in the water after such a long absence, and anyone he'd known would have long since forgotten all about him. Max would have to start from scratch at the age of forty, and although some more optimistic souls might see his predicament as a clean slate, all Max saw was a bottomless chasm of his own insignificance.

TWELVE

Hugo stopped at a crossroads and reined in his horse, taking a moment to decide on a course of action. Going to Salisbury seemed pointless. Both armies had moved out in the first week of December. The Battle of Reading, however, had taken place only ten days ago, so it made more sense to head in that direction. If Brad were indeed with the Royalist Army, then someone would know something of his whereabouts.

Hugo dug his heels into the horse's flanks and took off for Berkshire. The day was cold but bright, and the mud on the road was minimal due to the cold temperatures. Hugo estimated that Reading was about fifty miles away, so if he stopped for dinner at midday, he could easily reach the town before nightfall. Traveling on horseback for hours in the middle of December was not advisable, but he had little choice.

By the time Hugo stopped at a nondescript tavern in some tiny hamlet, he was stiff with cold and ravenously hungry. He hadn't eaten anything but a hunk of day-old bread and a piece of cheese before leaving at dawn, since the new cook hadn't been up yet, and he'd grabbed whatever he could find. The tavern was tiny, with only a few scarred tables and two attic rooms available to travelers, but the food was surprisingly good and fresh. Hugo ate a bowl of stew, rich with meat, gravy and root vegetables, and then agreed to a slice of meat pie which the publican's wife was trying to press on him. It was rather good; the crust flaky and buttery, and the meat flavored with onions and spices.

Hugo leaned back in his chair by the hearth and allowed himself a few more minutes of warmth, posing as just a traveler taking his ease to listen to the talk around him. The men in the tavern were a poor lot, their clothes threadbare and not nearly warm enough for the weather, but they were in good spirits, drinking to the health of William of Orange, who would save them from the uncertain future they would have had under James II and his Catholic dynasty.

Hugo threw on his cloak, pulled on his gloves, and adjusted his sword before heading out into the cold again. He couldn't bear to hear another word. In truth, he could understand the feelings of the common man, but as a Catholic, it cut him to the quick to hear of their fears. Not that they weren't based in fact. Mary Tudor had single-handedly destroyed any faith the people might have in a Catholic monarch. Her fanaticism had left deep scars among the people, who would sooner welcome a foreign prince rather than risk another monarch who might bring the Inquisition to their doorstep. He couldn't blame them. What Hugo wanted was a country in which its citizens were free to practice their religion, whatever it happened to be, without discrimination or suspicion, but, as things stood now, that wasn't going to happen for many centuries to come.

Even in the twenty-first century there were still wars of religion, although they were fought on a somewhat different battlefield than in his own time, or the centuries before when the Crusades were seen as the will of God, rather than a senseless slaughter of people who happened to worship differently and live in a way that was unfathomable to Europeans. Of course, it was all a play for power, as most wars were, and a bid to control the Holy Land using the common people's superstition and hatred to swell the ranks of the army and do the killing and pillaging.

William of Orange was not a man who would rape and pillage; he was a well-respected ruler and statesman, one who was well-versed in the politics of the time, and more grounded than the autocratic Louis XIV, whom the ill-fated James hoped to emulate. The notion of Divine Rule was still strong in France and Spain, but the people of England wanted a ruler who understood its people, not one who craved absolute power and ruled through fear and subjugation. For the first time in the history of Europe, the monarch would have the religion of his people, rather than the people being required to have the religion of the monarch. Hugo was well aware, though it hurt him to the core, that very soon a law would be passed, which would still be in effect in the future, that a British monarch could not be Catholic, nor could marry a Catholic.

What damage the Catholics had done to their image with their burnings and thumbscrews, Hugo mused as he trotted along the road. He had never been a fanatic himself, nor had he known anyone who believed in the eternal fires of Hell which would consume anyone who didn't share their faith, but unfortunately, to some degree, he was a minority, and that realization turned his stomach. Hugo's father had been a staunch Catholic, but he was also a consummate politician, a man who understood that there was nothing to be gained by alienating those in power and worked the establishment to his advantage, as he hoped Hugo would do. Joss Everly believed that faith was something between a man and his God, not to be sullied by politics or financial gain. He never had misgivings about pretending to be a Protestant to further his goals, nor did he sit in judgment of those who kept their faith secret in order to protect what was theirs.

Hugo smiled ruefully as he realized how much he'd changed since the days of his involvement with the Monmouth Rebellion. It had taken Neve to open his eyes, and a visit to the twenty-first century to truly bring home to him the effects of history on the future. He wished he could share his feelings with Brad, but there was no way he could explain to his friend what he'd come to understand without divulging the source of his knowledge, and that he couldn't do. No matter how much he trusted Bradford Nash, he couldn't endanger his wife by exposing her for a time-traveler or breathing any life into suspicions of witchcraft. Brad was a kind, educated man, but, like most people of the time, he still held on to superstition and a belief that the Devil and his disciples were among God-fearing folk, tempting, perverting, and spreading like cancer.

Hugo pinched the bridge of his nose, his head suddenly aching unbearably, made worse by the bright sunshine and blinding whiteness of the colorless sky. *A pair of sunglasses would come in very handy right about now,* Hugo thought as he pulled his hat lower, *and a car with a heater and a radio.* There were so many things he missed about the future—not being in constant danger being one of them.

THIRTEEN

Liza Timmins gazed into the leaping flames of the fire as she stirred a pot of porridge to keep it from burning. The porridge would have to last through today and tomorrow, and serve as both breakfast and dinner for her and Johnny.

Liza put down the wooden spoon and climbed to the loft to check on her son. Johnny was two and a half, but he was a sturdy little lad, one who could easily pass for a boy of three. He had a quick mind and a sweet face, dominated by a pair of dark, thickly lashed eyes. Liza felt the boy's forehead. Thank God the fever had broken and the child was sleeping peacefully. Liza took off her shawl and spread it atop the thin blanket to make sure that Johnny was warm enough. He'd have to stay abed today to make sure that the illness was well and truly gone.

Having climbed back down, Liza continued her inspection of the ill and infirm. She pulled aside a curtain which shielded the bed in the alcove of the cottage. Her mother's breathing was raspy, her thin chest barely rising and falling as she waited to breathe her last. Liza brushed the thin hair away from her mother's forehead before she adjusted the blanket and closed the curtain. Her mother had been hale and hearty once, but now, at fifty-two, she was a sack of bones, her sunken eyes a testament to her pain. The village wisewoman said it was a malady of the stomach, which had spread into the other organs. There was no cure, but the wisewoman had charged plenty for potions that helped relieve the pain and brought on hours of blissful sleep. Her mother barely ate these days, but she did take the potions, desperate for anything that would dull the pain and let her rest.

Liza poked her head outside. It was bitter cold out there. What was keeping the girls? Liza's sisters were in charge of milking their one cow and feeding the chickens and the horse. They'd gone out over an hour ago, but there was no sign of them. If Liza knew Avis, Tess, and Molly, they were up to no good—or at least Avis was. She was sweet on the boy from the neighboring farm and put her younger sisters to work while she met him by the stile. *Little strumpet*, Liza thought angrily. It was just a matter of time before those two announced their intention to wed, and Liza would be left with a dying mother, two younger sisters who still needed years of supporting, and a fatherless son. The money she'd taken off Lionel Finch was not stretching as far as she'd hoped, and soon she'd have to think of a way to start supplementing their income. There were jobs to be found in the nearby town of Haslemere, but taking a job as a maid would mean leaving Johnny and her mother to be looked after by the girls, one being too young, another too frivolous, and the third with her head permanently stuck in the clouds as she dreamed of her wedding.

FOURTEEN

Reading, Berkshire

As Hugo drew closer to Reading, he saw few signs of the recent engagement. William's forces had moved on, and as far as Hugo knew, William was already in Windsor. James's troops had dispersed after their sovereign had fled and had submitted to the conqueror when he came upon them during his advance through the Thames valley. The town of Reading looked peaceful and sleepy in the December twilight; the windows glowing with candlelight, and smoke from the chimneys curling and dissolving into the darkening sky. In exactly a week, James would flee the country, but, as of right now, he was still engaged in negotiations with William, presumably to buy time to plan his escape.

Hugo trotted up Broad Street and looked around. He didn't want to draw undue attention to himself, so turned onto Basingstoke Road instead and dismounted in front of a small establishment called The Globe Inn. He found that when fishing for information, it was best to avoid the more popular haunts and go somewhere nondescript, where the owners were so delighted with unexpected custom that they were especially gracious and forthcoming. The pub was much as he expected, with low ceilings, dark wooden beams dissecting walls of dirty plaster, and a heavily carved wooden bar which took up a good third of the taproom. Only one table was occupied, and by the looks of it, the patron was so deep in his cups that he could barely stand up.

Hugo took the table closest to the hearth and stretched out his legs, happy to be out of the saddle after hours of riding. A pleasant warmth from the fire spread through him as he waited for service, so he removed his cloak and gloves and tossed them over an empty chair.

He didn't have long to wait. A thin, haggard woman made a beeline toward him, her face wreathed in a happy smile at seeing an unexpected customer. "Welcome, sir. Welcome. And what can I get ye this evening?"

"Do you have brandy?" Hugo asked, guessing that they probably didn't. A place like this served ale and beer, and possibly apple cider, but finer spirits were not their bread and butter. They catered to simple folk, with simple tastes. But Hugo wanted to make the woman doubt if he'd stay—a move which would make her more eager to please.

"No, sir," she muttered, her smile faltering. "But we do have ale, small ale, and some excellent cider."

Hugo waited a moment, giving the impression of debating whether he should remain or not.

The woman looked fearfully toward the back before coming to a decision. "The first tankard of ale is on the house, sir."

"Well, that's most generous of you, mistress. I'll have the ale then, and whatever you have on the menu tonight for supper," Hugo replied, smiling at her graciously. "Roast beef, is it?"

It smelled nothing like roast beef, which dismayed the poor woman even further. "No, sir, 'tis rabbit stew, but it's fresh and hot. I made it meself just this afternoon."

"That sounds delightful," Hugo nodded to the woman. "And some bread please."

The woman scurried off to get his drink, leaving Hugo to hope that he'd get what he came for. He took a long pull of the ale the publican's wife pushed toward him before running off to the kitchen. It was cold and sour, but not unpleasant. In France, he'd gotten accustomed to good wine and fine cognac, but old English ale was sometimes just as good.

The stew, when it came, wasn't quite as advertised, and Hugo strongly suspected that the rabbit wasn't so much a rabbit as something else entirely, but he wasn't there for the food.

"Tell me, mistress, has your family been much affected by the recent battle?" Hugo asked conversationally as he forced himself to swallow some gristle artfully disguised in gelatinous gravy. The battle hadn't been a bloody one, and the only royal troops to have participated had been a detachment of Irish Catholics who were loyal to James. Hugo didn't expect Brad to have even been in Reading, but he needed to speak to someone who'd actually been here and knew what had happened first-hand. Perhaps they'd know something of Brad's whereabouts.

"Oh no, sir, not at all. Why, me husband and son took up arms against the Irish, taking shots from the windows of a house on Broad Street. Scattered like marbles, they did. Even left their dead for us to bury. Now, what kind of decent folk would do that, I ask ye? But these were not decent folk; these were Catholics," she said with great satisfaction at having come to that conclusion.

"So what became of the dead?" Hugo asked noncommittally as he gave up on the stew and reached for a hunk of bread.

"Buried at St. Giles, they were, those heathens. Should have left them to rot, I say, but it wouldn't be the Christian thing to do, the vicar said, so they are now buried with our own dead. It's shameful, it is." Blotches of anger stained the woman's cheeks, and she stuck out her meager chest in righteous indignation.

"Shameful, indeed," Hugo agreed. "Were there many casualties then?"

"Two dozen or thereabouts, I s'pose. A couple of wounded, too."

"What happened to the wounded?" Hugo asked as he took another sip of ale.

"The ones as could walk just made themselves scarce, and the ones who were seriously wounded were taken to the vicar."

"I see," Hugo replied. "Well, mistress, never have I eaten a more satisfying meal. Now, if you'll excuse me." Hugo tossed a coin on the table and rose to leave, eager to get away.

"But ye haven't finished, sir."

"Can't eat another mouthful, I'm afraid." That, at least, was true.

Hugo stepped out into the cold evening. He had to find a room for the night since it was doubtful that he would find the vicar at the church now. He supposed he could go visit the man at home, which might actually prove to be a better plan. People tended to be more honest when not in the house of God, even its humble servants.

Hugo was pointed in the direction of the vicar's residence by the first person he asked. It was a modest house next to the church; the windows of the ground floor spilling light onto the snow in a most welcoming way. Hugo tethered his horse and knocked on the door, hoping he would learn something of value. The vicar was his only hope, since he doubted that anyone in the town could tell him more than the woman at The Globe.

A middle-aged servant answered the door and directed Hugo to a small but comfortable parlor, where the vicar sat reading by the fire. He set aside his book and rose to his feet, quickly hiding his look of surprise at having an unexpected visitor at that time of night.

"Reverend Creswell, my name is Richard Tully," Hugo began, using his alias. There was nothing to be gained by announcing his true identity, especially since he was still technically an outlaw. "I apologize for disturbing you at such a late hour, but I'm afraid I'm in need of some information, and can't wait."

Reverend Creswell smiled broadly and indicated a chair by the fire, inviting Hugo to sit down. He was in his thirties, with kind dark eyes and a narrow face framed by wavy brown hair. He had a rather prominent nose, but was blessed with a pleasant smile, which probably made him popular with the females of his parish. An approachable and attractive vicar was always a bonus when church services were mandatory, and the vicar was often his parishioners' only beacon of hope in times of hardship. "Please, warm yourself by the fire. May I offer you a brandy? I must admit it's one of my vices," the vicar confessed shyly. "I look forward to having a small brandy after supper. It is rather an extravagance, but it's such a pleasure that I'm afraid I simply can't give it up. Never did care for ale or beer," he admitted as he poured Hugo a measure of brandy.

"Thank you, Vicar. That's most kind. I'm rather partial to brandy myself."

"I've never been a believer in denying oneself small pleasures," the vicar confided as he handed Hugo the glass.

Hugo took a sip of brandy. It was quite good, and almost washed away the nasty taste of the stew from his mouth.

Hugo didn't like to jump to conclusions about people, but he liked this man. Unless he was much mistaken, this was someone who served the people rather than an institution and would readily put dogma aside to help his fellow man.

"How may I help you, Master Tully?" Reverend Creswell asked after topping off his own glass of brandy and taking a sip with a small sigh of pleasure.

"I've come in search of a dear friend who I believe might have passed this way in recent days. My friend felt it his duty to join His Majesty's forces, and although the army had disbanded, he hasn't returned home. I thought to start my search here in Reading, since I honestly don't know where else to try."

Reverend Creswell set down his glass next to the book and nodded in understanding. "That must be very distressing for you. In truth, I have very little information about the whereabouts of the royal supporters. The Battle of Broad Street, as the residents are calling it, was rather quick and decisive, with an undisputed victory for the Dutch."

"I was told that there were casualties who were buried at St. Giles and a few wounded who'd been left behind."

"Yes, there are about two dozen men who were interred at St. Giles. They are Irish Catholics, but since we have no Catholic priest here, I did my best for them, believing that they would understand. I have a list of names, if you'd care to look it over. There were also three men who were wounded. They were taken to a farm a few miles north of here to be tended to by Widow Starkey."

"Does she have some knowledge of medicine?" Hugo asked.

"No more than most, but I felt it wise to remove the men from the town, given the hostility toward them, and Widow Starkey was given a small sum to compensate her for her trouble," the vicar replied apologetically. "It was the best I could do under the circumstances."

"You did what you felt was right, Vicar. I would like to speak to the men after I've taken a look at the list of the fallen."

"I pray your friend is not on it," the vicar replied as he rose to go fetch the list.

Hugo scanned the page, relieved to see that Brad's name wasn't there. He didn't expect it to be, but needed to be sure. As long as he knew that Brad was alive, there was hope of finding him, although Hugo had no idea where to look. The trail was cold, and once he left Reading, he had no clue which way to go. Speaking to the survivors was the only logical next step.

"Where would I find this woman's farm?" Hugo asked as he rose to leave.

"Master Tully, it's late, and bitterly cold. I have a spare room which I would be happy to offer you, and I will direct you to the farm come morning. Do say you'll stay."

"Thank you, Vicar, that's a most generous offer, and I gladly accept, but only if you allow me to buy you a bottle of brandy as payment."

"I don't require payment," the vicar protested, but Hugo noticed a gleam in his eyes. Perhaps the good vicar indulged in more than one small brandy, as he claimed. Well, everyone had their vices, he supposed.

"A gift then, from one connoisseur to another," Hugo suggested with a smile.

"It would be churlish to refuse," the vicar replied, accepting Hugo's offer graciously.

"It would indeed."

The room at the top of the stairs was small, and the mattress lumpy, but Hugo had slept in less comfortable places. At least it was relatively warm, and the bed linens were clean. Hugo undressed, got into bed in his shirt, and blew out the candle thoughtfully provided by the servant. He thought he'd fall asleep immediately, but sleep wouldn't come, leaving him feeling restless and annoyed. And then he realized what was bothering him; this was the first time in years that Neve wasn't lying next to him. The last time he'd slept alone was when Neve was in Newgate Prison, and he'd been tormented by despair, terrified that he'd lose Neve and their baby.

Hugo folded his arms behind his head and stared at the darkened ceiling. Only last night he'd shared a bed with Neve and the children. They'd been warm and snug, and he could still feel the slight pressure of Elena's small body as she curled up next to him. He'd been overjoyed by the birth of Michael, but, deep down, Hugo had to admit that Elena was the child of his heart. There was just something about her which neither of the other children had. Valentine was willful and, at times, manipulative. Michael was quiet and too fearful for a boy. But Elena was pure joy. She was sweet, affectionate, and incredibly brave for a child of one. Her natural curiosity overrode any fear she might have, and she plunged into things with an innocent abandon, eager for new experiences.

And Hugo was her favorite as well. Valentine was attached to Archie, perhaps because he didn't give in to her tantrums, and she instinctively felt that she needed to win him over. Michael was closer to Neve, his eyes always searching for his mother. But Elena was a daddy's girl, toddling toward him and climbing into his lap as she wrapped her arms about his neck and planted sweet kisses on his cheek.

Hugo began to feel drowsy at last, thoughts of the children relaxing him and soothing his anxiety. He hoped he'd learn something at the farm tomorrow which would lead him to Brad since he hated to be away for long. He felt ashamed of his selfish thoughts, but he was desperate to return home to his family.

FIFTEEN

Hugo burrowed deeper into his cloak as he set off for Widow Starkey's farm after delivering a bottle of brandy to Vicar Creswell's servant with his compliments. The vicar had already left for the church by the time Hugo awoke, but the servant had made sure he had a hearty breakfast before leaving and had even given him a small parcel containing a pork roll and some cheese for his midday meal.

A dense fog had descended overnight, making visibility less than two feet. Hugo had been able to orient himself in the town, but once he reached the outskirts, an ominous silence descended all around him, making him feel as if he were riding through a thick cloud. To add to the illusion, the air was so saturated with moisture that Hugo's face felt damp, and his horse's coat glistened in the half-light. The vicar had said that the farm wasn't difficult to find as long as Hugo followed the road, so he ambled along, listening for any sounds of life. No farm was quiet. Even if the inhabitants were inside, there were animals, who rarely felt the need for silence.

Hugo was beginning to debate the wisdom of his plan when after about an hour, he was still in exactly the same predicament. He hadn't seen nor heard anything. He wasn't particularly hungry, but he took out the pork roll and began to chew on it out of sheer boredom. It was cold and a little soggy, but still better than the horrible stew from last night. Hugo finished the roll, brushed the crumbs from his gloves, and continued on his way. Eventually, this fog would lift, but by that time, he might have passed the farm altogether.

About twenty minutes later, Hugo heard something that might have been the bleating of a sheep. A ghostly outline of a barn melted out of the fog as he drew nearer, and a rutted track led off toward the farmhouse. The house itself was of decent size, but looked as if it could have used some attention. It had a depressing, run-down air about it, as if the inhabitants didn't care enough to spend time on its upkeep. A thin plume of smoke rose from the chimney, but the shutters were still closed despite fresh tracks in the snow which led to the barn.

Hugo dismounted and rapped on the door, hoping that this was the place.

The door eventually opened just a crack. "What'ya want?"

"I'm looking for Widow Starkey," Hugo answered in as friendly a voice as he could muster in the face of the woman's hostility.

"I'm Mistress Starkey. What's it to ye?" she demanded.

"I was hoping to speak to the Irish soldiers. I'm looking for someone."

"Go away, whoever ye are."

"I'll pay you," Hugo said and held out two coins where the woman could see them through the crack. She hesitated for a few moments, then finally opened the door.

He'd been expecting a woman of middle years, but instead, Hugo was confronted by a girl hardly older than Frances, with a baby on her hip. Mother and child were thin, and seemed to be wearing all the clothes they owned to keep warm. The fire in the hearth was burning low, the room cold enough to make

Hugo's breath come out in white puffs. The girl might have been pretty once, but she looked tired, her face gaunt from lack of nutrition. A few dirty strands of hair escaped her cap, and she brushed them away with impatience, eager for the money, but clearly annoyed by Hugo's presence.

"Mistress Starkey, may I speak with the men you're looking after?" Hugo asked politely. He didn't see anyone in the house, nor did he hear anyone upstairs. If the rest of the house was as cold, they'd likely frozen to death.

"There were three of 'em to start with," the girl replied. "Two died right quick though. They's up in the loft, ye may go up if ye wish."

"It must be freezing up there," Hugo remarked. He didn't mean to sound judgmental but couldn't help feeling sorry for the poor man, who was obviously not being cared for very well.

The girl looked at him, her eyes narrowing at the affront. Two bright spots of color appeared in her sallow cheeks. "Oh, aye, 'tis freezin' up there. And 'tis also freezin' down 'ere. Me 'usband died over the summer. 'E was brawlin' in town, got a beatin' 'e richly deserved, and died of 'is injuries, leavin' me alone with a newborn babe. Do ye think I've 'ad much time to chop wood? I don't know if we'll make it through the winter, so don't expect me to use me meager resources on someone who's naught but a stranger and an imposition. I only did it for the money, and the value of yer coin is runnin' out. If ye wish to speak to the man, do it, or else leave me in peace."

Hugo stared at the girl, chastened by the tongue-lashing he'd just received. Of course, she was right. She was barely surviving, and to keep a fire going in the upstairs room would quickly diminish her already inadequate pile of firewood. He wished he could help her, but there wasn't much he could do short of giving her some money, which would reduce her burden. She had spirit; he'd give her that.

"Show me," Hugo said as he cut his eyes at the stairs.

The girl seemed reluctant to go up, but finally relented. Hugo followed her up the narrow stairway. It was dark despite the early hour, and the upper floor was lost in shadow since the shutters were closed against the morning light. A terrible smell seemed to permeate the loft, something the girl was well aware of since she hung back and pointed to the right. "Over yonder," she said.

Hugo was nearly knocked off his feet by the stench as he got closer to the silent shapes by the wall. He pulled out his handkerchief and held it to his nose as he threw open the shutters to admit some light and approached the men carefully. As Mistress Starkey had told him there were three of them on the floor, but two were clearly dead, and had been for several days. The cold slowed down decomposition, but putrefaction had set in. Hugo noticed that anything of value had been stripped from the men, including their boots. Their bluish bare feet stuck out from beneath the threadbare blankets which had been pulled up to cover their faces. Widow Starkey would sell what she could as soon as she got to town.

Hugo ignored the corpses and carefully approached the third man who was lying in a fetal position in the corner, one arm over his head. He wasn't wearing the uniform of the Irish detachment, but was dressed as a civilian. His breeches were drenched with blood, some dried, some fresh, and yellow pus stains suggested that the man's wound had festered. Hugo briefly wondered when the man had last eaten. It seemed that the good widow wasn't spending much time up here. There was a thick layer of dust on the floor, and mouse droppings were scattered over the bare boards. The mice had probably fled for lack of any edible crumbs.

"Sir," Hugo addressed the man. "Can you hear me?"

The man moaned in response but shifted the arm covering his face by a few inches. His face was smudged with dirt, and his hair was so greasy, it was difficult to tell its color.

"Is there anything I can do for you?" Hugo asked. "Some water perhaps? Have you eaten anything?"

"Your voice," the man mumbled. "So familiar."

"Pardon me?" Hugo asked as he inched closer to the man so as not to alarm him.

"Hugo," the man breathed. "You sound like Hugo."

"Oh, dear God," Hugo gasped as he closed the space in two long strides. "Brad, is that really you?" How was it possible for a man as brawny and healthy as Brad to be reduced to such a state so quickly?

"Delirious," Brad whispered to himself. "Hugo is in France."

"Brad, it's me, and I'm going to get you out of here." Hugo crouched next to his friend and put his hand over Brad's. "It's really me. I'm here, Brad."

Brad's eyelids fluttered as he tried to open his eyes. His face was haggard from pain and lack of food, and his normally powerful frame had whittled down considerably. Brad's shaggy blond hair was crusted with grime, and the stench from the wound was unbearable.

"I'll be right back," Hugo said as he strode from the loft and thundered down the stairs.

"How could you allow a man to get to such a state?" Hugo roared at the defiant girl. "He's dying up there, and probably not even from his wound. When was the last time you fed him or gave him a drink? And what about the corpses of those soldiers? Will you let them lie there until they rot?"

"Now, ye listen to me, Master 'Igh and Mighty. I 'aven't got the strength to drag 'em down by meself or to bury 'em. I thought 'twas the more decent thing to do rather than leave 'em to the animals. I was goin' to tell the vicar come Sunday and ask 'im to send someone to 'elp me. Thought the third 'un would be dead by then."

"So, you were hoping he'd die, so you could strip him and sell his belongings?"

"And what could I do for 'im? I gave 'im food and water, but I barely 'ave enough to feed meself. 'Is wound festered. 'Twas just a matter of time."

"Do you have an outbuilding where the bodies can remain until help arrives?"

"'Tis out back," the girl answered sullenly.

"Give me something to wrap them in," Hugo ordered.

"I ain't got nothin' I can spare. Use the blankets; they're ruined anyhow."

"Boil some water, get me clean strips of linen, and heat some porridge. Lay a fire in the loft. I'll pay you," Hugo added as he saw the gleam of defiance in the girl's eyes.

He didn't wait to see if she would comply but went back upstairs to remove the first corpse. The blanket was barely enough to wrap around the man, but Hugo did his best and carried down the bundle, maneuvering the body to avoid hitting the walls. The man was unbearably heavy, but Hugo didn't set him down until he was outside the house, then he grabbed him by the feet and dragged him to the outbuilding. He didn't have the time or the strength to dig through frozen ground to bury the men, and it would be best if they were buried at St. Giles, next to their comrades. They deserved that much.

The second man had been thinner and not as heavy. Hugo was surprised to notice that he didn't seem to have any obvious fatal wound. There was some blood on his upper right arm, but it appeared to be more of a flesh wound. The wound didn't look infected, so he must have died of something else. Had the poor man frozen or starved to death? Hugo didn't have time to ponder the cause of death since he had to see to Brad. He left the two men laid out side by side, said a quick prayer, crossed himself, and commended their souls to God.

By the time he returned, Mistress Starkey had boiled the

water, prepared some rags, which were far from clean, and heated up porridge that must have sat in the pot for at least a week. Before tending to Brad, however, Hugo rummaged in the trunk at the foot of the narrow bed fitted into an alcove and separated from the main room by a curtain. He found what he was looking for: breeches, shirt, and an old coat. Widow Starkey's husband wouldn't be needing these. Hugo poured some hot water into a basin, took the rags and the clothes, and made his way up the stairs.

A small fire burned in a brazier. It did little to warm the freezing room, but at least it gave some additional light and enough warmth if one stood very close. Hugo dragged Brad as close to the fire as he could and began to clean his face. He'd give him a drink and feed him first, then see to the wound.

Hugo didn't think Brad would be able to eat, but he swallowed the porridge in seconds. "Is there any more?"

"Get more," Hugo barked at the girl. She took the bowl and left.

The baby appeared to have gone to sleep, so Mistress Starkey left him downstairs where it was warmer. She brought another bowl of porridge, then reluctantly assisted Hugo in removing Brad's soiled clothes. She refused to touch the wound, however, which was just as well. She seemed to know nothing of healing, or cleanliness. An odor of stale sweat emanated from her person, and the child had recently pissed down the front of her skirt, leaving a smelly stain. It was too cold to bathe, but it didn't take much to heat some water and freshen up from time to time, Hugo mused as he went about his task. He supposed he'd gotten used to Neve's standards of cleanliness. He might not have even noticed the girl's unhygienic state before, just taking it for granted that she was a peasant who didn't know any better and likely bathed only once a year.

"Do you have any medicinals in the house?" he asked, already knowing the answer.

"No."

"What about wine or ale, or anything alcoholic?"

"What d'ye think this is, a tavern?" she countered, annoyed.

"You must have something."

"I 'ave some mead." The girl looked furious but went down to fetch it.

Hugo took a new rag and soaked it in the mead, to the girl's utter horror. He dabbed the mead over the wound, hoping that the alcohol and honey might do something to disinfect it. The wound itself didn't appear to be too deep and would have healed properly had it been attended to in time. Hugo hoped that he wasn't too late. Brad just lay there shivering; his eyes glazed as he stared at the flames.

"Do you have a wagon?" he asked the girl.

She stepped from foot to foot, glaring at the floor defiantly.

"I'll take that as a yes. Get your baby. We are going to town. You're going to help me bring my friend to Reading, then return here in your wagon. While in Reading, I will buy you some food and firewood. It won't last you the winter, but it will help, and I will talk to Vicar Creswell about getting you some assistance."

"I don't want no charity," the girl mumbled, but Hugo could see that she was pleased by his offer.

"It's not charity; it's payment. And the vicar has a responsibility to you as a member of his parish. If you need help, there's no shame in asking. Now, do we have an agreement?"

"Well, since ye put it that way," the girl said and went to get her child.

Hugo hitched a malnourished horse to the wagon, spread the bed with some clean straw, which the girl could little spare judging by the state of the livestock, and brought the wagon as close to the door as possible. Brad couldn't walk, so he had to carry him down and lay him in the wagon. Hugo briefly considered using the filthy blanket to cover him but changed his mind. He took off his own cloak and tucked it in around Brad to keep him warm, then mounted his horse. Widow Starkey laid the sleeping baby next to Brad and used a piece of the cloak to cover the child before taking up the reins and turning toward town.

Brad was silent, but awake, his eyes taking in the colorless sky and swirling fog. He breathed deeply, filling his lungs with clean air. Hugo kept a close eye on him until the motion of the wagon lulled Brad to sleep, his chest rising and falling, a slight smile on his face.

SIXTEEN

Hugo considered taking a room at an inn, but bringing a wounded man who'd fought for King James II into a town whose citizens had asked William for help and fought on the side of the Dutch was not safe, so he directed Widow Starkey straight to St. Giles. He would ask Vicar Creswell for help.

As they got closer to Reading, the girl seemed to lose some of her defiance and huddled deeper into her shawl, her face set in lines of resignation. Hugo could see that she was waging some internal battle and left her to it; it was of no concern to him.

"Please, don't tell 'im," she implored Hugo as they finally stopped in front of the vicar's house. "I did what I could. I know I should 'ave done more," she added, her face turned up to Hugo in supplication, "and I will carry the deaths of those men with me till the day I die."

Hugo doubted that Widow Starkey would think of those men past next week, but there was no point in saying anything to the vicar. He was angry with the girl, but it was plain to see that she was barely surviving, and the money she was offered for taking in the men was too good of an opportunity to refuse.

There wasn't much she could have done for them on her own, but she should have at least fed them and tried to keep them warm. Hugo was sure that the vicar wasn't aware of the extent of the girl's situation, never having been to her farm, and she had too much pride to beg for help.

"I won't say anything," he finally replied. "You have my word."

The girl breathed out a sigh of relief, her expression of remorse instantly replaced with a haughty look of defiance. Under different circumstances, Hugo might have admired her spirit, but at the moment, he was still annoyed.

He went to fetch the vicar, who was at home for his midday meal.

"Vicar Creswell, this is the man I've come to find," Hugo explained as he led the reverend to the wagon. "He's still alive, but his wound has festered, and he needs help. The other two men are dead. Widow Starkey did what she could, but their injuries got the better of them. I've removed the bodies from the farmhouse and left them in the shed until someone can come out to the farm to collect them and bring them to St. Giles for burial."

"Of course," the vicar replied, suddenly flustered. "I should have gone to the farm myself to check on them and offer any succor I could, but I must admit that I was remiss in my duties. I will send Mistress Lacey to fetch the physician for your friend. In the meantime, let's get him settled in the spare room."

Between them, they were able to carry Brad to the room where Hugo had spent the night. It seemed like an awfully long time ago, although it had only been last night. The vicar began to lay the fire, while Hugo pulled off Brad's boots and soiled coat and settled him under the covers.

"Vicar, Widow Starkey doesn't have enough firewood, hay, or provisions to last her two weeks, much less until the spring. Both her and her child will die unless the parish comes to her aid. I will purchase some necessities before she returns to her farm, but unless someone sees fit to help her, she will not survive."

"I hadn't realized it was as bad as that," the vicar replied. "She's a proud lass, and something of an outsider in this community. Doesn't have any family or friends. Came here after marrying Harry, but he was recently taken from her. She doesn't like to accept charity, but I will see to it that she is looked after."

"Thank you. I will return shortly," Hugo replied as he went to rejoin the girl who was waiting in the parlor and warming herself by the fire. Her baby was awake now, gazing at his surroundings with wonder, his eyes round with curiosity. "Come, let's get you what I promised."

Hugo couldn't help noticing the relief in Widow Starkey's eyes. She likely thought that he would renege on his promise once he'd brought Brad to town. He hadn't realized how tense she'd been until a bright smile split her tired face.

"Thank ye," she said as she hoisted the child higher on her hip. "Ye're a real gent."

"Don't mention it."

Had it been market day, Hugo would have been able to stretch his coin further, but he had to buy whatever he could, and spent nearly all his money by the time the girl's wagon was loaded and she was ready to return home. Hugo handed her into the wagon and passed her the child, who was now snugly wrapped in a new woolen blanket instead of the threadbare one he'd had earlier.

"Thank ye, sir," Widow Starkey said again as she took the baby from Hugo. "I mean that."

"Best of luck to you, Mistress Starkey."

"'Tis Judith," she said shyly, gazing at Hugo in a way that suggested that all he had to do was ask, and she'd be his for the taking. A woman in her position needed a man to take care of her, and he'd proved himself worthy in her eyes.

Hugo just tipped his hat to her, eager to see her on her way. The girl read his rejection in the gesture and took off, her back ramrod straight as she stared ahead.

Hugo turned and went back to the vicar's house to face whatever bad news he had to, for surely nothing the doctor said would be too optimistic. The local physician had already arrived and was examining Brad. He was a modestly dressed middle-aged man, his russet-brown wig shorter and less voluminous than was fashionable, but at least it didn't get in his way as he examined the patient. The physician had a pinched look as if he were suffering from a headache. Perhaps he was, or perhaps he found the smell emanating from Brad to be offensive. Now that Brad was inside a small room, the reek of a man who hadn't washed for weeks and had been lying for several days in his own waste was so thick that it made the poor man's eyes water. Hugo noticed the doctor discreetly taking a whiff of the pomander he wore about his neck to counter the effects of sweat, pus, and dried urine.

Brad was lying on the bed with his eyes closed, but Hugo was sure he was awake. His breathing was shallow, and a telltale flush spread across his cheeks and neck, a sure sign that he was fevered. The doctor had removed the breeches Hugo had appropriated from Widow Starkey and was staring at the wound with the aid of a magnifying glass.

"Master Clarke, this is Richard Tully, a friend of the patient," Vicar Creswell announced, forcing the physician to look away from Brad's leg to acknowledge Hugo's presence.

Doctor Clarke straightened up and faced Hugo across the bed, the magnifying glass still in his hand.

"What say you, Master Clarke?" Hugo asked, bracing himself for the worst.

"It appears that Master Nash has been wounded by a

sword, rather than shot, which, in fact, is actually good news as there's no bullet to extract. However, since he didn't receive proper treatment immediately, the wound has festered. Your friend is fevered, and likely has been for several days, and quite delirious. He also shows signs of malnutrition," the doctor said, his expression one of puzzlement. Despite the borrowed clothes, Bradford Nash was clearly no peasant, and would have been adequately fed as a supporter of the king. The fact that he appeared to be half-starved pointed directly to Widow Starkey, something Vicar Creswell deduced right away, judging by the look of horror in his eyes.

The vicar opened his mouth to say something, but Hugo cut across him in an effort to redirect blame from the poor girl. He had a strange desire to protect her, one he couldn't explain given Brad's condition.

"Will he live?" Hugo asked, his voice rising with hope.

The doctor pinched the bridge of his nose and stared at his toes before finally raising his eyes to meet Hugo's. "Master Tully, the only way to ensure that your friend lives is to ampu-tate his leg at mid-thigh to stop the putrefaction from spreading."

"No," Hugo exclaimed before the doctor even finished. "There must be another way."

"Master Tully, I am not insensitive to the feelings of my patients. A man with one leg is an invalid, a cripple. He will never be able to lead a full life, and the emotional toll of losing a leg can sometimes be even greater than the physical one," Doctor Clarke replied, his eyes full of compassion, "but that's the only way to save a person's life when the contamination has spread."

"Is there anything else you might attempt before amputa-tion?" Hugo asked stubbornly.

"The only other course of treatment would be to apply compresses, which might draw out the infection. However, if sepsis sets in, your friend will die very quickly, and even amputating the leg at that point will do little good. I will give him willow bark tea for the fever and apply honey and garlic poultices. Unfortunately, that's all I have to work with. If your friend is strong, he will fight off the infection, and if not..." The doctor shrugged his shoulders, allowing Hugo to draw his own conclusions.

"Do what you must, Master Clarke, but try to save his leg."

The physician nodded in acknowledgment as he turned back to Brad, who seemed oblivious to the conversation that just took place. He'd fallen asleep, which was probably for the best under the circumstances.

"Master Tully, come and have a cup of hot broth. You look done in," the vicar said as he took Hugo by the arm and led him from the sickroom.

"I am, rather," Hugo agreed as he allowed himself to be deposited before the fire and relieved of his hat and sword. A cup of hot broth actually sounded very good at the moment, especially if it came with some bread. He was hungry, tired, and heartsick.

Of course, saving Brad's life was a priority, but Brad wouldn't be the same man if he lost his leg. He'd always been fairly bursting with vigor and good health, but having a stump for a leg would curtail all of Brad's activities. He would be relegated to sitting by the fire with a rug over his legs as he was waited on hand and foot. Mounting a horse would become an impossibility, and walking, even for short distances, would be painful and awkward. Brad would do anything to survive for Beth and the children, but he would never fully recover his independence. His helplessness would gnaw on him day and night, eating away at his confidence and spirit until the man left behind was a mere shadow of the man he had been.

SEVENTEEN

Hugo woke up with a start as the first light of dawn began to seep through the mullioned windows. He felt stiff from lying on a pallet on the floor all night, and his head ached from lack of sleep. It had been a restless night with Hugo tending to Brad, who had alternated between fitful sleep and delirium. Doctor Clarke had instructed Hugo to change the bandage and apply a fresh poultice once the bandage became saturated, so Hugo had checked on the wound approximately every two hours. When he'd peeled away the soiled bandages, he'd nearly gagged from the smell. Blood, pus, honey, and minced garlic were to the senses what a tidal wave was to a dinghy. Hugo would have opened the window to air the room out, but Doctor Clarke gave strict instructions, telling Hugo not to allow any bad humors into the sickroom. Hugo didn't believe in ill humors, having been to the twenty-first century, but he was afraid that the frigid air from the window would chill Brad to the bone, especially since his shirt was soaked with sweat brought on by doses of willow bark tea.

Brad had slept more peacefully for the last few hours, his delirium replaced by the deep slumber of a man who was hopefully recovering. He was still flushed, but his eyes were clearer, and he seemed lucid as he gazed at Hugo from the bed. "Hugo, is that really you?" he asked.

"Yes, it is me, and I'm getting too old to be sleeping on the floor," Hugo replied crankily as he sat up and rubbed his lower back.

"I don't understand. What are you doing here? And where is here, exactly?" Brad queried as he looked around the small, unfamiliar room.

"We're in Reading. Beth asked me to look for you after you failed to return."

"You came from France to look for me?" Brad asked, clearly confused.

"No, Brad. Neve and I returned to England just over a week ago. I wrote to you, but it seems that you never received my letter."

"No." Brad seemed muddled as he thought this bit of news over. Now was not the time to explain the timing of their return or the implications of King James's actions, so Hugo tried to change the subject.

"What happened, Brad?" Hugo asked gently.

Brad appeared momentarily confused by the question, his eyes glazing over with pain and fatigue as he tried to move his leg. He closed his eyes, the silence stretching between them as he seemed to fall back asleep. Sleep was the best medicine for Brad at the moment, so Hugo let him be and busied himself with poking some life back into the fire. The room had grown considerably colder during the night, but the frigid draft also dispelled some of the stagnant odor. Hugo had slept in his clothes, but that couldn't be helped since it wasn't warm enough to undress, and he needed to be up every few hours anyway. He brushed the creases out of his shirt, ran a hand through his hair, and splashed a bit of cold water over his face before shrugging on his coat and pulling on his boots.

"I've been wounded," Brad suddenly said, as if no time had passed by since Hugo's question. "Hugo, please take me home. If I'm to die, I'd like to do it there. And I long to see Beth and the children one last time."

"You are not fit to travel, nor will you die. Not if I can help it. I'm here to nurse you back to health."

Brad leaned back on the pillows, exhausted by the exchange. "All right, then," was all he said before dropping off into sleep again.

Hugo let himself out of the room and went in search of Mistress Lacey. She was already in the kitchen, kneading dough and heating up yesterday's porridge.

"Good morning to you, Master Tully," she said without pausing in her work. "May I offer you some breakfast?"

"Thank you, Mistress Lacey," Hugo replied as he took a seat at the table. "Would you be so kind as to heat some water for me while I eat?"

"Of course. And how is your friend this morning?"

"A little better, I think." Perhaps Hugo was being too optimistic, but at least Brad wasn't delirious anymore.

"I'm that glad to hear that he's on the mend. That woman..." Mistress Lacey said, pursing her lips in disapproval. "Wouldn't trust her with a dog, much less an injured man."

"Got something of a reputation, does she?" Hugo asked, curious about Widow Starkey.

"Oh, aye. Drove that poor lad to drink, she did. Had to marry her because she was in the family way, but who fathered that babe is anybody's guess. 'Twas six months ago now that it happened. Someone made a comment about Judith Starkey's loose ways in the tavern. Didn't say nothing that wasn't true, mind you, but Harry felt he had to defend that trollop of a wife. A fight broke out. It would have all blown over after a few minutes of high spirits, but Harry Starkey was too drunk to keep upright when hit, and bashed his head on the corner of the mantel as he went down. Dead as a doornail within minutes, he was. And now, that slattern is the parish's responsibility, the good vicar says. Can't manage the farm by herself. Well, she should just give it back to Harry's kin and go back where she came from." Mistress Lacey attacked the dough with renewed vigor, which was obviously fueled by righteous indignation.

"Where had she come from?" Hugo asked.

"Oh, I don't rightly know, and neither does anyone else hereabouts. Just showed up one day. Said she was searching for work. Not a month later she'd wed our Harry. He were a good sort, Harry was, until she came along."

"Thank you for breakfast, Mistress Lacey," Hugo said as he pushed his bowl away. He didn't care to hear anything more about Judith Starkey. She was clearly not liked in this town, and he felt pity for her. Life was hard enough when you had family and friends, but when you were a friendless young woman who'd been branded a whore, living in a town full of hostile inhabitants, it was that much harder. Perhaps her reputation was well-deserved, but it didn't matter. He had more important things to deal with, and Widow Starkey wasn't one of them. Whatever happened to her was out of his hands.

Hugo experimentally stuck a finger into the water to check its temperature. It was warm enough, so he poured the water into a pitcher and grabbed a basin and a towel on his way upstairs.

"Mistress Lacey, would you mind bringing some food for Bradford, in about fifteen minutes, say?" Hugo asked.

"Not at all, Master Tully, not at all," the woman replied as she deftly fashioned lumps of dough into loaves.

Brad was awake when Hugo came upstairs with the water. The smell in the room was still overpowering, but beneath the stench of the wound was the smell of a man who hadn't washed in weeks.

"I'm going to give you a bath," Hugo announced as he went about pulling the shirt over Brad's head. "You stink."

Brad pulled a face. "I do stink, but the thought of you bathing me stinks even more."

"Nonsense." Hugo wet a towel and rubbed it on a cake of soap before beginning to apply it to Brad's neck and chest. He methodically moved down, scrubbing everything except the area of the wound. It was difficult to wash the soap off without wetting the bed linens, but the result was well worth it. Brad was clean, but the water in the basin was nearly black.

Hugo tossed the contents out the window and went back to the kitchen to get clean water. Mistress Lacey had already put the loaves in the oven and was preparing a tray for Brad.

"Is he decent then?" she asked as she prepared to deliver the food.

"Just five more minutes, Mistress," Hugo replied as he went back to finish his task.

He carefully moved Brad over to the side of the bed, suspending his head over the floor. It wasn't a comfortable position, but made it possible for Hugo to wash Brad's hair and rinse it without soaking the bed.

"Thank you, old friend. I feel so much better," Brad said as Hugo helped him with the shirt.

"Mistress Lacey will be here directly with your breakfast. You need to eat."

"Hugo, I meant what I said. Please, take me home."

"You can't sit a-horse, old man," Hugo replied as he took a peek under the dressing and judged it to be adequate for another hour.

"I have some money. Perhaps you can buy a cart of some sort."

"You had money," Hugo corrected him. "The good widow relieved you of it some time ago, but perhaps buying a cart is not a bad idea. Are you sure you're up to traveling? It will take us the best part of a day to get back to Cranley, and it won't be a luxurious ride."

"You won't hear a word of complaint from me," Brad promised.

"All right. Let me see what I can find," Hugo promised as he held the door open for Mistress Lacey, who was bringing broth, bread, and a bowl of porridge for the patient.

EIGHTEEN

By midmorning, Hugo had managed to procure a rickety cart—the only conveyance he could afford. His purse was now depressingly empty, which made him doubly thankful for the generosity of the vicar, who bid Mistress Lacey to provide two old blankets and a pillow for Brad to rest his head on, and a parcel of food. Hugo made the cart as comfortable as possible before asking Vicar Creswell to help him lift Brad onto his makeshift bed. Brad could barely walk, much less climb into the wagon. His condition had vastly improved since Hugo had found him at Widow Starkey's farm, but that wasn't saying much.

Brad was still flushed with fever, and his thigh was swollen and putrid with infection. The only thing that would truly help at this stage was a dose of antibiotics, but, of course, penicillin would not be invented for centuries to come. The natural antibacterial agents in honey and garlic could only do so much against an infection which had been allowed to fester for days. Brad would survive the ride back to Cranley, but Hugo had no idea what to expect beyond that. He tucked in the blankets around Brad to keep him warm but reclaimed his cloak. He couldn't ride all day without it. He was chilled to the bone despite being constantly in motion.

"Vicar, Mistress Lacey, thank you for your kindness," Hugo said as he shook the vicar's hand. "I don't know what I would have done had you not welcomed us into your home."

"I have no doubt you would have found a solution, Master Tully. You appear to be a very resourceful man. Bradford is lucky to have such a devoted companion. I do hope he recovers. I will pray for him," the vicar added piously. Vicar Creswell walked around to the side of the wagon and shook Brad's hand before Hugo pulled away. "Go with God," he called out after them.

"Are you all right back there?" Hugo asked as the wagon rattled down a rutted track through the outskirts of Reading. The impenetrable fog of the day before had lifted, and the sky was clear and bright, but the cold December air was still bitter.

"I am more than all right; I am utterly blessed," Brad replied, the smile evident in his tone.

"Really? I had no idea that getting wounded and being left to starve would have such a heartening effect on your disposition," Hugo remarked, amazed by Brad's good spirits. Most people would feel bitter and angry after such an ordeal, but Brad seemed unusually light of spirit this morning.

"A few days ago, I was sure that I would die in that loft, Hugo, and be left there to rot like those two Irish soldiers. I've seen death before, of course, but never this close. I had to share a room with two putrefying corpses for days, acutely aware that it was just a matter of time until I joined them in death. I'd never felt as alone or devoid of hope as I did then. I tried praying, but somehow the words seemed hollow, as if no one was listening—no one at all," Brad confided. He'd always been a pious man, a man who believed in the power of prayer. It wasn't just a balm for the soul to Brad; it was a direct line to God, a two-way conversation where the other participant was often silent, but sympathetic and eager to help none-theless.

"I knew I was dying," Brad continued, "and would have welcomed death had I been offered even a glimpse of Beth and the children one more time, but I knew that was not to be. Even the notion of being buried at home seemed like a paradise I couldn't hope to attain. I'd be buried in a strange place with no one to mourn me or even carve my name into the cross. Beth would never know what had happened to me; would not even know where I was buried. And then, I heard your voice. I thought an angel was calling to me."

"Well, I've been called many things before, but this is defi-nitely a first," Hugo replied with a grin. He tried to keep the mood light, but he understood Brad's anguish all too well. Neve had expressed a similar sentiment after being locked up in Newgate, alone and without hope, torn from him without so much as a word of warning. Dying with the knowledge that Hugo would never know what became of her and their baby made the prospect that much more painful, more senseless.

"Don't ridicule me, old friend. I know I may still die, but knowing that I will see my family before I do, and will be buried in a place where my wife and children can visit my grave and pray for me, gives me peace of mind. I know you can under-stand that."

"Yes, of course I can." Dying was never desirable, but there were different kinds of death, and dying in your own bed with your loved ones around you was likely the best death anyone could ask for. There were some who believed that dying on a battlefield fighting for a cause was an honorable end, and perhaps it was, but having come close to death only a few years ago when he was shot in Paris, Hugo could understand Brad's heartfelt desire to be with his family. Having Neve near, and holding Valentine as she fell asleep, was the best medicine Hugo could have asked for, so perhaps Brad's family would be the cure that tipped the scale in favor of life. "Try to sleep, Brad. We have a ways to go, and you need your rest."

"I suppose I should," Brad replied, his voice thick with emotion, "but I keep thinking that this might be my last glimpse of the sky. I don't want to miss a moment, Hugo, in case I am no longer here tomorrow. I'd rather talk, if you don't mind."

"When have I ever minded talking to you?" Hugo replied, stunned by Brad's revelation. Was he really about to lose his closest friend? Brad had followed his conscience, did what he felt was the only thing to do under the threat of invasion by a foreign, Protestant king, but now that it was all over, his sacrifice seemed so pointless. William's ascent to the throne was inevitable, but, of course, Brad had no way of knowing that. How different life would be if everyone had the same knowledge he'd been gifted through Neve, Hugo mused.

"Hugo, how did you come to be back in England at just the right time? If James II is deposed by William, then you will be pardoned," Brad theorized. "You couldn't have known what was about to happen."

Hugo mulled the question over for a moment, unsure of what to tell Brad. Part of him wanted to tell Brad the truth, but despite their friendship, Brad was still mired in superstition, as he himself had been before his eyes were so forcefully opened by Neve. Besides, Hugo didn't want to say anything which might endanger Neve. Any hint of witchcraft could result in Neve's imprisonment and death, and traveling through time was about as "witchy" as one could get—in any century.

"Oh, you did know," Brad concluded from Hugo's silence. "She foresaw it, didn't she, your wife? I keep forgetting she is a seer."

"Yes," Hugo said simply.

"What else did she say? She has quite a gift, Neve. She's like the Oracle of Delphi," Brad said, his voice trembling with awe.

"All oracles are fallible," Hugo replied, reluctant to share what he knew with Brad.

"Come, Hugo. I know she foretold something. You can trust me; you know that." Brad suddenly sounded offended, instinctively sensing that Hugo was holding something back. "I wouldn't betray Neve any more than I would betray you."

"She foresaw that there will never be another Stuart king on the throne of England, or another Catholic for that matter." The words were simple enough when spoken out loud, but they summarized the demise of all hopes and ambitions that Hugo and Brad had harbored and fought for. The dream of being able to practice their religion openly during their lifetime came abruptly to an end, all hope extinguished through the certain knowledge of the future to come.

"Poppycock," Brad replied angrily. "This invasion won't last. James will rally his forces and drive William from the shores of England. This is a temporary setback, nothing more. Perhaps Neve misinterpreted what she saw. You just said yourself that no oracle is infallible. We haven't seen the last of the Stuart kings, I tell you, especially now that there is finally a male heir." Brad sounded unusually defensive, his attitude full of bluster he clearly didn't feel.

"Tell me what happened to you, Brad," Hugo suggested in an effort to change the subject. Talking about the future left him feeling unsettled.

Hugo heard Brad's sigh as he shifted his weight to make himself more comfortable on the hard bed of the wagon. The road was a bit smoother now they had left Reading behind, so the going was easier. They'd passed a farmer a few minutes back, but otherwise, they were alone. Even the livestock were indoors, the winter grass not suitable for grazing. Hugo hoped Brad was warm enough under his blankets. He pulled the cloak closer around his body. When traveling on horseback, he had the warmth of the animal to dispel some of the chill, but now that he was sitting on the bench of the wagon, he was numb with cold, his fingers stiff on the reins.

"I was really happy when the little prince was born," Brad began, his voice wistful. "It seemed a good omen of things to come. Finally, the succession was assured, and we Catholics had some hope of a better future. I didn't think that change would come overnight, but with a Catholic prince as next in line, I hoped that the attitude toward Catholics might begin to soften," Brad confided, his voice strangely disembodied as he spoke.

"I was feeling hopeful all through the summer, until rumors began to circulate. I confess, I found it hard to believe that a foreign prince would be preferable to an Englishman, one who had a legitimate claim on the throne and had provided an heir, but the rumors grew more persistent. A part of me still hoped that common sense would prevail and the invitation to William of Orange would be revoked, but, as you know, that wasn't the case."

"So, you joined James's army?"

"I felt it my duty, Hugo. I know that I'm only one man, and not a very good fighter at that, but if there were more like me who felt that they should volunteer, perhaps the tide could be turned."

"What was it like at Salisbury?" Hugo asked. He already knew the answer from reading historical accounts, but wanted to hear it from Brad, who had been there to witness the events in person.

"It was awful, actually. James's troops were well-armed but reluctant to fight; the general feeling being that their cause was doomed and not worth risking life and limb for. There were even some officers who voiced their support for William of Orange, utterly unafraid of being taken up on a charge of treason," Brad related, still unable to believe what he'd seen and heard.

"And James? Did you see him?" Hugo asked, curious as to whether the accounts had been accurate.

"His Majesty seemed to be experiencing some sort of crisis of faith. He worked himself up into such a state that his nose began to bleed profusely, which he took to be a bad omen— a sign from God that he should order his troops to retreat. He appeared to be looking for signs rather than trying to inspire his men and focusing on strategy."

Brad sounded incredulous, still amazed by the all-too-human weakness he'd witnessed behind the mask of the ruler he'd admired.

"There were some who said that James II actually referred to the wind which helped William cross the sea as a 'Protestant wind.' Does wind have religious beliefs now?" Brad asked with undisguised disgust.

"Then what happened?"

"The Earl of Feversham proposed retreat. His Majesty might have dismissed the suggestion had Lord Churchill of Eyemouth not deserted to William the very next day, soon to be followed by the king's own daughter Anne. He lost heart after that and fled to London."

"How did you come to be in Reading?" Hugo asked, still trying to piece together the circumstances that had led Brad to Reading on the day of the battle.

"Not being an officer, I had no real idea of what was going on. There was confusion and chaos, and many speculated that the king feared execution and was using his negotiations with William as a means of stalling for time while he planned his escape to France. James sent a detachment of Irish troops into Reading to engage the Dutch, who'd been summoned by the residents for protection. I wasn't meant to be there at all, not being part of the Irish Brigade, but was asked to deliver a message. I could hardly refuse, could I?" Brad remarked, his voice bitter with defeat.

"I had no idea where I was going or how to find the Captain of the Guard to whom the missive was addressed. There was fighting in the street, the menfolk of Reading firing at the soldiers from upper-story windows and from behind corners and walls. The streets were overrun by the Dutch. The Irish soldiers sought cover in doorways and behind trees as they returned fire, but they were grossly outnumbered. My horse was shot out from under me before I had the sense to dismount and get out of the street," Brad confided.

His moment of inaction clearly still rankled, but Brad was no trained soldier, which made it all the more strange that he had been chosen to deliver a message. Unless he had volunteered.

"I tried to get out of the way and take refuge in a livery stable," Brad continued, "but there was a Dutch soldier directly in my path. I suppose he might have taken me for one of the inhabitants of Reading and left me be had I not engaged him. He was a skilled swordsman and had me disarmed and on my back in moments. He went to finish me off, but I rolled out of his way and his sword struck my thigh instead of my chest. He could have easily killed me, but just left me to bleed as something else drew his attention. I crawled behind a hedge and stayed there until the end of the battle. I was bleeding profusely and must have lost consciousness, because when I awoke, I was in that loft with the Irish soldiers."

"It seems that no one came to collect the wounded or dead. The fallen soldiers were buried at St. Giles by Vicar Creswell. He didn't say so outright, but I believe they were tossed into a mass grave since there was no one to pay for the burial, and no names to go with the corpses," Hugo explained, his voice laced with disgust. James's army had left their men behind.

"I would never say this to anyone but you, Hugo, but I was ashamed," Brad confessed, his voice pitching low as if he could be overheard on the desolate road they were now traveling.

"You have no reason to feel shame," Hugo countered. "Better soldiers than you have been disarmed and killed in battle."

"Not quite what I meant," Brad smirked.

"What then?"

"All my life, I've been taught that the king is God's representative on Earth, a man who is as close to divinity as the Pope. But seeing that frightened, panicked man at Salisbury forced me to realize that the king is naught but a man; a vain, selfish man, fearful for his own skin. A person becomes a sovereign by accident of birth, not through merit or wisdom, which, in the grand scheme of things, doesn't seem right, does it? I'm ashamed to say that giving up my own life for his cause suddenly didn't seem like a fair exchange." Gone was the bluster of their earlier conversation. Brad knew the truth and was ready to face it at last. James would never rule England again.

Hugo was glad that Brad couldn't see his expression. What Brad had just said was not only treasonous but dangerously democratic; something that men like him wouldn't come to embrace for centuries to come, their free-thinking ideals delayed by centuries thanks to the catastrophic failure that had been Oliver Cromwell's Republic. Instead, thousands would lay their lives down to restore James to his throne. They would lose their families, their livelihoods, and any chance of a decent future to fight for a man who saw the throne as his due but had done very little to deserve the loyalty and self-sacrifice he called for. Brad couldn't know of the slaughter that was to come, but Hugo was well aware of the consequences of James's defeat.

"Perhaps it's not a fair exchange," Hugo agreed. "These past few years have been eye-opening, to say the least."

"You've changed, Hugo," Brad remarked, his tone one of amusement rather than judgment. "I suppose it takes a much greater sacrifice to martyr yourself when you have a wife and children than when you have nothing to lose. I've learned that the hard way as well. All I could think of as I lay in that loft was that my boy would grow up without his father, and my daughter wouldn't have anyone to arrange her marriage or protect her honor. My wife would be left widowed, lonely and shunned by polite society, which is not welcoming to women who are without husbands. And for what? For a man who decamped at the first opportunity, and ran away like a coward rather than staying and fighting for his country and his throne."

Hugo was taken aback by Brad's vehemence, but not by the sentiment. He'd experienced a similar kind of disillusionment, but just because he no longer cared to lay his life down for a monarch who would never again sit on the throne didn't mean there weren't other, equally dangerous situations which couldn't be avoided.

"Brad, I've done something while in France," Hugo confessed. "Something which might still threaten both myself and my family."

"What have you done, Hugo?" Brad asked warily.

"I've sold my soul to the Devil," Hugo replied, his voice as tense as the set of his shoulders.

"What have you done?" Brad repeated, his tone no longer philosophical, but full of apprehension.

"Louis would never welcome me into his Court unless I had something of value to offer him. I am a man who plotted against his fellow Catholic king and cousin, so whatever I offered had to be of great value."

"No, Hugo. Please, say I'm not hearing you correctly," Brad pleaded.

"You are. I offered to spy for France if William took the throne. You know the volatile history between Louis and William. Any insight that Louis can gain into William's affairs is valuable to him—more valuable than the honor of his cousin, whom he secretly considers weak and deluded."

"Spying is treason, Hugo, and treason is punishable by death, as you well know."

"Yes, but I had little choice, Brad. I couldn't very well stay in France for nearly three years without reclaiming my name or providing for my family. Louis had agreed to a stipend, one that helped me support us while in exile. Now that what Neve has predicted has come to pass, I must fulfill my end of the bargain, and it turns my stomach to have to honor it. I've no loyalty to William and Mary, but what I've promised to do is dishonorable and cowardly, and there's no way out of the bargain. Louis will have me killed if I fail to deliver, and I must think of my family."

"Yes, you must," was all that Brad said before falling quiet. What more was there to say?

NINETEEN

The last remnants of a winter sunset glowed in the western sky, a mauve band encircling the horizon and highlighting the dark limbs of bare trees, which looked like gnarled fingers pointing at heavenwards. A few shy stars already twinkled overhead upstaging the pale crescent of the moon. The snow crunched beneath the wheels of the wagon, the distant lights of Nash House at the end of the drive a welcome sight.

Brad slept for the best part of the journey, leaving Hugo to his own thoughts, which were unusually jumbled and nonsensical. Hugo woke up with a start several times, surprised that he had nodded off while driving the wagon. That wasn't like him. Fragments of strange dreams swirled in his mind, confusing images overlapping each other in puzzling sequences. Hugo shivered beneath his cloak as a blast of cold wind found its way inside the folds. He felt unusually tired and achy. Hugo sat up straighter and urged the horse on, eager to get to their destination. The poor animal didn't need much prodding; it was just as eager for their journey to end.

Hugo finally drew up in front of the house and ran up the steps to pound on the door. Beth's frightened face appeared briefly at one of the downstairs windows, and then she was outside, with just a shawl over her shoulders, trying to peer over the side of the wagon at Brad's immobile shape.

"Oh, dear God," she moaned as she saw her husband. "Is he badly hurt? Is he dead?" she whispered as she tried to reach for Brad's hand.

"He's alive, Beth, but he needs a physician urgently. I'll need some help to bring him inside. Summon one of the grooms and send someone for a medick right away."

Beth opened her mouth to reply, but then thought better of it and went running back into the house. A moment later, two strapping lads came rushing from around the corner. They must have been having their supper in the kitchen when Beth summoned them. The boys lifted Brad out of the cart and carried him into the house and up the stairs to the bedroom he shared with Beth.

Brad smiled at Beth dreamily, his eyes half closed. He was barely lucid, but some part of him registered that he was finally at home. "Beth," he breathed. "My sweet Beth."

Beth bent down to kiss his forehead, drawing back in shock. "He's burning up," she whispered to Hugo, her eyes huge in her pale face. Her hands were shaking as she held Brad's large hand in her own, but Beth was never one to fall apart in times of crisis. She drew herself up, her expression going from one of shock to one of determination. "Bert, go fetch the doctor. Quick as you can. Harvey, bring up some hot water and clean linen bandages. And tell Cook to send up some hot broth and brew willow bark tea. Hugo, is there anything I need to know?" Beth asked, eyeing him over the vast bed.

"Brad's wound is not deep, but it had been left to fester, and there's no telling how far the infection has gone. The physician in Reading advised amputation, and it might come to that if the putrefaction has spread."

"How you must have suffered, poor lamb," Beth spoke

soothingly to Brad as she went about removing his clothing. "You are home now, and I will take good care of you. The children have missed you so very much. They'll be so happy to see their papa. Where did you find him, Hugo? Was he well looked after?" she asked, her voice low.

"He was at a farmhouse outside Reading." A partial truth. Hugo couldn't bear to tell Beth of the condition he'd found Brad in. "Beth, is there anything else I can do for you?"

Beth glanced at Hugo, suddenly aware of how of tired and disheveled he looked. "Oh, Hugo, I am so sorry. You must be cold and tired. Would you like something to eat? Can I get you a brandy or some hot broth? There are no words to express the depth of my gratitude. I'm indebted to you, and to Neve for sparing you. Please forgive my rudeness; I was somewhat overcome."

"Beth, there's nothing to forgive, and you don't need to thank me. There's no debt, and never will be. I only hope that Brad recovers. But I must get back to my family."

"Yes, of course. Please, have a drink before you go. You look worn out."

"I won't say no to brandy," Hugo conceded. "I'm chilled to the bone after that ride."

Hugo was surprised to see a decanter of brandy on a table by the window. Few people kept spirits in their bedchamber.

"I've had trouble sleeping," Beth confided as she poured Hugo a healthy measure of brandy. "Brandy helps calm my nerves. I needed to stay calm for the children."

"There's no need to explain. Thank you," Hugo said as he accepted the crystal glass. He drained the brandy in one gulp and held out the glass for more as a pleasant warmth began to spread through his chest and belly. He needed to get going, but suddenly felt too tired to do anything but remain in this warm, cozy room in front of the roaring fire. He felt a pleasant drowsiness settle over him as he sat down and savored the second glass, closing his eyes for just a moment.

"Hugo," Beth's gentle voice recalled him from near slumber.

"I must go," he said again as Harvey made his way carefully into the room carrying a pitcher of hot water, clean bandages, and a bowl of broth.

"Shall I walk you out?" Beth asked, but her eyes were on Brad.

"You see to your husband. I'll check back tomorrow."

Hugo's limbs felt unnaturally heavy as he unhitched the cart and left it for the grooms to deal with before vaulting onto his horse and galloping away. He was desperate to get home to Neve and the children. He'd never been away from them, and this separation had hurt more than he expected. Only the light of the moon was there to guide him, but he knew the way by heart and breathed a sigh of relief when he saw the lights of Everly Manor in the distance.

TWENTY

Hugo was relieved when a young man emerged from the stables to take his horse. He didn't recognize him, but the groom obviously knew him.

"Welcome home, Your Lordship," the young man said as he took the reins from Hugo and bowed respectfully.

"Thank you, eh..."

"Robbie, sir," the young man filled in helpfully. "Master Bowden hired me for the position of head groom."

"Very good," Hugo replied absentmindedly. "Carry on."

The young man led the horse away as Hugo strode toward the door, happy to be home at last. It was just past eight in the evening, so the children would already be in bed, but if he hurried, he might still have a chance to kiss them goodnight.

The door had not been locked for the night yet, so Hugo let himself in. The house was quiet, a single candle burning in the foyer, and casting shifting shadows onto the walls and the breastplate of Bruce's suit of armor which stood in the corner, the armor polished to a dull shine. Hugo's heart soared as he heard a child's voice. Not too late then. He took the stairs two at a time but slowed down before bursting through the door so as not to startle Neve or the children.

Neve was sitting in bed with Elena in her arms. Elena's dark curls were unruly, as always, and her eyes bright with tears, but her face lit up when she saw Hugo.

"Papa," she squealed. She still pronounced it the French way, which Hugo found charming.

"Hello, my darling," Hugo whispered as he scooped up the little girl. She pressed her face to his chest, her arms going around his neck in a sweet embrace. Hugo inhaled the intoxicating smell of babyhood as he kissed the top of her head.

Elena raised her face and planted a kiss on his lips. "Love Papa," she said as she buried her face in his shoulder. She was wearing her nightdress and bare feet dangled from beneath the hem, pink in the firelight.

"I love Papa too," Neve said as she smiled at them. "I'm so glad you are back. Have you found Brad?" Neve's voice sounded casual for Elena's benefit, but Hugo could see the tension in her face.

"Yes, Brad is at home, but he's wounded and in rather a bad shape. Beth has summoned the physician," Hugo added as he set the child back on the bed and planted a kiss on Neve's head before shrugging off his coat and sitting down by the fire to remove his boots. "Where are the others? I was so hoping to see them."

"You're too late, I'm afraid," Neve replied as she tucked Elena in next to her. "Michael is already asleep; he tired himself out with a temper tantrum right after supper, and Valentine asked Frances to tell her a bedtime story and fell asleep in her bed. And I haven't laid eyes on Archie since this afternoon. He's been personally training the new grooms—or terrorizing them, I should say."

"Anything happen while I was gone?" Hugo asked as he climbed into bed, bracketing Elena between himself and Neve.

He was hungry, since he hadn't eaten since midday, but he was too tired to go down to the kitchen in search of something, and the servants had already retired for the night. He'd just wait till morning.

Elena snuggled up next to him and closed her eyes in contentment, her hand on Hugo's as if she were afraid that he would leave again.

"Reverend Snow called the banns for Frances and Archie at Sunday service," Neve whispered meaningfully over Elena's head.

"Is that so?"

"Yes, it seems they've grown tired of waiting," Neve replied, watching Hugo for his reaction.

"It's their right to marry when they please. I haven't heard back from Gideon in nearly two years. Had he had something pertinent to tell me, he would have written. As far as I know, the elder Finch is still alive, so the estate is in his hands. It would be wise for Frances to wait just a little while longer, but I can understand her impatience."

"Hugo, perhaps they don't want Finch's money," Neve suggested.

"I am sure Archie doesn't, but I thought it would be good for Frances to have some independent means after what she'd been through. It would give her peace of mind."

"Perhaps, or perhaps it would drive a wedge between her and Archie."

Hugo shrugged. "It's their decision to make, and they've made it. I don't suppose they can wait much longer without bursting into flames."

"Would you have waited so long to marry me?" Neve asked coyly, smiling at him over the head of the sleeping child.

"I wouldn't wait a day longer than I had to."

"Then give them your blessing tomorrow," Neve said as she turned to blow out the candle.

"I will."

* * *

Hugo woke up sometime before dawn. The room was chilly, but he felt a searing heat welling up within him. His throat felt raw and swollen, and his head pounded worse than the day before. Hugo was desperate for a drink but felt too weak to get out of bed and go down to the kitchen. His limbs ached, and a heaviness settled in his chest, pinning him down to the bed. Hugo closed his eyes. He must have caught a chill while riding for hours without a cloak. It would pass in a day or two. He shifted further away from Elena just in case, but she shifted with him, eager to stay close even in sleep.

"Hugo, what is it?" Neve asked from the other side of the bed. She'd become a very light sleeper since Valentine was born, always listening for any sounds coming from the children during the night.

"Go back to sleep. I just have a bit of a chill, and my throat is on fire."

Neve reached out and felt Hugo's face. "You have a fever."

"I had to use my cloak to cover Brad," Hugo explained. "It was bitter out there." His voice came out as a hoarse whisper, and it hurt to talk.

"I'll go down and put some water on to boil. You need hot tea with honey, and I'll see if we have any mustard seed to make mustard plaster with."

"Can you add some brandy to that tea? I have a splitting headache."

"Of course."

Neve gently shifted Elena to the other side of the bed, away from Hugo, and tucked the blankets about her to prevent her from rolling off the high bed.

"I'll be back soon." She stuffed her feet into sheepskin slippers that Archie had made for her while in France and put on her woolen dressing gown. The house was even colder downstairs, with the fire in the kitchen having been out since the previous evening.

Hugo tried to go back to sleep, but it hurt to swallow, and his headache seemed to be intensifying. Elena was breathing evenly, her face angelic in sleep. Hugo reached out and lightly touched her cheek. Cool, thank God.

He was glad to see Neve slip back into the room. She presented him with a steaming cup of tea, liberally sweetened with honey and fortified with brandy. The tea felt good going down and relieved the throat pain for a few minutes, but it returned as soon as Hugo finished the drink.

Neve lit a candle and sat down on the side of the bed, looking at Hugo with concern. She set down the candle and wrapped her hands around his throat, feeling carefully with her fingers. "Your throat is swollen," she said. "I'm calling for the doctor."

"He might be at the Nashes," Hugo whispered as he rested his head against the pillow.

Neve went around the other side of the bed and lifted Elena into her arms. "Hugo, stay in bed, and do not interact with anyone. I will instruct Frances to keep the children away from you. Understood?"

Hugo could hear the fear in her voice. Any sign of illness sent Neve into a panic, and with good reason.

"Yes, of course," he replied. His eyelids suddenly felt very heavy. The brandy had dulled the headache but made him drowsy. Hugo dropped off as Neve carried Elena from the room and shut the door behind her.

TWENTY-ONE

I breathed a sigh of relief when I saw Robbie, the new groom, returning from Nash House with the doctor. I had never met Doctor Baldwin before, but had heard good things about him from Harriet and Cook, although the compliments were more on his bedside manner than his prowess at healing the sick. In our situation, beggars couldn't be choosers. Anyone with medical knowledge was better than nothing, and my meager supply of herbal remedies wasn't enough to combat any major illness. I tried not to overreact when someone ran a fever or had a bout of diarrhea or vomiting, but I couldn't help the feeling of dread that stole over me every time someone took ill.

Granted, most illnesses turned out to be nothing more than a cold or indigestion, but I lived in perpetual fear of someone contracting something more serious. The mortality rate in the seventeenth century was very high, especially for children, and I guarded my babies fiercely, instantly imposing a quarantine, whether the situation called for it or not. Hugo probably had nothing more serious than a sore throat, but I needed to be sure.

"Lady Everly, an honor to meet you," Doctor Baldwin said as he stepped into the foyer and removed his hat.

I instantly saw why the good doctor received such high praise from the ladies. He was in his early thirties and had a charming smile and luminous brown eyes which shone with kindness and compassion. I was sure that many a lass longed for a bout of indisposition just so that she could bask in the glory of that smile. According to Harriet, Doctor Baldwin was a widower with a fine house and a sizeable property—a catch indeed.

"How is Bradford Nash?" I asked, fearing the worst since the doctor had still been in attendance at Nash House this morning.

"On the mend, my dear lady. On the mend." He didn't elaborate, but I wasn't sure that he was telling me the whole truth. Perhaps he felt it unethical to discuss Brad's case with me.

I led the doctor directly to our bedroom, where Hugo was dozing fitfully. His face was flushed, and his breathing was ragged, bringing back horrid memories of his infected gunshot wound in Paris. Seventeenth-century medicine was brutal, but it had saved his life then, so I put my trust in Doctor Baldwin and stepped back in order to let him examine the patient.

I sucked in my breath when Doctor Baldwin removed a handkerchief from his pocket and held it over his face as he got close enough for Hugo to breathe on him.

Hugo opened his eyes, momentarily confused by the presence of the man leaning over him.

"Good morning, my lord," the doctor said soothingly. "I'm Cornelius Baldwin, the physician. Your wife tells me you've caught a bit of a chill. Let's have a look, shall we? Open your mouth for me, Your Lordship," he instructed and stared into Hugo's reddened throat, nodding to himself. "Any nasal discharge?"

"A bit," Hugo replied.

"Cough?"

"No." The doctor held a wooden tube to Hugo's chest,

listening intently. He removed the handkerchief as he finished his examination and stepped away from the bed. His face told me everything I needed to know, and I felt the cold fingers of fear coil around my heart as I sank into a chair.

"Your husband has the putrid throat, my lady. He must have come in contact with someone who'd been infected. Symptoms usually begin to show after a few days, so it must have been several days ago. As I am sure you are aware, it's highly contagious. His lordship must be kept away from the rest of the household, or the pestilence will spread. No one is to come in or out of this room except for the one person seeing to his needs, and that person must cover their face as the infection is carried upon the breath. If you have any children, keep them as far away as possible," the doctor advised sternly. "Give him an infusion of willow bark for the fever, have him gargle with salt water every two hours, and give him hot water with honey to drink. The honey will soothe some of the pain in his throat. I advise against solid foods during illness, but his lordship may have unlimited beef tea. If anyone else falls ill, call me at once."

"Will he recover?" I asked, suddenly terrified. The putrid throat was diphtheria, as it was known in my time, and was rampant in the seventeenth century. It often wiped out entire families in a matter of days, the close proximity and lack of hygiene allowing the infection to spread unchecked. I had been vaccinated for it as a child, but neither Hugo nor the children had any immunity against the disease. I could see the look of sympathy on the doctor's face as he faced me.

"My lady, I don't believe your husband's case is a severe one, but it might take a turn for the worse over the next day or two. If it doesn't, he will begin to recover. Don't lose heart."

"Thank you," I replied woodenly. Hugo must have come in contact with someone while he was searching for Brad. Did that mean that Brad had just brought the putrid throat to his family as well? Only time would tell. In a few days, we would know if anyone else had been infected, and if the whole village was in danger.

I saw the doctor out and rushed back inside to issue orders. Frances was in the parlor with Valentine and Michael, who'd already breakfasted in the kitchen. Elena was still asleep, having fallen asleep so late last night. The children were playing some game of their own invention, while Frances sat on the settee and gazed out the window, her look one of wariness.

"Neve, what is it? What's happened?" she asked as soon as she saw the doctor driving his trap away from the house.

"Frances, Hugo has the putrid throat. Keep the children away from him and from Elena as well. Wash their hands with soap and hot water several times a day. I will be looking after Hugo, so I cannot come in contact with them or anyone else in the house."

"Understood," Frances replied. "Give him my regards for a speedy recovery."

"Thank you, Franny. What would I do without you?"

"You would manage; you always do. I will look after the children; just see to his lordship."

I gave her a nod and fled from the parlor before the children got bored of their game and decided to follow me. I marched to the kitchen, knowing this part of it would be more difficult.

"Lord Everly is ill with the putrid throat," I told Cook and Ruby, who were in the midst of eating their own breakfast porridge. "You are to boil every dish and cup that he uses, and set them aside. You are to wash your hands before and after you handle food. You are not to touch anything his lordship has touched without using a cloth to shield your hands from infection. The cloth then has to be boiled as well. Is that clear?"

The two women stared at me as if I'd just told them to turn pewter into gold on demand, but they both nodded obediently.

No doubt they thought me strange, but I didn't care. I knew something of the way infectious diseases spread. It wasn't just through breath; it was also by touching infected surfaces, such as dishes that a sick person had used, or their chamber pot. I'd instructed Cook to wash her hands often, but I doubted she washed them as often as I would have liked, and not in hot water with soap. Both Abigail and Ruby were clean by modern standards, but they knew very little of hygiene and needed to be told what to do. I gave them both the gimlet eye and went on to talk to Harriet and her sister Polly, who were already going about their morning chores.

"Is it bad?" Archie asked as he met me on the stairs. I could see the terror in his eyes. Archie didn't fear much, and I suddenly made the connection.

"Was it the putrid throat?" I asked carefully. Archie's sister's children had all died within days of each other, leaving their parents desolate with grief. Their father had hanged himself in the barn after the funeral, and Archie's sister had eventually found her way to a convent, where she devoted herself to God, finding it impossible to survive her loss any other way.

"Aye," was all that Archie said as he gave my shoulder a squeeze and continued down the stairs.

"Don't panic," I told myself as I leaned against the wall, suddenly weak in the knees. But I was consumed by fear, especially since Hugo had been in contact with Elena last night. He'd held her and kissed her, and only a miracle would keep her from getting sick.

I finally peeled myself away from the cold comfort of the stone wall and went to check on my baby. Elena was still asleep in her own cot, her breathing even and clear. She was wrapped in the blanket, just as I'd left her, and I breathed a sigh of relief as I touched her face. No fever. There was hope, but if I continued to go between her and Hugo, I might carry the infection to her. I left Elena to sleep and retraced my steps to the kitchen.

Ruby was peeling turnips, having finished her breakfast, but she set down the knife when she saw me and glanced at Cook to see if she should continue.

"Ruby, you are one of eleven, you said?" I asked, smiling so as not to alarm the girl. I tried to be gentle with her, but every time I addressed her, she acted as if I were about to scold her or dismiss her entirely.

"Aye, me lady."

"So, you have some experience of small children?"

"Aye, me lady. I helped me mam rear all ten o' me siblings." Ruby looked confused, but I had no choice but to proceed.

"Ruby, Elena came in contact with Lord Everly last night. We won't know if she's been infected for a few days yet, but I need someone to look after her and keep her separated from the others while I nurse his lordship. Would you be willing to take on the task? You can say no, Ruby; I won't get angry," I added, feeling that I had to give Ruby a choice.

"I would be glad to help, me lady," Ruby said with another glance at the cook.

"Can you spare her?" I asked Abigail, more as a formality. She could hardly say no. Looking after Elena was more important than peeling turnips.

"Of course, Your Ladyship."

I gave Ruby a list of rules to follow and a large, clean handkerchief. "Wear this over your face. Elena will try to pull it off, but don't let her. Pretend it's a game. You must not get sick, Ruby. Do not touch your face after touching Elena and wash your hands thoroughly after every time you help her use the chamber pot or feed her."

"Aye, me lady," Ruby responded like an automaton. I could tell that she was scared, but there was no one else to ask except Harriet, who had recently been ill herself. She didn't have the putrid throat, but it seemed unfair to expose her to another illness so soon after she'd recovered.

I dispatched Ruby to mind Elena and went to fetch some beef tea for Hugo. The next few days would be crucial, and I had to be vigilant.

TWENTY-TWO

After three days, I was physically exhausted from taking care of Hugo, and emotionally overwrought from constantly worrying about the children. Being so small, they refused to understand why their parents wouldn't see them, and I heard their cries echoing through the empty corridors. Frances and Archie did their best to keep Valentine and Michael busy, but Michael only wanted me, and Valentine was throwing temper tantrums purely out of principle. Elena cried softly in the next room, begging Ruby to let her see her papa. She even asked for me from time to time, but it was Hugo she wanted.

Hugo spent the first two days lying prone, his eyes closed, and his breathing labored. His throat was swollen and hot to the touch, and his fever rose and fell all day long, giving me false hope before spiking again. Hugo gargled dutifully, drank hot tea with honey, and consumed liters of beef tea without complaining, but I could tell that he was feeling much worse than he was letting on.

Doctor Baldwin stopped in on his way to Nash House, but was satisfied with my report and didn't go up to see Hugo for fear of bringing the infection to the Nashes. He believed Hugo was on the mend, and I agreed with him. Another day or two and Hugo would be up and about, if the sudden increase in complaining was anything to go on.

I set down the tray with a bowl of beef tea on a small table and walked over to the bed to check if Hugo was awake. He was, so I reached over and felt his forehead. It was mercifully cool, and his throat looked better. He still had some difficulty swallowing, but he looked much better this morning, his color no longer a sickly gray. He wasn't contagious any longer, by my estimation, but I refused to allow him out of bed until he was fully recovered. Better to err on the side of caution.

"I think it's safe to say that you are on the road to recovery," I pronounced cheerfully as I brought over the bowl of broth.

"Can I at least have something to eat?" Hugo asked, sounding like a miserable child. "I can't take any more broth. I need food; I'm starving."

"All right; you may have some bread and butter, and a cup of milk for your dinner."

"Not exactly what I had in mind," Hugo grumbled.

"I know, but you must start slow. Eating meat might make you sick," I explained.

"I'll take my chances," he mumbled as I held out the bowl to him.

"Stop being such a grouch," I said with feeling. I was tired and cranky. All I really wanted was to curl up and go to sleep for a few hours, and then wake up and have a good meal. I'd barely eaten over the past few days, too busy running between the bedroom and the kitchen, and hiding from the children who wouldn't be able to understand why their mother refused to give them hugs and kisses. I wasn't ill, but I could be a carrier of contagion, and I would do nothing to put my babies in danger.

"Neve, why don't you have a lie-down? You look worn out," Hugo suggested gently. "I can fend for myself for a few hours. I'm hardly an invalid."

"Perhaps I should," I conceded. "I am tired, and hungry. And I miss the children," I added tearfully.

"It's been four days now, and no one else has fallen sick," Hugo reasoned. "Perhaps it's time to end the quarantine."

The incubation period could be as long as a week, in some cases, and I didn't want to take any unnecessary chances. I'd opened my mouth to state my case when a timid knock sounded at the door.

Ruby stood outside, her face the color of whey, and her eyes round with fear. She was stepping from foot to foot in her nervousness, as she raised her face to meet my gaze.

"Ruby, what's happened?" I asked as my heart sank.

"Lady Elena is ill, me lady," she replied. "She's fevered, and her throat is that swollen. She's crying for ye."

"I'll be right there. Wash your hands with hot water and soap and go to your room, Ruby. We must keep you from getting ill and infecting others."

"Aye, ma'am," she replied demurely. "I'm sorry, ma'am."

"You did everything you could, and I am very grateful to you. Now go wash your hands before you touch anything."

Ruby left in a hurry and I leaned momentarily against the door, willing my knees not to betray me. I had been so sure that everything was going to be all right and no one else would get sick, and now this.

"Neve," Hugo called through the door. "Is everything all right?"

"Elena is ill," I replied as I poked my head into the room. "I must go to her."

I could see the look of horror on Hugo's face. It was mirroring my own.

"I'm scared, Hugo."

"I am, too. May I see her?"

"No. I will keep all of you completely separate until this passes. Quarantine is the only way to contain cross-infection," I replied with more authority than I felt. Hugo was a grown man, but Elena was just a baby. She was susceptible to infection, and her immune system wasn't developed enough to fight off such a terrible sickness without the help of medicine.

"I know. Please let me know how she is," he appealed, his own complaints forgotten.

"I will."

TWENTY-THREE

When I came running into the nursery, Elena was lying on her cot, her face flushed, and her body limp. Her eyes were partially closed, and her breathing ragged. Her chest rose and fell along with the cloth dolly she clutched with both hands. The child seemed to shrink into herself every time she needed to swallow. My heart nearly burst at the sight of her, but I smiled calmly and lifted her into my arms.

"How are you, my darling?" I asked as I brushed the damp curls off her forehead.

Elena barely opened her eyes, but she melted into me, eager to be comforted. I nearly gasped in shock at the heat coming off her body. She was like a tiny furnace.

"Hurts Mama," she whispered.

"I know. You're going to be all better in a few days; I promise. Papa is feeling better already, and he will come to see you tomorrow. In the meantime, you need to drink some broth. It will make your throat feel better."

Elena stubbornly shook her head. "Hurts," she repeated.

I would have done anything to take the pain away, but my choices were few. All I could do was be there and keep her hydrated. I managed to get her to swallow a few spoonfuls of broth before she fell into a fitful sleep. I climbed into bed next to her and curled around her little body, offering whatever comfort I could. I must have dozed off but woke up with a start when Elena woke up crying. She was rubbing her eyes and clutching at her throat as she tried to swallow.

"Take a sip of water," I begged her, but Elena pressed her lips together, refusing to drink. Hot tears ran down her face, her eyes begging me to make her feel better. "Darling, please," I pleaded. "Take a sip of water with honey. It will ease your throat."

"No," she moaned stubbornly.

"All right," I conceded. "Let's try something else."

I poured some cool water into a basin and began to sponge Elena's face and upper body. The coolness brought some relief and helped to reduce the temperature, enough to allow her to sleep comfortably for several hours after drinking half a cup of honeyed water. But Elena's temperature spiked again during the day, and she went from being weak to being lethargic. The only thing that roused her was the horrible cough that seemed to tear straight from her chest and sounded like the barking of a seal. The coughing fits left her drained and gasping for breath.

I cried with fear and frustration as I sat by her cot all through the day. Elena needed antibiotics, but there was no way for me to get any without physically taking her to the twenty-first century. The thought had crossed my mind, but I was afraid of taking a sick child out into the bitter cold of a December dusk. I had nowhere to go once I came out on the other side, and the village doctor might not be able to see us given the lateness of the hour. I would have to find my way to the nearest hospital, something that would not be easy given the fact that I had no money, and, once there, would have much explaining to do since my child was not registered with the National Health Service.

I didn't even have the heart to reprimand Hugo when he stepped into the room. His face was haggard in the light of the single candle, his eyes haunted. Hugo sat down next to me and took Elena's hand.

"How is she?" he asked.

"She's worse, Hugo. The illness seems to be progressing much faster in her. What should we do?"

He knew what I was asking and nodded in understanding.

"We'll take her to a hospital if she's not better by morning," he said. "I'll sit with her. You go get some rest. You look done in. You've hardly rested in four days."

I was about to argue, but my body was already responding to Hugo's suggestion. I was swaying with fatigue, my eyelids drooping from lack of sleep. I wanted to stay with Elena, but I could barely keep from falling off the chair. The half-hour nap I'd taken earlier wasn't nearly enough to keep me going through the night.

"I'll just lie down here on Michael's cot for a half-hour. Wake me if you need me," I said as I curled into a fetal position and instantly fell asleep.

TWENTY-FOUR

When I awoke, the candle was guttering, the flame wavering and casting wild shadows onto the wall. I wasn't sure what woke me at first, but then I saw Hugo sitting on Elena's cot, his body bent over hers as he held her against his chest. He seemed to be rocking back and forth, his head resting against Elena's forehead. Her hair was plastered to her face, and her skin looked strangely pale in the glow of the candle. Elena's eyes were closed, her lashes fanned against the swell of her cheeks. I got to my feet but couldn't take a step. Elena looked like she was asleep, but I knew. My heart knew.

A low growl tore from Hugo's body, the sound of a mortally wounded animal that knows that there's no hope. I wanted to go to him, to them, but my body failed me, and I crumpled onto the floor, my legs buckling under as the magnitude of the loss washed over me. An all-encompassing blackness swallowed me up, my body cushioning me against the agonizing blow.

When I came to, the room was almost completely dark, only the pearlescent light of the coming dawn bleeding through the cracks in the shutters and outlining the furniture and the man still sitting as he had before. Hugo seemed to be frozen in his grief, his shoulders stooped like those of an old man, and his eyes closed in what was either a refusal to look upon his child or prayer.

I finally managed to get up and came up behind him, my heart hardly beating. I wrapped my arms around Hugo and Elena. I wished I could scream and release some of the unbearable pain in my heart, but my voice seemed to have deserted me. Hot tears rolled down my face into Hugo's hair. He reached out and pulled me down next to him, his arm around my shoulders in a half-measure of comfort. He was too numb to do more.

I reached out and touched my daughter's face. It still retained a tiny bit of heat, but already the cold was seeping in, laying claim to its victim. Elena lay still in Hugo's arms, her little face peaceful. There was a small smile on her lips, which gave me a tiny bit of comfort. She had died peacefully in Hugo's arms, still clutching her dolly. Her hand was now cold, rigid around the cloth poppet.

"Hugo," I called softly, but there was no answer. He was lost in his grief. I tried to take his hand, but he pulled it away. He rose unsteadily to his feet and laid Elena on the cot before striding from the room without a backward glance. "Hugo," I called after him, unable to cope on my own, but Hugo ignored me and melted into the darkened corridor.

It was only then that I was able to really cry. Loud, wracking sobs tore from my body as I wrapped my arms around my middle to keep myself from coming apart. I couldn't breathe, couldn't see, couldn't hear. I was consumed by my loss, unable to imagine a life in which I could ever be whole without my little girl. As Hugo had done before me, I clutched her to me, kissing her face and her hands, begging her to wake up when I knew she never would, and baptizing her with my tears. She was gone, gone forever, to a place I couldn't follow. I had my other children to think of, so I couldn't do what my heart called for me to do—I couldn't go with her.

It was Archie who tore me away. He unfolded my fingers one by one from Elena's hands and took the child from me, laying her on the bed. Archie pulled me to my feet and held me until I began to regain some sense of control, tiny though it might be. "You must be strong," he whispered in my hair. "You must survive. Don't let it destroy you."

I knew he was talking about his sister Julia. She had never fully recovered from the death of her children, and at this moment I completely understood. Was it really possible to recover?

Archie walked me to the door, and toward my own room, where he removed my shoes and laid me on the bed. "Sleep," he said. "I'll take care of everything. You needn't worry."

I didn't think I could possibly sleep, but I felt so eviscerated by what had happened that I fell into a heavy sleep, desperate for that temporary escape from the horror of my reality. I didn't dream. I seemed to have fallen through a black vortex where there was only silence and endless space. I felt myself floating, disengaging from everything and everyone, my mind cushioning me from a full breakdown through some primal method of self-preservation.

* * *

Hugo was still gone when I woke up. The house was quiet, no sounds of laughing children or running feet heard over the deathly pall. Someone had left a glass of brandy by the bed, which I drank in one gulp, needing whatever strength I could find to face this new life in which Elena was no longer mine.

I finally got out of bed and made my way downstairs. Frances was in the parlor with the children. Michael was playing happily, but Valentine looked frightened, her eyes full of questions.

"Oh, Neve," Frances breathed as I walked into her arms.

We cried together, our tears mingling as they slid down our cheeks. We clung to each other for what seemed like hours until the children began to cry, sensing, as children do, that nothing would ever be the same. Frances gathered them up and took them to the kitchen, leaving me to just sit and stare into the flames. I wanted to hug and kiss Michael and Valentine, but I was afraid to touch them for fear of infecting them. They had to be kept safe.

Archie walked in, stomping snow from his boots.

"Where is Hugo?" I asked absentmindedly.

"Let him be," was all that Archie said.

"Where've you been?" I asked, not really caring.

"I spoke to Reverend Snow about holding the funeral on Saturday, if that's agreeable."

"Yes," I breathed. The thought of putting Elena in the ground caused a fresh flood of tears.

Archie came and sat next to me. He held me until I was able to formulate words again, which was a while. Strange, that in my state of impenetrable grief, I noticed little things like bits of wood on Archie's boots. He must have been chopping wood.

"I will make the coffin myself," Archie said when he noticed me looking. "I don't trust anyone else to do it right for our Elena."

I nodded, unable to speak. Saturday was three days away, days during which I would have to lay out Elena's body, prepare for the funeral, and find a way to get through the day without coming apart at the seams. I felt numb, almost as if I were floating outside my body, but I knew that eventually this feeling would pass and I would be swallowed up by my grief, and the unbearable pain of Elena's loss waiting to ambush me just beyond this moment.

TWENTY-FIVE

Blood-red rays of the rising sun streaked the murky winter sky, painting the crust of frozen snow in shades of mauve and pink. Several crows erupted above the tree line, their plump bodies looking like smudges of black against the vivid skyline. Thin plumes of smoke rose from chimneys in the village, people already awake and going about the business of starting their day. Hugo's breath came out in white puffs as he stumbled forward. He'd fled the house in his shirt, not having the presence of mind to put on a coat and cloak. He didn't feel the cold; he didn't feel anything except the pull of the yawning chasm that had opened up when his baby had breathed her last.

He knew he should have woken Neve when he'd realized Elena was dying, but he couldn't let her go, couldn't give up a single moment with her. He'd held her to his heart, whispered words of love, and prayed with all his might that her passing would be easy. She'd opened her eyes in that final moment and looked directly at him, the suffering gone from her expression, and only a blinding hope in her little face, still believing that her father could help her, could save her. She'd tried to lift her hand to his face but couldn't find the strength. "Papa," she'd whispered before closing her eyes. A small smile had appeared on her face as she'd let out her breath in a sigh of contentment or release. And then she was gone. Just like that, Elena was gone. Gone forever, and it was all his fault.

Hugo had no idea where he was going when he fled the house; he just knew that he couldn't spend another moment there or he would go mad. He found himself at St. Nicolas's Church. The interior was tomblike and freezing cold, the unlit candles white vertical shapes in their holders. The church was lost in shadow, except for the cruel sunrise, the brilliant light of which shone through the high windows, filling the church with a rosy glow that crept down the nave. The day had come; life went on even when all you wanted was to die.

Hugo didn't often pray at this church. He attended services as was mandated by the realm, but he did his real praying at home. But, today, he needed to be in the house of God, any house, and if it had to be a Protestant church, then that's where he would be. He prostrated himself on the cold stones; feet together, arms outstretched, forming a human cross, and prayed. He prayed for his Elena, prayed for Neve and the other children, but, most of all, he prayed for forgiveness because Elena's death was his fault. He'd brought the sickness into the house, had held and kissed Elena, passing the deadly pestilence to her. It should have been him that died, not that sweet, innocent baby, but she was gone, and he was here, and he had to live with what he'd done for the rest of his miserable life.

Hugo barely noticed when Archie came into the church. He spoke softly to Reverend Snow, who'd left Hugo to pray in peace. Their voices washed over him like warm water, soft and soothing. Hugo hadn't even realized that he was crying until the tears began to solidify on his face from the chill of the floor, and still he couldn't get up. He had no strength to even sit up, much less get to his feet and face the day in which Elena was no longer living.

"Lord Everly," Reverend Snow said gently as he knelt beside him, "it was God's will. There is nothing you could have done to save Elena. If you accept Christ as your Savior, then you must accept His will. This is a test of your faith."

"To hell with Him then," Hugo roared as he jumped to his feet and fled the church, leaving Reverend Snow staring after him openmouthed.

The reverend shook his head sadly, then lifted his hand in benediction, saying softly, "You might forsake Him, but He will never forsake you, my son. He understands your pain and forgives you."

TWENTY-SIX

Hugo did not come home the day Elena died. At any other time, this would have caused me great concern, but, today of all days, I could barely keep it together. I needed him to share this pain with me, but instead, he'd chosen to run off and lick his own wounds.

Somehow I had gotten through the day—the first day. I could barely remember what I'd said and done, but the one thing I would remember forever was laying out my daughter. Frances had offered to step in, but I needed to do it on my own. It was the last time I would wash her, or dress her, or brush her unruly hair. It was the last time I would be alone with her, the last time I would be able to touch her and hold her, and kiss her.

Once she was laid out in her coffin on the dining-room table, she would no longer be mine. She would be a corpse waiting to be buried; a shell devoid of the mischievous, funny, brave little girl who'd inhabited it. I took my time preparing Elena for her last journey. I tried to memorize every detail of her face, the silky feel of her hair, and the shape of her hands. I'd placed her dolly on her stomach and folded Elena's hands over it, feeling marginally better that Elena wouldn't go to that dark place completely alone.

Perhaps it was a morbid thought, but I wished I had a camera so that I could take a picture of my baby. Her features were burned into my brain, but I knew that, with time, they would begin to blur, and her face and the sound of her voice would begin to fade, leaving me to grope in the darkness for faded memories and little mementos. Already, she seemed so far removed from me, so untouchable.

Valentine and Michael were subdued, aware that something irrevocable had happened. They didn't ask about their sister, but their eyes were watchful, full of fear as they tiptoed around me, not wanting to disturb me. They were constantly close to tears, as was everyone in the house. Someone would stay with Elena at all times until the lid would be nailed on and the coffin transported to the churchyard for burial, but I wanted to stay through the night. I left candles burning at the head and foot of the coffin, and the flame cast eerie shadows, playing tricks on me and making me believe that Elena had blinked or pursed her lips.

Archie came in some time after midnight and forcefully lifted me off the chair. I tried to struggle, but he carried me upstairs and laid me gently on the bed. "Sleep now. I will watch over her until morning."

"Where is Hugo?" I asked. If anyone knew, it would be Archie.

"In Hell," was all that Archie said before quietly leaving the room and closing the door behind him.

Well, that makes two of us, I thought as I sank into the pillows, suddenly devoid of any will to go on.

* * *

Hugo materialized on the morning of the funeral, carrying the tiny coffin on his shoulder as we made our way to the church. The day was warmer, the road muddy and slippery. A weak sunshine peeked through the clouds, and a gentle wind caressed my face as I tried not to stare at the little box that held the remains of my child. Hugo hadn't said anything, hadn't offered any explanation or apology; he seemed to be someplace else, his eyes hollow and his shoulders stooped. At any other time, I would have confronted him, but he was so clearly eviscerated by grief that I just walked next to him silently, holding Valentine's hand until we reached the church. Archie carried Michael, and Frances walked next to him, her arm linked through his in a mute appeal for support.

There were already people at the church. I knew some of them from before, but a lot of them were strangers to me. They'd come out of respect for Hugo, and probably out of curiosity. They wanted to see Lord Everly's family, since we hadn't been to the village since our arrival in Cranley. Godfrey Bowden stood off to the side with his wife, who was looking at me from beneath her lashes, not wanting to be caught staring. The only friendly face I saw was Beth's. She came toward me, and I walked into her arms and buried my face in her shoulder. She didn't say anything, just held me in that way that friends do, offering a quiet, rock-solid support.

"How is Brad?" I asked, having finally found my voice.

"Still holding on," Beth replied tearfully. "He will recover; I know he will. He must. Especially after such a sacrifice."

"What do you mean?" I asked, suddenly alert.

Beth looked away, two bright spots of color blooming in her pale cheeks. "Brad thinks one of the Irish soldiers had the putrid throat. He wasn't badly wounded, but died soon after they were brought to that farm. He complained of a sore throat and was burning up with fever. It's a wonder Brad didn't catch it, but

Brad never went near him," Beth confided. "They'd been transported in different wagons."

"And Hugo?" I asked.

"Hugo helped remove the corpses from the farmhouse. Perhaps he became infected then."

It was entirely possible. If Hugo had touched a contaminated corpse with his bare hands, he might have been exposed to some bodily fluids or live bacteria. I was sure he'd washed his hands, as I had drilled into him time after time, but perhaps something had remained beneath his fingernails or on his clothes. These infections were strong and infected countless people, causing epidemics if not stopped in time. It was a wonder that Brad hadn't been taken ill, considering that Hugo had tended him just before beginning to show symptoms himself.

"Come, sit down," Beth said as she led me to the front pew, where Archie and Frances were already sitting with the children. Hugo stood with his back to the church, his head bowed as he looked down on the coffin.

"Ahem, we are ready to begin, Your Lordship," Reverend Snow said tactfully.

Hugo didn't reply, just took his seat. He sat next to me, but there was a distance between us that had never been there before, and the gap seemed unbreachable. Did he blame me for Elena's death? I suddenly wondered.

I barely listened to the words of the reverend as he spoke of God's mercy and divine light. I didn't care. There was no mercy in a child's death, and there would be no light for any of us, not for a very long time.

We all shuffled out into the graveyard, where a small grave had already been dug. It looked like a scar on the snow-covered expanse of the sleepy cemetery. Michael began to cry, but Valentine stood silently next to me, her eyes dry in her solemn face.

The coffin was lowered into the ground, and clumps of dirt hit the lid with heartbreaking finality. That sound would haunt me for the rest of my days.

I reached for Hugo's hand, but he just stared straight ahead, his hand rigid in mine. He walked away alone as soon as the funeral ended, going toward the village rather than home.

Cook put out some food and drink for the mourners, but I just couldn't face the trial of having to be social after burying my daughter. I hid in Hugo's study, comforted by the indifferent stares of distant relations glaring at me from the paintings, and the dusty smell of books and maps.

"May I come in?" Archie asked as he entered the room.

I shrugged. He could hide with me if he wanted to.

Archie sat down and looked at me. I didn't make eye contact, but his gaze was fixed on my face, demanding that I respond.

"He needs you," Archie said bluntly.

"I don't recall turning him away."

"He's suffering," Archie replied, still holding my stare.

"As am I."

"You don't understand. He blames himself," Archie explained patiently.

"It wasn't his fault any more than it was mine. It happened," I replied brusquely.

I couldn't tell Archie that in the darkness of a sleepless night, I blamed myself as well. Had I taken Elena to the future, she might have lived. She might have been saved with something as simple as a dose of antibiotics. But I'd hesitated. I'd waited. I'd listened to Hugo when I knew that the situation was critical. Hugo had recovered, and I'd foolishly assumed that Elena would too. In my stupid twenty-first-century brain, I'd still believed that everything would always be okay; everything would blow over, the way it had done in the past. There would be an eleventh-hour miracle, a happy ending for all.

Elena's death was my first real encounter with tragedy. Sure, I'd lost my father when I was a child, and then watched my mother drink herself to death, but those events had been the result of choices, choices that ruined my childhood, but might have been prevented had my parents cared more about me than they had about themselves. Elena's death was not a choice—or was it? Was it the result of my own selfishness and ignorance?

"He brought the sickness from Reading," Archie said. "He passed it on to Elena."

"Archie, he couldn't have known," I rounded on him. What was the point of allocating blame? "Hugo didn't feel ill until the next day. Had he known, he'd never have gone anywhere near Elena. There's no sense in blaming anyone. It won't bring her back."

"No, it won't," Archie agreed, "and there's no sense in blaming anyone, but that's what people do when they are grieving. They look for answers. They go over every detail in their mind and try to rewrite what happened in an effort to make sense of it all. Deep down, Hugo knows that he's not to blame, but he can't accept that this was a random act. He must give it meaning, and by blaming himself, he has someone to rage at other than God."

I stared at Archie, suddenly seeing him in a new light. He was always stoic, reticent, and a little intimidating. I would trust Archie with my life without giving it a second thought, but as of this moment, I trusted him with my heart as well. I never understood how deep his waters ran, or how intense he was under that gruff exterior. I remembered seeing him for the first time years before and dismissing him as a callous youth, a pretty boy who was ignorant and beneath my notice.

I didn't say anything, just walked around the desk and laid my head on Archie's shoulder as his arms came around me like steel beams of support. I loved this man with my whole being, but not in any kind of romantic way. Archie was the closest thing I'd ever had to a brother, and to a real friend, and at this awful moment, I felt blessed.

TWENTY-SEVEN

Hugo stared balefully at the grimy walls of the cottage. He'd been hiding out here for days, the way he had when he was a boy. The old ramshackle dwelling belonged to an old wise-woman who had lived in the woods. She was nothing more than a harmless old woman knowledgeable in herbal cures, but the previous clergyman had run her out of the village under the threat of being burned as a witch. Reverend Wilkins had not been as compassionate or progressive as Reverend Snow. He'd been a brimstone and fire minister who believed that God's will had to be obeyed at all cost, and, therefore, any type of interference, in the form of herbal cures, was a direct affront to the Almighty. The fact that the old woman had helped countless women miscarry unwanted children hadn't helped her case.

The cottage still smelled of herbs despite being vacant for nearly two decades. Parts of the roof had rotted away, and it was colder inside than out, but Hugo didn't care. He simply couldn't bear to be around anyone. A nearly empty cask of brandy sat next to him on the floor, and some bread and cheese were left over from last night, now the feast of hungry mice.

Hugo leaned his head against the wall and closed his eyes.

He couldn't hide here forever, but the thought of going home made his stomach twist into knots. How could he face Neve when he was solely responsible for Elena's death? How could he go on living when Elena was gone? There had been terrible moments in his life, but he'd never felt as forsaken as he did now. Was this God's way of punishing him for allowing his children to be baptized into the Protestant Church? Was this the price he had to pay for trying to give them an easier existence? How did he go on knowing that his decisions had cost Elena her life? How could he be a husband to Neve when his own ignorance had torn her heart out?

Hugo poured out the rest of the brandy and gulped it down in one swallow. He couldn't have known that he'd been exposed to the putrid throat. He might have gotten it from handling the corpses of the dead soldiers, but he had no way of knowing. He'd come in contact with numerous people while searching for Brad, from innkeepers along the road to Widow Starkey. Any one of them could have been carrying the sickness. But he had known that he wasn't well when he got home. He'd felt feverish, and there was that telltale tickle in his throat, but he'd been so desperate to see Neve and the children that he'd ignored the signs and allowed himself to hold and kiss Elena and Neve. Neve was immunized against the disease, but not poor Elena. She'd been an innocent victim of his own stupidity and selfishness. And now she was gone, and he was left behind to carry his guilt for the rest of his days.

Hugo drew up his knees and rested his head on his folded arms. He had to go back; had to do his duty by Neve, the children, and the estate; had to live, but he wasn't at all sure how to start.

"Get up!" The words came from somewhere above his head, and Hugo opened up one eye to see Archie towering over him. "Enough of this!" Archie physically hauled Hugo to his feet and glared at him from beneath the brim of his hat. "I've given you three days to feel sorry for yourself, *Your Lordship*," he said with biting sarcasm. "And now you will pick yourself up and go home to your grieving wife and your frightened children, or, so help me God, I will beat you to a pulp." Archie looked like he meant every word. His hands were balled into fists at his side, and his eyes were blazing with anger.

Hugo gazed back at Archie, a bitter smile spreading across his haggard face. "Thank you, Archie," was all he said before walking out into the cold December twilight.

TWENTY-EIGHT

Hugo came home that night: cold, unshaven, and heartbreakingly distant. He called for a bath, and remained lying prone in the steaming water with his eyes closed, his profile reminiscent of a stone effigy. Only the hard set of his jaw and the furrow between the eyebrows indicated that he was still awake, and tense as a bow. He finally climbed into bed, but didn't reach out to hold me, or offer any words of comfort; just lay still, his eyes fixated on the embroidered tester. Hugo had never been one to just start analyzing his feelings, but I'd never known him to be insensitive or irrational—or so stoically silent. I could tell by his haggard face and haunted eyes that he was gutted by grief, and was torn between pity and anger, my own emotions boiling over after days of the terrible strain of trying to hold it together for the sake of the children.

"It wasn't your fault, Hugo," I finally said, needing to break the barrier of silence between us. I didn't care what he said as long as he responded to me and allowed me a glimpse into his tortured soul.

"It was," he replied tersely.

"It was just as much my fault as yours. I should have taken Elena to the hospital; I shouldn't have waited," I replied, finally putting my own guilt into words.

"It was I who advised you to wait. First, I infected her, and then I condemned her to death," Hugo replied through clenched teeth, his voice full of self-loathing.

I gaped at him, astounded by the depth of his guilt. I couldn't imagine any parent who didn't torture themselves with what-ifs after losing a child, but Hugo was being completely irrational, and given his need to punish himself, there wasn't much I could say, so I groped for the only line of reasoning he would respond to.

"Hugo, if you believe in God and His divine plan, you must see that Elena's death was His will," I reasoned. I didn't believe that for a moment, but I knew it would bring him some measure of comfort.

"Neve, I don't believe that God—to use a phrase I learned in the future—micromanages our lives. We had a choice, and we made it. *I* made it. I told you to wait. Had you listened to your instinct, Elena would have lived."

I was glad that we were finally talking, but Hugo's reasoning made me want to throttle him. For the first time in days, I was angry rather than just broken and lost, and it actually felt good to feel fury coursing through my veins. It made me feel alive after days of walking the knife's edge between life and death.

"Yes, Hugo, we had a choice, and I made mine," I cried, desperate to get through to him. "I chose to wait. I could have argued with you, could have defied you, but I didn't. We made a grave mistake and paid with the life of our child. Must we wallow in self-pity? I need you to share my grief. I need you to support me, instead of indulging in this self-flagellation, or I'll go to pieces," I screamed at him, but his grief was so impenetrable as to block all reason.

"I'm sorry, Neve, but I am unable to do as you ask."

"Unable or unwilling?" I cried, my voice quivering with agitation. "You are not the only one who lost a child."

"I need time," Hugo replied woodenly.

"How much time?"

"As much time as it takes. I plan to leave for London come morning," he said with a heart-wrenching finality.

He was running away, something I'd never known him to do, and it scared me to death. He needed to deal with what had happened and his role in it, and he had to be here for the rest of us, rather than leaving us adrift in a sea of grief, while he did everything in his power to bury his feelings beneath a flurry of activity.

"You will do no such thing," I replied, my voice surprisingly strong despite the blind rage that was flowing through me.

"You can't stop me," Hugo spat out. "The king is gone, and things are changing rapidly. I need to be there."

"Tomorrow is Christmas Eve," I said, my voice now deadly calm. "You will *not* leave your family and go plot and scheme with the other parasites who are already picking over the bones of the corpse of this monarchy and are double-talking and maneuvering in a desperate effort to worm their way into the graces of the next."

"I'm going," Hugo replied, quietly, but firmly.

"Then you might not find me here when you return," I spat back at him.

"Meaning?"

"Meaning that I will not be treated this way. I know that you are sick with grief, but I am still your wife, and Valentine and Michael are still your children, and we need you. If you have no need of us, I know a place where we can have a better life, and a safer one."

That finally elicited a reaction. Hugo sat up and looked at

me, his eyes blazing with fury. "Are you threatening to leave me and take the children?"

"I am."

"You wouldn't," he whispered. "You wouldn't do that."

"Try me."

"You are mine to command," he said, finally blowing the lid off my fury.

I threw myself at him, pounding my fists against his chest. "Yours to command, you righteous bastard? How dare you? How dare you treat me like I'm your chattel rather than a human being who is overcome with sorrow and guilt?" I punched him until he finally lost it and flipped me onto my back, his hands pinning my wrist to the bed. "Go ahead," I goaded him. "Show me what it means to be your wife. Exercise your husbandly rights. Are you going to beat me too? Isn't that the acceptable form of punishment for a disobedient wife?" I was panting now, but I couldn't turn back, couldn't stop. I was taunting him intentionally and cruelly, but he had crossed the line, and at that moment, I despised him and wanted no part of him. I saw that realization dawning in his eyes as Hugo lost that last shred of control.

His eyes blazed with the kind of rage I'd rarely seen, his mouth twisted with anger. He drove his knee between my thighs, pushing them apart as he rammed himself into me. I tried to throw him off, but he was too strong. I clawed at his hands and bit his lip as his face came closer to mine, but my body betrayed me, my hips grinding against his in a fierce need to connect with him in any way I could. This wasn't making love; this was him punishing me, and me punishing him in return. He released my hands, and I scratched his face, drawing blood with a growl of satisfaction.

Hugo's mouth came down on mine, swallowing my fury. His thrusts became more vicious, but I welcomed the assault, meeting him thrust for thrust. I was in pain, but I didn't care.

Pain was better than hopelessness and grief. Pain was better than stony silence. Pain was life.

I wasn't sure when the anger turned to a need for forgiveness and a plea for love. Hugo's head dipped into my shoulder as he collapsed on top of me, his body shaking with sobs. He'd held in his pain all these days, but now that the floodgates had opened, he was a drowning man, unable to stop. I'd never seen a man cry like that, never felt the depth of another's grief so intensely, but as my tears mingled with his, we held each other, silently renewing our bond and offering each other forgiveness.

"I'm sorry," Hugo finally breathed. "I am so sorry. I would give my life in a second if I knew it could bring our baby back."

"I know," I whispered to him as I brushed the hair from his face. "I know."

"My life is worth nothing without you and the children," Hugo said as he rested his forehead against mine. "I'd be adrift, as I had been before I met you. Please, Neve, please don't ever leave me, no matter how foolishly I behave. You are my reason for being."

"And you are mine," I replied, as I kissed him tenderly with my swollen lips.

"I didn't mean what I said," Hugo continued. Now that he was talking, he had to get it all out, had to make me see what was in his heart. "You are my love, my partner, and my best friend. It is I who am yours to command," he pleaded, needing to hear that he was forgiven.

"I know you didn't mean it."

He buried his face in my neck, his breathing still ragged. The crying had unburdened him for the moment and allowed him a tiny bit of release, which would help him take the first step toward healing.

"Go to sleep, Hugo. You need your rest. And tomorrow, we will prepare for Christmas and celebrate with our children in a quiet, dignified way, respectful of Elena's memory."

"Thank you," Hugo murmured as he rolled off me and closed his eyes. Now that the storm had passed, he was exhausted, his voice slurred with fatigue. "Thank you for loving me."

I squeezed his hand as he slipped into a deep sleep, grateful to at least have my husband back.

TWENTY-NINE

I was glad to see the old year out, proud of myself for surviving Christmas and Boxing Day, on which the lord and lady of the manor were expected to visit the tenants and give them gifts. All I wanted to do was curl up into a ball and drift until the razor-sharp edges of my grief began to dull, and not disembowel me every time I so much as thought of Elena, but I didn't have that option; I had to function. Valentine and Michael were unusually subdued, their heads turning in unison every time a door opened, as if expecting their sister to come back. Valentine accepted our explanation that Elena had gone to Heaven, at least for the time being, but Michael kept asking for "Ena," and looking for her everywhere. Every night, Hugo carried him through the house so that he could check all the rooms to make sure his twin wasn't hiding somewhere. It broke my heart in ways I didn't know it could be broken.

I don't think I would have survived those first two weeks without the support of Frances and Archie, which made the thought of losing them even more painful. Soon, they would marry and leave us, and I would be parted from the only two people whom I could rely on besides Hugo. At a time like this, I felt my isolation very keenly. I had no family or friends to lean on, no support network, or enough mental distractions to find even temporary oblivion from my thoughts. Archie and Frances, as if by some unspoken agreement, had taken charge of the children; Archie doing his best to entertain Valentine, while Frances saw to Michael. They were giving us time to grieve and heal, and I was surprised to find that with each day that passed, we learned to accept the "new" normal and forge a way ahead. I went about my routine, taking each day as it came. I felt numb, but at least I was no longer sneaking off to an empty room to cry my heart out whenever something reminded me of Elena.

"Archie and I will postpone the wedding until the summer," Frances informed me as we sat in the parlor one January afternoon, watching Michael toddle from one piece of furniture to another. He still liked to hold on for support, even though he could walk. He was a cautious one, unlike Elena, who had always been the leader and risk-taker.

"Please don't, Frances," I replied, my eyes welling with gratitude. "You've waited long enough, and a little happiness is just what this house needs."

"How can we celebrate when you are suffering so?" Frances asked gently.

As I looked at her in the gray January light seeping through the leaded windows, I suddenly realized how much she'd changed. Gone was the wide-eyed, fearful girl, leaving a composed and self-assured young woman in her place. Frances was now eighteen, a woman in her prime by modern standards, no longer a child. She was right; the thought of a celebration seemed almost obscene, but we had no right to ask Frances and Archie to put off their wedding. It was their time, and Hugo and I had to swallow our bitterness and give Frances and Archie our blessing. They'd earned their happiness, and we would be happy for them.

"It's the cycle of life, isn't it? Hugo and I married a month after you lost Gabriel. Life is all about endings and new beginnings; I couldn't possibly ask you to wait any longer than you already have."

"And his lordship?" Frances asked carefully.

"He feels the same," I replied. I didn't think Hugo gave the upcoming wedding much thought, but I knew that he understood the importance of finding reasons to move forward. "I will miss you so much, Frances," I said tearfully. "You are like the sister I never had, but always longed for."

"Neve," Frances began, looking at my face in a searching manner, "Archie and I have been thinking..."

"What about?" I wasn't sure what Frances was going to say, but my voice trembled with hope.

"Staying."

"Really?" I could barely keep the relief out of my voice.

"This house is big enough for several families. The thought of leaving you after all we've been through feels rather like losing a limb... or two."

"How does Archie feel?"

Frances gave me a sweet smile, one that had Archie written all over it. "Archie needs a bed, something to toss in his belly, and a few horses to commune with. He doesn't care if we live in a cave. You know he's not a man of many words, but he loves you all with all his heart."

"Oh, Frances, I would be so happy." I froze momentarily, unable to believe that I'd just mentioned happiness. Was it possible to be happy after losing a child, even for a moment? The truth was that it was. The thought of Frances and Archie not leaving made me happy, and rather than push the feeling away and feel ashamed, I embraced it, and felt a tiny glow in my heart. I'd lost my precious baby, but at least I wouldn't be losing two more people that I dearly loved.

Frances watched the emotions playing over my face, and I could tell that she understood. She didn't say anything, simply walked over and put her arms around me, and we stood like that for a few moments until Michael squeezed himself between us and tried to hug us both with his little arms.

"It's time for your nap, young man," I said to Michael and scooped him up. He wrapped his arms around me and laid his head on my shoulder. He still smelled like a baby, and I inhaled the wonderful scent, thankful for the sweet little boy who loved me unconditionally. "I love you, darling," I whispered, savoring the moment.

Michael's eyes were already drooping, so rather than make him walk up the stairs, I carried him up. I hadn't realized how much heavier he'd grown, since I hadn't spent much time with him since Hugo had returned from Reading. Now it was time to get a handle on my grief and be a mother to my two remaining children.

"One day at a time," I told myself as I trudged up the stairs with Michael snug in my arms.

In the meantime, I'd thought of something that might make the wedding a slightly less somber occasion for all involved. I wasn't sure my plan would work, but I had to try.

THIRTY

Liza Timmins hitched the mule to the cart and made sure Johnny was sufficiently bundled up for the journey. It would take her close to two hours, but despite the cold, it was worth the trip. The news of Hugo's return had dominated the gossip in the tavern for several weeks, poor folk having nothing to do but speculate about their betters, but the last piece of news got Liza's full attention. Poor people's children died all the time, and no one cared, but when a lordling's child died, it was all anyone talked about. She did feel sorry for the little lass's passing, God rest her soul, but it couldn't have come at a better time. Too bad it wasn't the boy who had caught the pestilence, Liza mused as she set off for Cranley.

The local gossips said that it had been Hugo himself who'd brought the sickness home, a fortuitous coincidence. Hugo had always had a longing for children, and Liza knew with absolute certainty that he would be devastated by the loss of his child; not only devastated, but feeling guilty and vulnerable, especially with Christmas just come and gone. Now was the time to strike, if there ever was a right time, and she would not let this opportunity pass. She'd taken her chances with Lionel Finch and had assured herself a life of comfort for over two years, and now she would take her chances with Hugo. They'd been close once, and she knew how to manipulate him better than he might expect. Hugo would never respond to threats or demands, but he would respond to kindness and humility. She only hoped that witch of his wasn't there to ruin the moment. Liza would have to bide her time and catch him out on his own.

Johnny fell asleep soon after they got on their way, so Liza laid him down in the cart and enjoyed her solitary ride. It wasn't often that she was out and about, enjoying the day, cold though it was, rather than doing endless chores and looking after her mam. Well, today the girls could do it while she saw to their future. If things went her way, they could be set for life—all of them.

* * *

The pitched roof of Everly House came into view shortly before noon, and Liza felt a momentary panic before she admonished herself and drew a few calming breaths. She just had to stick to the plan, and everything would be right as rain.

Going up the drive might alert Lady Everly to her arrival and get her hackles up, so Liza stabled the cart at the inn in the village and walked the rest of the way. Johnny was heavy in her arms, but he was awake now, looking around with interest as they approached the big house. Liza positioned herself behind a large oak where she had a good view of the front door. She hoped Hugo would come out soon since it was cold, and she could do with a warm drink and a meat pie for her trouble.

Liza was beginning to despair when the door finally opened, and Hugo strode out. He took her breath away as he stopped on the top step for a moment to pull on his gloves. She hadn't seen him in over three years, but the draw was still there, the heart still not indifferent to the man who'd once shared her bed. Hugo had changed in subtle ways; his hair now longer and his face leaner. He was a little thinner, but he looked stronger and perhaps a little meaner, or maybe those were only the lines of grief etched into his face.

Hugo walked down the steps and set off for the stable, likely to fetch his horse. He liked to ride without a saddle whenever possible, so wouldn't have been expecting a groom to lead out the horse.

Liza took a deep breath and stepped out of her hiding place, materializing before Hugo like a restless ghost. She didn't say anything, just curtsied prettily, not an easy thing to do with a child on her hip.

"You dare to show your face here?" Hugo demanded as he took her measure. He didn't look angry, just wary, and tired.

"I've come to offer my condolences on your loss, Hugo," Liza answered demurely, her eyes searching his face for signs of weakness. If only she could find the chink in his armor.

"It's Lord Everly to you, and I have no need of your sympathy," Hugo replied, his head tilted to the side, his eyes watchful.

"'Tis a terrible thing to lose a child."

"What do you want, Liza? Don't imagine that I don't know you betrayed me to Lionel Finch. So how much was my life worth?" Hugo asked, a bitter smirk on his handsome face.

So, he knew. That would make her mission more difficult, but not impossible, Liza mused as she tried her best to look contrite. He hadn't walked away, so there was still a chance she could talk him round.

"Your life is priceless to me," Liza replied, her color rising in indignation. "You don't understand, Your Lordship; he threatened me. I was frightened, and had no one to turn to."

"Really?" Hugo asked conversationally. "And how did Lionel Finch come to know of you, or of your connection to me?" Hugo asked, leaving Liza momentarily speechless. She hadn't thought of that, but it didn't matter.

"He was a very resourceful man, Lionel Finch was," Liza replied, hoping that would put the matter to rest.

"Leave now," Hugo said. His voice was quiet but laced with threat. "If you were a man, I'd have you horsewhipped."

"I thank you for your mercy," Liza persisted. "I only wanted to tell you that you have other children, besides the one you've lost."

Hugo remained silent, waiting for her to go on. This was her big chance; the reason she'd come.

Liza took a step forward, turning Johnny to face Hugo. Johnny was wide awake, his dark eyes studying the man before him. He was a friendly child and smiled at Hugo in his disarming way. Liza noted the softening of Hugo's features. He wasn't indifferent to the child, so perhaps this would actually work.

"You have a son, Hugo. This is Johnny. Won't you come and meet him?" Liza cajoled, inching closer to Hugo.

Johnny reached out a chubby hand and Hugo took it, despite his obvious misgivings.

"And how old is Johnny?" Hugo asked as he studied the little boy.

"Why, he's nearly three," Liza replied proudly. "A few months older than your eldest girl. And a fine, strong boy he is; just like his father."

Hugo remained silent as he studied the boy, so Liza, feeling emboldened by his silence, went on.

"I didn't come to ask you for anything; just wanted you to know that you have another boy. Your eldest, you might say," she added.

Hugo suddenly smiled. It was a smile she recalled well, warm and genuine. He'd smiled at her like that before that slattern who was now his wife had showed up. Well, she'd done it.

She'd hooked him. Was it really going to be so easy? Liza wondered as she smiled back, already hearing the jangle of coins in her nearly empty purse. Hugo would take care of his boy; he'd take care of them all. Despite his gruff exterior, he was a kind and honorable man. He'd take care of his spawn—not like so many other men who left a trail of bastards in their wake, as indifferent to their fate as they were to the fate of the women they'd ruined. She'd trusted her instinct, and once again it had seen her right, Liza crowed to herself as she stepped closer still, bringing Johnny almost face to face with Hugo.

"I would dearly like to strike you," Hugo said softly, "but that would be ungentlemanly and might frighten the child. So, I will put this in a manner you will understand. If I ever see you here again, or if you ever again presume to try to trap me, you will live to regret it, and so will your poor fatherless bastard. Get off my property, and never show your face here again."

"I took you for an honorable man, Hugo Everly," Liza fumed. "A man who would not turn his back on his own flesh and blood."

"And I wouldn't, except that this child is neither."

Liza took a hasty step back as Hugo moved toward her, his eyes filled with menace.

"I'm going," she spat as she turned on her heel and fled. Liza didn't stop until she was halfway down the drive, her heart hammering in her chest like a jackrabbit.

Johnny was smiling happily, having enjoyed the bumpy ride. "More," he begged, as he tried to bounce in her arms.

"Sorry, my lad, but you'll have to walk from here," Liza said as she lowered him down on the ground.

Johnny gave her a pouty stare, but accepted her hand and began to walk, his attention instantly taken up by two squirrels who seemed to be fighting over a pinecone.

Liza stood quietly for a few minutes, allowing Johnny to watch the squirrels while her heart slowed down to a normal pace. Her scheme had backfired. She always knew it might, but she'd been so close. Hugo had seemed taken with the boy, and he had listened to her, rather than just throwing her off his land at first glance. Perhaps he would have a think and change his mind, but if he didn't, there was more than one way to skin a cat, as her mam used to say, and she was far from defeated.

THIRTY-ONE

Hugo watched Liza hurrying away, her back rigid and her arms straining with the effort of carrying the child. He wouldn't have actually done anything to hurt her, but she'd taken his threat seriously, the fear visible in her eyes. The boy gazed at Hugo over her shoulder, his dark eyes watchful as if sensing his mother's distress. He was a sturdy child, with round cheeks pink from the cold and a sweet smile, which he bestowed on Hugo before turning away. Hugo mentally wished him well and turned toward the stables.

Seeing Liza had been unexpectedly disturbing, and Hugo felt a sudden twinge of guilt gnaw at his soul. He'd never made advances to Liza, but she had been an ambitious girl who had made it clear that she was there for the taking should he wish it. And he had wished it. He hadn't realized how lonely he'd been until Liza had come to his room one night and simply climbed into his bed. He had meant to tell her to leave, had opened his mouth to chastise her, but the need for human contact had proved stronger, and he'd taken what she was giving, allowing himself a few hours of emotional and physical release. Liza had not been a virgin, and she knew what she was about, in bed and out. She was lively, playful, and knew how to lighten his mood, which was often dark in those days.

Their association—for he couldn't call it anything else—had lasted for about a year. No promises had ever been made, and no future had been discussed. What future could there have been? Hugo liked Liza, indulged her when he could, and tried to make her feel appreciated, but she was a servant. They both knew their place—or so he'd thought. Hugo had taken every precaution against pregnancy. He wasn't the type of man whose morality was elastic enough to allow for bastards. There were those who gave no thought to the consequences, but Hugo was not one of those men. Had Liza ever gotten with child, he would have taken care of her and his offspring, but this child couldn't be his, especially given the timing. But the fact that Liza had chosen to approach him at a time when he was at his lowest proved once again that she wasn't as naïve or helpless as she had once pretended to be. Liza was a survivor, and she would latch onto any opportunity that presented itself to further her own ambitions. She'd nearly cost him his life once, and if he knew anything, it was that Liza wasn't finished with him. Not yet.

Hugo mounted his horse and took off for Nash House. He hadn't seen Brad since he'd left him in Beth's care just over two weeks ago. It'd been seventeen days, but it felt like seventeen years. Seventeen days ago, he'd had three children. Seventeen days ago, he'd been whole. But he had to be grateful; he still had Neve and the children.

Hugo smiled ruefully as he thought of Neve, his fingers going subconsciously to the scratches on his face. What had he done to deserve a woman like her? Whatever his past transgressions, God had seen fit to put Neve in his path that fateful day—a day that had changed both of their lives forever. Neve was his lifeblood, his heart. She understood him like no other, and although he was deeply ashamed of his behavior the other night, he knew that his wife had known exactly what to do to break through his self-imposed exile. Had she allowed him to leave for London, their marriage would have been irrevocably altered, their relationship forever fractured. Perhaps some part of Hugo felt that he no longer deserved to be loved or have a family, but Neve had brought him back. She'd broken through the wall of grief he'd erected around himself and allowed him to release some of his pain without blaming him or seeing him as being weak.

There were times when Hugo wished that he could erase all previous liaisons from his past, but, as Neve pointed out, his experiences made him who he was, and shaped him as a man. She didn't seem to mind that he'd been married before, or that he had taken other women to his bed. And he felt a deep sense of relief at the knowledge that he could tell Neve about Liza's visit without having to hide the truth. Neve knew he'd been with Liza before he'd met her, and she would believe him when he said the child wasn't his. *Strange what it takes for a man to realize how blessed he is,* Hugo thought as he galloped toward Nash House, his heart suddenly lighter than it had been in weeks.

THIRTY-TWO

Brad was fully dressed and downstairs, sitting by the fire in the front parlor with a book in his hands. His injured leg was propped up on a stool, and the thickness of his thigh beneath the cloth of the breeches indicated that it was heavily bandaged, but at least he felt well enough to get out of bed. His normally ruddy complexion had lost some of its healthful glow, and he'd lost weight, but he looked remarkably well for a man who'd been close to death only a few weeks ago.

Beth sprang to her feet from her seat by the window where she'd been working on some embroidery. Her face was anxious as she approached Hugo, her needlework forgotten. "Hugo, how are you?" she asked, her question encompassing everything from his physical well-being to his emotional state.

"I'm all right," Hugo replied as he took Beth's hands in his. "Really."

"And Neve?"

"She's managing. We all are."

"I suppose that's all anyone can expect," Beth replied as she threw a grateful look at her husband. "I'm sure you two have much to talk about. I'll leave you to it."

"Thank you, sweetheart," Brad said as he smiled tenderly at his wife. "Just have Millie bring some refreshments for us."

"As if you have to remind me," Beth remarked with an indignant scowl, which instantly transformed into a smile as she saw the look of contrition on Brad's face. She blew him a kiss and left the room, closing the door softly behind her.

"Hugo," Brad said as he clasped Hugo's hand warmly. Brad looked sick with grief as he beheld his friend. "Nothing I say can possibly make up for what you've lost, and I feel so responsible for the part I've played in Elena's death. Is there anything, anything at all I can do?"

"It wasn't your fault, Brad. There's nothing either of us could have done differently."

"I know, but the knowledge brings me no comfort."

"Nor me, but there's no use laying blame. Some day we will be able to think of her as she had been, and remember the love we felt for her, but right now the grief is just too raw."

"You saved my life, Hugo. I would have died in that loft had you not come for me, and you lost your child because of it." Brad looked miserable. "If only you'd known."

"Do you think I would have forsaken you?" Hugo asked. "You are my oldest and most trusted friend. I would have still come for you. Had I known that soldier had died of the putrid throat, I wouldn't have touched him with my bare hands, nor would I have exposed anyone to the disease, but I had no way of knowing, Brad. It was a tragic mishap. Now, tell me, how do you feel?"

"Better. For the first few days, I could barely move my leg. The smell was awful, but the physician irrigated the wound every day, and put on a fresh poultice until the infection started to loosen its hold. Had it not, he would have taken the leg off to save me," Brad added, still unable to believe that he was a whole man.

"I'm glad it didn't come to that."

"As am I," Brad replied with a sigh of relief. "So, what now?" he asked. "What are your plans?"

Hugo shook his head miserably. "I suppose I must go to London and petition the new king for a pardon, but I have no heart to do anything. I just want to lose myself in the running of the estate. I no longer have a taste for politics. But, sooner or later, de Chartres's men will find me and demand that I make good on my promise, and for that, I need to lay the groundwork."

"Is there no way out for you?" Brad asked, his face creased with concern.

"None that I can think of. Oh, and Liza came to see me today," Hugo added conversationally, eager to change the subject.

"Never. Not after what she'd done." Brad's face was slack with shock. "What did she want?"

"She wanted me to acknowledge her son as mine. Claimed he was my firstborn," Hugo replied dispassionately.

"Her son?" Brad echoed. "I must give credit where credit is due; that woman has the bollocks of a man. I hope you didn't make her any promises. Everyone knows that child was fathered by the captain who'd been sent to Cranley to arrest you."

"I know the child is not mine, but I'm afraid she'll make trouble, Brad. Liza is not the innocent I believed her to be."

"No, I'd hardly call her that," Brad agreed. "But what can she do?"

Hugo shrugged. "I don't know, but I'm sure she'll think of something."

Hugo accepted a cup of ale from the serving girl and helped himself to a pork roll which was still hot from the oven.

"Actually, there's something I wanted to ask you about. I'd written to Gideon Warburton two years since but heard nothing back. I wanted him to look into Finch's estate and see if Frances might benefit from his death. He replied to the first

letter, promising to do what he could, but subsequent correspondence went unanswered."

Brad suddenly looked uncomfortable, his eyes sliding away
from Hugo's in a way that suggested that Brad had something to
hide. He reached for a roll, but held it in his hand without biting
into it, his expression pensive.

"What is it, Brad?"

"Gideon is gone, Hugo," Brad replied, suddenly replacing
the roll on the plate as if it disgusted him.

"Gone, as in dead?" Hugo asked, a sick feeling of foreboding
spreading through his chest. People died all the time from
illness, but judging by Brad's expression, this was something he
didn't care to share with Hugo.

Brad just nodded, his face clouding with sorrow.

"What happened to him?" Hugo asked as he sat forward in
his chair, refreshments forgotten.

"Nothing. Never you mind," Brad responded brusquely.
"What's done is done."

"Tell me," Hugo insisted quietly. Gideon's death clearly had
something to do with him, and he needed to know.

Brad shrugged in resignation, his gaze fixated on the fire in
the grate. "Gideon did not have an easy time of it after you left.
There were many, especially at Court, who felt that he had
committed an act of treason by defending a known traitor, and
passions ran even higher when it became known that Jeffreys
had been bribed by Gideon to commute the sentence from
beheading to deportation. Gideon received threatening letters,
and people often threw rotten vegetables and excrement at him
when he left the house. Perhaps a stronger man might have
weathered the storm, but Gideon was rather sensitive. He all
but isolated himself from the world, which certainly didn't help
his prospects. Work dried up, since no one came to him for even
the most basic of legal undertakings. He was in despair. It was
at that time that he met a man named Julian Covington. I am

not sure where they met, but it seemed that this man offered a sympathetic ear and the companionship that Gideon so desperately needed at that time. I found this newfound friendship to be a bit strange, since Gideon had always been something of a loner, but Beth and I were glad that he'd found someone to lean on in his hour of need."

"Go on," Hugo prompted as Brad grew quiet.

"I met Julian Covington once when I visited Gideon in town and was astounded by how much the man resembled me. Even Beth remarked on it. It was uncanny. But Gideon seemed very taken with him. It was almost as if..." Brad grew quiet again, his face reddening.

"What are you getting at, Brad?" Hugo asked, wondering if he'd understood correctly.

"I believe they were lovers, Hugo. And I think Gideon was supporting this man, possibly even paying him for his 'companionship.'"

"So, what happened?"

"Gideon's situation became dire since he could no longer earn a living and his finances were dwindling. He took the decision to sail to the colonies—a decision which I believe was prompted by Master Covington. Gideon thought that a fresh start in a place where his skills might be something of an advantage would be just the thing. Julian Covington was meant to go with him, but it seemed that he missed the boat, or some such nonsense. I received a letter from the captain of the ship many months later, being Gideon's closest male relative, informing me that Gideon had drowned himself the day after leaving port. A letter from Julian Covington was found among his possessions, telling him that he would not be joining him in Virginia and that their association was over."

"He did away with himself?" Hugo asked, incredulous.

"There's more," Brad added sourly. "It seems that Gideon had made a will in which he left all his worldly goods to Julian

Covington. He didn't have much in the way of coin, but he did have his house in London, and there were other valuables. Master Covington is now residing in Gideon's house with another gentleman, who he claims is his kinsman."

"And you don't believe that?"

"Not for a moment."

Hugo felt a wave of despair assault his senses. There it was again, another casualty of his refusal to die. Gideon Warburton had lived a quiet and solitary life, making a comfortable living from his profession. Had Hugo died when he was supposed to, Gideon Warburton would still be alive. Neve had thwarted history by taking Hugo to the twenty-first century, and so many lives had been altered, so many people affected. Now, he was indirectly responsible for the death of Gideon as well, a man innocent of any wrongdoing, whose life had been made a living hell thanks to his association with Hugo. The poor man had been vulnerable, and susceptible to someone who saw an opportunity to use that vulnerability to their own advantage.

"I must go, Brad." Hugo got to his feet and turned to leave. He just needed to be alone for a while.

THIRTY-THREE

Liza brushed the crumbs off her skirt and wiped Johnny's mouth. He'd had two slices of bread and butter and a cup of milk thoughtfully provided by the publican's wife. Liza was hungry, but to pay for a meal seemed too extravagant. She would wait until she got home. She finished off Johnny's milk and the crust he hadn't eaten and got up to leave.

The day outside had warmed up a bit, a hazy winter sun shining glibly onto the sleepy village. She used to like it here, used to like working at Everly Manor. Soon, she would have to look for work—work which would separate her from Johnny unless she took in washing, which didn't pay much. Poor people didn't pay someone to do their dirty work, and the rich had servants to do it.

Liza retrieved her cart and settled Johnny in for the ride home. She couldn't help looking up at Everly Manor sitting proudly on the ridge. She'd seen Hugo going into the stables after she'd left. He'd gone out, but his lady was probably at home. Liza turned the cart toward the manor house. She'd be damned if she didn't try harder to get what she came for. Hugo might have been hard to sway, but perhaps she could still manipulate the situation to her advantage. And, if nothing came of it, she'd have the satisfaction of knowing that she'd sown seeds of doubt and pain in the woman who'd taken Hugo from her.

Liza stopped the cart in front of the house and got out, hoisting the child onto her hip. She walked up to the door, brazen as you please, and used the heavy knocker to announce her presence.

"I'd like to see Lady Everly," she announced to Harriet, who gawped at her as if she'd just risen from the dead. They'd been friends once, and Liza was glad to see Harriet looking so well. But she had no time to chit-chat.

"Liza, are you mad?" Harriet asked, staring at the child. "If you've come for a job, this is not the way to go about it."

"I'm not here for a job, Harriet. Now tell Lady Everly that I am here."

"Wait here," Harriet said and left her to wait in the foyer. Visitors were usually invited into the parlor, but Liza wasn't good enough to be offered a seat. She had to stand and wait for a handout. Well, she'd see who had the upper hand in the end.

Liza stiffened as she heard the sound of footsteps. Lady Everly was coming. She would have one chance, and one chance only, to play her trump card.

THIRTY-FOUR

I'd never been a proponent of physical violence, but if I ever succumbed to the urge to beat someone to a pulp, it would be Liza Timmins. Seeing her standing in the foyer, cool as a cucumber, made my blood boil. Liza didn't look too different from when she'd worked at Everly Manor. She was a bit grubbier, and her cheeks weren't as plump as they had been, but she had the same lively brown eyes, and the dark ringlets that escaped from beneath the plain linen cap she wore framed her face becomingly. I strove for control as I looked at her smug expression, and fought an uncontrollable urge to slap it off her face. But I wasn't just plain Neve Ashley anymore; I was the lady of the house, and, unfortunately, I had to behave appropriately—no brawling for me.

I motioned Liza into the parlor, not because I wanted to give her the honor of being received, but because there were currently at least three pairs of ears straining to hear what was about to be said, one of them being Harriet. I liked the girl, but she did love to talk, and between her and her sister, the whole village would know my business by teatime.

Liza walked in, her posture imperious, and took a seat

without being invited. She set down her son, who stood next to his mother, timidly taking in the room. His eyes alighted on the carved horse left there by Michael, and I suppressed a churlish desire to snatch it up and hide it. The child picked up the toy and looked at it with wonder, likely never having seen a toy of any kind in his short life.

"You wished to speak with me?" I asked. I didn't sit, but continued to stand, letting Liza know that this would be a short interview indeed.

Liza adjusted the shawl about her shoulders and folded her hands in her lap before answering, taking her time just to annoy me. And she was succeeding admirably. I was vibrating with impatience and dislike.

"Yes, my lady," she replied finally. The "my lady" was uttered with dripping sarcasm, which wouldn't help her cause, whatever it was.

"Go on then," I prompted.

"It would appear that I can no longer support my son, so I brought him here. I trust his father will acknowledge his responsibility and look after the child, while I seek employment which will enable me to care for my ailing mother and three sisters."

I allowed my eyes to slide to the boy, who was now sitting on the floor and tracing his finger over the pattern in the rug, the horse momentarily forgotten. He seemed amazed by the pretty colors, his face wreathed in a smile as he mouthed "flower," completely in awe of such beauty.

"Perhaps you should present your case to my husband, and not to me," I replied, clasping my hands behind my back to avoid them strangling Liza of their own free will.

"I have. He denied all knowledge of his own child. Few men are honorable enough to acknowledge their bastards before the world."

I could see the gleam of satisfaction in Liza's eyes as she studied my reaction. I was livid, and she knew it, but that was part of the fun. She not only wanted to provide for her son, she wanted to humiliate me, and tarnish Hugo's reputation. Allowing her to leave the child would be paramount to acknowledging Hugo's paternity, but that wasn't what she wanted. Liza had come for money, of that I was sure. She wanted us to buy her silence, and to keep buying it every time she ran out of funds. Well, this wouldn't happen on my watch. If Hugo had denied paternity, then this boy wasn't his. I knew my husband well enough to know that he would never shirk responsibility for his own child, even if that child were the son of a woman who'd betrayed him and wished him dead. This was blackmail, pure and simple, and if I gave in to it once, it would never stop.

I looked from the boy back to Liza. She was a clever girl, I'd give her that, and clever girls needed to be outwitted, not threatened. I'd have one chance to nip this in the bud, and my chance was now. I hated to be callous where an innocent child was concerned, but the child was too young to understand what was being said, and I had to gamble with his future in order to be rid of his scheming mother once and for all.

"Of course," I replied, nodding my head in affirmation, "Lord Everly should take responsibility for his flesh and blood. And he is such a fine boy, your son, hale and strong."

Liza's face lit up at she glanced down at the boy. He was rather sweet, I had to admit, with his dark eyes and wavy dark hair. I walked over to the child and patted him affectionately on the head. The boy was clean and well-fed, and I could tell from his demeanor and the way he kept smiling at his mother that he was also well loved. His cheeks were still rounded with babyhood, and I judged him to be under the age of three.

"How old did you say he was?"

"Just gone three," Liza replied happily, eager to prove to me that he had been conceived once I was already in Hugo's life. Well, I knew better.

"I suppose you'd best say goodbye to him then," I suggested. "You won't be seeing him again."

"Why is that? You'd keep a mother from seeing her child?" Liza asked, fear suddenly showing in her eyes. She hadn't expected that.

"I would never keep a child from his mother, but, as I am sure you understand, to keep the child here would be an embarrassment to me, as well as to his lordship. You didn't really think he would be raised under the same roof as our own children, did you?" I asked innocently, driving the nails into the coffin one by one.

"Well, I..." Liza faltered. "He can stay with me if his father will look after him financially."

"Not a chance," I replied calmly. "You just leave him here, and we will do right by him. As a matter of fact, I have family in the Netherlands. They are fine people, well respected, and deeply religious. Yes, I think we will send him there. It's not a long sea voyage; I'm sure he'll be just fine. Of course, they wouldn't treat him as one of their own, but they will be happy to give him a place in the household and raise him to be their faithful servant."

I almost smiled when I saw Liza blanch. She had no way of knowing that I'd never been to the Netherlands, much less if I had any family, but many Protestant families had been exiled to the Dutch Republic after the execution of Charles I, so it wouldn't be odd for me to have relations who settled there permanently.

"No," Liza cried. "You won't take him away from me."

"But, Liza dear, if Hugo is indeed his father, he has rights. He can take him away from you any time he likes," I added spitefully, driving the final nail in with resounding finality.

I allowed myself a small smile as Liza grabbed the boy and fled from the room, crashing through the front door just as Hugo came around the side of the building after stabling his horse and walked toward her trap. I saw the look of horror Liza threw at a bemused Hugo as she tossed her son into the trap and took off, glancing back at the house fearfully. I waved to her from the window just as Hugo walked into the parlor.

"What was that all about?" he asked, looking at me as if I were a ticking bomb. "Was she making trouble?"

"She was, but she won't be anymore," I replied cryptically and left the room. I suddenly felt an overwhelming need to hug my children.

THIRTY-FIVE

Liza was relieved that Johnny slept most of the way home, giving her time to fume. She was hungry, cold, and tired, but, most of all, livid. She'd underestimated that wife of Hugo's, expecting her to be the same frightened, lonely woman she'd known when she had first stumbled up the ridge from her sanctuary at the church. Neve Ashley was now Lady Everly, and she was a formidable opponent. She'd gambled and won, correctly deducing that Liza would not be parted from her boy. Neve understood a mother's love and had used it against her. Well, if she understood that, perhaps she would also understand that a mother had to do everything in her power to give her child a better life.

Liza huddled deeper into her shawl and stared at the road ahead. Life was full of opportunities, if one was clever enough to recognize them, and Liza was cleverer than most. She'd taken ten crowns off Lionel Finch, so perhaps she could use the same method to obtain another windfall. Hugo wasn't willing to give her any money for the boy's upkeep, but perhaps Josiah Finch would. He would never fall for the story that Johnny was Lionel's son, but perhaps he would be interested to learn that

Hugo Everly was back in England and sharing a house with Lionel's errant wife.

No one in Surrey would readily make the connection between Frances Morley and Frances Finch, but having been in London during the trial and having heard the gossip, Liza surmised that it was too much of a coincidence that a young woman by the name of Frances was living with Hugo Everly—the very man who'd been accused of abducting her from her husband. Liza couldn't fathom what Hugo's interest in Frances Finch might have been, considering that he was already ensnared by the comely Neve Ashley, but whatever drove him to remove Frances Finch from her home must have been very powerful, since he was still supporting her and offering her his protection after all this time. And if Frances Morley was indeed Frances Finch, then there was one man whom she'd need protecting from—Josiah Finch.

As far as Liza knew, Lionel had been Josiah Finch's only child, so now his widow stood to inherit the estate once the old man died. Perhaps that could be worked to Liza's advantage somehow. Would the old man want the girl back, or would he perhaps want to punish her in some way for her role in his son's death? Had Frances never run off with Hugo, Lionel would still be alive and well, an heir to the vast fortune that was the Finch estate. Surely the bereaved old man could spare a few coins for a woman who had known his son and only wished to comfort him in his grief by bringing him information about his daughter-in-law.

Liza snapped the reins, urging the horse to go faster. Now that she had a plan, she felt infinitely better. She'd need to find out how to get to Finch House and arrange with her sisters to look after Johnny for a few days. It wouldn't do to drag the child with her. She'd even offer to pay the little witches to mind their nephew. She could afford to be generous.

THIRTY-SIX

I touched a taper to the candlewick and walked out of the room on silent feet. Hugo was fast asleep, his lashes fanned across his lean cheeks. He looked so tense these days, so guarded. He did his best to act normally around the children, but he had a harder time of keeping up the pretense when we were alone. I tried not to harp on to him about his increased drinking, nor to point out that he wasn't eating enough. Only a month had passed since Elena's passing, so he was coping as best he could. Tomorrow would be a hard day, a day when Hugo would give Frances away in marriage, as he would have given Elena someday had she lived. Hugo would never disappoint Frances, but I knew what it would cost him to stand at the altar and take on the role of her father—a role that he would never again play with his own daughter.

I tried to keep busy during the day, desperate for any distraction which would keep my mind off our loss, but it was at night, when the house was quiet and everyone was asleep, that the pain came and wouldn't leave again till morning when I got up to see the sleepy faces of my two surviving children. I often went down to the library and sat in silence, surrounded by the creased spines of books and the comforting smell of leather. I wasn't sure why it brought me peace, but it did.

I padded down the corridor, surprised to see a flickering light beneath Frances's door. She should be asleep, dreaming of her wedding, not lying awake. I rapped gently on the door. Perhaps she'd fallen asleep and forgot to blow out the candle, but I heard light footsteps as Frances opened the door and motioned me inside.

"What's wrong, Frances? Are you nervous about tomorrow?" I asked as I took a seat by the hearth.

Frances looked small and frightened; her face, although much more mature than it had been when I'd first met her, that of a child. She threw a shawl over her shoulders and joined me by the fire. Frances remained silent for a few minutes, but I knew her well enough to realize that she needed to talk; she was just gathering her thoughts. Spending time with Archie had taught her to value words, and to phrase things in the most efficient manner. She no longer prattled on the way she had when she was younger. Or maybe it wasn't Archie's influence, but just the residue of her experiences, having taught her that sometimes it's best not to say too much, or share something which couldn't be taken back.

She finally tore her gaze away from the fire and looked at me, now more composed. "When I married Lionel," she began, "my father counseled that I should obey my husband in all things, and all would be well. I was thirteen years old, and I took him at his word."

"But now you don't believe that? Are you having second thoughts about marrying again?"

"I'm frightened, Neve," Frances admitted as her eyes slid away from mine.

"You are afraid of Archie?" I asked, incredulous. Archie was always kind and patient with Frances and the children, but perhaps something had happened in private that had put her on her guard. I wasn't sure if the two of them had consummated their relationship and didn't dare ask, but hoped that if they had, Archie had been gentle.

Frances shook her head stubbornly. "I am not afraid of him; I am afraid *for* him. I couldn't bear to lose him, Neve. I've waited so long for someone to love me, the thought of losing that love is worse than any beating or physical torment."

"Why would you lose his love?" I asked. I was confused, but Frances needed to tell me in her own time. She'd obviously given this a lot of thought.

"There are so many things that can go wrong, aren't there?" Frances whispered plaintively. Her fingers were pleating at the fabric of her nightdress, and one foot began to tap nervously on the wooden floor.

"Are you referring to having children?" The doctor in Paris had said that Frances might be barren after she had tried to self-abort, especially so soon after giving birth, but she wouldn't know unless she tried to get pregnant.

"Yes, there's that, too. What if I can't give him a child, Neve? Archie said that it wouldn't matter, that he'd love me anyway, but you know how men are; they want sons."

"Frances, you can't put that kind of pressure on yourself. Time will tell. You are still very young, and you have many years of fertility left. It might not happen right away, but it will happen in time. Don't work yourself up into knots over this."

"There are other things as well," Frances continued as if I hadn't spoken. It seemed that having children was not her primary concern after all.

"Like what?"

"Archie is a man of blood, of violence," Frances stated flatly. She didn't appear to be judging him, just articulating a simple fact.

"Has he hurt you in some way?"

"No, of course not, but he's not cut out to be a farmer. Lord

Everly is talking of going to London, to see the new king, and
Archie will go with him. Change is coming, and when there's
change, there's violence. Look at what happened to Master
Nash. He would have died had his lordship not found him and
taken him to a medical man straight away. I'm afraid of losing
him, Neve. So afraid."

I wished I could reassure her and tell her that everything
would be all right, that Archie would grow to be an old man and
bounce his grandchildren on his knee while telling them stories
of his youth, but having lost a child only last month, I could
make no such promise. We all lived and loved at our own risk.
I'd nearly lost Hugo, and he'd come damn close to losing me. I
suddenly remembered the words of my foster father. "Life's a
crapshoot, Neve. Remember that." I think he'd heard the phrase
in some American film and liked the sound of it, but perhaps
he'd been right. We were all like grains of sand on a vast beach,
subject to winds, tides, and erosion.

But, of course, I couldn't tell Frances that the night before
her wedding, so I walked over, put my arms around her, and
kissed the top of her head. "Trust in your love, and all will be
well," I said, hoping desperately that I was right.

Frances nodded like a marionette against my shoulder, but
her shoulders were rigid, and her foot continued to its staccato
on the floor.

THIRTY-SEVEN

An indistinct murmur of voices could be heard coming from Frances's room on the floor below. It seemed that she was wakeful as well on this final night before their wedding. Archie couldn't help wondering what Frances and Neve were talking about. Was Frances too excited to sleep, or were fears and reservations keeping her awake? He hoped it wasn't the latter. Archie normally fell asleep as soon as his head hit the pillow, but tonight he felt restless as well, his mind refusing to settle down. He had to admit that he was excited, and a little nervous as well. He'd sworn often enough that he would never marry, but here he was, a fretful bridegroom, spending his last night as an unmarried man alone in his attic bedroom, waiting for the morning to come.

Tomorrow everything would change, and he hoped that after years of longing and steadfast friendship, he and Frances would be able to transition to being man and wife. The thought of finally making love to Frances made Archie burn with a slow heat that had been building over the past few years, and at this point, it was about to consume him. He'd never made a conscious decision to remain celibate once he declared his love to Frances, but although it was perfectly acceptable for a man to satisfy his urges elsewhere before marriage, it seemed wrong, and, truthfully, the thought of being with other women left him cold. It was Frances he yearned for, and Frances he would have —tomorrow.

Archie folded his arms behind his head and stared into the impenetrable darkness of the night, the conversation with his father replaying in his mind. He'd been excited and nervous about seeing his father after such a long absence. His father wasn't a man of letters, so a correspondence had been out of the question. Asking someone else to read Archie's letters and have them write back would leave Hugo too exposed, so Archie had no idea what to expect after a three-year silence. The cottage had seemed in good order when Archie had approached, a plume of smoke curling from the chimney and a good-sized pile of wood neatly stacked and covered against the damp.

Archie's breath had caught in his throat as he'd knocked on the door, hoping his father was in. He'd have heard that Lord Everly was back if he'd gone to the tavern, but if he were ill, he'd not have heard the news. The door swung open to reveal his Da, a huge smile on the old man's face as he pulled Archie into a bear hug.

Horatio Hicks had been a man to reckon with in his day, but although he'd shrunk and lost weight as he aged, he was still strong for a man of seventy. The bright hair of youth had faded to an ashy gray, and the cornflower-blue eyes which had many a lass sighing with longing were now rheumy, but still had that twinkle.

"Archie, my boy, what a wonderful surprise. Come in, son, come in. I was just about to have my dinner. Get a plate and cup. 'Tis been a long time since you and I had a meal together."

Archie felt something unclench in his heart as he sat across from his father. He seemed well, and that was more than Archie had hoped for. He knew that his friends, Arnold and Bill, would have looked after his father while he was gone, and the large pile of firewood and repairs to the cottage attested to the fact that they'd kept their promise, but no kindly neighbors could make up for the loss of one's wife and children. With his wife long gone, his daughter moldering in a convent, and his son God only knew where, Horatio Hicks might have succumbed to old age and melancholy.

"Tell me everything, or whatever you can tell me," Horatio said as he poured Archie a cup of beer. "I have always longed to see foreign shores. Ah, to see Paris," he sighed. "Is it much different from London?"

Archie tucked into the pottage his father offered him, surprised by how tasteless and unsatisfying it seemed after the fine meals he'd had in France. His mother always made pottage, it being the most economical and filling meal, but now the unappetizing mix of oats, stale bread, bits of vegetables, and dried peas tasted like mud. Archie pushed his plate away and told his father of the past years. He made his time in France sound like a wonderful adventure, a glittering holiday filled with trips to Versailles and gallops through the woods of Fontainebleau. He left out anything which might have made his father feel less than proud of him, such as killing a man in cold blood to avenge the attempt on Hugo's life, although Horatio's hands had seen their share of blood. His father had fought in the Civil War on the side of the Roundheads.

"And Jem? Has he come back with you? I know how attached that boy was to you," Horatio said as he helped himself to Archie's plate of pottage.

"Jem is gone, Da. His father came to fetch him, and he is now the heir to the Marsden estate."

"You don't say," his father gasped. "Well, what good fortune for that boy. The way his mother carried on, 'tis a wonder anyone knew who his father was at all. Nicholas Marsden, you say? Oh, I do remember him. A friend of his lordship's, he was. A good man, if a bit wild."

"Not so wild now. He's got an invalid for a wife and no legitimate children of his own. I can't help wondering if he'd been so keen to take Jem from us if he'd had a child with his wife before her riding accident."

"Probably not, but it worked out well for our Jem, didn't it? I always had a soft spot for that boy. There were those in the village as said he was his lordship's bastard, but I always knew there was nothing in those rumors."

"I did think they might be true, but Lord Everly denied it, and I believed him," Archie said, putting an end to that particular discussion.

"And what about you, son? Any thoughts of settling down? You'll be looking at thirty before the decade is out."

"I've been betrothed these two years, Da," Archie said, finally sharing the news he'd come to tell his father. "It's Frances Finch, although she calls herself Morley now."

"Frances? That little chit you rescued from Lionel Finch and took to our Julia?" Horatio asked, gazing at his son with newfound interest.

"Yes, the same."

"How old is she now?"

"She just turned eighteen, Da. Old enough to know her mind."

"Well, I would hope so. Any girl should know her mind when agreeing to marry. Is she not somewhat above your station, son?" Horatio asked carefully.

Archie shrugged, ignoring the question. "I love her, Da."

Horatio Hicks leaned back in his chair, his eyes never leaving his son's face. His head was tilted to the side as if he were studying him and coming to all the wrong conclusions. Archie had expected a less than enthusiastic response to his forthcoming marriage, his father being a proponent of marrying a girl of your own class, and preferably one whose family was known to him, but his father's silence was strangely ominous.

"Is it because she was married before that you disapprove?" Archie finally asked, needing to know his father's mind.

"I've never met your Frances, but I remember all too well you telling me about her when you returned from the convent. Heartbroken you were over that girl's treatment at the hands of her husband; your protective instinct aroused. I know you, Archie; ever since you were a little lad, you had that sympathy in you, that kindness. If ever there was a wounded bird or an injured puppy, you'd nurse them until they were well, and pine for them once they were gone."

"Frances is not a wounded bird," Archie retorted, suddenly annoyed. Why did parents always do this? Why couldn't his father just be happy that he'd found someone to love?

"Isn't she? She is a fragile girl who has been broken beyond repair. Just make sure she doesn't fly the coop once her wings have healed, 'cause then it's you who'll need mending."

"Da, I am a grown man, and I am not exactly an innocent, am I?" Archie demanded. "I do know something of women, and Frances is not just a broken thing; she is a grown woman who knows her own mind, and she loves me, Da. She loves me for who I am."

"And I suppose his lordship has given his blessing? He's another one you can't break free of. He stole your heart when he fished you out of that river when you were seven, and you've followed him about like a faithful puppy ever since. I do hope he has your best interests in mind."

"He's never asked me for anything I wasn't willing to give, and he does approve of the marriage. Frances and I are fated," Archie said with surprising finality. He didn't believe in fate, which made his declaration all the more startling, especially to himself.

"Glad to hear it. Then marry her and give me a grandchild to love before I breathe my last."

Archie nodded, unable to tell his father that there might not be children. He'd assured Frances that it didn't matter to him. He'd seen what losing children did to families, his sister's especially, but Frances wanted so desperately to have a baby. There was no way of knowing if she would be able to conceive, but if she couldn't, it would tear her apart.

"I have to go, Da," Archie had said, rising to his feet. "I'll come by next week to see you."

"And I'll be waiting, my lad. I'll be waiting."

THIRTY-EIGHT

Thankfully, the snow had stopped, but the road was nearly impassable. Liza's horse ambled along, picking its way through the snow, its nostrils flaring every time it felt less than secure on the slippery path. The winter day was drawing to a close, the lavender shadows of dusk already pooling between the trees and painting the snowy landscape in purples and blues. The temperature was dropping, and the wind was picking up, forcing Liza to dig her heels into the poor animal's flanks. She had to get to Finch House before nightfall. Perhaps Josiah Finch would invite her to spend the night, Liza mused, but then again, if he were anything like his son, he'd throw her out into a storm and not give a toss if she froze to death. She'd have to find a place to shelter for the night. If he paid up, she'd get a room at an inn and a hot meal. If not, she'd try to bed down in a barn or some other outbuilding, with or without permission.

At last, the lights of the house came into view, and Liza pushed the tired horse, desperate to get out of the cold. She hoped a friendly groom would give the horse some water and hay, but that was unlikely.

Going up the drive took another half an hour, the house

being so far removed from the road, but at least the tunnel of trees sheltered Liza from the piercing wind. Normally, she wasn't a fanciful sort of person, but today she kept seeing shadows lurking behind the dark outline of ancient tree trunks, and imagined countless eyes boring into her back, glowing in the dark with ill-disguised menace. She knew the eyes belonged to small forest animals, like foxes and rabbits, but in her mind, they grew to mythical proportions, becoming monstrous in their form.

"Stop it, you foolish girl," she muttered to herself. "There ain't nothing in those trees other than God's creatures, who are hungry and cold just like yourself."

But the unease wouldn't leave her, so she kept her eyes on the glowing light of a tower room situated just above the studded front door. The place must have been a fortress once, but the leaded windows of the room had to belong to a parlor. In Liza's mind, it was warm and snug, the type of room that would be the heart of the home. Of course, houses that size had no heart. They weren't like the dwellings of poor folk, where the family gathered together of an evening whether they liked it or not, for lack of any place else to go. It was either sit by the fire or go to bed, which wasn't something you did by yourself either. When she was a girl, Liza had shared a bed with her sisters, and now she slept with Johnny. She liked sleeping with him. He was a warm little bundle next to her, a reminder that despite her transgressions, the good Lord had been kind enough to bless her with a beautiful child, a child she loved with all her heart and would do anything for.

"Stupid cow," Liza said to herself to dispel the eerie silence of the forest. "Who does she imagine she is thinking she can take my boy away?" To Liza, the Netherlands might as well be on the moon. She'd never see her Johnny again. "Witch," Liza said louder, and then repeated it again. His lordship might not see what he was dealing with here, but Liza wouldn't be fooled by a pair of guileless eyes and a pretty smile. Neve Ashley was a witch, no question about it. She'd come from nowhere, and she served her dark master— poisoning Hugo's mind with her visions and false concern for his well-being.

Perhaps I should start having visions, Liza thought spitefully. *Mayhap I'll bag a lord as well.* That was a nice dream—a dream that might have come true had that bitch not appeared on the scene. Hugo had been lonelier than even he understood. He'd succumbed to Liza's advances easily enough. He'd never have married her, of course, but he might have set her up as his mistress, lavishing beautiful gowns and expensive jewels on her. And maybe he'd even have given her a little cottage on his estate, a cottage she could inhabit for the rest of her days, free of charge.

She would have loved that dearly, would have loved him, had he seen her as a human being, and not just a warm body to stick his cock into when he was feeling the urge. Liza had to admit that she rather enjoyed his attentions, and she felt the urge as often as he did, something no decent woman would readily admit to. Yes, she liked it, and look where it got her—a woman scorned, with a fatherless child, and nothing to show for it, save the few crowns she took off Lionel Finch with her scheming. Well, she'd been scheming again, and with any luck, his father would be as gullible as the son.

Liza finally reached the house and continued on toward the stables. A young boy emerged from the shadows, clearly annoyed at being disturbed by an unexpected visitor at such a late hour. He gave her a quizzical look, but she decided that a brazen approach often worked best with servants.

"Feed and water my horse, boy," she ordered as she slid off and threw the reins to the groom. "I've urgent business with Master Finch. He's expecting me," she added for good measure.

The boy just shrugged but did as he was told and walked

the horse to the stables. Well, at least one of them would warm up and eat tonight.

Liza held her head high and her shoulders back as she walked up to the front door. She banged for several minutes before a middle-aged servant finally opened the door a crack, staring at her as if she'd lost her mind. She didn't expect that many people showed up at the Finches' door unannounced, at least not if they hoped to live to see the next morning.

"I have important business with Master Finch. Tell him I am here," she informed the servant imperiously.

"And who might you be?" the woman asked, glaring at Liza with an air of one who knew exactly what she was up to.

"My name is Liza Timmins. I was a friend of Lionel Finch."

"Lionel Finch had no friends," the woman grumbled, but allowed Liza into the house. "Wait here."

Liza stomped her feet on the stone floor, grateful for a respite from the cold, not that the square foyer was much warmer. This part of the house must have been a keep at one point, the thick stone walls unbroken by windows and immune to any form of warmth. No amount of heating would make this space warm or cozy. It was also completely dark since the servant had taken the candle with her, leaving Liza to just stand there like an interloper.

She finally came back and gestured for Liza to follow her up the stairs. Sure enough, they came to the room just above the foyer—the parlor Liza had imagined when she saw the house. The parlor was much warmer, the rugs and tapestries doing their damnedest to keep in the heat from the fire.

Josiah Finch sat in front of the hearth, his feet perched out on a low stool in front of the fire. He looked relaxed, but his eyes were fixed on the door, his mouth pursed as he beheld his unexpected guest. Liza wasn't sure what she'd expected having met the son, but the father did not resemble him much at all. Josiah Finch was bald as an egg, and had deep-set, lively dark eyes, so different from the colorless, venomous stare of Lionel. His complexion was ruddy, that of a man who spent his time outdoors. Lionel had been as pasty as unbaked dough, his thin lips the only slash of color in an otherwise blanched face.

"Stop gawping and tell me what'ya want, girl?" he growled as Liza advanced farther into the room. He didn't invite her to sit or offer her any refreshment, but at least he allowed her to come closer to the fire, which was a blessing. She could hardly feel her feet, her thin-soled shoes offering little protection from the frozen ground outside.

She timidly stepped onto the rug, her feet sinking into its warm softness. What a luxury to have something other than straw rushes to cover the floor.

"You'd best start talking," Finch said more forcefully, clearly losing his patience.

Liza tore her eyes away from the warming flames and met Finch's stare head-on. Men were like dogs; they sensed fear. She had to be aggressive, and fearless.

"I had a brief association with your son in London before the trial," Liza began.

"Yeh? So, what's that to me? Got a bastard you want to foist on me now that Lionel is gone? I've had a few of Lionel's whores try, and I showed them the back of my hand fast enough."

Liza said a quick thanks for not trying that one on Finch the elder. Had she done so, she might have lost her chance almost at once.

"I have some information that might be useful to you," Liza said softly, waiting for the man to take the bait, but he turned away and stared into the flames.

"I can't imagine anything you might tell me which might be of any interest to me," he finally replied.

"I know the whereabouts of certain people," she offered, her eyes never leaving Finch's bald head. He wasn't looking at her, but she saw a minuscule change in his facial expression. He was listening.

"Oh, yeh? Like who?" he asked casually, still not turning his head to face her fully.

"Like Hugo Everly and your daughter-in-law," Liza supplied. She suddenly realized that her information might be worthless. Gossip traveled fast, so Finch might already be aware of Hugo Everly's return, but he would surely not know about Frances.

Josiah Finch finally turned to glare at Liza, his color high, either from the heat of the fire or from emotion. Liza couldn't tell which.

"Hugo Everly—damn his eyes—is back from wherever he's been hiding, looking no worse for the wear considering that he was supposed to have been working off his indenture in the West Indies, and with a family in tow, no less," Finch supplied. "And my daughter-in-law is of no interest to me."

Liza opened her mouth to reply, but suddenly realized she wasn't sure what to say. She groped desperately for some angle that would distract Josiah Finch from his belligerence and focus his mind on future action. "Don't you want revenge?" she finally asked. "Hugo Everly and that girl were responsible for your son's death."

"Now, that's where you are wrong, girl. My son was responsible for his own death, and no one else," Finch countered. Liza thought he was finished with her, but he obviously needed someone to talk to about this, and she happened to be there. "My son was a weak, cruel man who took pleasure in causing pain. 'Twas the only way he could get a cockstand, I imagine. Frances was the ideal wife: a young, pretty girl who could be molded and subjugated, but my son wasn't happy with that. He tortured her until she finally found whatever backbone she had and ran off with the first man who was chivalrous enough to offer his help. Can't say I blame her. At least she got out alive, but it was a near thing, I tell you."

Josiah Finch turned back to the flames, his voice taking on a dreamlike quality, almost as if he were talking to himself. "I suppose Lionel got to Everly somehow after the trial, although God only knows who the man on trial was if he wasn't Hugo Everly. Lionel wanted revenge for the slight to his honor, but if I know Everly, he is not a man to go meekly to his death. An idealistic fool that one, but a fighter. Hugo Everly is not the type of man to sit at home and count his blessings. Oh, no. Everly is the type who thinks he can change the world, and maybe he can. Look, we got us a Protestant king after all, even if it isn't the one Everly was backing. So, best of luck to him and to Frances," Finch finished, his eyes finally meeting Liza's.

"But they were responsible for the death of your only son and heir," Liza tried again.

"I have an heir," Josiah Finch announced proudly, gratified to see Liza's look of astonishment. "After Lionel's death, I had no choice but to marry again, and I have a son and heir sleeping peacefully in his cradle after getting his fill of his mother's ample breasts. And I will get that woman full in the belly again as soon as I can. Now, as you can see, your information is worthless to me, so get out of my sight, and take yourself back where you came from before I have you thrown out."

Liza swallowed back tears of frustration as she left the room and made her way out the door through the darkened foyer. There was no one to show her out, nor was any hospitality offered, not even a warm drink. The snow had started again. She would freeze to death in the barn, even if she managed to get in undetected with her horse. No, she had to leave. Josiah Finch didn't seem like a man who made idle promises. He would have her thrown out and would likely cause her bodily harm if she didn't do as she was bid.

Liza felt in the pocket of her skirt for the coin she'd hidden there. It'd be enough to pay for a room, but she couldn't afford to eat too. Her stomach growled in protest as she made her way back through the dark tunnel of the drive, eager to get away from the place. Even her horse was spooked by the eerie silence.

Damn the lot of them, she thought bitterly. Hugo Everly and his wife, Lionel Finch and his father, and most of all, Captain Norrington, who'd left her pregnant and heartbroken. She was woman enough to admit defeat this time, but she was a fighter, and she would rise again. There was still one more card she had to play. It was a dangerous one, but it just might pay off.

THIRTY-NINE

JANUARY 24, 2015

Surrey, England

Simon gazed around the church from his vantage point by the Cheshire Cat pillar, as he liked to think of it. He'd always loved that little face, especially when he was a boy coming to church services with his mother. He liked to pretend that it was the real Cheshire Cat from *Alice in Wonderland* and it appeared and disappeared at will, materializing in different parts of the church during the sermon and playing clever tricks on the limited imagination of Reverend Lambert.

The reverend had been younger then, but just as boring. *Blimey, if boring was a sport, the good reverend could bore for England, and no doubt qualify for first place,* Simon thought as he recalled those long-ago hours spent sitting in the hard wooden pew. But today he wasn't here for the service. The church was decorated with white flowers and gauzy swaths of fabric, making it look like a garden in full bloom in the middle of winter.

Heather had done a lovely job organizing the wedding, no thanks to him. He hadn't seen her dress, but he was sure her gown would be beautiful; understated and classy. Heather had good taste, especially in men, as she liked to point out.

The church was filling up, pews dotted with the colorful outfits of the ladies who wore elaborate hats despite the dreadful weather. It had snowed the night before, but today was a combination of sleet and rain, which made the short trip to the church perilous. Still, everyone was on time. There were people from the village, including Doctor Lomax and his wife, who sat next to his mother as if he were family. Stella Harding was wearing an outfit in lavender with an elaborate hat, which completely blocked the person sitting behind her. Simon wasn't quite sure if his mother had chosen lavender, the color of mourning, for his wedding as a not-so-subtle message. She never uttered a word of reproach, but he was beginning to realize that she didn't care for Heather or her campaign to become the next Lady Everly.

Simon supposed that no one would be good enough for him in his mother's eyes. She was the only person in this world who loved him unconditionally, and he returned that love tenfold. He hoped that his mother and Heather would get on but knew with a dead certainty that if he were ever forced to choose between the two, his mother would always be the winner. Heather had once called him a "mama's boy," but he wasn't so much a mama's boy as a grateful son who realized what his mother had given up to give him a good life and keep him in the orbit of his indifferent father, in the hope that one day maybe a relationship would finally blossom between them, or, at the very least, his father would feel guilty enough at the sight of him to do something for Simon's future.

"Are you ready, old boy?" Jack asked as he came up behind Simon. Jack was his best mate and his best man. He'd thrown an epic stag do which Simon was still recovering from, truth be told, but he hadn't done anything to be ashamed of. He didn't want to disrespect Heather that way. Some men felt that it was their last chance to sow their wild oats and shag some nameless slag, but Simon felt no such urge. Heather was insatiable when it came to sex, which, in his mind, made her a good candidate for a wife. His friends always complained that their girlfriends made constant excuses to avoid sex, but he'd never complained himself. He was very happy in that department; it was the other stuff that worried him.

"Yes, I suppose I am," Simon replied reluctantly, touching his fingers to the sly smile of the gargoyle. "Wish me luck, old friend," he muttered to the amazed reaction of Jack.

"Have you been drinking?"

"No, but I suddenly wish I had," Simon said as he made to step out from behind the pillar.

"The bride is here. Her limo just pulled up, and her father is helping her out of the car. He'll have to carry her if she hopes to keep her dress from getting soaked. It's nasty out there."

Heather was there. Simon suddenly felt a tightness in his chest. He'd felt it last night as well, but now it was that much worse. He couldn't breathe—couldn't think straight. What the hell was he doing? He'd succumbed to Heather's emotional blackmail and put a ring on her finger, but deep down he knew the truth—he didn't want to marry her, at least not yet. He was barely twenty-six. His life was just beginning, and he was about to nip it in the bud. He had two friends who were already married. Charlie was hopelessly whipped, needing his wife's permission to so much as set foot into the pub with his friends for a few hours, and promising to do extra night feedings and nappy duty just to get an evening off. While Giles supplemented his unsatisfying sex life with Brandy every chance he could, frequently lying to his wife and saying that he was working late while he was out carousing. Giles said he couldn't live on starvation rations, but his wife was the same woman who'd foregone underwear all through university for the sake of ready access and sucked Giles off on the motorway while he drove, nearly causing a motor accident more than once.

Marriage changed people, especially women. Beautiful, sexy girls turned into tired, frustrated middle-aged women who traded in their short, tight dresses for tweeds and twin sets. Heather had already changed, he mused. She'd been fun and easygoing, but now she was suddenly acting as if she were royalty, practicing for her new station in life. Simon supposed he loved Heather as much as he could love any woman, but he simply wasn't ready to get married and start a family. Heather had already announced that she wouldn't be taking her birth-control pills on their wedding trip to Morocco. She wanted a boy, she said, an heir to the estate. That had been a jaw-dropper. What the hell did she think this was, the seventeenth century? An heir to the estate?! But Heather was determined.

"I'm ready, and you'd better be too, lover. I expect you to shag me stupid and bring me back home with a baby in my belly. Marcia said that doing it standing up against the wall ensures a better chance of having a boy," Heather had added. A year ago, Simon would have thought she was pulling his leg, but she was deadly serious.

Well, he could handle the shagging stupid part, but he didn't want a baby. And, if Heather failed to get pregnant, there'd be IVF treatments, ejaculating into a cup, and constant hysterics. Sex would become a chore, something to be done with a purpose and at the proper time. Besides, he wasn't ready to be a father any more than he was ready to be a husband. This wasn't just a case of cold feet; this was his gut instinct telling him the truth, and if he didn't listen within the next two minutes, it would be too late. But how could he humiliate Heather by leaving her at the altar in front of all these people?

"Simon, are you all right? You look pale, mate," Jack observed as he clapped him on the back. "Shall I get the smelling salts?" he asked with mock concern, clearly enjoying Simon's panic.

"I just need a minute alone," Simon muttered. "Be right back."

Simon hastily crossed the nave without making eye contact with any of the guests and bounded down the steps to the crypt. He hadn't planned this, hadn't even considered it until that moment, but he knew what he had to do. He strode over to the tomb of the knight, and ran his fingers frantically along the darkened wall until he found the six-petaled flower. The scraping of stone seemed deafening, but it really wasn't all that loud.

Simon poked his head into the passageway. He could just make out a thin band of light beneath the wooden door at the top of the worn steps. He closed the passage and walked toward the light. He would just hide out for a few hours until everyone left, then come right back and take off for London as soon as his mother finished giving him the bollocking of his life. He would go see Heather in a few days, explain, and apologize for being such a wanker. She would be hurt and angry, but a called-off wedding was better than a bitter divorce.

Simon's hand shook slightly as he reached for the heavy iron ring on the door. He had no idea what he was going to find, but somehow the unknown wasn't nearly as frightening as the future he'd just left behind.

FORTY

Surrey, England

I sat in the second pew next to Valentine, who'd begged to come to the church. Cook remained at home to prepare food for the wedding, and Michael opted to stay with Harriet, who was only too happy to be excused from her chores to keep him entertained. Ruby and Polly sat in the pew behind me despite all the empty space next to me. They didn't think it appropriate to their station to sit next to the lady of the house, and I didn't insist. Archie's father sat across from me, dressed in his best coat, which had seen better days and had probably been made at least a decade ago. But his iron-gray hair was brushed and his beard neatly trimmed for the occasion. He held his hat in his gnarled hands, his eyes fixed on the altar.

Arnold and Peter, Archie's friends from the village, sat next to Horatio Hicks, their bearded faces almost identical from my vantage point. Archie said they were cousins, but they looked more like brothers, with their thick dark hair and broad shoulders. I had met them several years ago when I'd first come to the seventeenth century, and they bowed to me respectfully upon entering the church, painfully conscious of my new role as Lady Everly.

Beth and Brad had come as well, and sat in the front since Brad found it painful to bend his leg in order to slide into the narrow pew. He looked well, and Beth glowed with happiness as she glanced at her husband.

All in all, not a bad turnout for a dreary January day. Normally, weddings and christenings took place in the church porch for all to see, but taking the weather into account, everyone agreed that it was best to hold the wedding inside. After all, few would doubt the authenticity of the ceremony given that there were plenty of witnesses and an entry in the parish registry.

Frances had chosen a light blue damask gown trimmed with ecru lace for the occasion. The color accentuated her eyes and reminded one of a clear blue sky on a spring day. Her hair was dressed in the fontange style and adorned with matching lace. I, myself, didn't favor the style, but it was all the rage in seventeenth-century England. It made Frances look more mature than her eighteen years, but she was very pleased with the way it came out and patted it self-consciously just before Hugo walked her toward the altar.

Archie had also dressed up, wearing his one good suit of midnight-blue velvet with a new shirt, its wide collar trimmed with lace. His hair was tied back with a leather thong, and his boots gleamed with polish.

Hugo, having done his duty, now came to sit next to me, his eyes on the happy couple who were about to make their vows. I couldn't help thinking that even if Frances and Archie were dressed in rags, they'd still be the most handsome couple I'd ever seen, not due to their youth and good looks, but because of the light of happiness which shone from their eyes. If ever love triumphed, this was the moment, and I chose to put aside my own pain and savor it.

I discreetly glanced toward the back of the church when I heard the opening of a door. I had so hoped that Nicholas Marsden had received my letter and brought Jem to the wedding. It would be a wonderful surprise for everyone, especially Hugo. We hadn't seen Jem since Nicholas took him back to England in the summer of 1686, and had only had one letter from Nicholas since, assuring us that Jem was well and was settling into his new life. Nicholas had promised to write regularly and keep us abreast of Jem's progress, but either he wasn't much of a correspondent, or life simply got in the way.

Hugo and I often spoke of Jem, and although we both knew that we'd done the right thing in letting Jem go, we still worried about his well-being and missed him terribly. Jem's departure left a gaping hole in our hearts, which would never fully heal. He wasn't our biological child, but both Hugo and I thought of him as an adopted son, and longed to see him again.

I craned my neck to get a better look, but the door to the church remained firmly closed. *I must be hearing things*, I thought as I turned back to the front. Perhaps Nicholas couldn't get away, or maybe my letter had gone astray. Either way, it didn't seem they'd be coming. I was glad I hadn't told Hugo of my intended surprise. At least he wouldn't feel as disappointed as I did.

The Reverend Snow was just about to pronounce Archie and Frances man and wife when a young man, wearing a twenty-first century morning suit in dove gray with a striped ascot, erupted into the church and froze at the sight of the congregation. His hair was disheveled, and his cheeks stained pink with embarrassment as he realized his mistake and tried to step back into the shadows.

Hugo and I exchanged a look of surprise, having grasped the significance of this apparition, and recognizing him for what he was rather than just a strangely dressed man who'd stumbled into someone's wedding.

"Oh, dear," I murmured as the young man looked from side to side, clearly searching for a graceful way out of his predicament. He looked vaguely familiar, and I suddenly realized where I'd seen him. There was a picture in Max's study of him and the young man in rugby gear. Simon. Simon Harding, son of Stella the housekeeper. "Simon," I hissed. "Over here." I patted the space next to me, inviting him to come and sit.

Simon looked bewildered, but decided not to make a scene and slid into the pew next to me as if we were old friends. He fixed his eyes on the front as Reverend Snow, having regained his composure, proceeded to conclude the marriage ceremony.

I forgot all about Simon and drank in the newlyweds, involuntarily grinning from ear to ear. Valentine clapped her hands in delight, her eyes large with wonder.

"You may kiss your bride," Reverend Snow announced.

Archie's mouth stretched into a joyful smile as he took Frances's face in both hands and kissed her soundly. She blushed prettily, which was most becoming to a new bride, according to Ruby, who whispered to Polly just behind me and sighed dramatically. She found Archie and Frances's story to be unbearably romantic, as did Polly, who whispered back to Ruby that she hoped she'd be the next to marry.

The bridal couple headed for the door, accepting good wishes as they made their way down the nave. Hugo scooped up Valentine, who looked displeased by Archie's lack of attention toward her, and carried her off, giving me a chance to speak with Simon. Soon, we were the only ones left in the church. Simon sat next to me rigidly, unsure of how to begin.

"Came from a wedding, did you?" I asked conversationally. "Is the weather as dreadful there as it is here?"

"Worse," he replied, although he had no way of knowing what the weather was like since he hadn't left the church yet.

"Whose wedding was it?" I asked. I had a pretty good idea

but wanted to get Simon talking. He appeared to be a little shell-shocked, and I hoped to put him at ease.

"Mine," he replied, the blush on his cheeks deepening.

"I take it your escape wasn't accidental?" I enquired casually as Simon finally turned to face me.

"No, it wasn't. I left her at the altar like a total coward." The telltale blush crept up his cheeks again, making him look very boyish. Simon hung his head in shame. "U.L.M.F.," he spat out with disgust.

"And that is?" I asked, smiling despite his misery. He had a disarming quality about him, which made it impossible to judge him. Any man who left his bride at the altar would be an unforgivable wanker in my eyes, but Simon looked so genuinely distressed that I actually felt sorry for him.

"Utter Lack of Moral Fiber; one of Mum's favorite expressions. Anyhow, I stood in the passage for what felt like an hour, telling myself to go back and face up to my responsibilities, but I couldn't. I just couldn't. Any place seemed better than the place I'd just left. Where am I, by the way, and how do you know my name?"

"You are in 1689, and I saw a picture of you on Max's desk a few years back."

"Oh God, you're that woman who vanished. Natalie? Nancy?" he tried again.

"Neve. Yes, I am that woman."

"Well, bugger me, never fancied meeting you on the other side," Simon said, eyeing me with interest. "So, you live here now? And was that...?" He glanced at the door.

"Yes, that was. Hugo Everly. I'm sure you've seen the portrait a few thousand times."

"Blimey," Simon said, clearly bowled over. "Look, Neve, is there any way I can just bide with you for a little while? I can't go back now. Heather will rip my balls off if she lays eyes on me."

"Can't say I blame her," I added helpfully.

"I know, I know. I was a total prat, but marrying her would have been an even bigger mistake. I'll go back, explain, and apologize. I just need a place to stew for a little while. Besides, you guys are family," he added. He no longer seemed as embarrassed; more fascinated by the situation he found himself in.

"Are we?" I asked, confused.

"Yes, well, you see, I didn't find out until after Max had gone. All my life, my mother told me that my father was some bloke she'd met at a music festival. Didn't even know his name. But I never really believed her; she's not that kind of woman."

Few men could imagine their sweet, twin-set-and-pearl-wearing mother shagging wildly in the back of some car with a stranger, but in this case I had to agree. I'd met Stella Harding, and I couldn't imagine her having a one-night stand with a faceless stranger. I thought she'd been married at some point, but it would seem that her ex-husband wasn't Simon's father.

"My father was Roland Everly, Max's father. Seems he and my mother carried on behind his wife's back for over twenty years." Simon actually looked as if he were about to cry. Clearly, the knowledge of the affair had upset him, or maybe it was just that he'd never gotten to know his father.

"All right, Simon, you may stay, but you need to change out of those clothes, and come up with a convincing lie. Why would I suddenly let you stay at Everly Manor? Who are you?" I asked, forcing Simon to stop feeling sorry for himself and try to think practically.

"I'm Hugo's cousin a hundred times removed," Simon suggested with an impish grin.

"We've already had to explain Max, whom no one's ever heard of. Perhaps with your light hair, you'd do better to be my cousin. From London. Do you know anything at all about the late seventeenth century?"

"Only what I've seen in films, but I think I can pull it off. I have a good imagination," Simon added.

"What do you do in your real life?"

"I'm in banking. Is there banking in this time, or does everyone just barter chickens and such?"

"Of course there's banking. It's the world's oldest profession besides prostitution," I quipped. "Just say you are a clerk at the Bank of England, and you work at Mercer Hall. Don't divulge anything more."

"Understood." Simon gave me a conspiratory smile as he took me in—upswept hair with tendrils framing my powdered face, silk gown trimmed with fur, and velvet cloak with a silver clasp at the throat. "My, I really missed you, Cousin Neve. It's been such a very long time. Why, we haven't seen each other since we were children, playing in the narrow alleys of Black-friars with our hoop and stick."

"Don't overdo it, Mister," I said, but couldn't help smiling. Simon was getting over his bout of remorse and beginning to enjoy himself. "Come on then."

FORTY-ONE

Simon felt like a right prat wearing hose and a shirt that would have been more appropriate on a pirate, but Neve and Hugo had been very kind to him, and he was grateful. It seemed wrong somehow to join the wedding celebration, so he asked if he might just sit in the library and read for a while.

Simon moved closer to the fire, amazed at how cold the house was without central heating. The rest of them seemed immune to the chill, but Simon added a few extra logs to the fire after Neve left to rejoin the party. A young maid named Ruby brought him a plate of food, which was actually quite tasty, or maybe he was just really hungry. He could hear sounds of chatter and laughter coming from the dining room where everyone was now assembled, and the gaiety brought a lump to his throat.

He couldn't say he had any regrets about what he'd done, quite the opposite, but he did feel sorry for the hurt and worry he'd caused. His poor mother would be frantic, and Heather would go from red-hot fury to confusion and fear for his safety. Wedding guests had seen him going down to the crypt, so he hoped that his mother would realize where he'd gone. They'd spent hours discussing Henry's journal and Max's disappearance. Stella Harding chose to remain skeptical, but she wouldn't be able to deny the existence of the wormhole after this. He couldn't wait to tell his mother of his adventure, but the cozy chat he anticipated might have to wait until she finally cooled down and was ready to listen. His mother might not be Heather's number-one fan, but she'd raised Simon to be responsible and have respect for the feelings of others.

A deeply unpleasant thought suddenly bloomed in Simon's mind, forcing him to sit up in the hard-backed chair. There was another parent who'd had a hand in his upbringing, a parent who had never so much as acknowledged him, but who was callous, shallow, and treated women with less consideration and respect than his Labrador, Tilly. Simon had behaved much as Roland Everly would have had he decided that he'd made a mistake and didn't care to deal with the consequences. His father had done as he pleased, and relied on his good looks and charm to talk his way out of any situation, managing to smooth the ruffled feathers of his harem of women. His mother could never stay angry for long, allowing her lover back into her good graces after a brief sulk.

Simon sat back and stared balefully into the flames, suddenly deeply ashamed of his behavior. He'd planned to charm Heather into forgiving him. He was Roland Everly through and through, and found the realization deeply disturbing, so much so that Simon decided to put the whole thing out of his mind. It was more interesting to analyze what he'd witnessed over the past few hours. Funny how people always had certain beliefs about the past, thinking that the people were ignorant, superstitious, and oblivious to the historical current of events that swept them along, usually with dire consequences.

Simon hadn't spoken to Hugo for long, just the few minutes they'd spent together while Hugo rooted in a trunk for some clothes which might fit Simon, but it was enough to completely crush any notion he had of the man. Hugo wasn't at all the pompous, overbearing, feudal overlord Simon always imagined him to be. He was well-mannered, intelligent, and obviously didn't lack for a sense of humor. But what really undid Simon was the hint of pain behind the eyes, the almost imperceptible fragility in both him and Neve which they were trying hard to hide. They had lost their daughter only a month ago, and under the façade of coping were two people who were still reeling from their loss.

Simon's mind was teeming with questions, all of which Neve promised to answer in due course. She had to return to her guests, but by the end of the day, Simon would finally learn what had happened to Max, and perhaps get some closure. But at this moment, Max's fate didn't seem as important as that of Hugo. According to the gravestone, which had still been there when Simon had gone back to check, Hugo would not live out the year. Simon had no idea if he would die of an illness or involve himself in another treasonous plot, but Neve was about to become a widow and find herself alone with her children in a hostile century with no family or friends. A woman in her position was only as safe as her husband made her, and her husband wasn't long for this world. Hugo didn't have any brothers or close male relatives who would assume responsibility for his family once he was gone, so Neve would be on her own with no one to turn to. There was a nephew somewhere, but he was still a teenager.

Simon froze in mid-thought, suddenly aware of what he'd forgotten. Hugo's nephew inherited the estate and title after his death, but Hugo was believed to have died without leaving a male heir. Was Michael Everly going to die as well? Simon suddenly wondered. He'd seen the little boy clinging to one of the maids and felt a stab of pity. He seemed like such a timid

child, frightened by the boisterous wedding guests and dangerously close to tears.

And then there was the older girl. Simon smiled at the
thought of Valentine. That one was a pistol, he could tell just by
looking at the determined look in her eyes. She had been at the
church and demanded to ride home in the carriage with the
bride and groom. The way she'd stared at the red-headed man
who married the lovely Frances, one would think that she was
experiencing the jealousy of a jilted lover. Archie had swept her
up off her feet and handed her off to Hugo, despite her protests.
"Not today, little lady," he'd said with quiet finality. "Not
today." Valentine had pouted but didn't cry as her father had
lifted her into the carriage and passed her to Neve. Valentine
had stared out the small window, still angry enough not to take
any interest in the strange man who had appeared at the church
and was now coming home with them. It might be the seventeenth century, but they were a family just like any other—a
family that would be decimated within the year.

Simon took a sip of ale and sighed. To warn Neve of what
was to come would be incredibly cruel, but to say nothing
seemed cowardly. But what could he tell her? He had no idea
what was going to happen or when, and to cast a shadow on
Neve's already fragile state just seemed wrong. Simon had
never seen a happily married couple firsthand, but after
witnessing the glow of affection between Neve and Hugo, he
realized that's what marriage was about. Romance and passion
based on respect, friendship, and a deeper kind of love, which
burned less bright than the initial heat of lust but was a steady
flame which kept you warm for the rest of your days, or until
death did you part. And that's something he never thought he
could have with Heather. They were both too selfish and too
independent to ever achieve that kind of a union of souls. Why
was it that the people who seemed to achieve that purity of love
seemed to always lose it?

Simon drained what was left in his cup and set it down with a decisive thud. He wasn't going to say anything to Neve; he just couldn't. He had no right. Whatever happened was going to happen regardless; all he could do was offer her sanctuary, should she ever need it.

FORTY-TWO

Frances smiled shyly as she bid everyone goodnight and turned to go upstairs. Normally, the bride and groom would go up together, eager to escape the raucous encouragement and bawdy advice from the inebriated guests, but Frances asked Archie to give her a few minutes to herself before coming up, so he was still in the parlor, drinking with the men, and good-naturedly accepting bits of wedding-night wisdom from Arnold and Bill. Hugo gave her a fatherly kiss on the forehead, and Neve smiled in encouragement, knowing that Frances had nothing to fear. Frances threw a final glance at Archie, whose look of naked longing turned her knees to water.

She'd anticipated this night for nearly three years, but now that it was here, she was paralyzed with anxiety. Frances refused to think of her wedding night with Lionel, but memories of making love to Luke were still fresh. The experience hadn't been unpleasant or painful, but neither was it what she'd expected. She had enjoyed the attention and the caresses, but felt no real passion or pleasure, glad to see Luke go and leave her blessedly alone. Frances was sure that Luke had done everything right, so it had to be her. Perhaps she was incapable of enjoying the physical aspects of love as other women suppos-edly did. And who knew if they were even telling the truth.

Frances was sure that Neve did not fear intimacy with Hugo, but was too embarrassed to ask her outright, and her only other points of reference were her scheming maid, Sabine, in Paris, who seemingly lied about everything, and the ladies of Louis's Court, who giggled prettily and blushed as they gossiped about their lovers. If there was anything that Frances had learned over the past few years, it was that you couldn't really believe anyone, especially people who had something to gain by pulling the wool over your eyes. She did trust Neve, though, and the warmth and ease she saw between Neve and Hugo made Frances believe that a happy marriage was possible, not that they didn't have their ups and downs. Hugo's reaction to Elena's death had taken Frances by surprise, since she'd always viewed Hugo as stoic and indestructible, but seeing the depth of his grief only made her love him more, for he wasn't just her savior and guardian, he was a man who truly loved, and in her experience, that was a rarity.

And Archie loved deeply, too. Frances had no doubts about the depth of Archie's feelings for her, but would his love for her change if she wasn't able to respond to him as a woman should? He'd enjoyed plenty of women in his day, so he would be quick to notice if she failed to have the proper reaction. What if she didn't please him? What if he turned to other women to satisfy his needs now that they were married?

Frances's hands shook as she tried to roll down her stock-ings. She was more nervous now than when she was thirteen and about to be deflowered by a virtual stranger. She loved Archie with all her heart, so to disappoint him in any way would surely kill her. Frances tossed the stockings to the floor and reached for a decanter of brandy thoughtfully provided by Hugo. Perhaps the liquor would help.

She was on her second glass by the time Archie came up

and shut the door firmly behind him. He just stood and looked at her for a moment, his smile lazy and indulgent, but it seemed to falter as he realized the extent of her panic.

"Franny, don't," Archie murmured as he came up behind her and wrapped his arms about her waist, simultaneously removing the glass from her trembling hand and setting it on the mantel.

"Don't what?"

"Don't work yourself up. I know what you are thinking, and there's nothing to worry about. I won't hurt you, not ever."

"That's not what I was worried about," Frances replied, wondering if she should share her fears with Archie. She tried to relax, but her back was rigid against his chest, and her hands felt cold despite the roaring fire in the hearth.

"Then what is it?" Archie asked, clearly concerned. "Are you having second thoughts?"

"I'm afraid I won't please you," she mumbled as she turned in his arms. She needed to see his face to know if he shared her concern.

"I reckon there's only one way to find out," Archie whispered as he pulled her closer and covered her mouth with his own.

Archie's kisses had always been tender and sweet, but this kiss was possessive and demanding—the kiss of a man who would no longer be denied. Frances stiffened in Archie's arms as he turned her around, undid her lacings, and helped her out of the bodice and skirt. Frances was left in her shift, which she hugged about herself, suddenly feeling self-conscious. Archie had never seen her unclothed. What if he thought her too skinny or lacking in bosom?

Archie didn't insist that she remove her chemise the way Lionel had. Lionel had made her turn around while he looked at her appraisingly and stroked himself, enjoying her terror as his cock thickened and grew longer in his hand. But Archie just let her be. He removed his own clothes, but kept his shirt on, still modestly covered.

He poured a glass of brandy for them both and handed one to Frances. "To us, Franny," he said, but waited to drink until Frances took a sip of her own brandy. The fiery liquid did help and made her feel slightly less agitated, but the more she chastised herself for being foolish, the more anxious she felt.

Archie took the empty glass from her and set it aside before coming up behind her. He didn't pull her against him as she expected but moved her hair away from her shoulder and planted feather-light kisses on her neck, eventually catching her earlobe between his lips and sucking gently. Shivers of pleasure raced down Frances's spine, making her legs feel weak. She thought that Archie would now take her to bed, but he seemed in no rush. He moved back down to her neck, lifting her hair with one hand and kissing her nape before paying court to the other side. Frances relaxed a fraction and allowed herself to lean against Archie as he wrapped his arm around her middle. She could feel his arousal against her lower back, hard as a wooden cudgel.

She felt momentary panic, but it meant that Archie wanted her, and she was pleasing him. The thought helped her relax, and she let out a small sigh as she closed her eyes. Archie's warm hand crept up to her breast, and he slid it inside the shift, cupping her and caressing her nipple. Frances hardly noticed when she arched her back to press her breast into his hand, or when Archie pushed down the shift to expose both breasts. He gently rolled her nipples between his fingers, making her moan with pleasure as she savored the sensation. She felt a strange ache somewhere deep in her lower belly, as if her body were asking for something, but she attributed it to her nervousness.

"May I?" Archie asked as he came around and lowered his head to her breast.

Frances buried her fingers in his hair as he sucked on her

nipple, sending ripples through her belly which seemed to culminate between her legs and make her feel strangely moist.

"Oh, Archie," she breathed as he continued to suckle her breasts. It felt so different from when Gabriel had nursed, gumming her nipples until she nearly screamed from the pain.

Frances didn't protest when Archie slid her shift over her hips, leaving her completely exposed. She was no longer embarrassed, but pulsing with a yearning that was unfamiliar to her. Was this what it meant to feel desire? Frances wondered dazedly as Archie pushed her onto a settee and sank to his knees in front of her, pushing her legs apart. Frances let out a startled gasp and dug her hands into Archie's shoulders as his tongue slid inside her, moving slowly and deliberately until her legs were vibrating with tension, and her senses swam with indescribable pleasure. Archie pulled her lower down and continued his exploration, using his fingers to penetrate her while he teased the small bit of flesh which she'd never paid much attention to before his tongue brought it to startling life.

Archie lifted Frances's legs and placed them on his shoulders. He buried his face deeper between her legs as his tongue probed her with deadly intent and his fingers continued to work their magic. The sensation was so intense that all thought fled from Frances's brain as she gave herself up to the pleasure Archie was giving her.

She suddenly felt as if something came undone within her. Her womb began to convulse, and she threw her head back with a cry of surprise. She was quivering all over, waves of exquisite pleasure washing over her, her limbs heavy and languid.

Archie looked up at her, his lips moist, and his eyes shining with satisfaction as he moved up, pulled off his shirt, and covered her body with his own. "You look like you need a few minutes to recover, my sweet," he said innocently as he kissed her hard, grinding his hips against hers.

Frances didn't want to recover. She wanted more, so she arched her hips against Archie's in mute demand.

"Yes, madam," he whispered into her ear as he slid inside her and began to move.

He felt big and hard, but she didn't resist him. Frances wrapped her legs around him and began to move with him, urging him to go faster. She had no idea what she was doing, but at this point she was being guided by pure instinct.

"Please, Archie," she gasped as he pulled back for a moment, then thrust into her hard.

"Please what?"

"Please don't stop."

"Oh, I won't," Archie promised as he grabbed her hips and lifted her pelvis for deeper penetration.

Frances cried out in ecstasy as she surrendered all remaining control to her husband. Her body was no longer hers, but an instrument that Archie was playing with such skill that it sang in his hands and made the type of exquisite music it never knew it could.

Frances went limp as a rag doll as Archie collapsed on top of her, his body damp with perspiration. He was still inside her, but he no longer stretched and filled her as before. He seemed vulnerable somehow now that he was no longer hard, and she wrapped her arms around him, holding him tight as a joyful smile spread across her face.

"Is it always like this?" she asked him as he looked down at her, clearly satisfied with his efforts.

"No."

"No?" Frances asked, a stab of disappointment piercing her heart.

"No, it gets better."

"How can it possibly get better?" Frances asked, confused. What more could he do to her?

"Franny," Archie said with a wicked smile, "there's going to be a rosy blush on those cheeks in the days to come as you imagine all the things I will do to you as soon as I get you on your own."

"And will you do those things?" Frances asked innocently.

"Only if you ask me to," Archie growled and bit her earlobe, making her squeal. "I don't ever want you to feel that you have no say and must submit to me whether you want to or not. I will never force you or use you unkindly, Frances."

"That means more to me than you can possibly imagine," she said as she took his face in her hands and kissed him tenderly.

Frances was shocked to feel Archie growing hard inside her again, his eyes clouding over with desire, but he held back, waiting, his body poised on the brink. Frances gazed at him in confusion as she moved her hips against him, but he remained motionless, his eyes on hers. Did he not want her again? Frances wondered. His body indicated otherwise, but he didn't seem in any rush to make love to her again. And then she understood.

"Make love to me, Archie," she said as her cheeks blazed crimson. She'd never demanded anything before, but if Archie didn't take her now, she'd burst. Her body was thrumming, the point of their joining wet with longing.

"I thought you'd never ask," Archie replied as he plunged into her, banishing all further thoughts from her head.

FORTY-THREE

After seeing our guests off, Hugo and I went to see Simon in the library. He'd been understandably reluctant to join the party, having been in the past for only a very short while. It was a shock to the senses, so to have to immediately socialize with people he'd never met and try to come up with the right historical responses was daunting, to say the least. Besides, he'd just made a life-changing decision, and although Simon seemed to have no regrets, I was sure that he was putting on a brave face. He might not have been ready to marry his Heather, but he'd been with her for several years, and must love her to some degree if their relationship got as far as the altar. Perhaps there would be recriminations tomorrow, especially after spending what was supposed to be his wedding night alone in a strange house filled with people he'd only ever heard about, mostly on Halloween. I recalled Max telling me about a spooky tale he'd made up about the restless ghost of Hugo Everly haunting Everly Manor on Halloween to scare a young Simon.

Simon had been dozing by the fire, but woke up and sat up straighter as we came in, eager to talk. I knew he was full of questions, but planned to present him with an abridged version of events. We hadn't seen nor heard from Max in over two and a half years, so, most likely, he was dead. There was no point in tarnishing Max in Simon's eyes, especially when the younger man clearly grieved for him and missed him. Also, now that Simon was here in the seventeenth century, I didn't want to give him any encouragement to stay. I didn't think he would want to, but if he believed that his older brother was alive, he just might decide to go in search of Max, which likely wouldn't end well, especially for Simon.

Hugo had just finished telling Simon about his visit to the twenty-first century, leaving out the more colorful bits about Max's attempt on his life, and making the whole episode sound like a delightful holiday which he had fond memories of. No mention was made of the frustration or lack of direction that Hugo had felt during those months, or the deep-seated desire to get back to his real life where he was a man of rank and property, a man able to offer me marriage and a better station in life.

"So, you were able to avoid arrest by wearing colored lenses and coloring your hair?" Simon asked, clearly impressed with Hugo's ingenuity.

"I don't suppose I would have fooled too many people in the future, since changing your appearance is not unheard of, but with no benefit of photography or forensic evidence, it was easy enough to pull off here," Hugo replied modestly. "No one truly knows what you look like unless they've met you in person, and a general description in a broadsheet is worthless if it's inaccurate."

"You know about forensics?" Simon asked, gaping at Hugo. He had a hard time accepting that Hugo could talk to him on his own level, still distracted by the clothes and trappings of seventeenth-century life.

"Rather a fascinating subject," Hugo replied with a small smile.

"Was it difficult for you to come back?" Simon asked, giving Hugo an appraising glance.

"Yes, and no," Hugo replied noncommittally. "Coming home always feels right, even if the home in question is not perfect." Hugo threw me a guilty look, realizing that there'd be no coming home for me. "But, of course, I was acutely aware of the ignorance and lack of scientific progress in my own time, especially in medicine. I had visited the dentist in the future," Hugo confided, "and although it wasn't a very pleasant experience, he was able to save a tooth which would otherwise have had to come out at some point, having been bothering me for some time."

Simon was oblivious to the change, but I'd noticed the sudden tightening of Hugo's mouth as his eyes slid away from him. He was thinking of Elena, and what modern medicine could have done for her had we had the foresight to act in time. There would be that "what if" all our lives, no matter how much time had passed since our baby's death.

There was a sudden knock on the door, distracting me from my morbid thoughts. Ruby entered the library, curtsying to Hugo as she always did. He'd told her repeatedly that it wasn't necessary, but she couldn't help herself.

"Sorry to disturb yer lordship, but Michael is crying and won't settle down. I think he might have a bellyache," she added apologetically. "He doesn't normally eat so much afore bedtime, but he did overindulge on some sweetmeats." I was just getting to my feet when Ruby interjected, her face a mask of embarrassment, "It's his lordship he wants, me lady. He's asking for his papa."

Hugo was instantly on his feet. "Do excuse me, Simon. I'll come back as soon as I can. In the meantime, my wife will keep you company." Hugo bowed to Simon from the neck. The formality was unnecessary, but it was too deeply ingrained.

Simon made to rise to his feet, but Hugo held up his hand to forestall him before leaving the room.

"He's not at all what I imagined," Simon said after the door closed after Hugo.

"No, he's not. I had some preconceived notions about him myself, mostly based on what I'd heard from Max. Hugo is the best part of me," I added, my voice quivering with emotion.

"I think you might be the best part of him as well," Simon replied, looking at me intently.

I nodded in acknowledgment, suddenly feeling vulnerable in front of this young man who didn't seem like a stranger anymore.

"Neve, is Max really dead?" Simon asked, eager to change the subject. "I found something online, which stated that Lord Hugo Everly died shortly after arriving on a sugar plantation in Barbados. Since Lord Hugo Everly just went up to nurse his son's bellyache, I can only assume that it was really Max who died."

"Simon, I don't know exactly what happened to Max after the trial. He'd been sentenced to transportation, and Barbados was as likely a place as any for him to be sent to, but he either never made it to the West Indies or managed to escape somehow since Hugo and I saw him in Paris in June of 1686."

"Really? Did you speak to him?" Simon asked, eager for details.

"It wasn't really a social occasion," I replied, loath to tell Simon of Max's plans for Hugo and myself. Max had been calm and collected, which made him that much scarier. Somewhere along the line, the charming man I'd met in the twenty-first century, who pursued me so gallantly, had become completely unhinged. His actions didn't seem to be driven by passion, but by cold reason, his plan having been well thought out. Max had no qualms about killing an innocent man or abducting a woman and child who'd done nothing to harm him. Whatever humanity he had once possessed seemed to have been stripped away by his experiences, the line between right and wrong completely obliterated by his desire to preserve that which was his.

Simon nodded in understanding, his expression going from hope to one of sadness. "Was he ill, do you think?"

"Possibly. He looked unwell. I would think that if he were alive, he'd have returned by now. It's been over three years since he went through the passage in the crypt," I pointed out gently.

"I hope you don't mind me asking, but were you two an item before you went into the past? Max spoke of you as if you were involved, and then didn't mention you to me again. Of course, we didn't speak as often as we used to once I became serious with Heather. We did meet up in London from time to time, for a drink or dinner."

"Max seemed to have something of a fixation with me," I replied carefully, "that pitted him against Hugo and prevented any civil interaction between them." That was the understatement of the year, but that was all I was willing to say. There was no reason for Simon to know the truth.

"I thought as much," Simon said as his eyes met mine.

"What do you mean, Simon?"

Simon looked uncomfortable as he shifted in his seat and stared into the fire for a moment, trying to determine how much to tell me. "Neve, Max never told me outright, but I had it on good authority from my mother, who'd known Max since he was a boy, that he suffered from something called the Histrionic Personality Disorder."

"I'm sorry, but I don't really know anything about it. How does it manifest itself?" I asked, trying to recall if I'd ever heard anything. Being able to google the symptoms would have been very handy at the moment, but I had to rely on Simon for an explanation.

"Supposedly, Max's case was mild," Simon replied, still

uncomfortable with the subject. He probably felt as if he were betraying Max, or his memory, but it seemed important enough that he felt the need to explain. "Max started showing symptoms when he was a teenager, so his mother promptly took him to some hotshot therapist in Harley Street who told her that the onset of puberty often brought on manifestation of the disorder. Max never took any medication for it, but he did have ongoing therapy, which his parents kept hush-hush. I am no expert on the disorder, but my mother told me that the person tends to distort relationships in their mind, thinking them more intimate than they really are, always wants to be the center of attention, and suffers from mood swings and occasional paranoia. Did you have a relationship with him, or did he just conjure it up in his mind?" Simon asked, still curious.

"We had a few dates, that was all, but Max seemed to think that we had a definite future. Now I understand why he became so territorial and took such a dislike toward Hugo. He seemed to believe that Hugo had come to the twenty-first century to usurp his life, and blamed Hugo for his arrest when Hugo was nowhere near Cranley when it happened."

Simon nodded in understanding. "Max worked really hard to control his symptoms, but there were times, particularly when he got emotional over something, when he lost control. His last fixation had been running for Parliament. His mother was very much in favor, but my mother thought that the stress of life in politics might cause him irreparable harm. Country life suited him best, and if he'd found a woman who loved him, I believe that his condition could have been managed with patience and support."

I decided not to point out to Simon that Max's case was probably a lot more severe than he thought. What was the point? Max was gone, and Simon would soon be gone as well. At least his explanation had shed some light on Max's irrational behavior and thirst for vengeance.

"Will you tell Hugo?" Simon asked, his eyes asking me not to.

"Would you rather I didn't?"

"I don't feel right about betraying something so personal. Max would be really angry with me if he knew. It's enough that you know. Isn't it?"

"Simon, you have my word. There's no need for Hugo to know. It's all in the past now anyway. Or in the future. Depends how you look at it," I joked lamely.

"I do wish he would have found his way back," Simon said wistfully.

"So, you believe he is dead?" I asked carefully, needing reassurance that Simon had no plans of a rescue mission.

"What would he be doing in France for two and a half years? Surely, he would have found his way back by now if he wished to return. The most likely explanation is that Max died. I am truly the last of the Everlys now," Simon sighed, "not a distinction I ever wanted. I don't want Max's life, Neve. I don't care to be the lord of the manor. I just want my life back."

"I understand." And I did. Being Lady Everly had changed my life as well, and I often felt like an impostor, pretending to be someone I wasn't. I was just Neve Ashley, not a noblewoman with a houseful of servants and people curtsying to me as if I were the bloody Queen of England. Sometimes I missed being a nobody.

"I suppose it's safe for me to go back now," Simon said reluctantly, his gaze on the folds of Hugo's coat.

"The church might be locked up for the night. Why don't you stay? Things always look brighter in the morning," I suggested, knowing that Simon really wasn't ready to go.

"Thank you, Neve, I would like that. I'm just not ready to face the music. Not yet."

"Will you be able to sleep?" I asked, feeling sorry for him despite his dishonorable behavior.

"I think so. Actually, I feel emotionally drained. This has been one of the most dramatic days of my life," he added with a rueful smile.

"Let me show you up to your room then. I'll send one of the maids to light the fire. I assume you are not very handy with tinder and flint."

* * *

Simon stayed the night, but, by morning, having had a hearty breakfast, was ready to go back. All the wedding guests would have departed, and it was safe to return to Everly Manor and face the consequences of his escape. I had to admit that it was a relief. Having Simon with us made me feel unsettled, especially when he was full of news of the life I'd left behind. We had spent some time talking about music, books, and films before Simon finally went up; things that I missed dreadfully. Simon had even imparted some gossip about the royal family and world events. I had to confess that I missed watching the world do its thing from behind the safety of the walls of my flat, watching politics playing out on television rather than in my own house.

I returned Simon's morning suit, but lent him Archie's cloak to wear over it on the way to the church so as not to attract too much attention from the villagers. I'd walk over with him and distract Reverend Snow if necessary while Simon made his getaway.

Simon was pensive as we walked toward the church, his mind already on his own time and the bollocking he would get from Heather. I'd never met her, but from everything I'd heard, she didn't seem the type of woman who would let Simon off without inflicting a few battle scars.

I was surprised when Simon stopped in the churchyard and glanced toward Elena's grave, as if he knew it'd be there. "I'm sorry about your daughter," he said. "I can't imagine how painful it must be to lose a child."

"Thank you, Simon," was all I could say with the huge lump lodged in my throat.

"Look, Neve," he began, his eyes sliding away from mine for a moment, as if he were afraid I'd see too much in them. "There might come a time when you decide that this life is no longer for you. If ever you come back, know that I would be happy to help you with whatever you need: money, a place to stay, a convincing story..." Simon pulled a card out of his wallet and placed it in my hand, folding my fingers around it. "Don't throw this away."

"Simon, is there something you are not telling me?" I asked, as my heart did a summersault of foreboding in my chest.

"No, no, of course not. You've been so kind to me, so understanding. I just want you to know that I would be happy to return the favor."

We both knew he was lying, but I thanked him and slid the card into the pocket of my gown. I would keep it as a talisman. It was only when you lost something that you really needed it, so as long as I had the card, everything would be all right.

"Goodbye and good luck, Simon. It was a pleasure to meet you."

Simon pulled me into an embrace and kissed my cheek. "Goodbye, Your Ladyship," he said with a smile.

I stood in the nave for a moment, listening to the silence once Simon left. I felt strangely hollow as I walked slowly toward the door and left the church, my footsteps turning toward Elena's grave, as they always did.

FORTY-FOUR

Hugo stood by the parlor window, watching Neve as she walked up the hill toward the house, her eyes downcast, her step slow. Having Simon stay with them, even for a few hours, had unsettled her more than she cared to admit, and Hugo was glad to see the back of him. He didn't want to judge a man he barely knew, but Simon's actions were irresponsible and cowardly, not the actions of an honorable man. Granted, honor wasn't a highly valued commodity in the future; it was every man for himself, even if that man left a trail of bodies in his wake. Perhaps this Heather was lucky to have escaped marrying a man who was so easily spooked.

Hugo abandoned his position by the window and went out to meet Neve. He hadn't bothered to get his cloak or gloves, and the frigid air assaulted him the moment he stepped outside. His breath came out in clouds of vapor, and his face prickled with the cold, but he had something that would take Neve's mind off Simon and the twenty-first century, something she would be excited about despite her glum mood, and he didn't want to wait a moment longer to tell her. Two letters had been delivered yesterday, but Hugo had waited to open them, saving them for a time when he would be able to read them in peace and share them with Neve.

"Is he gone?" Hugo asked unnecessarily as he met Neve halfway up the hill. Her cheeks were pink from the cold, and she gladly accepted his hand since her leather boots didn't have much purchase on frost-covered grass.

"Yes, he is. I was actually sad to see him go," Neve said. Her tone was one of surprise, but Hugo could understand her reaction to Simon. Simon was an added complication, one they didn't need in their life, but he had been a messenger from the future—a window into the life she'd left behind. Neve rarely spoke of the future, but Hugo knew that there were moments when she missed that other world, and some of the people in it. "Why aren't you wearing your cloak?" Neve asked reproachfully as Hugo shivered. She was terrified of anyone getting ill, especially now.

"I only came out for a few minutes. I'm fine, really. Come inside, I have something to show you," Hugo said as they finally crested the hill and walked up the drive.

Neve undid the clasp of her cloak, pulled off her gloves, and removed her hat, handing them all to Harriet, who looked unusually tired, having joined the wedding party last night. She had imbibed her fair share of the mead that Brad had contributed to the festivities, and the effects were obvious. Cook looked a bit sluggish this morning as well, her normally rosy cheeks pale beneath her puffy eyes.

"Any sign of the newlyweds?" Neve asked Harriet, who blushed as if it were her wedding night instead of Frances's.

"Not yet, Your Ladyship."

"Good," Neve replied, making Harriet blush even deeper as she turned to put away Neve's things.

"Harriet, bring some mulled wine, please," Hugo called after the maid as he invited Neve into his study.

"So what do you want to show me?" Neve asked as she

settled in the chair closest to the hearth and held out her hands to the fire.

Hugo triumphantly held up two letters. "Letters from Jem and Clarence. Which should I read first?"

He knew exactly what Neve would say. The letter from Clarence would not be nearly as interesting as the one from Jem. Clarence wrote to Hugo about once a year, a perfunctory reply which told Hugo that he was well, and the estate was prospering. What Hugo read between the lines was actually more informative. Clarence never asked after Hugo or the family, and never implied that he would like a reunion. In fact, as time went by, the letters actually grew terser, which led Hugo to believe that Clarence still blamed him for Jane's death, and his resentment grew rather than abated. But now that they were back in England, Hugo hoped to repair his relationship with his nephew and had said as much in the letter he'd dispatched a month ago.

"Read the one from Clarence first," Neve said, her voice indifferent.

Hugo broke the seal and glanced over the letter. It was only about three sentences, but it said it all.

Uncle,

I was surprised to hear of your return to England. Thank you for your invitation, but a visit would not be convenient at this time as I am much occupied with estate matters. Perhaps we will see each other at some point in the future.

I hope you and your family are in good health.

Clarence Hiddleston

"As expected then," Neve said as she looked over at Hugo. "He doesn't wish to come here, nor does he invite you to visit him in Kent. Will you keep trying?"

"He's my only nephew, Neve. I know he blames me for Jane's death because it's easier than accepting the truth, but, in time, perhaps he will be ready to hear me out." Hugo wasn't convinced this was true, but he meant to keep trying. Clarence had been only thirteen the last time he saw him, and he was a sullen, often spiteful boy, but Hugo had seen a different Clarence when they'd gone fishing and hunting a few times. Clarence took a while to warm up, but once he did, he'd enjoyed himself, and forgot to sulk long enough to tell Hugo something of his hopes and dreams. Perhaps Hugo could manage to appeal to that Clarence and try to mend the fences one post at a time.

"Read the letter from Jemmy," Neve said, no longer interested in Clarence. "Oh, I do miss him, Hugo. I'd sent a letter a few weeks back inviting Nicholas and Jem to the wedding. It was to be a surprise," Neve added sadly, disappointed that no one came.

Hugo unfolded the letter, which was a lot longer and written in the neat hand of someone who wanted to make a good impression. They hadn't had a letter from Jem in over a year, so any news would be welcome. The letter was dated two weeks prior, so it had been written shortly after Nicholas had received Neve's letter inviting them to Everly Manor. Jem wrote:

Dear Lord and Lady Everly,

Thank you for your kind invitation to Archie and Franny's wedding. Father and I so wanted to come and see you all, but stepmother Anne took with a terrible chest cold and passed in her sleep three days later. We were all saddened by her passing, but I think Father was also partially relieved as things between them have been less than cordial. Father is quite fond of a certain young lady, and I think I might have a new stepmother before the summer is out. She is beautiful and charming, and reminds me of her ladyship, so I look forward to this most welcome change.

Father engaged a tutor for me as soon as we returned to

England, and I have been hard at work. Master Thompson is a man of five and twenty and has a talent for making history come alive. I'm still not over-fond of mathematics, but Master Thompson says that I'll do. I am learning Latin and Greek, and as a reward for my efforts, Master Thompson has gifted me with a book on Greek mythology, which I quite enjoy.

When not applying myself to my studies, I am out on the estate with Father. He is teaching me the running of the place, and I must confess, I find it more interesting than I thought I might.

Father bought me a splendid horse. It's a chestnut mare, and I called her Coco because she reminds me of the chocolate Frances and I used to drink for breakfast. Please tell Archie about the horse; I think he would be much impressed.

I hope you are all doing well. I miss everyone and would have liked to be there to tease Frances on her wedding day. I know she was a beautiful bride, and a clever one if she managed to bring Archie to heel.

Uncle Luke has also gotten married. He married in Constantinople, but is now back in England, having lost the taste for politics. He sends regards, as does Father.

Your obedient servant,

Jeremiah Marsden

"He hardly even sounds like the Jemmy we knew," Neve observed as she glanced at Hugo's reaction to the letter. "Do you think he had to show the letter to Nicholas before sending it?"

"I don't know," Hugo replied glumly. He tossed the letter onto the desk and glanced out the window, needing a moment to get his feelings under control. Jem sounded happy and well-adjusted, so why did he feel a pang of resentment? It was childish and made Hugo feel ashamed of himself, but rather than rejoice in Jem's good fortune, he felt almost disappointed that Jem expressed no desire to return to them.

"You are so transparent," Neve said with a gentle smile, as she got up and came to stand behind him and wrapped her arms around his waist. "Hugo, it's all right to feel a little hurt. You took him in and loved him, and now he doesn't need you anymore. Your feelings are natural."

"Are they? I feel a fool," Hugo grumbled.

"No one likes to be replaced. Jem will always love you; you know that."

"He has a real father now, one who bought him a chestnut mare," Hugo replied churlishly. He could almost feel Neve smiling indulgently behind him.

"Why don't you go read a story to your son? Perhaps one day you can buy him a chestnut mare and teach him to ride it," she suggested gently.

Hugo smiled wistfully at his own foolishness. "You are right, as usual. I look forward to spending time with Michael as he gets older. I'll take him hunting and fishing and teach him all about the running of the estate. I think he will be good with numbers, he's got a logical mind."

"And you deduced this how?" Neve asked, laughing.

"He always looks at the pages of the book in sequence and never jumps to the end the way Valentine does, and he likes putting things in order. Haven't you noticed that?"

"I have. He is rather meticulous, unlike our unruly Valentine." Neve grew silent as her mind went to Elena and what she had been like, but she didn't say anything, knowing that it would bring Hugo pain.

"Neve," Hugo said, his voice full of hope, "do you think there's a chance...?"

Neve shook her head stubbornly. There would be no more children, not unless it happened by accident. The birth of the twins had been brutal, and the loss of Elena had brought Neve to her knees. She was done with babies, she'd made that clear, so

Hugo had gone back to using the prophylactics after the birth, telling himself that too many men lost their wives in childbirth, but he wouldn't be one of them. As much as he longed to have more children, he was glad not to put Neve at risk, for life without her would be meaningless.

FORTY-FIVE

JANUARY 1689

Devon, England

Jem waited until the house was quiet and everyone abed for the night before pulling Lady Everly's letter from beneath his pillow. He fancied it smelled of her perfume but knew he was being silly. Neve didn't wear much scent, and even if some had gotten on the letter while she was writing, it would have surely evaporated by now. Jem didn't open the letter; he knew the words by heart, just held it close, needing to feel even the most tenuous connection to the Everlys. He managed to keep his mind occupied during the day, focusing on his studies and accompanying his father when he went out on the estate, but when everyone retired and Jem was finally alone in his room, he felt a soul-crushing loneliness that had nothing to do with being alone.

His father never actually saw the invitation to the wedding. Jem had noticed the letter with the Everly seal lying unopened on the desk in his father's study, and palmed it before anyone else had a chance to see it. What he'd written to Hugo was partly true, but he'd allowed himself some license with the timeline. It was true that his stepmother had passed away, but it had actually happened just after the summer, and although his father did feel some sorrow at his wife's passing, what he seemed to feel was mostly relief. The marriage had been strained, to say the least, and Jem's arrival did little to improve relations between Nicholas and his invalid wife, who saw Jem as a constant reminder of her failure to produce a son and heir.

Anne Marsden had been surprisingly kind to him, but she was a woman who'd lost nearly all interest in life in the decade since her riding accident, and spent most of her time either reading or staring out the window at the world she could no longer enjoy. She'd been an accomplished horsewoman once, a woman who loved to dance and take long walks through the countryside. Her accident had put an end to all that, her only exposure to the outside world being weekly trips to church and an hour or so outdoors on fine days. A burly groom named Wilfred, who smelled of horse manure and sweat, appeared every day at midmorning to carry Anne outside and settle her in her chair with a rug over her legs where she had a lovely view of the lawns and the park. Wilfred returned just before the midday meal to carry Anne back inside.

To Jem's knowledge, the two never spoke or even looked at each other, but Wilfred carried Anne Marsden as if she were made of fine china, and gazed on her with undisguised affection when she wasn't looking. They'd been friends once, in the days when Anne went out riding every day, with Wilfred galloping after her on orders from her husband to make sure that she was chaperoned and safe. After years of confinement, her death was probably just as much of a release for her as it was for her husband, and the only person who seemed to grieve for her was Wilfred. He was a man of few words, but Jem had seen him kneeling by Anne's grave several times, an expression of abject misery on his face as he cleared away the fallen leaves and used his sleeve to wipe the dust off the inscription.

Jem covered his ears as he heard the mewling of a baby coming from down the corridor. *Anne died just in time,* Jem thought bitterly as he pressed his face into the pillow. Nicholas had married his pregnant mistress only a month after the funeral, and now he had a new son, a legitimate son, whose mother would fight tooth and nail to make sure that her boy got what was coming to him, and that the bastard son of her husband would not usurp what was rightfully her son's.

Nicholas spoke to Jem of the new baby many times, reassuring him that his brother would not in any way change what he felt for Jem or alter the order of the inheritance, but Jem didn't believe that for a minute. Had Anne died a few years before, his father would have simply remarried and produced an heir, instead of coming all the way to France to find a child he had fathered years ago with a woman who was hardly more than a whore. Jem had loved his mother once, but now he knew too much about her to feel any love or respect for the woman who'd given him life. She seemed to have lain with just about every man in Cranleigh, and quite a few in London. She'd had no honor, no decency, and no modesty.

Jem tried to remember her as she was when she took him to church on Sundays, but all he saw in his mind's eye was a dark-haired woman, her head thrown back and her eyes closed in ecstasy as she rode Archie, her full breasts bouncing up and down, a cry of pleasure escaping her pouty lips as she ground her hips against his.

There was a time when Jem thought that Hugo Everly was his natural father, or that Archie might marry his mother and they'd be a family, but his mother didn't wish for a husband. She liked having lovers—many of them. Archie wasn't the only man she'd taken to her bed; there were at least half a dozen that Jem had seen her with. She often caught him watching through a curtain around the alcove that contained his cot and winked at him, completely unashamed of her nakedness or carnality. He'd been frightened when Margaret died, but then came the best years of his life.

Hot tears ran into the pillow as Jem remembered his time with the Everlys. He would never be Hugo's son, but he'd felt a sense of belonging, and a quiet, steady love that he hadn't known since. His father would have taken him to the wedding had he asked him to, but Jem couldn't bear to see all of them again and feel the pain of separation. He could never go back, and to see them all would just be salt on the wound of his broken heart. He'd excel at his lessons, learn about the estate, and hope that, in time, his father bequeathed him enough money to allow for some kind of independent existence. He didn't expect more than that, nor did he hope for more.

Jem eventually fell asleep with the letter still clutched in his hand, dreaming of walking by the Seine with Hugo and stopping off for a freshly made crepe liberally spread with butter and strawberry jam. How happy he had been then, and how naïve.

FORTY-SIX

MARCH 1689

London, England

Archie glared out the window at the darkness outside. A few windows still glowed with candlelight, but for the most part, the city was dark. Archie could have gone to bed, or out to a tavern for a game of dice, but he kept his vigil by the window, waiting for Hugo to return. He would have preferred to stay at an inn rather than Bradford Nash's London house, where the two doddering old servants floated about like ghostly specters. They were so used to their routine that having unexpected guests sent them into a near-panic, especially since Archie and Hugo needed food that required chewing. The old retainers barely had five teeth between them, and subsisted on pottage and gruel. Hugo assured them that he and Archie would just eat out at nearby taverns, but they insisted on preparing meals for them, going to more trouble than was worth since the food was barely edible.

Archie resumed his pacing. Next time, he would follow Hugo and keep an eye on him rather than sit around the house waiting like a neglected wife. His own wife wasn't too happy with him going off to London with Hugo, but she understood his duty to his master. Besides, a few days apart were healthy, in his opinion. Frances seemed happy, but Archie knew what was on her mind. She'd just gotten her monthly courses before he left, and he'd seen the look of despair in her eyes. No amount of assurances from him convinced her that he wasn't disappointed by her failure to conceive. It had only been two months since the wedding, so a child was hardly on Archie's mind, but Frances thought of little else.

He would have thought that constant exposure to Valentine and Michael would put a damper on Frances's urgent need for a baby. Archie loved the children, especially Valentine, who, in his opinion, should have been born a boy. She was willful, clever, and fearless, unlike little Michael who was afraid of his own shadow. The poor boy spent all day surrounded by women who fussed over him for lack of anything better to do. Of course, the child needed to be kept safe and healthy, but an occasional fall on his behind wouldn't hurt him. He needed freedom to explore his surroundings and learn from his mistakes. Neve, especially, hovered over the poor boy, walking behind him should he falter in his step, or running to soothe him the minute he began to cry.

Archie smiled as he remembered his own mother. She'd let him have the run of the house as soon as he could walk, and he had many a scorched smock and bruise from going where he shouldn't. His sister Julia had always been clean and tidy, and it drove his mother to near madness when Archie came home covered with mud or horse manure. She scolded him nonstop, forcing him to wash with cold water, something he'd hated.

Archie said a brief prayer for the souls of Julia's dead children and husband. He wished that his sister would rejoin the world of the living before their da passed, but that would never happen.

Pouring himself a cup of ale, Archie sat down in front of the fire, tired of pacing. He actually hoped that Frances would get with child, not because he was so eager to be a parent, but because it would put her mind at rest. She was so worried about what she'd done in Paris that nothing would pacify her, save a baby in her arms. Well, it certainly wasn't for lack of trying. Archie shifted in his chair, uncomfortably aware of his sudden arousal. Frances had been afraid at first, but her worry had evaporated after their wedding night, and she'd become quite the demanding madam, eager to perform her marital duties. Archie grinned at the thought. He loved that she was finally able to tell him what she wanted in bed, and that he was able to satisfy her. It warmed his heart to see her happy; her maidenly blush, when she ran into him during the day, sending a clear message of what was on her mind.

If he were honest with himself, Archie was terrified of having a child. He didn't love many people, but when he loved, he loved deeply and forever, and the thought of the vulnerability a child would bring scared him. He rarely thought of Julia's children now, but seeing the unbearable pain Elena's death had caused, he remembered only too well what it was like to lose someone you loved so dearly. It would destroy Frances, too. She'd already lost one child. What if she lost another?

"You are fretting like an old woman," Archie grumbled to himself. Perhaps it was time he found his bed, and actually slept for a change. He was getting a lot less sleep these days thanks to his lusty bride, but he was genuinely happy—an emotion he'd never thought to achieve.

FORTY-SEVEN

The door closed behind Hugo with a soft click, leaving him alone in the street. It was deserted at this hour, the sky overcast, with scuttling clouds obscuring the moon for brief intervals during which the street was nearly pitch-dark. It was dangerous to be out alone at this hour, even in this part of London populated by the wealthy and the titled.

Hugo glanced around and, seeing nothing to arouse his suspicions, set off for Brad's house, where Archie was no doubt waiting for him like a devoted wife. Hugo had considered bringing the young man along but had left him behind since a man-at-arms might draw attention to what would otherwise be perceived as just a social call, which is what this was meant to appear as.

Henry FitzRoy, 1st Duke of Grafton, had received Hugo graciously enough, although he did appear somewhat taken aback by the late hour. Henry was something of a night owl, so Hugo's visit was meant to catch the young man alone and in private. His wife, Isabella, had already retired, and Henry was reading in the library when Hugo was announced. He was normally a man of high fashion who favored long, curly wigs like his father Charles II, but at this hour, he was wearing just breeches and a linen shirt, his feet and calves covered only in mustard-yellow stockings. Henry's hair was cropped short, making him look more boy than man, and his face was remarkably smooth for such a late hour when most men would be covered in a day's worth of stubble.

Hugo had chosen not to write ahead of his visit, but to take Henry by surprise to gauge his reaction. The Marquis de Chartres had instructed Hugo to send all his intelligence through the Duke of Grafton, who was a loyal supporter of his uncle James II and a secret Catholic, having converted not long after his father's death. But Hugo couldn't bring himself to put his trust in the illegitimate son of Charles II and the notorious Barbara Villiers, the Duchess of Castlemaine. Henry's parents had both been shrewd and seasoned political animals, and with the recent events surrounding the abdication of James II and William's ascension to the throne, Hugo couldn't help questioning Henry's loyalties. He might be genuinely devoted to his uncle's cause, or biding his time to see which way the wind would blow. Hugo had met Henry FitzRoy some years ago at the Court of James II, but Henry had been too young at the time to leave much of an impression. He'd been a handsome youth, in an ostentatious kind of way, but Hugo couldn't recall anything of his character.

"Lord Everly, what a surprise," Henry had exclaimed as he'd invited Hugo to sit and offered him a cup of very good claret. "So, you've discovered my secret. I stay up half the night reading and pursuing various interests of mine when no one can disturb me." He shared this confidence in a low voice, as if it were a great secret and someone might overhear them. But the only person within hearing distance was the servant who'd let Hugo in, and he was fully aware of his master's habits.

"I do apologize for the interruption, Your Grace," Hugo supplied smoothly, taking the casual comment as a chastisement for calling so late. "I'm afraid I've come on a rather delicate matter and hoped to find you alone."

Henry set aside the magnifying glass he'd been using to study some point of interest on a spread-out map, and leaned back in his chair, affecting the air of someone ready to give his full attention to an unwelcome visitor.

"I believe we have an acquaintance in common," Hugo began, watching Henry like a hawk from beneath hooded lids.

"Oh?"

"The Marquis de Chartres sends his regards," Hugo said casually.

"Very kind of him, to be sure. I trust he's in good health?"

"He seemed to be the last I saw him," Hugo replied, waiting for Henry to say something else, but the young man remained quiet. Henry was giving nothing away, so Hugo had to proceed very carefully. He supposed it was encouraging that Henry FitzRoy didn't immediately take the bait and incriminate himself, but Hugo had no wish to incriminate himself either.

"The Marquis was under the impression that you might be able to help me contact some friends in France. Letters do take such an awfully long time to arrive, don't they? And are so often lost along the way," Hugo mused as he took a sip of claret.

"Yes, I do have a means of getting messages to France securely," Henry replied with a small smile. "A good nephew must always inquire after his uncle's health and send regards to the family. And Cousin Louis is such a dear, always eager for news of his kin, despite the demands of his kingdom."

"No one would fault you for taking an interest in your relations, Your Grace," Hugo agreed. "Keeping up with family is so important."

"I do, however, find that some people tend to take too much of an interest in our letters, mistaking affection and duty for something rather more sinister," Henry remarked as he continued to study Hugo with undisguised interest.

"These are uncertain times, Your Grace," Hugo replied smoothly.

"Indeed they are, which is why if I wish to say anything of import, I do so in code. A childish game really, but a necessary one. A precaution, if you will." Henry was enjoying himself now. His eyes were sparkling with good humor, and his full mouth was stretched into a knowing smile. They were speaking the same language now—the language of espionage.

"And a very wise one. Are you of the opinion that I should employ a cypher when writing to my friends?" Hugo asked casually.

"Without question. It's quite fun really. Once you get the hang of the thing, it's ridiculously simple. Shall I show you?"

"Please," Hugo said, leaning forward as Henry reached for a clean sheet of paper and a quill. Hugo had wondered how he would learn the necessary cypher since the Marquis never revealed to him the method of communication. Now he realized that Henry had been instructed to teach him the intricacies of secret communication.

"I've been using a simple substitution cypher in which I've moved the alphabet by six letters to start with. Therefore, A would be F, B would be G, and so on. Of course, if the letter is intercepted, it appears to be utter gibberish, but unless anyone can break the cypher, they are in the dark. To continue using the same cypher is risky, so every month I revise the cypher, moving the corresponding alphabet by two. So, the following month, A would be H, and B would be I."

Henry's eyes were now lively, and a charming blush appeared on his cheeks as he wrote out a short message to demonstrate his method. It was simple enough to code and decode if you knew the key, which was childishly simple. Hugo was tempted to point that out, but refrained, not wishing to offend Henry and imply that his cypher was simple-minded. Anyone who was able to decode the first letter would figure out the method easily enough and play with the first few words until they hit on a pattern which made sense.

"To write more than once a month is dangerous, so I would ask you to get your report to me by the middle of every month. I will consolidate your message with other sources and send the information on to our friend the Marquis. You may write down anything you think is of importance, no matter how trivial. Sometimes minor details reveal a bigger picture. I will expect your first report just after the coronation. Oh, and I would like your report in plain writing. I will do the coding since I am the only one who knows the order of the letters on a particular month. I will burn your report as soon as I've transcribed it. Are we agreed?"

"Yes, Your Grace," Hugo replied and rose to leave.

"I look forward to reading your intelligence," the duke said thoughtfully. "The Marquis de Chartres has despaired of you ever honoring your end of the bargain, so he will be glad to see that you are a man of your word after all. And I am sure he will be pleased to hear that you appear to be in good health. After all, so many misfortunes might befall a man in these turbulent times, wouldn't you agree?"

Hugo bowed to the duke stiffly and left the library. The servants seemed to have retired, so he let himself out into the street and closed the door behind him. The last comment was a veiled threat, Hugo was sure of that, and once again he felt an unwelcome tightening in his chest. The Duke of Grafton now held all the cards, which placed Hugo in a vulnerable position. He'd heard rumors that Henry FitzRoy had thrown in his lot with William after learning of his uncle's shameful and cowardly behavior. Either his support for William was a wise political move meant to camouflage his spying activities for James II and Louis XIV, or perhaps his loyalty had truly shifted, in which case Hugo had just walked into a trap. The only way Hugo could protect himself was to disguise his writing when composing a report, and make sure never to sign his name or use his own seal. As long as the report couldn't be definitively traced back to him, he was safe.

FORTY-EIGHT

Archie came downstairs in the morning to find Hugo sitting in front of the cold hearth, twirling a chess piece in his hand. He'd come in late last night and retired to his room, but Archie had heard him pacing for an hour at the very least, the floorboards groaning under his weight. Perhaps the meeting did not go as planned. Now, Hugo seemed completely preoccupied, his eyes glued to the black bishop as if all the answers could be found in the ebony depths.

"All right?" Archie asked as he sat across from Hugo.

"Hmm," Hugo replied, still staring at the piece, which he deftly moved between his fingers. "Have some breakfast. I've already eaten."

"I think I'll just purchase a pork pie," Archie replied. Billingsley's porridge did terrible things to his guts, forcing him to remain within close proximity of the privy for at least two hours after consumption. The old servants didn't bother with bread, since it was too crusty to chew, so there was nothing to break the fast on except the offensive porridge.

"Perhaps you'd like to purchase that pie in Cheapside," Hugo suggested, finally setting the bishop back on the board.

"And why would that be?" Archie asked with interest.

"Because that's where Gideon Warburton used to reside," Hugo replied cryptically.

"I don't follow."

Hugo leaned back in the chair and faced Archie, his head cocked to the side as if he were deep in thought. Archie remained silent, knowing Hugo too well to rush him. He was obviously on to something, but he was still thinking the details through.

"Gideon Warburton fell on hard times after Maximilian's trial," Hugo finally said. "Public opinion was against him for attempting to defend a traitor. According to Bradford Nash, Gideon fell in with a man called Julian Covington during this time, and then made the sudden decision to travel to the American Colonies. Gideon threw himself overboard shortly after leaving the shores of England, and the said Julian Covington was named in Gideon's Last Will and Testament as his beneficiary. Covington didn't get much money, but he did take possession of the house and all its contents," Hugo explained.

"And you suspect foul play," Archie concluded.

"I do."

"What's that to do with us?"

"Gideon Warburton suffered because of his involvement with me, Archie. I'd only met the man once, but he didn't strike me as someone who would be easily manipulated or driven to suicide. He was analytical, practical, and emotionally detached. What would drive a man like that to throw himself overboard, especially en route to a new life? Even if he'd changed his mind, he could have returned to England in a few months. Why kill himself?" Hugo demanded, daring Archie to give him a good answer.

"I don't know. It does seem strange, now you mention it."

"See what you can learn of this Julian Covington," Hugo said as he rose to his feet. "We can meet back here at noon."

"Am I permitted to ask where you're off to, Your Lordship?" Archie asked as he followed Hugo outside into the foggy March morning. The fog had rolled off the Thames during the night, and figures seemed to emerge from the mist, floating like apparitions. Even the usual morning sounds were muffled, giving the street a church-like hush.

Archie thought that his question had got swallowed up by the mist, but Hugo finally responded, his voice thoughtful.

"I'd like to pay someone a visit, Archie."

"Another private assignation?" Archie quipped, but there was a note of anxiety in his voice. He was worried, and he had good reason to be, but not this morning.

"Perhaps you can wait for me at the coffeehouse on the corner. We can get dinner and save our stomachs from another one of Mistress Billingsley's culinary creations."

"You don't have to ask me twice," Archie responded happily.

"And, as it happens, I'm going to see Mistress James," Hugo replied to Archie's earlier question.

"Right."

Hugo could hear the note of relief in Archie's response.

"I'll see you at noon then," Hugo said as he pulled on his gloves and set off on foot, keeping close to the houses for fear of getting under the wheels of some wagon that came out of the fog.

This particular call had nothing to do with treason—at least not of the political kind. Hugo hadn't seen Magdalen Hiddleston since she'd married Percy James some seven years ago. He'd been invited to the wedding and had attended, less to see Magdalen married, and more to spend time with his sister and nephew. Living alone at Everly Manor had weighed heavily on him then, his own failed marriage and childless state often on his mind. It had been a pleasant visit, with Jane seemingly excited by the wedding plans and probably eager to get rid of the stepdaughter she'd never particularly cared for. Ernest was in good spirits as well, although signs of illness were clearly visible, especially in retrospect.

Magdalen and her husband lived near Bishopsgate, a part of the city known for its coaching inns used by passengers setting out on the Old North Road. Hugo knew that Percy was a prosperous merchant of some sort, and it served his business interests to be in that particular location, but he couldn't claim to know exactly what Percy's business was. The Jameses' house was just up the street from the Catherine Wheel Inn.

A skinny child came toward him, her frail shoulders barely supporting the tray of oranges slung over them, her lips blue with cold. Having seen children in the twenty-first century, Hugo always felt an overwhelming pity for these poor urchins, who were cold and hungry at the best of times, and freezing to death and starving at the worst. This child had probably never had a proper meal or even a bed of her own. Her parents sent her out day after day to sell oranges—an occupation that would probably be her life's work until an untimely death.

Hugo pushed his morbid thoughts aside and approached the girl. "I'll take the lot," he said and handed her enough money to buy double the amount of oranges in the tray.

"I don't got no change, sir," she mumbled, terrified that Hugo would change his mind and leave.

"Not to worry. Just give me the whole tray. I don't have anything to put the oranges into."

The girl happily took off the tray and handed it to him after removing the strap. She looked stunned by her good fortune, unable to believe that she'd made enough money in under a minute to probably last her family a whole week. She smiled at Hugo shyly, her buckteeth strangely out of place in the little face. "Thank ye, sir." The girl gave an awkward curtsy and ran off before he could reconsider his impulsive purchase.

Hugo looked at his bounty. Neve was always going on about

the need for vitamin C to avoid scurvy, and after the long winter, Magdalen's family could probably do with a dose. Of course, they didn't know that, but they would simply enjoy the fruit.

Hugo knocked on the door and stood back a bit, surveying the house. Although built in the typical Tudor style, the ground floor was made of stone, which was a sure sign of prosperity, and the ornamental chimneys rose proudly from the slate-covered roof, not the usual thatch. The first floor extended over the ground floor, casting the front door in permanent shadow, but the diamond-paned windows were rather wide and gleamed in the near white light which tried to break through the morning mist, now being slowly burnt off by the weak sun.

A young girl of about twelve opened the door and stared at Hugo, her mouth open in surprise. Perhaps it was too early in the day for visitors, or perhaps it was his appearance, which was highly at odds with the tray of oranges he held in front of him.

"Master James is not at 'ome, sir," she supplied timidly.

"I'm here to see your mistress. Please tell her Lord Everly wishes to speak with her. And take these. They are a gift for Mistress James."

The girl gaped at him as if he were the king himself. She didn't have much interaction with members of the peerage, and Percy's business associates were likely wealthy men, but not titled ones. Hugo also realized that she'd probably never even had an orange.

"Take one for yourself," he added.

"Ah, aye sir. Please come in, sir," the girl stammered as she led Hugo to a parlor and ran upstairs to get her mistress.

The room was lost in shadow due to the overhanging upper floor, but it was clean and lavishly decorated with soft cushions on the wooden settles and tapestries on the walls. Hugo turned from studying the tapestry when he heard light footsteps on the flagstone floor.

"Your Lordship, what a surprise," Magdalen said as she sailed into the room, her belly preceding her. She was clearly in the last stages of pregnancy, but it became her, giving her a healthy glow instead of a patina of exhaustion.

"I seem to be surprising people a lot these days," Hugo replied with a smile, glad to see that Magdalen didn't seem put out by his visit.

"Shall I call for some refreshments?" she asked, gazing into the dim corridor to see if the maid was there. "Or would you like an orange?" she asked with a chuckle.

"No, thank you, and the oranges are for you. I hope you enjoy them. My wife always asks that I bring some back from London," Hugo added by way of explanation. "Actually, I won't take much of your time. I'm glad to see you looking so well, Magdalen," he commented.

Magdalen had always been a pretty girl, but many a pretty girl lost her looks after marriage. Magdalen wasn't one of them. Her blonde curls artfully framed her full face, her cheeks and lips rosy with good health, and her wide blue eyes sparkling with good humor. There was nothing of her father in her features, and now that Hugo knew the truth about Ernest, he understood why. Magdalen probably wasn't his natural daughter, but a child conceived with a handsome groom or some local man from the village. Ernest's interests did not extend to women, as both his wives would attest to had they been alive.

"Is this your first?" Hugo asked, nodding at her belly.

"Oh no, my lord. 'Tis our third. We've already got the two girls, so hoping for a son this time. I do think it might be," she confided happily. "And if not, there's always next time."

"When do you start your confinement?" Hugo asked.

"Not for another month at least, and thank the Lord for that. I do so want to see the coronation procession. I would be that heartbroken if I had to be shut away in a dark room and miss all the fun."

"So, you approve of your new king then?" Hugo asked with a grin. Her good humor was infectious.

"'Tis not for me to approve or disapprove, but I'm always keen on a good celebration. 'Twill be a day to remember, I'm sure."

Magdalen settled herself by the hearth and invited Hugo to sit down across from her. Her hand rested on her belly as she sighed with pleasure.

"I don't get to sit much during the day, not with two little ones. They do keep me busy, so thank you for this welcome break."

Hugo realized that Magdalen was too polite to ask what brought him to her door, so it was for him to broach the subject. He almost dreaded talking of what had happened, but at this stage, Magdalen was the only person who could shed any light on what was going on with Clarence.

"Magdalen," Hugo began, "I've written to Clarence from France several times over the past few years, and once since returning to England, but although he was polite enough to respond, he seems reluctant to see me in person."

Magdalen shifted in her seat, her eyes thoughtful as she considered her response. Hugo knew she didn't wish to offend him, but she wasn't the type of girl to moderate her answers, which was something he'd always liked about her. Neve would say that Magdalen was "real," and he agreed.

"Clarence was torn up when his mother died. It would have been bad enough had she passed as a result of an illness, but going the way she had nearly destroyed him. He was in shock, and probably still is. Clarence wanted more than anything to believe that his mother hadn't chosen to take her own life; that she'd been driven to it," Magdalen said, her eyes sliding away toward the fire.

"So, he blamed me," Hugo supplied.

"Yes, he did. Clarence needed to excuse his mother's

actions and blaming you for driving her to suicide allowed him to do that."

"But I didn't actually do anything," Hugo protested.

"I know you didn't, but by the time Jane died, her mind was so twisted, she could explain away anything. I do believe that her suicide was a form of self-punishment. She believed that she didn't deserve the glory of Heaven and everlasting life, so she made sure she'd be damned for eternity. Clarence wanted to believe that his mother killed herself because she couldn't live with the guilt, but I think the truth is quite different."

"How so?" Hugo asked, curious to hear Magdalen's take on Jane's fatal decision.

"I suppose Jane felt some guilt over what she did to your lady, but she believed she was doing it to protect her son's future, so her remorse was fleeting. What Jane really dreaded was the prolonged illness, which would leave her incapable of caring for herself and would rob her of all reason. She'd seen what it had done to my father and to his secretary, John Spencer, whom she'd had a liaison with. She didn't think I knew of their trysts, but I was a very observant child, and they weren't all that careful. I hope that doesn't shock you," Magdalen said, suddenly realizing that Hugo might not want to know such intimate things about the sister he'd loved.

"No, I was aware of her relationship with Spencer. She told me of it herself the last time we met."

"Jane had nursed the man during his last months, believing it to be her Christian duty, but I think there was a part of her that still loved him, despite the fact that he probably gave her the illness," Magdalen said, her voice sad as she contemplated the broken lives of the people who surrounded her during her childhood. "The idea of wasting away in both body and mind was more than she could bear, so she decided to die on her own terms, believing herself to be damned already for her infidelity."

"Is there any advice you could give me about Clarence?"

Hugo asked wistfully. "I would like to see him and talk to him in person. I can understand his anger and resentment, but I refuse to be held accountable for my sister's death."

"Forgive me for saying this, Your Lordship, but Clarence has always been a spiteful, irrational boy. He was filled with venom while he stayed here after his mother's death, and truth be told, I was glad to see the back of him, as was Percy. You can force a reconciliation and hope for the best, but I would just let him stew for a time. He needs to see for himself that you are not to blame and that he has no right to your estate, which he sees as having been snatched away from him."

"I see," Hugo said as he got up to leave. "Thank you for seeing me, Magdalen. I do wish you well and hope we will see each other again before too long."

"You are always welcome here, my lord. Percy will be sorry to have missed you."

Hugo took Magdalen's hand and kissed it respectfully before walking out the door. Magdalen hadn't said anything he hadn't suspected himself, but hearing it from her did make him feel somewhat lighter. Perhaps she was right, and he should leave Clarence be. The boy was old enough to know his own mind, and putting pressure on him would accomplish little of value. Until he was ready to see that Jane had made her own bed, there wasn't much he could do, nor would he apologize for getting married and siring an heir despite Jane's hopes that her son would remain his beneficiary. He'd apologized for his behavior long enough; now he had to look to the future and see his family safe.

FORTY-NINE

Archie slowly approached the house in Cheapside. It was in Bow Lane, one of the narrow side streets off the main thoroughfare, and not at all far from Bradford Nash's house. Archie had considered his plan of action as he walked over, but still had no idea where to begin. Simply knocking on the front door would not get him the answers he needed, and watching the house would accomplish little since he couldn't see inside, and the weather was too foul for anyone to be out.

Archie stopped across the street and looked up at the damp façade for a few minutes before he spotted a serving girl stepping out with a shopping basket slung over her arm. She looked up at the gray sky and huddled deeper into her shawl, ready to brave the elements. Archie approached the girl with a bright smile. "Hello, my pretty," he called out, leaving enough space between them so as not to make her feel threatened. Having a strange man approach a woman in an empty street rarely boded well for the woman in question, and the last thing Archie wanted to do was spook her or give her reason for alarm.

The maid was in her twenties, with a rosy complexion and merry eyes. She raised her chin defiantly in an effort to show that she wasn't afraid, but instinctively took a step back toward the house just in case.

"Hello, yourself," the girl finally answered. "Looking for someone, luv?" She remained standing in front of the house, where she could dash back inside should the situation demand it. Archie didn't blame her; a woman on her own was never truly safe, not even in some of the better areas of London.

"Yes," Archie replied, improvising on the spot. "A man of law used to live here. Gideon Warburton. I am in need of some legal counsel, and he comes highly recommended."

The girl shrugged. "Never heard of him, but then, I'm fairly new here. Came down from Lincoln with my master and his family not six months ago."

"Is he a man of law, your master?" Archie asked hopefully.

"Oh, no. He's a silversmith. Has a shop two streets over. Master Forsythe is his name. He might not be a man of law, but he does fairly well for himself, that I can tell you. Well enough to afford this grand house. This is a right palace compared to the modest dwelling him and his lady had in Lincoln."

"That must be nice for them," Archie commented, eager to keep her going. He could see that she welcomed the chance to vent her ire and was only too eager to listen. People often revealed more than they intended when allowed to talk, especially if the listener appeared sympathetic.

"Nice for them it is. Not so nice for the rest of us. Three times as much to clean and dust, and all for the same meager wage. And now them be wanting to eat like the nobility too. No more pottage and stew for the likes of Master Forsythe. Oh no. Cook sends me to the market near every day in search of choice cuts of meat and fresh fish. The master desires a more sophisticated table to impress his new friends. Well, 'tis only himself he seems to be impressing."

"Aye, it must be hard for you, lass," Archie agreed, nodding his head. "A comely thing like you should have her own home and hearth to tend to, not some master's."

The girl's expression instantly soured. Archie had clearly hit a sore spot. "Well, I should, shouldn't I, but my sweetheart let me go off to London without so much as a by-your-leave, he did. Said he wasn't ready to be wed. So, no; I don't have my own home and hearth and won't for some time. Now, what of you? Are you a married man?" she asked, suddenly recognizing the opportunity and making the decision not to let it pass her by.

She was a fiery thing, Archie would give her that, but it was time to take himself off. There was nothing more of value he could learn from this serving girl.

"I am to be wed next month, as it happens, and it's rather fortuitous that your master is a silversmith as I am in need of a ring for my future wife," he confided, lowering his voice. He felt momentary pity for the look of disappointment in the girl's eyes, but she'd get over it soon enough. She was too pretty to remain alone for long.

"Best of luck to you then," the girl replied as she began walking away, the handsome stranger suddenly not nearly as interesting. Archie noted her rigid back and hurried step. She'd assumed he was interested in her and probably felt humiliated by his perceived rejection.

Archie turned on his heel and began to walk in the opposite direction. Her feelings were of no consequence to him.

Archie returned to Cheapside and found Forsythe's shop in mere minutes. The man was standing behind the counter, having just opened up for business. Archie liked him on sight, despite what his maid said. He was portly and balding but had a welcoming smile and a twinkle in his eye, indicating a friendly nature. It was always easier to glean information from a person who was willing to talk rather than some surly sod who was much harder to engage in conversation.

"Good morrow," the silversmith said as Archie entered the shop. "How may I be of service?"

The shop was small and dim, but it looked clean, and the wooden counter and heavy armoire made up of rows of little drawers shone with polish. A workbench was situated in the corner closest to the window where the man must make his wares. Several unfamiliar tools were on display, and scraps of silver littered the surface.

"I am to be married, and need a wedding ring for my betrothed," Archie replied as he approached the counter.

"You've come to the right place then, my good man. I have several different styles to choose from. Do you know her size?"

"Her ring finger is the same size as my little finger," Archie supplied, holding up his hand.

"Splendid. And what type of ring did you have in mind? Would your lady prefer something delicate or something more substantial, with perhaps some gemstones or an engraved pattern?"

Archie gave this question some thought. Frances would probably like something dainty. Her hands were small with long, graceful fingers, so a heavy band would look out of place.

"I think perhaps something delicate," Archie replied. "But I am sure she'd like a bit of decoration as well."

"Allow me to show you what I have." The man turned toward the armoire and opened a few drawers, extracting several different rings. They were beautiful pieces with intricate patterns, some set with stones. Perhaps buying a ring for Frances wasn't such a bad idea. He'd placed a plain silver circlet on her finger when they wed, but Frances deserved something prettier, something that reflected her personality, rather than just a plain, unadorned band.

Archie considered all the rings and reached for a thin band of lacy filigree. He slid it onto his little finger and held up his hand to examine the effect. Frances would like it; he was sure of that.

"I've never noticed your shop before," Archie said as he continued to turn his hand this way and that.

"Oh, I am new to these parts," the man said, clearly eager to talk. "Came down from Lincoln."

"I've been there just the once. Beautiful cathedral," Archie replied eagerly. He'd never been to Lincoln, but had heard of its famed cathedral and knew that people from the city were very proud of it.

"Oh, indeed it is. One of the most beautiful in England, I would venture to say," Master Forsythe agreed.

"What brought you to London?" Archie asked casually as he set the filigree ring aside and chose another one to try on. "That's quite a long way."

The silversmith grew visibly uncomfortable, his eyes shifting away from Archie. "Oh, personal reasons."

Whatever the man had done didn't interest Archie. He was just making conversation and had no desire to pry.

Archie nodded as if he understood only too well and lifted his hand to admire the ring he was trying on. "Were you able to find a residence nearby? This part of town is so populated, difficult to find decent accommodation."

"Oh, yes." The man brightened, eager to continue chatting. "I bought a house two streets over, and for a very reasonable price. One man's loss is another man's gain, aye?"

"How do you mean?"

"Master Covington, from whom I'd purchased the house, had recently lost his wife, and found it unbearable to remain in the home they'd made together. Sold the house with everything in it. Wanted a fresh start, he said. We did bring some bits and pieces with us from up north, but only what we could load in the wagon. Imagine getting all the furniture, household goods, and even paintings without having to spend a fortune," the silversmith exclaimed, clearly still amazed by his good luck.

"Fortuitous, indeed. And what became of Master Covington?"

"He said he was sailing to the American Colonies in April. Had the passage already arranged." The man scratched his balding head as if trying to remember something. "The ship had an odd name. Now, what was it? Ah, yes, the *Persephone*. Never heard of such a name in all my life."

"An odd-sounding name if I've ever heard one," Archie agreed. "I'll take this one," he said, picking up the filigree band again.

"A splendid choice. Your lady will be most pleased. Shall I package it up for you or will you wear it?"

"Package it up, Master Forsythe," Archie replied as he paid for his purchase.

He watched as the silversmith placed the ring into a small pouch made of soft leather and handed it to Archie. Archie felt a momentary glow as he imagined giving the ring to Frances and stuffed his purchase deep into the pocket of his coat. He'd have to wait for Franny's reaction until returning home tomorrow.

FIFTY

Archie inhaled the aroma of roast mutton as the plate was placed in front of him by a serving wench, grateful for a good meal to sink his teeth into. He'd forgotten to get a pork roll that morning and was ravenously hungry. Hugo didn't appear to be as impressed with his meal as Archie, but he did drain his mug of ale and held it out for a refill. Archie couldn't quite gauge his mood after the visit to Mistress James, so decided not to ask. Hugo's visit to Magdalen was on private business, and if he wanted to talk about it, he would.

"Have you learned anything, Archie?" Hugo asked as he took a bite of his meal and chewed thoughtfully. Hugo never fell on his food, even if he were starving—a true mark of a gentleman in Archie's opinion. Archie wanted to devour his mutton but had to restrain himself to one mouthful before replying to Hugo's question.

"Julian Covington sold Gideon's house some months ago. The buyer got the lot: furniture, household goods, and even pictures. Seems Covington didn't wish to keep anything. Told the buyer that he'd lost his wife and couldn't bear to remain in the house."

"Is that all?" Hugo asked, his face dropping in disappointment.

"No, there's more," Archie said through a mouthful of mutton. "He said he was sailing to the American Colonies in April, on a ship called the *Persephone*."

Archie was gratified to see a change come over Hugo as he put down his knife and spoon, his mouth stretching in a satisfied smile. Clearly, this information meant something.

"What did I say?" Archie asked, surprised by the reaction from his master.

"Plenty. Brad mentioned that Gideon sailed to the New World on a ship called the *Persephone*. It's a strange coincidence that Master Covington should mention the same vessel."

"Strange name, too," Archie mused. "Doesn't sound English."

"It's not. It's from Greek mythology. Persephone was the goddess of the Underworld."

"Even stranger then," Archie observed. "Why would you want to name a ship after someone who is known to rule over the dead? I'd think that's inviting bad luck, don't you?"

Hugo shrugged, unimpressed with Archie's theory. He was lost in thought. "April, you said?"

"Yes, why?"

"I'd like to have a word with this Julian Covington. Or, rather, I'd like you to have a word with him; see what type of man he is."

"And what shall I ask him, should I find him? He's not likely to tell me outright if he'd done something to defraud Master Warburton," Archie pointed out reasonably.

"No, I don't suppose he is," Hugo agreed as he returned to his meal, now eating with more relish.

"Shall I use more persuasive methods?" Archie asked innocently.

"Use whatever methods you see fit," Hugo replied. "I trust

your good judgment, Archie. I would like to return home tomorrow, so perhaps today would be a good day to start making your enquiries."

"In that case, I'd like another serving of mutton. Making enquiries is hungry work," Archie grumbled. He hadn't liked Gideon Warburton, nor did he care what befell him. True, the man had agreed to help Hugo, but he was handsomely paid for his services. He reminded Archie of a dead pig—his beady eyes devoid of any emotion and his body dumpy and shapeless. And it wasn't just his appearance that put Archie off; there was just something about the man he didn't trust, even if he was Master Nash's kin by marriage.

Archie prided himself on being a student of human nature and someone who took notice of things others might not. He didn't care to bring this up with Hugo, but there was something about Gideon Warburton that struck him as odd. It wasn't just his appearance; it was something in his demeanor. Lady Everly was not the type of woman most men would look through, but the man had hardly given her a glance, instead focusing most of his attention on Bradford Nash and Lord Everly. It was normal that he should, them being his clients, but it was the way he had looked at them. There was a spark of interest there—sexual interest, especially when he had glanced at Bradford. Hugo had mentioned that Julian Covington bore a striking resemblance to Bradford Nash. Was that significant? Archie wondered.

"You are not doing it for Gideon Warburton; you are doing it for me," Hugo clarified, as if reading Archie's thoughts. "I can't rest easy knowing that a man took his life because of me. I must know what really happened."

Archie gave Hugo a nod of acquiescence, not wishing to discuss the subject any further. *Sod Gideon Warburton*, he thought savagely. *I just want to get back to my Franny.*

FIFTY-ONE

After four fruitless hours of going from tavern to tavern, the only thing that Archie could claim was that he was footsore and annoyed. Either Julian Covington was a man who didn't frequent public houses, or he used another name. Or, perhaps he'd left London already, having changed his plans. It was the end of March, so ships had started sailing across the Atlantic. Mayhap the man was in a rush to leave England, and the memories of his wife, if he ever had one, behind. Archie had been to at least a dozen taverns around Cheapside and Blackfriars; perhaps he needed to go farther afield. Five more taverns, and he was calling it a day. Hugo would just have to accept that the man was not to be found in one afternoon, if at all.

The rain of that morning had cleared up during the afternoon, but a chill breeze blew off the Thames, and the temperature dropped once it began to grow dark. The raw damp of being close to the river penetrated Archie's cloak and made him feel unusually cold, the reek of wet mud and rotting fish infuriating him further. It never got this cold in Surrey in his opinion, nor did it smell as bad, but, then again, he rarely just walked around for hours searching for a needle in a haystack. Archie pulled his hat lower over his eyes and huddled deeper into his cloak, as he continued down the street in search of his next stop.

Two more taverns yielded no results. It was getting near to supper time, and Archie found that despite two helpings of mutton at noon, he was hungry. Thirsty too. He would eat at the next tavern and then visit a few more and go back to Bradford's house. He continued toward the Strand and was glad to see the sign for the Lamb and Flag tavern a few feet up ahead. He'd try that one.

Warm light spilled into the darkened street, and the smell of food wafted through the door as it opened and closed, disgorging patrons into the street. Although it seemed that more people were going in than out. This was the time of day when working people finally closed up their shops and abandoned their stalls and headed home or to their favorite public house for some supper and a well-earned rest.

Archie sighed with pleasure as he stepped into the smoky warmth of the Lamb and Flag. This tavern wasn't as dingy as some of the others, the patrons being men of means rather than just poor folk who could ill-afford a tankard of ale. It smelled much like any other tavern, of spilled ale and too many bodies, but the customers were somewhat better dressed, and several wore curly periwigs, a sure sign that this place catered to a more refined clientele.

Archie spotted an empty table in the corner and made his way over, eager to sit down after walking for so long. He smiled to himself ruefully as he realized how disgruntled he felt. It wasn't like him to be so out of sorts, and he had to grudgingly admit that he was angry to be away from Frances for so long. They hadn't been apart for any length of time since he had fetched her from the convent in the woods on their way to France, and had shared a house with her every single day since then. This was their first separation, and he was feeling the pangs of homesickness, not a feeling he was readily familiar with.

Archie hadn't felt homesick since Julia's family had died of the putrid throat all those years ago. His parents' home went from being a place of warmth and love to a place of loneliness and grief, especially after his mother died and only his father remained. Archie visited his father as often as he could, but couldn't bear to stay too long, still hearing in his mind the laughter of Julia's children when they visited, and the soft voice of his mother as she talked to his sister or sang to herself while she prepared supper.

Archie pushed his melancholy thoughts aside and signaled to the barmaid, who wove her way between the tables and approached him with a smile of welcome. She was a young girl, no older than seventeen, with a mass of dark curls spilling from her cap, and sparkling blue eyes. The girl was pleasantly plump, and had deep dimples when she smiled, her jolly expression suddenly dispelling Archie's glumness.

"What's on offer tonight?" Archie asked. He didn't care as long as it was hot and would fill his belly.

"There's boiled beef with mashed turnips an' mutton stew. I'd go for the beef meself," the girl advised Archie quietly, giving him a meaningful look.

Archie didn't bother to inquire what was wrong with the stew. He'd had mutton for his midday meal anyway. "All right, boiled beef it is, and a tankard of ale. Bring some bread, too," Archie instructed.

"That'll cost ye extra," the girl said as she continued to study him.

"I'll pay." The girl turned to leave, but Archie had to ask her about Julian Covington. He had no expectations of finding the man here, but he might as well be diligent. "What's your name, love?" Archie asked playfully, eager to keep the girl from leaving.

"Moll."

"Would you know of a man called Julian Covington, Moll? I've been searching for him all day."

"Are ye a friend of 'is then?" the girl asked suspiciously. Archie noticed a twinge of distaste on the girl's round face.

"Aye, I am. Do you know him?"

The girl's smile vanished from her face, leaving her eyes stormy and mistrustful. "Didn't take ye for 'is sort," she mumbled as she tried to back away.

"And what sort is that?"

"Never ye mind," Moll replied stubbornly. "'E comes in 'ere most days. Sits over yonder." She pointed to an alcove in the corner, which was empty at the moment.

"What sort, Moll?" Archie persisted, eager to know as much as he could about the man.

"I ain't supposed to talk about it. And if ye're 'is friend, ye'd know, wouldn't ye?"

With that, Moll walked away to get his food. Archie stared after her, his mind awhirl. So, he had found the watering hole of Julian Covington, but there were things he needed to know about the man before approaching, and Moll wasn't about to tell him without further inducement.

Archie looked up as Moll returned with his beef and ale, a coin already in his hand. He skillfully twirled the coin between his fingers, making sure that the girl noticed it as she set down the plate of beef. Fragrant steam rose from the plate, making Archie's stomach growl with hunger, but eating had to wait. Again.

Archie stopped twirling the coin and held it up in front of Moll's face. "Tell me what I need to know, and the coin is yours."

"'Ow do I know ye'll really give it to me?" She was a mistrustful one, and probably with good reason.

"Here." Archie placed the coin on the corner of the table

closest to Moll. "Place your hand over it if it makes you feel better. I will pay for the information, but it best be worth the money."

"Oh, o'right." Moll glanced around nervously as she placed her hand over the coin. "Julian Covington likes gentlemen," she whispered. "'E comes in 'ere, orders a brandy, and waits for 'is opportunity. Many a night 'e doesn't find what 'e came for, but 'tis no' only carnal pleasure 'e's after. 'E befriends gentlemen, wins their trust."

"And then what?" Archie asked.

"I don't know 'xactly, do I? No' like I'm invited to sit down with 'em for a quiet palaver."

"Come now, Moll; a serving wench knows all, especially about men who come in regularly. And you look like a right clever girl."

Moll colored with pleasure at the compliment but moved the coin closer to the edge of the table. "I think 'e murders 'em," she whispered.

"Why would you say that?" Archie demanded, taken aback by her answer.

"Cause no' long after meetin' 'im, they stop comin' in."

"Is there anyone he meets with regularly?" Archie asked as he placed his hand over Moll's to keep her from running off.

"There's one man 'e meets with from time to time. A sea captain."

"Does Covington like to make small talk, or does he keep himself to himself?" Archie asked.

Moll gave him a dubious glance, wondering why he'd want this type of information about someone he supposedly knew. "'E generally keeps to 'isself when 'e first comes in, but 'e likes his brandy, 'specially when 'tis paid for by someone else. 'E is a tight-fisted sod, 'e is. The drink loosens 'is lips, and right quick. 'E can't hold 'is liquor for naught. And that's all I mean to tell ye, or I'll lose me position an' I got a nipper to feed. Not worth lettin' me babe go 'ungry over the likes of ye."

Moll pulled her hand from beneath Archie's, grabbed the coin and fled, leaving Archie to ponder the information. He always thought better on a full stomach, so he tucked into his meal with relish. The beef was rather good—not too dry, and clearly fresh. And the mashed turnips were moist with melted butter. Archie tore off a chunk of bread and popped it into his mouth as he considered what Moll had said.

So, Julian Covington was a homosexual who used this tavern as a place to meet potential lovers. If Gideon Warburton was a homosexual, as Archie suspected, then that would explain the connection between the two men. Archie gazed around, suddenly wondering if this place catered to those types of men, but didn't see anyone who stood out. He supposed they knew each other somehow, or maybe of each other. There were at least two brothels that Archie knew of that were for men who liked boys, but perhaps Julian Covington was after something else. Moll had said that the men disappeared shortly after meeting him, just as Gideon Warburton had. And what of this sea captain? Was that a factor?

Archie stopped chewing as he noticed a well-dressed man enter the tavern. He wasn't wearing a wig over the thick golden hair that fell to his shoulders. The man's face was lean, dominated by warm, blue eyes which crinkled when he smiled. He nodded to several patrons and took a seat in the alcove Moll had indicated but didn't summon a serving maid. A cup of brandy was placed before him within moments of arrival, and there was a minute of cheerful banter between him and the serving wench before she accepted payment for the brandy and left. Archie continued to eat as he discreetly studied the man. There was something of Bradford Nash about his looks, just as Hugo had suggested, and he carried himself like a gentleman. Archie snuck a peek at Covington's hands. They were white and smooth; not the hands of a man who'd ever done any work. So, he was a man of means, inherited or otherwise.

Archie considered his options. Approaching the man seemed pointless as he'd either just dismiss him or feed him a pack of lies. He'd finish his meal, have another tankard of ale, then leave the tavern and wait for the man to make his way home. Hugo gave him leave to use any means possible, and he would. Covington looked like the type of man who'd run away from a fight and would divulge anything Archie needed to know if threatened. There was no need to cause the man any actual harm, but if it came to it, Archie wasn't averse to showing him who was in charge of the conversation. Either way, he'd get what he came for.

Satisfied with this strategy, Archie leaned back in his chair, having finished his beef, and took a long pull of ale. Archie was taken by surprise when he noticed the man's gaze settle on him. Covington's head was tipped to the side and his mouth stretched into a seductive smile, the kind of smile a man would bestow on a woman he hoped to win. Archie swallowed a sip of the ale and returned the smile, raising his tankard in a toast. Two could play that game. Hugo always jokingly said that Archie was pretty; well, perhaps he was pretty enough to attract the attention of Julian Covington and extract the information he needed. It would be preferable to use his wits, instead of violence for a change.

Archie pushed the plate away and cradled his tankard, still acutely aware of Covington's gaze. The man was watching him, but Archie wasn't ready to make a move just yet. It was too soon. He signaled Moll to refill his cup and leaned back in his chair, sated and relaxed. At least he needn't continue his search; he'd found his man, and would put an end to this business tonight, as Hugo had requested.

Archie took a sip and finally turned his head, making eye contact with Julian Covington. The man's eyes glowed, that sardonic smile still on his face. Archie stiffened in surprise as the man rose from his seat and began to slowly walk in his direction. The game was afoot.

"Good evening," Covington said as he approached Archie's table. "I must confess that I hate drinking alone. It makes one feel so isolated from his fellow man."

Archie swallowed down the desire to point out that it was difficult to be isolated from your fellow man in a tavern full of people. Everyone was talking and laughing, and all one had to do was leave the sanctuary of the alcove and join the crowd at the bar to feel a part of things.

"Yes," Archie replied. "I was meant to meet someone, but I'm afraid he failed to show."

"Would you join me for a drink?" Covington asked.

Archie motioned toward the empty chair at his table, but Covington shook his head.

"Come to my table. It's so much quieter. Easier to talk. And get to know each other," he added softly.

Archie bowed in acknowledgment, picked up his tankard, and followed Covington toward his table. Julian Covington slid back into the alcove gracefully, folding his elegant hands in front of him on the table. Archie couldn't help noticing that the man was a bit older than he first took him to be. He was forty, at least, but his skin was smooth and clear, and his physique was lithe, no signs of thickening around the middle or softening of the jowls. He was a very attractive man, but there was just a hint of femininity about him, and something flirtatiously playful, which was oddly disturbing in a man of his age.

Covington tipped his head to the side again and glanced at Archie from beneath his lashes, as coy as a young maiden. "Do you have a name, or shall I just call you 'Red'?"

"It's Archibald," Archie replied softly. "And you are?"

"Julian. A pleasure to meet you, Archibald. Is it Archie for short?"

"To my friends."

"Then I beg the pleasure of being your friend," Julian replied flirtatiously.

Archie just smiled back, unsure how to reply. The man was certainly forward. Instead, Archie motioned for the barmaid to bring Julian another brandy. Julian inclined his head in thanks and reached for the drink.

"You are not from around here, are you?" Julian asked as he studied Archie's rough hands and serviceable attire.

"No, I come from Surrey. I've come up to London looking for work," Archie added. "My employment was terminated recently, and a friend from my village thought he might fix me up with a job."

"And what was it you were employed at?" Julian asked, but raised his finger to forestall Archie's answer. "No, let me guess. You are strong, but you don't have the look of a farmer about you. A blacksmith perhaps?"

"Why do you say that?" Archie asked, suddenly enjoying this game. The man really was entertaining.

"You have such strong hands." Julian Covington reached over and took one of Archie's hands, his eyes never leaving Archie's face.

"No, not a blacksmith."

"What then?"

"I was a man-at-arms," Archie confided, waiting to see what Julian would make of that.

"Ah, a fighting man. A protector. How very appropriate. And what happened to your master, Archie?" Julian asked, curious.

"Let's just say that the current political climate didn't suit him."

"I see. So, you find yourself adrift in the world." Julian made it sound as if Archie were a drowning man, but his eyes caressed Archie as if he were offering to save him.

"Not adrift, exactly, but searching for a safe harbor." Lord, did he really just say that? Archie felt a blush creep up his neck. He was sitting here playing coy with a man. Thank the Lord Franny wasn't here to see this display, or Hugo. He would find this deeply amusing.

"Hmm, I wonder if I might be of help to someone of your particular talents," Julian mused out loud.

"Are you in need of protection, Julian?" Archie asked, eager to see where this conversation would lead.

"I might be. Someone like me is always in danger, wouldn't you say?"

"Someone like you?"

Julian Covington didn't reply but took Archie's hand again and began to stroke Archie's palm with his thumb, moving it in sensual circles. Archie wanted to yank his hand away, but he wasn't finished with Covington yet, and this was surprisingly diverting.

"I have rooms not far from here," Covington whispered, almost as if to himself. "They are quite comfortable, and you are welcome to spend the night if you wish."

Archie pretended to think while buying himself some time to evaluate the situation. He was sure that Covington would be a lot more forthcoming in private, but he might also expect Archie to respond to sexual advances, and Archie wasn't prepared to go that far—not even for Hugo.

"I wouldn't dream of abusing your hospitality, Julian. Unless you were offering me lodgings as my future employer," Archie improvised.

"I bet you're good with your sword," Covington smiled happily. "All right, I suppose I could give you a try. I need a man of discretion, one who wouldn't ask too many questions."

"I am not interested in what you do, just in how much you pay," Archie replied.

"Is it just payment in coin you're interested in, or would

something a little more pleasurable interest you as well?" Julian
slid his right hand beneath the table. Archie nearly jumped out
of his skin when he felt the man's hand on his cock, massaging
lightly. Archie willed himself to sit still and ignore the man's
touch, but his traitorous cock began to stiffen, bringing a smile
to Julian's face. "I see that's open for discussion."

I have to finish this up before things get out of hand, Archie
thought as he carefully removed Julian's hand from his crotch.
Covington wasn't pleased, but he placed his hand back on the
table where Archie could see it, deterred, but not defeated.

Archie ordered Julian another brandy to soften the blow of
his rejection. Julian eyed it greedily before taking a slow sip. He
wasn't drunk, but he was pleasantly intoxicated and steadily on
his way to full-blown inebriation.

"I want to know exactly what it is you'd wish me to do,"
Archie said to Covington.

"Have a conscience, do you?" Julian asked playfully.

"No, but I set a value on my services based on what's
required of me," Archie replied, his attitude now businesslike.

Julian Covington's face went from playful to closed, his eyes
narrowing in speculation. He was wondering if he could trust
Archie, so Archie just sat back, his own expression as bland as
he could manage. He didn't expect Covington to confide in him,
but maybe he could glean something he could work with.
Archie crossed his arms and waited, watching the internal
battle wage within the man. Did he think that Archie would
submit his body if he got hired? Perhaps he needed to reassure
him.

Archie forced himself to relax and reached for Julian's
hand. He squeezed it gently as he smiled into his eyes. Julian
froze for a moment, but then relaxed and returned Archie's
smile. Still, he remained silent.

"Will I be expected to kill?" Archie tried again.

"No, you won't. What would give you such an idea?"

Covington asked, widening his eyes in mock astonishment. "I would require your services more for protection of my person."

"And who does your person need protecting from?" Archie asked with a smile, trying to cut through Julian's reluctance to talk.

"Why don't you come back to my lodgings, and I'll explain," Julian Covington suggested. "We can't talk freely here."

"All right," Archie replied, suddenly uneasy. This wasn't going quite as he'd planned, but he couldn't give up now. He was onto something, and he intended to find out just what game Julian Covington was playing, and with whom.

FIFTY-TWO

Archie followed Julian Covington out of the Lamb and Flag into the swirling darkness of the March evening. He wasn't wearing a sword, since he didn't think it necessary, but he did have faith in his fighting skills should things get nasty, and a dagger tucked into his boot if he needed a weapon. He liked to be prepared for every eventuality, but there was no reason to worry. Julian was hardly steady on his feet, and the alcohol made him appear mellow rather than belligerent. Julian reminded Archie of a nervous maiden, one who was overcome with longing, but too embarrassed to act on her desires—for the moment.

Archie forced himself to relax and walked close to Julian through the thickening mist. The buildings had been swallowed up the fog, and only the occasional muffled cry and a splash of oars reminded Archie of the proximity of the river. The normal cacophony of daytime was now a sinister hush, the sound of footsteps and conversation muffled by the fog. An orb of light from a window occasionally materialized out of the mist, but, otherwise, all was quiet and dark.

Archie had no idea where they were, but figured they had to

be somewhere close to the Strand since they'd walked for no more than ten minutes. Julian used a key to unlock a door and ushered Archie inside, closing the door behind him. A single candle burned on a small table by the door, another door firmly closed with no sounds coming from inside the room. Archie inhaled the scent of the house. You could tell a lot by the way a house smelled. This one smelled of wax polish and wood. The houses of the lower classes reeked of poverty; a unique smell comprised of human waste, rotting vegetables, and despair. The houses of the wealthy often smelled of flowers, perfumes, and food, if the kitchens were not located in an outbuilding. This house didn't smell lived in, nor did it stink.

Julian picked up the candle and lighted their way as they ascended a flight of stairs and stepped into a parlor. The room wasn't large but was comfortably furnished with cushion-covered settees and rugs on the wooden floor. A merry fire crackled in the grate, and several candles were placed around the room, dispelling the gloom of the evening. Two doors led off the parlor, likely bedchambers.

Julian invited Archie to sit down and went to pour them a drink before knocking on one of the doors. Archie wasn't sure what to expect; he'd assumed they would be alone.

"Don't worry, Archie," Julian said, seeing Archie's eyes fixed on the door. "I only want to introduce you to someone."

Archie rose to his feet as the door finally opened, and a man came out to greet them. He was of about the same height as Julian, but at least a decade older and more thickset. He had the same mane of hair, but his was a few shades darker and care-lessly pulled back with a leather thong, thick strands escaping the binding and falling about the man's face. His dark eyes were watchful in a weather-beaten face, and his skin ruddy in the glow of the fire. There was a hint of familial resemblance between the two men, but it wouldn't be instantly noticeable if one weren't looking for it.

Archie remained standing where he was as the man drew closer. They appraised each other openly, neither hostile, but not friendly either. Archie was sure that he could take Julian if it came to that, but this man was bigger and stronger, and the one to watch out for, especially since he appeared to be stone-cold sober. Archie's chances wouldn't be good if it came down to two against one.

"Jared Covington," the man finally introduced himself as he took a seat by the fire and accepted a drink from Julian.

"Jared, this is Archie. I think he would do very well for the opportunity we'd discussed."

"Oh?" Jared answered noncommittally.

"Archie has been employed as a man-at-arms for several years and has just recently relocated to London."

"Indeed," the man said, taking a sip of his drink.

By this point, Archie was beginning to seethe with anger. He'd assumed that he'd have an inebriated Julian to himself to question at length, but now the situation had changed entirely. Julian's flirtatious manner had been replaced by something else. He seemed in awe of the other man, and there was a nervousness in his demeanor that hadn't been there before.

Archie refused the offer of a drink and stood with his back to the door facing both men. "Now, look here," he said with all the indifference he could muster, "if you wish me to stay, then be so kind as to tell me straight out what it is you do and what would be required of me. If you have no interest in my skills or don't trust my person, then let's not waste each other's time. A good evening to you both." Archie waited a few moments before turning on his heel, ready to leave.

"Archie, wait," Julian called after him desperately.

Archie made a pretense of considering for a moment before he turned around.

"Please, don't be hasty," Julian pleaded as he glared at Jared, whose expression was closed. "Have a seat. Let's talk. My brother is a cautious man. He always says I'm too impulsive," Julian blathered.

Archie made a show of reluctantly taking a seat and crossing his legs. He looked calm and collected, but ready to leave at any moment. He'd learned to trust his instincts, and his gut feeling was telling him not to get too comfortable.

"Archie, Jared is a captain of a ship called the *Persephone*, which makes several voyages between England and Virginia every year. Trading with the colonists is a profitable venture, but not enough to make one a wealthy man," Julian explained.

"And you wish to be a wealthy man," Archie stated, watching Julian through narrowed eyes.

Julian opened his mouth to reply, when Jared rose to his feet, his face filled with anger. Julian had obviously said too much.

"A word, if you please," he growled to Julian as he strode off into the bedchamber.

"Please, excuse me a moment. Don't go," Julian whispered, giving Archie a lovesick look.

"I'll be right here," Archie promised.

He was seated as far away from the other room as possible, but as soon as the door closed behind the two men, Archie sprang to his feet and tiptoed toward the door. The voices were low, but if he stood close enough, he could just make out what they were saying.

"I don't trust him," Jared stated, his voice flat. "You're blinded by lust as usual. I turn a blind eye to your proclivities, but I will not allow you to endanger our operation. Your job is to attract the right sort of man, and mine is to see to the rest."

"But he's exactly what we've been looking for. The fact that he happens to be attractive is an added bonus, Jared," Julian whined.

"No, it isn't. I have plenty of men on board who can do what needs to be done and do it discreetly. They know better than to question their captain, or they'll end up going into the sea should they grow too curious. You know nothing of this man. He can betray us, or grow greedy and demand a piece of the profits. I won't have it."

"Jared, let me talk to him. I got a really good feeling about him."

"I forbid you to say anything more to him. Take him to your bed if you must, use him for pleasure, but do not involve him in our business. He's not as harmless as you take him to be."

"He's nothing more than a sweet young thing from the country," Julian protested. "Let me have him, brother."

"Have him if you must, but don't ever bring him here again. He has neither money nor a reputation to lose, so there's naught to be gained from him. Now, get rid of him."

Archie sprang back from the door and took a seat, looking about the room as if he hadn't moved an inch. He could see that Julian was upset, a flush creeping up his cheeks and neck.

"I'm sorry, Archie, but the position we discussed is no longer available. My brother has someone else in mind."

"Disappointing, to be sure," Archie remarked, "but not unexpected. I think your brother would prefer a man he can relate to," he said, hoping that his comment would get under Julian's skin. His brother tolerated his homosexuality, but it clearly disgusted him, and Julian felt angry and misunderstood. "Allow me to buy you a drink to show you there're no hard feelings," Archie suggested, giving Julian a slow smile.

"All right. Let's get out of here."

The fog had dispelled somewhat, giving Archie a glimpse of his surroundings. He didn't wish to return to the Lamb and Flag, so instead, he took Julian to a quayside tavern full of rowdy, drunk men. Julian was so angry with his brother that he never even noticed.

Archie forced a tankard of ale into Julian's hands and maneuvered him to a table in the corner where he sat closer to

Julian than was strictly necessary. This was his last chance to learn anything. Once Julian cooled off, he'd realize that his brother probably had a valid point, so Archie had to get him talking while he was still angry and hurt.

"Archie, I need to ask you a question," Julian said, watching Archie with an expression of dejection, his mouth pouty. He was drunk, having had several brandies and now working on the ale.

"Go ahead."

"Have you ever been with a man?" Julian asked softly. This was obviously a test, which could only be passed by lying.

"I have," Archie replied, mentally asking God to forgive the lie.

"Then you understand what it's like. My brother thinks it's a choice, something that can be turned on and off, but he can't possibly understand that this desire cannot be controlled or ignored. Jared likes women and spends much of his time indulging his lust. He is like a rutting bull who'll stick his cock into any willing, or sometimes unwilling, female. But it's not like that for me. I want to feel a connection, a delicacy of feeling. I long to be loved and desired for who I am."

"And you should be," Archie replied, his eyes never leaving Julian's. "Have you not met anyone you thought could genuinely care for you?"

"There was someone once, but Jared wouldn't allow it. He couldn't stand that I was happy. He used my proclivity to his own advantage and forced me to take part."

"In what?" Archie asked.

Jared sighed like a heartbroken woman and gazed up at Archie. "Will you stay with me tonight, Archie?"

"If you want me to, but I must understand the hold your brother has over you," Archie replied. "I don't wish to put myself in danger."

"Oh, you're not in danger from Jared," Julian laughed.

"Jared is only interested in those who have something of value to lose."

"Why?" Archie asked, watching Julian in a way he hoped encouraged him to talk.

Julian took another gulp of ale and closed his eyes, his face a mask of suffering. "You know how vulnerable men in our position can be. To trust someone with our secret is dangerous because the consequences of such trust can be dire. Blackmail, denouncement to the church, and ridicule are high on the list of consequences. That's why it's safer to have a steady lover rather than indulge in random trysts," Julian began.

"Go on," Archie said, still wondering what the point was.

"I frequent several taverns where the patrons are of a—shall we say—more privileged class. They are men of wealth, and often power. I watch and I wait, and approach only when I am certain. Some men reject me outright, but there are those who are so lonely and vulnerable that they open up to me like a flower. So, I take them in, love them, encourage them, and win their trust until the groundwork is laid."

"Groundwork for what, exactly?"

"I collect mementos and love letters from my lovers, then threaten to expose them unless they give me what I want. Few can weather the storm that such exposure would bring, but they are usually defiant until the end."

"What end would that be?"

"I 'convince' them to make out a will leaving all their worldly goods to me should any misfortune befall them. Within a few days, they find themselves aboard my brother's ship, heading to the New World. Oh, they do rage and make threats, but sadly, not one of them has reached Virginia alive. The seas can be so treacherous during a crossing," Julian added meaningfully.

"And what of those who won't comply with your demands? Are they the ones who need to be 'persuaded' into signing over their possessions to their dear friend Julian if they hope to see the next sunrise?" Archie asked, trying to keep the anger out of his voice.

"Precisely."

"So, you prey on those who trust you and lead them to the slaughter, all the while getting richer off your victims," Archie said, his voice dripping with disgust.

"Please, don't judge me so harshly, Archie. I owe my life to Jared. I can't refuse him."

"Why not? You're a grown man; you can decide for yourself."

Julian shook his head. He was truly maudlin now, the alcohol sloshing in his bloodstream and making him careless. "Jared is my half-brother, you see," he said as if that explained everything.

"So?"

"He's fifteen years older than I am. My mother died when I was two, and our father had no use for me. I was a bastard he didn't care to acknowledge. He was a vicious drunk, and a bully. Jared was seventeen at the time and had just gotten married. He felt sorry for me and took me in, treating me as if I were his own son. His wife, Dulcie, was a kind woman, and she looked after me when Jared went to sea. If not for the two of them, I would have died on the streets. By the time I was fifteen, Jared was the quartermaster of a ship called *The Lady of the Sea*. He took me with him on several voyages, but saw very quickly that I wasn't cut out to be a sailor. The captain of *The Lady* saw me for who I was and took me to his bed, swearing me to secrecy. We were happy for a time, but, eventually, Jared found out. He blackmailed the captain into signing over everything to him, then pushed him overboard one dark night. Jared was suddenly a wealthy man with his own vessel, and he liked the taste of his success. Dulcie might have appealed to his better nature, but she was gone by then. God rest her soul."

"Was that when Jared began using you as bait?" Archie asked, disgusted.

"No. Jared genuinely thought that the captain had taken liberties with me, and that once he was no longer about, I would grow into a 'real' man, as he put it, but he eventually learned that that would never happen. He tried beating me, calling me names, and forcing me to lie with women, but after a time, he gave up. It was a few years later when I developed a relationship with a wealthy courtier that Jared saw his opportunity. I loved the man, but I loved Jared more. I owed him, so I went along with the plan."

"How many have there been, Julian?"

"Oh, a few."

"And Gideon Warburton?" Archie asked carefully.

Julian turned his alcohol-glazed eyes on Archie. "How do you know about Gideon?" he asked, suddenly suspicious.

"Oh, I remember him from the trial of Lord Everly. He left for Virginia shortly after, aboard the *Persephone*, if memory serves." The explanation was a weak one, but Julian was so deep into his cups, he didn't question it, especially not once Archie put his arm about his shoulders, drawing him closer in a gesture of forgiveness and acceptance.

"Gideon was the easiest of them all," Julian giggled drunkenly. "He was so pathetic, so needy. He'd never acted on his desires, preferring to hide from the world. He was a virgin, you know. Innocent as a newborn babe. I think there was someone he worshipped from afar, but he didn't have the courage to act on his feelings. It didn't take much for him to succumb to someone who pretended to love and understand him. Jared wanted to make sure I consummated the relationship, since Gideon was too smart to give in to blackmail if nothing happened. It was like lying with a pillow," he said with a shudder of revulsion.

"I had a hard time getting aroused enough to take him, but

he was so besotted that he was willing to do anything. I taught him how to put his mouth to good use. It was worth it, too. He was a wealthy man, a man who had no one to spend his money on. Jared put me onto him after that disaster of a trial. Gideon was so vulnerable that he would have signed everything over to me without so much as uttering a word of protest, but Jared wanted him out of the way. He'd served his purpose. He's at the bottom of the Atlantic now, where he belongs, the feckless cretin."

"Serves him right," Archie mumbled through clenched teeth. He hadn't cared for Gideon, but he did feel pity for the man. And a blind hatred for the man who was now trying to slide his hand inside Archie's breeches.

"Come, Archie. Let's go outside. There are plenty of dark alleys hereabouts. No one will be the wiser. I can't wait much longer."

"I need to go for a piss first," Archie replied. "I'll meet you out back in five minutes. Be ready for me," he whispered into Julian's ear.

"I'm ready for you now," he replied, slurring his words.

Archie slipped out of the tavern and walked away at a brisk pace. His guts were roiling with rage, and his hand felt soiled where Julian had held it. He couldn't understand feeling sexual desire for a man, but he supposed people like Julian couldn't help it. He didn't condemn him for that. Using these men's weakness against them was what made him want to kill the man. It was low and cowardly, and blaming it on his brother was just an excuse. Julian enjoyed a life of privilege and comfort, and he chose to sell his soul time and time again for a bit of silver. Like Judas.

FIFTY-THREE

Hugo remained strangely quiet while Archie told him what he'd found out about Julian Covington and his brother. He sat in front of the fire, his elbows resting on the armrests of the chair, and his fingers laced in front of his stomach. Hugo's eyes were half-closed, his expression pensive.

"So, what will you do?" Archie asked, having finished his recitation. "Will you report them to the authorities?"

"Pointless," Hugo replied, still preoccupied. "I have no proof to present to a magistrate, so it's my word against that of Julian Covington. And my reputation is not exactly sterling these days."

"What then? You want me to do away with them?" Archie asked reluctantly.

Hugo finally roused himself and fixed his dark gaze on Archie. "I would never ask you to murder anyone in cold blood, and committing murder to avenge a murder is not my way of doing things. There are other ways."

"Care to elaborate?" Archie asked, amused by the mischievous expression which Hugo was now wearing. He had a plan; he'd just been thinking it through while Archie was talking.

Hugo sat forward, his lips stretching into a smile. "The Covingtons are thieves, first and foremost. And one way to get back at a thief is to steal that which he's stolen. I have no doubt that Captain Covington's vessel has been financed by these clandestine liaisons with unsuspecting men," Hugo explained, leaving Archie just as much in the dark.

"And so?"

"You said that the *Persephone* is due to set sail next week. It stands to reason that if the vessel is getting ready to sail, it's already in the process of being loaded and provisioned. A large portion of the cargo bound for Virginia should already be in the hold—cargo that Captain Covington is responsible for," Hugo stated patiently, waiting for the penny to drop.

"It would also mean that there are sentries on duty," Archie pointed out reasonably.

"Yes, it would mean that," Hugo agreed, his eyes dancing with merriment.

"After you," Archie said as he got to his feet and gave Hugo a mock bow.

"We need a few supplies first," Hugo replied as he strode toward the door. "Get some rope, cloth strips, and oil."

"Yes, Your Lordship," Archie replied happily.

* * *

It was well past midnight by the time Hugo and Archie got to the docks. Ghostly hulks of ships bobbed in the water, their outlines barely visible against the pitch-black sky. Water splashed against the wooden quays, the stench of the river not nearly as bad at night as it was during the day. A few stragglers were just leaving the waterfront tavern located about one hundred yards from where Hugo and Archie were; otherwise, all was quiet.

There were only three ships in port that were large enough

to be contenders, so Hugo and Archie walked softly in the dark, peering at the names on the hull. The *Persephone* was the last one, its figurehead that of a fierce-looking woman draped in a white tunic. She stared straight ahead toward London, her dilated pupils just dark pinpoints in white-painted eyes.

"Wouldn't want to meet her in the Underworld, or anywhere else for that matter," Archie said as he looked up at her, his expression one of mock horror.

Hugo chuckled and motioned for Archie to follow him. They lifted a wide wooden plank and carried it over to the *Persephone* to use as a gangplank. It produced a loud thud as it made contact with the hull, but nothing aboard the ship stirred.

"Come," Hugo whispered.

Archie and Hugo walked carefully up the plank and were on board in less than a minute, their swords drawn. They needn't have worried. The two sentries who were supposed to stand guard over the vessel were fast asleep, empty bottles next to them. They were snoring in unison, their heads lolling as they leaned against the main mast. They truly were a sorry sight.

Hugo nodded toward the sentries, giving Archie the go-ahead. Archie took out a small cudgel from his belt and hit each man over the head, rendering them unconscious, or more unconscious than they already were. He then gagged them and tied them up. Neither man stirred. Then Archie followed Hugo down into the hold.

Hugo had already lit a candle, which cast a pale glow into the cavernous space. It was full, as Hugo had predicted. Barrels and crates filled the area, strange smells mixing into an unpleasant stench magnified by lack of fresh air. There was salted pork, tack, and fish for the sailors, plus barrels of ale, and the cargo itself, which took up more than half the hold. It was hard to tell what was inside the crates, but the colonists needed luxury goods, such as cloth, lace, and ceramics. They paid in tobacco and furs they'd traded from the natives, which Covington brought back and made a hefty profit on.

Archie took a leather flask off his belt and began to pour modest amounts of oil between the crates, making sure to create small puddles all around and connect them with a trail of oil. He shook the flask upside down, letting the last drops of oil plop onto the wooden floor.

"Ready?" Hugo asked as he backed toward the steps.

Archie nodded.

Hugo set the candle to the nearest pool of oil, the liquid igniting with a satisfying hiss. The flames began to lick the sides of the crates and spread from one pool of oil to the next with frightening speed. Hugo and Archie didn't wait around to watch. They climbed the ladder and went back for the sentries, who were still insensible. It took no more than ten minutes to carry the men off the ship and deposit them on the quay.

"Shall we untie them?" Archie asked as he looked at the silent lumps at his feet.

"They'll be out for some time," Hugo replied. "Might as well."

They quickly untied the sentries and disappeared into the shadows, positioning themselves behind a dark warehouse to watch. It took no more than a quarter of an hour for a rosy glow to envelop the ship. Thick tendrils of smoke escaped the cargo hold and curled upward, disappearing into the moonless sky. Sparks flew as the crackle of the hungry fire became audible over the slapping of water against the hull. The *Persephone* was burning from within, the flames devouring everything below deck before bursting onto the deck and spreading up the masts, setting the rolled-up sails alight. The last to succumb was the goddess herself, her eyes staring in now-appropriate horror as the fire began to roast her feet and move up her torso to finally engulf her face in a halo of orange and red.

Screams tore through the night as men ran toward the

flaming ship, buckets in hand. But it was too late; something they realized as soon as they reached the inferno. They turned back defeated after dumping their water into the Thames.

The sentries were now awake, cursing loudly, their voices laced with fear. They would pay for their lack of vigilance.

The crossbar of the mast detached itself from the ship and crashed onto the deck, a shower of sparks lighting up the night sky. The ship creaked pitifully as it began to slowly sink into the river, but it wasn't deep enough to swallow the whole thing. Part of the hull and the three burning masts stuck out of the black water, eerie in their demise.

"Let's go home," Hugo said with an air of satisfaction as they left their hiding place and headed toward Bradford's house.

"You know it won't stop them, don't you?" Archie asked as they crossed the road and disappeared into a side street.

"I do, but it will set them back financially a great deal, and that's all the punishment I am able to mete out without getting the authorities involved," Hugo replied. "I can't save every gullible man who allows himself to be blackmailed, but this is all I can do to avenge Gideon's death. The rest is out of my hands."

"Fair enough," Archie replied.

FIFTY-FOUR

I threw on my cloak and stepped outside, certain that I would find Archie either in the stables or chopping wood. Hugo had returned from London in the afternoon, having been gone for the better part of a week. Despite Hugo's smiles and assurances that everything was well, I could tell that he was in a black mood as he stomped off directly to his study. I knew he wouldn't tell me anything, mistakenly believing that he was protecting me. Hugo was used to keeping secrets, and I could honestly say that this lack of full disclosure was the biggest issue in our marriage. I told myself that he did it because he loved me and thought he was sparing me worry, but I actually worried more when I didn't know what I was up against. Well, I would go to the next-best source—Archie.

As expected, Archie was in the stables, brushing down Hugo's horse with a clump of clean straw. We had grooms for that, but he found comfort in doing it himself, and often spent hours with the horses, just mucking out stalls and exercising them, when weather permitted. Archie gave me a nod and continued with what he was doing.

A young groom froze in the act of mucking out a stall,

surprised to see me in the stable. After years of living in the seventeenth century, I would still have given anything for a car, preferably one with a working heater and a good stereo system. Horses made me uneasy, not having a control panel or a brake pedal.

"Give us a moment, Joe," I said to the groom, who was only too happy to scamper to the kitchen for a warm drink and a bite of something. "Archie, what is he up to?" I asked without preamble. Making small talk with Archie was pointless, and there was a directness in our dealings with each other which suited us both.

Archie shrugged, his eyes firmly fixed on the horse. No one would ever accuse the man of being chatty.

"Are you just going to ignore me then?" I demanded, irritated by Archie's lack of response.

"You know I can't tell you," he replied in that matter-of-fact tone that drove me crazy sometimes. In Archie's mind, it was a foregone conclusion that the trust between him and Hugo was not to be questioned and that I was violating some unspoken rule by asking him to betray a confidence.

"Archibald Hicks, I swear to God that I will wrestle you to the ground if you don't answer me," I fumed. Of course, I probably couldn't even budge him, but I knew my threat would illicit some sort of response.

"I am almost tempted to let you try," Archie replied with an amused smile. "It would be most ladylike, Your Ladyship," he added with a sarcastic chuckle.

"Archie, please. I'm going mad with worry, and Hugo won't tell me anything."

"He's only trying to protect you," came the predictable response.

"Yes, so I've been told. Will you at least give me some mono-syllabic answers if I ask you something? Shouldn't be too hard for you," I added sarcastically.

Archie gave a nod of agreement, so I plunged on.

"Is he putting himself in danger?"

"Aye."

"Is it the kind of danger that can lead to imprisonment and execution?"

"Quite possibly."

"Is there anything I can do to stop him?" I asked, my voice laced with desperation.

"Not very likely."

"Do you approve of what he is doing?" I asked in an effort to trick Archie into revealing something.

"'Tis not for me to say."

I actually stomped my foot in frustration.

"Why did Hugo's coat smell of smoke?" I asked, remembering the acrid smell clinging to the fabric when Hugo came in and embraced me.

Archie actually smiled at that question, his eyes suddenly alight with some private joke. "We doled out some much-needed justice last night. Anonymously," he added when he saw my look of horror. Archie finally dropped the straw, patted the horse on the rump, and turned to face me, his face going from wry amusement to solemnity. "Neve, you know I will look after him, don't you? I will do everything in my power to keep him safe."

"I know that, Archie, but, sadly, your powers of protection are rather limited."

Archie didn't reply, but I knew that he agreed. He was one man, and he was no match for the law.

"Thank you, Archie."

I felt defeated and angry, but most of all helpless. And I would be damned if I was kept in the dark. Hugo wasn't forthcoming with information, but he usually answered my questions if I confronted him. I tried not to back him into a corner too often, but there was a persistent little twinge in my gut which told me that I should be concerned.

I stomped from the stables and went straight to Hugo's study, where he was poring over some document. His brows were knitted with tension, and his mouth pressed into a hard line, but he forced his features to relax as I entered the room, thinking he could fool me.

"Our bedroom. Now!"

"At your service, madam," Hugo replied, a happy grin spreading across his face. He actually thought I was after an afternoon tryst.

"Oh, don't flatter yourself," I spat out as I turned on my heel and took the stairs two at a time. I only wanted a bit of privacy, since talking in the study exposed us to too many ears which were attached to skulking servants.

Hugo followed obediently, probably still hoping to calm me down by getting me into bed.

I slammed the door shut and turned on him, my voice shaking with fury. "You are not leaving this room until you tell me the truth, and don't think I won't know if you are lying to me."

"I've never lied to you, Neve," he defended himself.

"No, but you've withheld things, which is almost the same."

"Is it? I didn't want you to worry; you have enough on your mind."

"Do you honestly believe that I worry less because I don't know what you are up to?" Only a man could come up with that kind of reasoning. "Hugo, I will ask you this only once, and God help you if you don't tell me the truth. What were you doing in London?"

"I've petitioned the new king for an official pardon, met with prominent members of Parliament in the hope of making some useful connections, and learned a cypher for coding reports for the Marquis de Chartres, which, if intercepted, would be viewed as an act of treason."

I think my mouth actually opened of its own accord at that last bit. "Did I just hear you correctly?" I breathed. "You are spying for France in the midst of the War of Alliance against Louis XIV? To what possible end? You know that James will never regain his throne. Are you completely raving mad?" I screeched, completely exasperated. "You will be executed on the spot if you are caught. Why? Why would you do this?"

I was breathing hard by this point, my mind refusing to accept what my instinct already knew. Hugo was putting his head on the chopping block, and sooner or later the executioner would arrive.

"Neve, I don't have a choice," Hugo replied quietly. "Did you really think that reclaiming my identity, funding our exile in France, and gaining entry into society would come at no cost? I did what I had to do for us to survive. I made promises."

"So, you are some sort of 'sleeper' agent who was activated upon return to England?"

"Yes, I suppose you can call it that. I was able to feed de Chartres bits of information I got off Luke, but, for the most part, I wasn't going to be fully active until my return to England. Now that William is at war with Louis, my information will be even more valuable. I have been contacted by a man who will get my intelligence to de Chartres."

"And who is this man?"

"He is a highly respected Member of Parliament, and a secret Catholic who wishes to see James II restored to the throne. He has channels through which he passes information."

I sat heavily on the chair in front of the empty hearth, my feet refusing to hold me up any longer. I thought we were finally safe, but what Hugo was doing now was probably even more dangerous than his scheme with the Duke of Monmouth.

"So, that's what Simon meant," I muttered.

"What are you talking about? What did Simon tell you?"

"Simon thought I would be returning to the twenty-first century in the near future. He knew something, Hugo, something he was afraid to tell me. Hugo, I beg you, stop whatever you are doing. It's not too late."

"It is too late," Hugo sighed. "Neve, I gave my word, I accepted payment, and I sealed my fate. Please promise me that if anything happens to me, you will go back to the future. I want to know that you will be safe, and that the children will have a better life."

"You think that living without their father on my pittance of a salary would be a better life? You are more deluded than I thought," I spat out. I was so angry, I could barely breathe. Angry and frightened. Perhaps Hugo had been right, and not knowing would have been easier.

Hugo reached for me, but I pulled away from him and left the room. I needed some air and a long walk to exorcize some of the terrible frustration I was feeling. Once again, Hugo was walking a tightrope, and this time, there was no safety net, because I had no inkling of what was going to happen and could do nothing to prevent it.

I grabbed my cloak and walked out into the garden. The shrubs were glittering with a sprinkling of frost, and the path was slippery beneath my boots, but I couldn't bear the thought of going back inside. My breath escaped in gossamer puffs and my face tingled with the cold, but I was oblivious to the discomfort. The winter-white sky seemed to go on forever, broken only by the intricate pattern of bare branches, which looked like tribal tattoos etched into eternity. Several crows were perched on the branches, watching me with interest as I huffed and puffed along, muttering to myself.

I was angry, oh so angry, but mostly I was scared. I had been naïve in thinking that anything could happen on its own or come without a hefty price. What a fool I had been to assume that Hugo would simply be accepted as Lord Everly in Paris and treated like exiled nobility. I had lulled myself into a false sense of security, needing to believe that we were safe at last, and that Valentine had a future after all. But was there a future? I was back to that niggling question. Was history still trying to right itself? Was it like a modern GPS that simply recalculated the route if you took a wrong turn and still brought you to the same destination? If Hugo died and I went back to the twenty-first century, Clarence would inherit and everything would be as it should have been, only with a slight detour. Was this "auto-correct" inevitable?

FIFTY-FIVE

MARCH 1689

Paris, France

Max stopped for a moment before entering the cathedral, oblivious to the driving rain that seemed to come out of nowhere and soak him in mere moments. Still, he hesitated. He'd been thinking of doing this for months, but now that he was finally here, he felt nervous and deeply ashamed.

The downpour seemed to stop as suddenly as it started, leaving the gutters spouting rainwater from the open mouths of the gargoyles, and puddles dotting the square in front of Notre Dame. The sky, which had been a milky blue only a half-hour ago, was the color of steel wool, the clouds so thick and dense that they gave the impression of blanketing the city and leaching all daylight, turning the early morning unnaturally dark.

Max suddenly felt very cold. He needed to go inside before he caught a chill. The cavernous cathedral was not much warmer, but at least he would be out of the wind which blew off the Seine and made him shiver in his damp clothes. He took a deep breath and pulled on the heavy iron ring attached to the massive wooden door. Max was greeted by the usual hush of the cathedral. Dozens of candles threw fanciful shadows onto the stone walls, and several people knelt in the pews, their heads bent in prayer. The funereal scent of flowers wafted from the arrangement at the altar and mixed with the heady perfume of incense and stone dust created by some minor repair. The masons weren't there at the moment, but their tools were still carefully arranged in the area, and several blocks of stone sat waiting to be lifted into their slots.

Max walked down the nave, his steps hesitant as he made his way toward the man who was gazing thoughtfully at the book on the pulpit, perhaps in preparation for the next sermon. Max had attended countless services at the cathedral, but the ones conducted by Father Mathieu seemed to resonate with him the most.

Father Mathieu was a man of middle years, with warm brown eyes and deep grooves bracketing his mouth, etched on his face by years of smiling. He seemed to be a kind and under-standing man, a man who truly listened to his parishioners and didn't just subscribe to the usual platitudes and dogma. He treated people as individuals who were in need of his help and guidance, which he was happy to provide.

There was another priest who presided over services, Father Marc, but he was a totally different manner of man, one who seemed harsh and unforgiving, fancying himself as the sword of God rather than His embrace. Max had seen several people walking away from Father Marc looking diminished and frightened, and that was not the kind of man he wanted to consult.

Max sat down in a vacant pew and bent his head, more in thought than in prayer. He needed a few minutes to compose himself, and the solemn silence of the cathedral always helped. The doubts of a few minutes ago were gone, replaced by a blessed calm. Max felt a familiar peace begin to steal over him as he soaked in the atmosphere. He could just sit for a while and go back home, but today his visit had a purpose.

There's no reason to rush, Max thought to himself. *I want to be sure.*

But you are sure, his mind replied. *You've been sure for months. Just go talk to him.*

Max finally worked up the courage to approach Father Mathieu, and left the safety of the pew. His steps echoed on the stone floor as he walked slowly toward the pulpit, hoping that Father Mathieu would look up. *If he looks up, it's a sign from God that I am doing the right thing.*

As if on cue, Father Mathieu lifted his head, his face breaking into a warm smile. He didn't seem to mind the interruption; just waited patiently for Max to speak as he rested his hands on the pages of the text he'd been perusing.

"Father, I was wondering if I might have a word," Max began, suddenly tongue-tied. He'd rehearsed his speech many times over the past few weeks, but now that he was actually here, his vocabulary seemed to be reduced to that of a child, and he forgot all the sophisticated phrases he'd prepared.

"Of course, of course," the priest said, closing the book and taking a step closer to Max. "How can I help?"

"I wish to make a confession, but I would like to do it in the open, not in a confessional. I don't require anonymity. I wish to confess to my sins to you and hear what you have to say to me without any barrier between us."

The priest looked somewhat taken aback but smiled kindly and nodded in agreement. "As you wish. I would be honored to hear your confession. Since you don't wish for anonymity, would you like to talk in the garden? The sun seems to have blessed us with its presence, and I could do with some fresh air."

Max gazed up at the stained-glass windows, surprised to see shafts of golden light filtering through and casting colorful patterns onto the stone floor and the pews, instantly brightening the atmosphere inside the church. The sun had indeed appeared, and Max suddenly wished for nothing more than to be out in the open, where he could talk without the fear of being overheard. Perhaps his confession would fly directly up to the heavens, and he would be afforded some measure of forgiveness.

Max followed the priest out to the garden behind the cathedral. At this time of the year, it consisted mostly of bare rose bushes, which in a few short months would be heavy with fragrant blooms. The garden was small but well-tended, and the bushes were covered with burlap sacks for the winter to protect them from the cold. A wrought-iron fence surrounded the garden, separating it from the busy streets behind the cathedral. The day was chilly, but the sudden burst of sunshine warmed the temperature by a few degrees and lit up the river with shimmering lights which twinkled on the surface, making the previously gray waters of the Seine come to life as they continued their timeless flow.

"I've noticed you attending the services," Father Mathieu remarked as he walked slowly down a stone path between the bushes.

"Yes, I try to come every week," Max replied as he worked up the courage to tell the priest what he'd come to say. "I am not even Catholic," Max confessed.

"You are English. A Protestant." It wasn't really a question, more a statement of fact which seemed to amuse the priest.

"Yes, I am, but I've greatly enjoyed your sermons."

"That's quite a compliment from someone who's not of the faith."

"Father, I've been in France for nearly three years now, but I am making plans to go home since there's no longer anything for me here," Max added ruefully.

"And there's nothing for you back in England," the priest supplied.

"No, not anymore. I must admit that I am rather apprehensive about returning."

"What is it you wish to confess, my son? Will your confession make it easier for you to return home?" Father Mathieu asked as he studied Max.

"Perhaps. You see, Father, there was a time when I considered myself to be a good man, a worthy man," Max began, but his voice trailed off as he tried to put a label to what he considered himself to be now.

"Tell me," the priest said softly. "I will not judge you, only listen."

"I allowed fear and greed to get the best of me. I wronged a man who came to me for help. I tried to kill him, thinking that he would take from me that which was most important to me."

"And did you?"

"No, he outwitted me, and instead of taking his revenge, he showed me mercy," Max confessed.

"He sounds like a good man," Father Mathieu said as he continued to walk, his face raised to the feeble rays of the spring sunshine.

"Yes, he is, but I went on to wrong him once again. I kidnapped his wife and child to lure him into a trap. I used those he loved most to bring him to his knees and planned to kill him as they watched. I believed that I could regain something I'd lost by getting rid of him. He outwitted me once again, only this time, he wasn't as merciful. I sustained injuries that nearly killed me, but I survived."

"Is it God's forgiveness that you seek or your own?" the priest asked, curious about this strange man.

"I think that God allowed me to live when surely I should have died. I want to know why."

"Perhaps God has a different plan for you. If you are repentant, then you should make amends. This man showed you mercy once, and spared you the second time as well. I suspect he could have killed you when he had the chance, but chose not to."

"Yes, he could have, and should have killed me. I left him no choice, but still he couldn't bring himself to end my life, especially not in front of his wife, whom I've lusted after for years. I planned to make her mine after his death and adopt his child. I wanted to obliterate him from their lives, and hear his daughter call me 'Father'."

"Is it love for this woman that motivated your actions?" Father Mathieu asked, trying to understand.

"In part, but I've since come to realize that I never actually loved her. I wanted her, desired her, and was furious when she thwarted me and chose him instead. I felt a need to prove to her that I was the better man, the stronger man. I wanted to show her that I could bring the man she chose to his knees, make him beg. There were other reasons as well."

"And would the lady have gone along with your plans?" the priest asked, looking at Max with open curiosity.

"No, she wouldn't," Max replied with a chuckle. "She's a feisty one. She probably would have slit my throat while I slept. Or maybe she'd do it while I was awake, so she could watch me die, and know that she avenged her man."

"Is there a particular bond between you and this man?"

"I suppose you could say that. We are related. But it's more than that; we can't exist at the same time. We are not meant to."

Father Mathieu grew quiet for a moment as he stood with his hands clasped behind his back, his eyes thoughtful. Max could see the priest's struggle to control his distaste despite his promise not to judge. How could he not? He was only human, and what Max had told him would make anyone despise him. He despised himself. This was why Max didn't wish for an anonymous confession. He had wanted to see Father Mathieu's face when he told him the truth—he wanted, and needed, to be judged.

At last, the priest turned to Max, having come to some decision. "My son, you've come to me for guidance, but it seems to me that you already know the answer to your question. I can see it there in your eyes. I can tell you that God forgives you and tell you to do penance, but that's not why you came. If that is what you were after, you would have simply gone to confession and walked out a much happier man."

"So, what is it that I want, Father?"

"You want me to tell you what to do, and I can't do that. You must listen to what your conscience dictates."

"What if I don't have a conscience?" Max asked desperately.

"You wouldn't be here talking to me if you didn't. You carry a heavy burden that only you can find the means to lift, and only you know what it would take to undo the harm you've done to this man and his family. God will forgive you, but you must forgive yourself, and the only way you can do that is by righting a wrong."

Max nodded in agreement. The priest was right; he couldn't forgive himself. He'd had much time to think over the past several years, and he'd come to realize that he couldn't live with the person he had become. He'd always been a bit selfish and self-absorbed, but he'd gone from being a prat to being a savage, a would-be-assassin of a man who'd done nothing more than try to stay alive and protect those he loved. Max had nearly robbed Neve of a husband she clearly adored, and would have gladly orphaned Hugo's daughter. He assumed that it was his God-given right to possess them, but God gave him no such power; he'd taken it for himself, and nearly paid for it with his life. And now it was time to make things right.

"Thank you, Father. You've been a great help to me," Max said as he smiled at the priest.

"Have I?" the priest asked cryptically.

FIFTY-SIX

MARCH 2015

Surrey, England

Simon glanced outside before swapping his shoes for wellies and tying a scarf around his neck for the walk to the church. It was nearly the end of March, but it was still unseasonably cold, and spring felt as far away as it had in January. Thinking of January always made Simon cringe inwardly, but now that two months had passed since his aborted wedding, he was starting to forgive himself. He supposed he might have allowed himself off the hook had Heather been really furious and abusive, but what he had found when he got back was a white-faced, hollow-eyed woman who'd forgiven him for ruining the wedding as soon as she learned that he went missing. Heather had spent two days agonizing over his safety, and, when he finally turned up, threw herself into his arms, sobbing with relief. Simon had expected a rant, or a massive hysterical outburst at the very least, but all he got were tears of joy that he had returned to her unhurt.

Simon knew at that moment that he stood at a crossroads. He could go on with his original plan and end things with Heather, or apologize profusely and reschedule the wedding.

He had to admit that he'd been torn. Once he saw Heather's haggard face, he wasn't nearly as sure as he had been when he threw himself into the passage, but eventually common sense won out. He knew now that Heather loved him deeply, just as he knew that he didn't love her enough to commit to her for the rest of his life. He liked her, desired her, but didn't wish to marry her. That conversation had been difficult, more so because Heather just listened silently rather than throwing crockery at him and calling him names. She had merely stared at the floor, her face going even paler than it already was, her hands folded demurely in her lap as if he were the headmaster and she was the student. At last, she had just got up, packed her things, and let herself out, leaving him feeling like the biggest wanker in the world.

His mother didn't help matters. She didn't say much, but the looks she threw him whenever she thought he wasn't looking were enough to convey her feelings. She'd never cared for Heather, but what he'd done was cowardly and selfish, and he should have been a man and faced up to his mistake instead of running away. "You are just like your father," Stella Harding's eyes said, and Simon felt himself cringing at the comparison. He didn't wish to be like Roland Everly, yet he hadn't had the backbone to stand up to Heather and give her the respect of telling her the truth. He ran away and hid like a little boy—a little boy who was afraid of taking his punishment.

It was all behind him now, but Simon's life had changed. He'd closed up his flat in London, made arrangements to work remotely, and moved to Cranleigh, where he devoted himself to running the thriving business Max had left behind and involving himself in the life of the village. He'd joined the football club, Cranleigh FC, and began to volunteer at the local art center, where he worked with kids. And now, he was on his way to the church the emergency meeting Reverend Lambert had called. Simon had no idea what the meeting would be about, but felt it his duty to attend, as Max would have had he still been alive.

Simon trudged down the soggy hill, glad that he'd put on wellies and his feet were mercifully dry. Try as he might, he couldn't avoid glancing at the gravestones of Elena and Hugo Everly as he walked up the path toward the church. Having actually met Hugo, he felt a pang of sorrow every time he saw the headstone, the memory of the man still fresh in his mind. What would befall him, and when?

His mother had asked him what had prompted him to rent out his flat and move to Surrey, but Simon couldn't tell her the truth. He needed a break from his London life. He hadn't seen Heather since the day he'd come back, nor had he even attempted to pull any girls at the local bars. He needed to be alone for a while to make sense of where his life was going, but he also wanted to be on hand when Hugo met his end in the seventeenth century. He'd felt a strange kinship with Neve, and if he only did one chivalrous thing in his life, he wanted it to involve her. If she came to him for help, he'd be there, ready to offer whatever assistance he could.

Simon walked into the church and took a seat in one of the front pews, returning the greetings of the other members of the Church Committee. Reverend Lambert was already there, standing in the center as one of the ladies—Simon couldn't recall her name—handed out cups of steaming tea in Styrofoam cups. Simon pulled off his scarf, unbuttoned his coat and accepted a cup of tea. If this meeting was anything like the reverend's sermons, then he'd be here a while.

"Ladies and gentlemen, thank you for coming," Reverend Lambert began. "I'm afraid I have some bad news. As you all know, this has been rather a harsh winter, with several significant snowfalls. There has been as much as an inch of water in the crypt once the snow began to melt, the water seeping through the cracks in the foundation. I'm afraid the repairs need to happen sooner rather than later, and, as usual, this requires funds. I've located a firm in Guilford which specializes in historic buildings such as our church, but, of course, this is a massive undertaking and will not only require funds, but will also disrupt the operations of St. Nicolas's."

Reverend Lambert took a sip of his tea as he allowed the information to settle. What he was really asking for were hefty donations, as well as ideas for raising money. The lady who passed around the tea was already talking excitedly about organizing a church fete, but the reverend's eyes were on Simon. As the proverbial lord of the manor, he would be expected to make a sizeable contribution, especially since the church was part of the tour which began at the historic Everly Manor Museum and gardens, and often ended with a visit to St. Nicolas's. Simon was sure that Max had made regular donations to the church, but they were hardly large enough to rebuild a foundation.

Simon sat patiently through another hour and a half, listening to half-baked ideas about booths for the fete and other equally useless suggestions. A fete would raise a few hundred pounds, not the thousands that would be needed to make repairs. At last, the meeting was over, and Simon slipped out the door after bringing his thumb and pinky to his face in the universal sign for "call me" to Reverend Lambert. They would need to meet in private to discuss Simon's contribution.

Simon refused to be drawn into further discussion by the ladies who were still firing on all pistons about a bake sale. He walked back to Everly Manor lost in thought. He had no idea what was actually involved in repairing the foundation and the cracks in the walls of the crypt, but he was fairly certain that the entrance to the passage would somehow be affected, possibly preventing Neve from returning from the past if she were in trouble. Simon had no way of knowing precisely when Hugo would die, except that it was some time in 1689, but he did know that once he did, Neve would be on her own, and would have no reason to remain in the past. Of course, she might choose to stay, but what if she wished to return?

Simon stopped midway up the hill, pondering the situation. Was it his responsibility to warn her, or was he being ridiculous and involving himself in something that was none of his affair? Neve had chosen to go back in time—twice. She was a grown woman, perfectly capable of making her own decisions, and although no one aspired to being a widow, being a wealthy, titled widow had its advantages.

Mind your own business, old boy, Simon thought to himself as he resumed walking. Neve didn't need him or his advice.

FIFTY-SEVEN

MARCH 1689

Surrey, England

I followed Hugo to his study and waited with trepidation as he broke the official-looking seal on a packet that had been delivered from London by special messenger. The young man was dressed in a splendid livery and had ridden all the way from London without stopping. I sent him to the kitchen for a meal and a hot drink while Joe took the horse to be fed and watered. Hugo offered the messenger the use of a guest room should he like to spend the night, but the young man announced that he had to return to London posthaste as he was needed at the palace.

I had never seen a royal seal before, but I was fairly certain this message came straight from the king. I hadn't realized I was holding my breath while Hugo scanned the missive. A smile split his face, my signal to breathe again.

"Is that what I think it is?" I asked, keeping my fingers crossed behind my back like a little kid.

"A royal pardon," Hugo announced happily, "as well as an invitation to the coronation. What do you think of that?" He was trying to remain composed, but I could see the relief in his eyes. A royal pardon meant that he could reclaim his place in society without the taint of treason always hanging over his head like a thundercloud. Even if there were those who still believed him guilty, their feelings would need to be kept to themselves out of respect for the king. Everything Hugo had hoped for was finally coming to pass, and we would be rejoicing if this wonderful news wasn't marred by Elena's recent passing.

"I think I'm in awe. I have never seen a live coronation, not even on television. Queen Elizabeth II was crowned long before I was born, and has been on the throne for over sixty years. That's probably the longest reign in British history."

"Do you have a gown to wear?" Hugo suddenly asked. He never concerned himself with fashion, but this was a big event, so I had to be appropriately attired, especially since all eyes would be on us after having been absent from Court for over three years following the trial. This would be Hugo's return to the life he was born to, and my official coming-out party. For the first time since our marriage, I would be introduced to members of the Court, and I hoped that this occasion would be easier than my presentation at Versailles, although I wasn't so sure. Courtiers were the same everywhere: vicious, spiteful, and insecure. The men might be less judgmental of Hugo's choice, but the women would be just as ruthless as they were in France. My lack of family, money, and connections would be examined and questioned. My hold over Hugo would be dissected, and Hugo's motives for marrying me would be ridiculed. The happiness I felt only a moment ago quickly evaporated, replaced by apprehension.

"I can wear one of the gowns I wore to Versailles. As far as I can tell, French fashion is still ahead of its time, so the gowns from two years ago will be right on time here."

"I suppose it'll have to do since there's no time to order a new one. The coronation is in less than two weeks—April 11."

"Hugo, our names will appear on the list of people who attended the coronation of William and Mary. People in the twenty-first century will be able to see it. As a matter of fact, people throughout history will be privy to this information. Do you know what that means?" I asked, suddenly anxious.

Hugo gave me a strange look as he placed the letter and the invitation into a drawer and locked it. "No, what does it mean?"

"It means that we have officially changed history," I breathed, suddenly aware of the magnitude of what that meant.

"Neve, we changed history the moment we met in 1685," Hugo replied, confused by my odd reaction. "Everything that's happened since then was never meant to happen."

I suddenly felt weak in the knees and slid into a nearby chair. Tears that were never far away these days spilled onto my cheeks, running into my open mouth as I stared straight ahead, unseeing.

"Neve, what is it? I don't understand why you are so upset," Hugo asked. He knelt in front of me and took my cold hands in his, gazing into my eyes in the hope of finding some explanation there, but he couldn't understand what I was thinking. I'd been harboring a terrible fear all this time, especially since Elena died, and it gnawed at me day and night, leaving me weak with relief every night when another day went by without incident. "Neve, please, tell me."

"I am not sure how to put it into words," I replied, almost reluctant to voice my concerns, for fear that saying them out loud would somehow jinx the future. I knew it was silly and completely unfounded, but there it was. "It's nothing, really. I'm just overwhelmed."

"I don't believe you," Hugo replied softly. "Now, please tell me what it is you've been carrying around all this time."

I looked down at our hands for a moment, reminding myself that Hugo was right, and we had actually changed the future

the day we met. Perhaps my fears were silly. I was very overe-
motional these days.

"Hugo, you were never meant to live past 1685," I began.

"Are you beginning to regret that I did?" Hugo asked with a
smile.

"No, of course not," I cried vehemently. "It's just that you
were never meant to have children. You went down in history as
having never married or fathered any biological children. You
and I are two people who were never, ever meant to meet. We
cheated the universe and combined DNA from the future with
that of the seventeenth century, creating children who are an
anomaly—biologically and historically. Ever since I was locked
up in Newgate, I began to worry that history would somehow
right itself. You know how a GPS just recalculates the route
when you make a wrong turn? Well, I began thinking that
history might do the same—simply recalculate and still proceed
to the same destination."

"Neve, I never did figure out how those GPS things work,
and history is not a conscious entity. It doesn't recalculate; it
just happens," Hugo replied patiently, already guessing where I
was going with this.

"Ever since Elena died, I've been fighting this terrible fear
that we will lose the rest of our children because they were
never meant to be born. I check on them a hundred times a day,
terrified that they will get a fever or have an accident of some
sort and be taken from us."

"And us going to the coronation and appearing in the
history books is proof that history can be altered?" Hugo asked,
finally making the connection.

"Yes. It's tangible proof that we changed history and
survived."

"Sweetheart," Hugo said softly as he pulled me to my feet
and drew me to him. "Countless children die every year, not
because they were never meant to be, but because it's the reality

of life in this century. Elena didn't die because we somehow upset the cosmic balance by meeting and having children. She died because she contracted an illness that kills thousands. Perhaps thinking that her death is part of some greater plan helps you to deal with her passing since it seems less random and meaningless, but as much as I hate to admit it, it was. It was random. Had Elena been asleep when I returned home, and not come in contact with me, she might never have gotten ill, and might still be with us today. Neve, I miss her every single day. I have dreams that she is sleeping in my arms, or bouncing on my knee, giggling, clapping her hands, and demanding that I bounce her harder. I feel the loss of her every minute, but I don't for a moment believe that she was taken because you and I were never meant to be."

I rested my forehead against Hugo's shoulder as his arms went around me. "I'm scared, Hugo. So scared. We are in uncharted territory. You've finally got your pardon. This could have truly been a new beginning for us, but instead, it's the beginning of a new chapter, in which you are once again in mortal danger. How do you plan to pull this off?"

"Neve, I spent hours at the library while I was in the future, studying the history of the Stuarts and reading up on the Glorious Revolution. I know what's going to happen. All I have to do is pass pertinent tidbits to the Marquis de Chartres to keep my end of the bargain. I can keep it up for years without ever putting myself in danger by trying to gather intelligence in any other kind of way."

"But what if someone learns of what you are doing? What if your 'tidbits' fall into the wrong hands?"

"I will be very careful. I promise. Will you trust me?"

"I've trusted you since the day you risked your life to save Frances. I knew then that you are an honorable man, despite your elastic moral principles," I joked, making Hugo smile. "I just want to keep you all safe; that's all."

"And you will. Now, let's go spend some time with the children. I can hear Valentine arguing with Ruby, and it's safe to say that Ruby is losing that particular battle."

"I think we need to get her a pony. You know how she wants one. It will make her feel special and grown-up, and give her some alone time with Archie. She misses him."

"Thank God she's only three, or we'd have a budding romance on our hands," Hugo joked as he followed me out of the room.

"I think we already do."

FIFTY-EIGHT

APRIL 1689

London, England

Henry FitzRoy, 1ˢᵗ Duke of Grafton, sighed with contentment as he rolled onto his side and rested his head on his hand, his gaze caressing the body of the woman next to him. Jocelyn never bothered to cover up after they made love, lying there in all her glory, her eyes frequently sliding to the gilded mirror which reflected her image to her satisfaction. Her silken skin glowed in the candlelight, and her abundant chestnut tresses spilled over her breasts as she flipped onto her stomach, giving him an eyeful of her delectable bottom. Jocelyn was brazen, and Henry loved that about her. The notion of his wife behaving in this manner would have sent him over the edge with fury, but in a mistress, this was a very desirable quality.

Jocelyn had another quality that he found desirable, and this one had nothing to do with her body. She was one of the most intelligent women he'd ever met, someone he could actually talk to, especially when he was sated but not quite ready to end their tryst and return to reality. Most times, the conversation led to another round of lovemaking, even better than the last since he usually lasted longer the second and third time. At first, Henry had been apprehensive about being too open with his mistress, but after nearly a year of secret assignations, he'd come to realize that Jocelyn could be trusted. Her opinion mattered to him, and he consulted her on all important decisions, putting aside that tiny twinge of guilt he felt at not discussing matters with his wife.

"Will you be attending the coronation with your charming wife?" Jocelyn asked playfully, knowing how much Henry hated any mention of his wife, especially in bed.

"You know I will, and I will no doubt be seeing you there with your husband," he answered gruffly, annoyed by the barb. "I am Mary's cousin, after all," he added.

"That you are, and also nephew to her father, who's currently cooling his heels in France while hoping to raise an army to reclaim his throne; and half-brother to the Duke of Monmouth, who's resting permanently these days after his failed attempt to dethrone his uncle. What a complicated family you have, Henry," she said with a giggle. "And you are a complicated man, which leads me to believe that you are not taking all this as meekly as one might expect."

"I don't take your meaning, madam," Henry replied, his eyes suddenly more alert. Jocelyn wasn't just being playful; she was implying something, and he didn't like her tone.

"Oh, you take my meaning very well, Henry. Just be careful. Very careful."

Jocelyn turned onto her side, raised herself on her elbow, and tried to plant a kiss on Henry's pouting lips, but he moved his head back, not ready to end the conversation.

"What do you know, Jocelyn?"

"I know that Mary, being the daughter of a Catholic monarch who has just been relieved of his throne, is very conscious of her position, and, although she's a Protestant and has been invited back to England to rule, will take no risks when it comes to her reign. Cousin or no cousin, she will strike if she has to, through her husband, of course," Jocelyn explained patiently as if Henry were a child. Jocelyn, who was Lady Devenish when at home, was one of Mary's ladies-in-waiting, so probably knew his cousin better than most. Prudish Mary would have a fit if she knew that one of her women was sleeping with her cousin, but that was all part of the fun, although Jocelyn's new position made her less available to Henry since she spent more time at Court, waiting on his frigid cousin.

"I am feverishly loyal to our new royal couple," Henry replied with a chuckle as he bent his head to plant a kiss on Jocelyn's breast, his pique forgotten. He didn't care to continue this discussion, but Jocelyn had given him something to think about. Her warning was thinly veiled, making him wonder if it had come directly from Mary herself. Perhaps his cousin wasn't as oblivious as he supposed.

Jocelyn pushed Henry down and suspended her hips over him, her hair trailing seductively over his chest. "It's my turn, my sweet," she breathed as she slowly impaled herself on his rock-hard cock. She threw her head back as he filled her and began to move, slowly at first, then with more intent, the conversation about Mary forgotten for the moment.

Henry lost himself in her, all his blood rushing to the place of their joining as he exploded embarrassingly fast, unable to take the exquisite pleasure any longer. Jocelyn raked her fingers over his chest, her face a mask of disappointment.

"You owe me," she breathed as she flipped onto her back and closed her eyes in expectation. Henry slid down between her legs, all too aware that there'd be hell to pay if he failed to satisfy his lover.

FIFTY-NINE

The summons from Mary came not twenty-four hours later, making Henry feel more nervous than he cared to admit. He hadn't seen Mary since she had returned to England with William, and even then, he'd been among the other nobles who'd come to welcome Mary and William to London. He hadn't seen her in private and didn't expect to have any communication with her until after the coronation, which was only a week away. If Her Royal Highness made time to see him now, it was because she had a good reason for seeking him out.

Henry dressed with care, choosing one of his most opulent suits, a midnight-blue velvet embroidered with silver thread and a perfect contrast to the snowy-white lace collar and cuffs of his shirt. He wore shoes with sapphire-encrusted buckles and white hose to match the shirt. His curly black wig, so like the kind his father used to wear, framed his lean face, the curls brushing his shoulders and hanging halfway down his back. He didn't want to upstage the queen, but he wished to remind her that despite being a bastard, he was still a force to be reckoned with. He was the son of a king, a duke in his own right, and a consummate courtier. He knew how the game was played as well as she did, and knew that this was an opening move in a game which would end very quickly if he countered with the wrong piece.

Henry nodded to various acquaintances as he strode through the corridors of Whitehall Palace, loath to be late for his appointment. Normally, he would stop to chat and indulge in the latest gossip and speculation, but today he had no time for such frivolous pursuits. His stomach was in knots, and his mind awhirl with possible reasons for Mary's summons. Had this been a social call, his wife would have been invited as well, but the summons had been for him alone. Henry stood erect and proud, despite his inner turmoil, as he was announced and admitted without delay.

Mary sat in a high-backed chair reminiscent of a throne, which was not a coincidence, of that Henry was certain. She couldn't be very comfortable, but she'd chosen it to remind everyone of her new position—as if they could forget. The room, which had been opulent at one point, had been stripped of some of its more elaborate decorations and now had a touch of austerity, so appropriate to the woman who sat with an open book on her lap, but made no pretense of reading.

Mary was surrounded by her ladies, who were working on their embroidery, their expressions unnaturally bland. Gone were the flamboyant gowns popular during the Stuart monarchy, the opulent fashions turning even the plainest of women into a glittering jewel. The ladies were all dressed modestly, their hair swept up and covered with lace headdresses. The ladies' faces were scrubbed clean, not a trace of powder or a beauty patch in sight.

Jocelyn, Lady Devenish, sat close to the window, her face serene as she bent over her work. There was no trace of the passionate woman who'd shoved his head between her legs only yesterday. This Jocelyn was demure and cool as marble, no sign of recognition flickering in her eyes as Henry walked into the room.

"Your Majesty," he greeted the queen with a deep bow. Henry was glad Mary was seated. She was a remarkably tall woman and made him feel dwarfed despite his own impressive stature. She was only a year older than he was, but appeared older, more mature, partly due to her royal reserve, and partly to the lines of disappointment which were etched deeply into the grooves between nose and mouth. Mary had longed for children but proved unable to carry to term. There was one known miscarriage, and several "illnesses," which were likely more lost babies. Henry did feel sympathy for her. For a woman in her position not to be able to bear a child was catastrophic and embarrassing. But Mary's pain was of a more personal kind. She wanted a child, longed to be a mother, and would have done so even if she had been the poorest of washerwomen or servants. Some women were meant to be mothers, and Mary was one of them.

Mary looked elegant as ever. She had never been one to overdress, choosing rich fabrics and simple designs over the ostentatious trends of the time. She wore a plain string of pearls about her throat, and her dark hair was dressed in flattering curls framing her face. She did look the part of the queen and had more composure and regal bearing than her father ever had.

"Your Grace," the queen countered, giving him the smallest of smiles. "A pleasure to see you." She made it sound as if he had simply dropped by, not been summoned by his queen to appear in front of her like an errant boy. "Leave us," Mary said to her women, who shuffled out without a word or a glance. They were used to being dismissed, and probably glad of a few moments of free time when they didn't have to attend on their sovereign.

What a bore it must be to spend endless hours of one's time trapped in a room with an all-seeing queen, and not be able to leave if one wished, Henry mused as he watched the women file past him.

Mary waited patiently until the door closed behind the last of the ladies before speaking. "It's good to see you, Henry. It's been an age. How are Isabella and your son? What is the boy's name?"

"Charles, Your Majesty. They are both well."

"Do give them my regards," Mary said, not without warmth.

"They will be honored by the attention, Your Majesty."

"Henry, I didn't summon you here to play the courtier, so let me speak plainly. I realize that the loyalties of a lifetime are not easily shrugged off, particularly at a time when those loyalties might still prove to be valuable, but a man has to make a choice and accept the consequences." Mary looked stern, but Henry could see a glimmer of sympathy in her eyes. She was a woman who'd had to live with divided loyalties her whole life, and now her husband occupied the throne from which her own father had been forced only a few months ago.

"I am not sure I know what you are referring to, Your Majesty," Henry replied smoothly. He knew exactly what she meant, but needed to find out how much she suspected, and how much she actually knew.

"Don't play the fool with me, Henry FitzRoy," Mary said, her tone now imperial. "I know you are in contact with my father, and I can only assume it's not to express your concern for his health and the well-being of the family. You are playing both sides and paving the way for yourself in case my father manages to take back his throne. Well, let me tell you something, cousin," Mary said with uncharacteristic venom, "my position as the daughter of James II is rather a unique one, so the people of this realm will expect me to prove myself. Should I smell even a whiff of treachery, I will not hesitate to act, particularly if it's against family. Am I making myself clear?"

"Crystal clear, Your Majesty."

"Now, I am going to ask this question just the once. Can William and I rely on your absolute loyalty, Henry?"

"Naturally, Your Majesty," Henry replied immediately, wishing desperately only to escape from Mary's clutches. Was it possible that Jocelyn had betrayed him in some way? Was their pillow talk designed to glean information for Mary? Jocelyn didn't seem the type, but who did? A good spy was not someone you'd ever suspect. He had started the relationship with Jocelyn long before William and Mary took the throne, but Jocelyn's position had changed, just as his own fortunes had shifted, and politics made strange bedfellows, as everyone was so fond of saying.

"I'd like a little token of your sincerity, cousin," Mary said with a small smile. Henry suddenly realized that she was much more comfortable in her new role than he'd realized. Mary wasn't torn at all; she was enjoying every moment of this, her new position taking her mind off her childlessness. This was her chance to prove herself to her husband and atone for some of the disappointment of failing to provide an heir. Mary could be ruthless, so Henry had to tread very carefully.

"A token, Your Majesty?" Henry asked, suddenly nervous.

"Only a small one. I want one name from you."

"Your Majesty?" Henry stammered. Dear God, did she expect him to betray people? He did have a sense of honor, after all, even if he wasn't really loyal to anyone but his own interests. To play both sides was canny; to give up one's contacts was deplorable.

"I want a name of a conspirator, Henry. Something I can take to my husband to prove to him that you are no threat to our reign. So, unless you care to spend the coming weeks in the Tower awaiting a trial, I suggest you come up with one quickly. And it best be a real name, not some wild goose chase which will end with us arresting an innocent man." Mary leaned back in her high-backed chair, her eyes slightly hooded as she contemplated Henry.

This was it, the moment of truth. If he refused to give a

name, or gave her a false one, he'd be sealing his own fate. If accused of treason, he'd go to the Tower at best, or get executed for treason at worst. As much as he didn't wish to give anyone up, he had no choice. This was self-preservation, pure and simple, and it was either his own future or someone else's on the line.

"A name," Mary repeated, her lips stretching into a sly smile. She had him by the stones, and she knew it. A refusal was paramount to political suicide. Giving Mary a name would not necessarily keep him safe, but it would buy time, the time needed to see if this monarchy would last. If Mary and William were here to stay, he needed their favor and trust. Oh, they would never trust him completely, given his parentage, but if he managed to keep his place at Court and his title and estates, that would be enough for now. And if his uncle managed to raise an army and mount an invasion, Henry could decide which side he chose to be on then, based on his uncle's chances of success.

"Hugo Everly," Henry finally said. He felt the bile rise in his throat as his stomach clenched in protest. There was no one else he could betray. Hugo Everly had a history Mary was well aware of. Having supported the Duke of Monmouth's rebellion, Mary might have some sympathy toward him since he openly fought for a Protestant monarchy. Perhaps this wouldn't have any serious repercussions for him.

"Everly?" Mary asked, clearly surprised. "Really? But we just granted him a royal pardon. He nearly lost his life in pursuit of a Protestant monarchy. Why would he now plot against us, Henry? It's nonsensical."

"People's motives are not always as clear-cut as they appear," Henry replied, inwardly cringing at his own choice of words. He'd just betrayed a man to save his own skin. His own motives were murky at best.

"Have you any proof?"

"Not at the moment," Henry replied evenly, hoping Mary

would leave it at that. Perhaps Mary would have someone keep an eye on Everly. The man was too clever to be caught, especially if forewarned. On the other hand, Mary would think that he'd lied to her, which would displease her and make her doubt his own loyalty. Either way, he was trapped.

"I want tangible proof before the coronation. If that man is truly plotting against us, I don't wish him to be present at Westminster. I expect to see you back here on April 10, cousin. Good day."

Henry FitzRoy bowed low and beat a hasty retreat, setting out in search of Jocelyn. He was thrumming with fury, every nerve ending on fire as he affected a bland expression for the benefit of the passersby. He found Jocelyn at last, sitting with a few other ladies in a comfortable parlor, awaiting the summons of the queen. In Henry's opinion, ladies-in-waiting were nothing more than dogs, kept on a leash all day by a lonely and demanding mistress. It was a great honor, to be sure, but not one he would ever want if he were a woman. It was a wonder Jocelyn managed to escape now and then, carving out time for a leisurely tryst. The rest of the time she was at the mercy of the queen and her own tyrannical husband, a man who treated her as a useful possession and a tool for his own advancement.

Henry bowed to the ladies, apologized for intruding on their peace in his search for his wife, and turned to leave, cutting his eyes at Jocelyn as he turned around. He couldn't just speak to her, so he'd have to wait around until she was able to escape for a few minutes and meet him in their spot.

The ladies smiled at him demurely, their faces betraying nothing, but Henry was certain that they guessed the reason for his unexpected arrival. His wife was actually at home, meeting with her dressmaker in preparation for the coronation.

Henry waited for nearly an hour until Jocelyn was finally able to get away. The queen dismissed the ladies while she went to chapel, preferring to pray in private rather than with her entourage.

Jocelyn slipped into the curtained alcove, her lovely face flushed. "I'm sorry; I couldn't get away," she apologized as she faced him.

"Jocelyn, please tell me it wasn't you," Henry said without preamble.

"Wasn't me what?"

"Tell me you didn't betray me. Mary knows about my activities. She's ordered me to declare my loyalty and give up a man as proof of my sincerity. I've just condemned a good man to possible death, so please tell me it wasn't you who gave me up." Henry intended to remain calm, but his hands were digging into Jocelyn's arms, his face inches away from hers as he searched her eyes for any flicker of uncertainty or guile.

"She knows about us, Henry. She is a shrewd and manipulative woman," Jocelyn replied, her face pale in the dim light of the alcove. "She threatened to tell my husband if I didn't tell her the truth about your loyalties."

"So, you sold me out to save your own skin," Henry hissed, furious. How could he blame Jocelyn when he'd just done the same thing?

"Henry, you know my husband. If he learns of our affair, he will send me away and never allow me to return. He might even ship me off to some convent as punishment for adultery. I couldn't bear that."

"Well, thank you for your honesty. I'm glad to know that your position is safe, and you can continue to enjoy yourself at Court while a man might face execution for trusting me, and that his family will be decimated by these charges."

"Henry, I am pregnant," Jocelyn breathed. Her eyes were huge with anxiety, a sheen of sweat coating her pale forehead.

"And what bearing does that have on the situation?" he demanded, his face dangerously close to hers.

"It's yours."

"And how would you know that, madam?" Henry asked. "Are you telling me that you haven't been performing your wifely duties?"

"Henry, Devenish was away for several weeks in February. Don't you remember? I am just over a month along, so there is no way it could be his."

"Don't worry, Jocelyn. He'll be so overjoyed to have gotten you full in the belly at last that he won't waste his time doing the math. He'll accept it as his own, not that it matters. Your condition doesn't justify what you've done. Don't ever speak to me again, you worthless whore," Henry ground out before walking out of the alcove. He would have been heartbroken to lose Jocelyn only yesterday, but right now, he felt nothing but disgust for the woman he'd adored. He hoped that if the child were indeed his, Jocelyn would miscarry. He didn't want that traitorous whore to be the mother of his offspring.

"Henry, I love you."

The words hung in the air as Henry stormed away, no longer interested in anything Jocelyn had to say. "Love," that was a strange word for what she'd done. He'd gotten off easily, but he could have been arrested and sent to the Tower, where he might have languished for years until either being released or executed. Hugo Everly would not get off easily though, not after the last trial. There would be no mercy for him.

SIXTY

APRIL 1689

Portsmouth, England

Max stared balefully at the group of men sitting around a large table in the center, laughing and talking as they downed one tankard of ale after another. The buxom wench who refilled their cups seemed to enjoy their ribald jokes, and dimpled at the men as she bent lower than strictly necessary when pouring the ale. She was going to make out well tonight if the men's good humor was anything to go by. Their camaraderie was there for anyone to see, and Max suddenly felt a deep sense of isolation as he nursed his tankard in solitude.

It had taken him over two years to finally return to the shores of England, but he was no longer the same person who could almost taste the rapture of his return to England while held captive in Barbados. His life in France had changed him irrevocably. Max genuinely missed Captain Benoit and Vivienne, but he especially missed the boys. By the time Max left the Benoits nearly a month ago, his pupils, Edouard and Lucien, spoke fluent English, were able to write and translate from English to

French and back, and knew more mathematics than their father ever imagined possible. They had been a delight, especially Lucien, who was the more sensitive of the two. Edouard had shaken Max's hand and thanked him for his efforts, but Lucien had flown into his arms and hugged him around the middle, visibly upset to see him go. The boys had spent more time with Max than they did with their own father, and their relationship was that of a father and his sons, or so Max liked to think, and the loss of that closeness left Max gutted.

Before saying a final goodbye, there was only one more thing Max needed to do. Hugo and his family were long gone, but there was one other person that Max wished to see. Despite his better judgment, Captain Benoit gave Max the address of the family that had purchased Banjo, the slave boy who'd come with him from Barbados. To openly visit Banjo would have been unacceptable, and possibly upsetting for the boy, but Max had waited outside the gate for several days until he finally saw Banjo's mistress leaving the house with her page in tow. Banjo had grown a few inches over the past few years, but he was still the adorable child Max remembered from the voyage aboard the *La Belle*. Banjo was dressed in a colorful outfit made of velvet and silk, and wore a yellow turban on his head; the front adorned with a large ruby pin to which a single peacock feather was attached. The feather fluttered in the spring breeze, the iridescent colors shifting from blues to purples to greens, mesmerizing in their beauty.

Banjo carried his mistress's train as she glided toward her carriage, a yapping puppy in her arms. She was no older than thirty-five, a woman of refinement and good taste. Her clothes were elegant and clearly expensive, and her face was a testament to an easy life and a healthy diet. Many women in their thirties already looked like old hags, but the woman's skin was still supple, her hair lustrous, and her teeth still in her mouth, as far as Max could tell from the small smile she bestowed on the dog.

Max watched as the woman alighted the carriage, leaving Banjo to ride up front with the liveried coachman. Just before Banjo closed the door, Max heard the woman's voice, and could almost see the smile on her face. "*Merci beaucoup, mon petite chou*," she said. Thank you very much, my little darling. She sounded kind, which is all a child in Banjo's position could ask for. The boy smiled, bowed, and jumped up on the bench after closing the carriage door. Max had seen what he'd come for, so he stepped behind a hedge before Banjo could see him from his perch. No need to upset the boy. Max walked away, satisfied that Banjo was well looked after. He had no idea what he would have done if he wasn't, but now he didn't have to worry about that. He hoped that someday Banjo would have a good life, a life in which he would be free to choose his own path, but, for now, he was far better off than he would have been cutting cane fourteen hours a day on a sugar plantation alongside his parents, if they were still alive.

Max finished his ale and made his way to his room at the top of the stairs. Tomorrow, he would set off for London. The original plan had been to go straight back to Cranley to confront Hugo before leaving this godforsaken century, but having heard about the coronation which was to take place in two days' time in London, Max couldn't resist the lure of the spectacle. So far, he'd lived history in a way that no ordinary person could even dream of, but he hadn't actually witnessed anything joyful or grandiose. Seeing the coronation would be a fitting end to his sojourn in the past, so a couple more days wouldn't make too much difference to his ultimate goal. He could be in Cranley within a few days; back to his old life before the end of next week. The thought, rather than bringing him joy, caused Max anxiety. He pulled off his boots, threw his breeches over a chair and climbed into bed in his shirt.

Three years was a long time to be away. What would he find on the other end of the passage? If Neve had borne a son, the entire line of succession would have changed. *What if I'd never even been born?* Max suddenly thought to himself. He supposed such a thing were possible. He might return to the twenty-first century to find that he simply didn't exist. What then? Would his mother still be there? Would Simon? If Clarence never inherited Everly Manor, it was reasonable to assume that Stella Harding wouldn't be there either, nor would her son. The more Max thought about his homecoming, the more anxious he became, tossing and turning for what seemed like hours before finally sinking into a fitful slumber, which was interrupted too soon by the sounds of activity from the wharf. It was morning; a cold and misty morning—the day he began his journey toward home.

SIXTY-ONE

APRIL 1689

Surrey, England

A lovely spring breeze caressed Liza's flushed face as she walked toward the church, having left her horse and cart at the inn. The trees were budding, and the sky overhead was a clear blue, not a cloud marring its pristine perfection. The road was blessedly dry, not the muddy mess of a few days ago caused by nearly a full week of rain. On any other day, Liza would have enjoyed the time to herself, but today her mind wasn't on the pleasures of nature. The past two months had been some of the hardest Liza had ever had to endure. Her remaining savings had been spent on tonic for her mother, which was really just laudanum sold for an exorbitant price by the local wisewoman.

Her mother had been in excruciating pain as she neared the end, so Liza couldn't bring herself to bargain or scrimp. Her mother had been the only person in her life who'd truly loved her; the only person who believed in her, and forgave her when she'd done wrong, as she so often had. She would have paid double if she had to in order to ease her mother's suffering but was still glad that a small sum was left over to get her mother a fine casket and a modest headstone. Sal Timmins had passed three weeks ago today, and then Johnny had gotten ill, sapping the last of Liza's strength and funds. Thank heavens Johnny had recovered, but something needed to be done to restore the family's fortunes. Her attempt to swindle Hugo Everly had failed, as had her gamble with Josiah Finch, but there was one more thing she wanted to try.

Liza passed beneath the lichen-covered gate leading to St. Nicolas's church and walked briskly up the path. It was mid-morning, so the church would be empty, and Reverend Snow free to hear what she had to say. Liza stopped inside the church porch, adjusted the shawl about her shoulders, and smoothed her skirts. She needed to look respectable for what she was about to do.

The door was heavier than she remembered; she had to use both hands to push it open before walking into the solemn hush of the church. It looked just as she remembered it: squat and dim, the smell of wood, candle smoke, and dust filling her nostrils.

The reverend was nowhere to be seen, so Liza walked toward the lectern, her worn shoes making almost no sound on the stone nave. She would take a seat in the first pew and pretend to pray while she waited for Reverend Snow to arrive. To convey an illusion of piety might predispose him toward her. In truth, she'd stopped praying years ago. What was the point when no one was listening? God had forsaken her long ago, probably around the time she had forsaken herself. Had she remained virtuous, she might have a husband now to take care of her and her family, but she was all alone, with no one to turn to in time of need.

She was acutely aware of what would happen to Johnny should she die. Her sisters would look after him until he was old enough to fend for himself, then set him out into the world with nothing to his name but his mother's shame. With no money, no education, and no apprenticeship under his belt, Johnny would be lucky to survive. She had to set money aside for his future, money that would go to furnish him with a skill which would ensure a living. He'd have to support a family someday, and he needed to earn a wage. What she was about to do wasn't for herself; it was for her son and his future.

Liza was sat with her head bent, her hands clasped before her when Reverend Snow came out of the vestry and closed the door softly behind him, as if he were afraid of disturbing God himself. Liza looked up, eager to see his reaction to finding her in his church.

Reverend Snow's look of surprise was quickly replaced by a smile of welcome as he approached her slowly. "Liza, is it not?" he asked, his head tilted slightly to the side as he tried to connect the face to the name.

"Yes," Liza answered timidly.

"I haven't seen you here since you left Everly Manor," the reverend commented, tactfully refraining from mentioning the circumstances of Liza's dismissal. "Have you found employment hereabouts?"

"No, Reverend Snow, I came here to speak to you."

"Oh?"

Reverend Snow would assume that Liza couldn't talk to her own parish clergyman because of something shameful that she had done, but she wasn't here to speak of her own shame. She'd led a blameless life for the past few years, taking care of her ailing mother, raising her son, and trying to be both mother and sister to her younger sisters. She was here for an entirely different reason.

"How can I be of service to you?" Reverend Snow asked as he took a seat next to Liza. She'd always liked him. He was an approachable and understanding man, not like Reverend Pettigrew at her parish church near Haslemere. Pettigrew was fanatical and cruel, a man who couldn't begin to relate to the problems his parishioners faced or give the support and guidance they needed. The God he served was as cruel and unforgiving as the clergyman, one who would see them all burn in Hell.

Liza lowered her eyes and began to pleat the fabric of her skirt, as if in apprehension. In reality, she wasn't apprehensive at all, but she needed to give the appearance of a woman who was wrestling with her conscience. Reverend Snow had to see that she was conflicted, torn even. Liza took a shuddering breath and let it out, before allowing herself a peek at the reverend. He just sat quietly, waiting for her to compose herself.

"I shouldn't have come," Liza said, making as if to rise to her feet.

"Come, Liza, tell me what's on your mind. The Lord is forgiving to those who repent for their sins."

"'Tis not my sin I've come to speak of," Liza whispered dramatically.

"Whose then?"

Liza finally raised her eyes to the reverend, ready to commence the performance. It was a gamble to be sure, but she not only had a great need of money, but of revenge. Hugo Everly had ruined her life. He'd used her; left her at the mercy of his vicious sister, who had dismissed her without a character reference or wages owed to her, and nearly got her killed by Lionel Finch. She knew that wasn't strictly true, but needed to believe her own lie in order to do what she must to survive and provide for Johnny.

"I've kept this to myself for several years, Reverend Snow, but I feel that I can remain silent no longer. My conscience won't permit me to allow evil to thrive."

"And what evil is that?" Reverend Snow had sat up straighter, his kind eyes no longer full of sympathy. He looked wary, almost frightened, which was what Liza had been hoping for.

She took another deep breath and stared at her shoes for a moment before squaring her shoulders and raising her head defiantly, ready to tell all.

"I saw things when I worked at Everly Manor—terrible things. I was too afraid to speak out, too fearful for my own soul, but I have worked up the courage to tell the truth."

"About what?"

"About witchcraft," Liza said, lowering her voice to a barely audible whisper. "I knew that Neve Ashley was a witch as soon as she came. Appeared out of nowhere, she did, and bewitched Lord Everly on the spot. Told him she knew things, could see things."

"There are those who have the Sight, Liza," Reverend Snow said sternly.

"Oh, aye, some do, but not her. 'Tis not the Sight she has, but black magic. I was there the day Lord Everly disappeared. I was watching from behind a tree. She spirited him away, turned him into a crow before my very own eyes. They flew away together, not to be seen again for months. Why, Captain Norrington and his men had seen it too, but were too afraid to speak of it. Afraid of the wrath of the witch."

"And have you seen any other signs of witchcraft while at Everly Manor?" the reverend asked. Liza had his full attention now.

"Oh, yes. There were times when I was still awake at midnight, working late to finish my daily chores, when I saw her performing strange rituals and intoning incantations in a language I didn't recognize. Spoke in tongues, she did, when no one was watching. I mentioned my fears to Mistress Hiddleston, and she became so frightened for his lordship that she dismissed me rather than face the truth. Why, you can ask Harriet. She's seen strange happenings as well," Liza added for good measure.

"Liza, are you making a formal accusation against Lady

Everly?" Reverend Snow asked. He wanted her to deny what she'd just said and go away, but Liza had come this far. She wasn't about to stop.

"I am."

"Accusing someone of witchcraft is a very serious matter. Are you prepared to testify before an ecclesiastical court?"

"Ecclesiastical court?" Liza asked, stunned.

"Yes, of course. I will have to make a report of this to the archbishop, and he will send a tribunal of experienced witch-hunters to examine Lady Everly. Your testimony will be required, since you are the one making the accusation."

Liza stared at Reverend Snow in shock. She hadn't considered that he might have to pass this on to a higher authority. The plan had been simple: make an accusation, watch the Everlys squirm as the whole village turned on Lady Everly in light of her nefarious activities, and then demand that Hugo Everly pay her off to withdraw the accusation. Oh, Liza did think there was something rather otherworldly about that woman, something odd and unspeakable, but she was no witch —not a good one in any case. Had she been a powerful witch, she would have saved her daughter from death, would have made a covenant with the Devil for the life of her child.

Well, there was no going back now. She would testify and get Harriet to testify as well. Everyone would learn of Neve Ashley's strange arrival and even stranger departure. Perhaps she would be burned at the stake or drowned, leaving Hugo in need of comfort and understanding. Once he recovered from being bewitched, he might even realize that Liza had saved him from a life of damnation.

Get a hold of yourself, you fool, Liza admonished herself. She was here for money and revenge, not scraps from Neve Ashley's table. She didn't want Hugo anymore, nor would he be stupid enough to believe a word of Liza's accusation. He would hunt her to the ends of the earth if she were responsible for the death of his wife. But he wouldn't have to suffer if he only gave her a small sum, enough to doubt her recollections and refuse to testify for fear of condemning a good woman to the fires of Hell.

"Leave it with me, Liza," Reverend Snow said sternly. Liza could see the disapproval in his face and the briskness of his manner, but she didn't care. Of course, he would take the side of Lady Everly. To offend Lord Everly might cost him dearly, but he had no choice now. He couldn't just ignore the accusation of witchcraft. He was compelled to act, whether he agreed or not. The wheels were in motion.

SIXTY-TWO
APRIL 1689

Essex, England

Jem stared balefully at the wall in front of him in order to distract himself from the terrible pain in his knees. There were a few interesting cracks, but nothing to really take his mind off the confrontation that had taken place an hour ago. These run-ins with his stepmother were happening more and more often, and although his father felt a certain loyalty to Jem, he had to side with his wife in order to keep the peace. Jem wasn't sure if his father realized what was going on, but it wasn't for him to enlighten him.

Anjelica Marsden was waging a military campaign against Jem, the bastard child who stood to inherit the Marsden estate instead of her own son. She was a shrewd and calculating woman who'd waited patiently for Anne Marsden to die so that she could marry her widowed husband, and managed to get with child just when it would make it impossible for Nicholas to have any second thoughts about marrying his mistress. And now she had a son, an heir, and his position was threatened by the by-blow of her husband's affair with a woman who'd been no better than a whore. Not only was Jem a threat to Will's inheritance, but he was a permanent reminder of the woman her husband once loved, a woman who still haunted his dreams and controlled Nicholas from beyond the grave through her son.

It had started innocently enough with Anjelica trying to assert "motherly" rights over Jem, but her demands were becoming more unreasonable, and the punishments more creative, like this torture she'd devised of making Jem kneel on his bare knees on a floor sprinkled with raw peas. The hard little pellets dug into his skin, making him want to cry. But he wouldn't cry, just as he wouldn't call that woman "mother." That had been her latest demand, which she knew he'd refuse. It was just a ploy to turn Nicholas against him and show him that all she wanted was to be a mother to his son, who refused to honor or obey her as a son should.

"Jemmy, would it be so difficult for you to respect Anjelica's wishes?" Nicholas asked, his voice tempered with a desire to be reasonable. Anjelica had come to him in tears a few minutes ago, stung by Jem's refusal to give her a chance. The tears were fake, meant to soften Nicholas's heart toward her and harden it toward the boy who took every opportunity to cause her pain.

"She is not my mother," Jem retorted, angry with his father for taking that woman's side. He had no desire to hurt her or disrespect her; he simply wanted her to leave him be, but that wouldn't achieve her aim of driving a wedge between Jem and Nicholas.

"I know that, but she is my wife and the closest thing you have to a mother in this world. Please, just do it to make me happy," Nicholas cajoled.

"The closest person to a mother I have in this world is Lady Everly," Jem answered calmly. "And the closest thing I've ever had to a father is Lord Everly, and nothing has changed," he spat out.

Jem enjoyed the shock in his father's eyes, quickly replaced by hurt. He hadn't meant what he said, well maybe a little, but he wanted Nicholas Marsden to feel the pain he was feeling at being ripped away from the family he loved; forced to accept a stepmother and a brother he despised and kept from doing anything he found even remotely enjoyable. Oh, how he missed tagging along with Archie and spending time with Lord Everly. His father was always busy, always distracted. He loved Jem, to be sure, but he hadn't actually devoted much time to him since returning from Paris. Jem was looked after, educated, given gifts, but the father-son bond that he'd hoped for had never developed, leaving Jem missing the people he truly loved.

Jem shifted his weight on his tortured knees and closed his eyes to stifle the tears which threatened to flow. He wasn't some parcel to be picked up and carried home, then discarded. He was a person, and he had feelings and desires, and his desire was to get away from this place and be with the people he missed, even if that meant forfeiting his inheritance, which Anjelica would find a way to strip him of anyway. The coronation was in a few days. He was sure that Lord and Lady Everly would be in London for the big event, and what fun it would be to see the procession and feel free of the tyranny he faced at home. All he had to do was find an opportune moment to get away. He had some money of his own, his horse, and a sense of direction. Getting to London wouldn't be that difficult so long as he kept to the main roads. His father would have no idea where he'd gone, and it would never occur to him to look for Jem in London.

Jem's eyes flew open, the tears no longer a threat. He'd dreamed of running away for months. Well, why not? What was the worst thing that could happen? Hugo Everly would eventually write to Nicholas, but at least he would have an adventure, and spend some time with the Everlys. God, he even missed Frances. A slow smile spread across Jem's face, his knees forgotten.

SIXTY-THREE

APRIL 1689

London, England

"Oh, I do wish I could go," Frances complained for the hundredth time as she ran her fingers reverently over my best gown. Ruby had cleaned and steamed it, but I needed to hang it up once we got to Brad's London house to avoid further creasing before I was to wear it tomorrow. Brad and Beth chose not to come to London for the big event; they had not been officially invited to the coronation, and had no desire to watch the procession from the sidelines, but they had kindly offered the use of their house since all the inns would be full to bursting. Archie and Frances came with us, eager to see the spectacle and enjoy a few days in London. Archie had recently returned from London, but Frances had never actually been. Lionel never allowed her to leave the estate, and she had spent time at the convent before leaving with us for France. She was bubbling with excitement, her eyes sparkling with the wonder of it all.

I had to admit that, just like Frances, I was giddy with anticipation. The city pulsed with excitement, ready for the procession which would take place tomorrow. Some said that the coronation would be more modest than that of King James II, William and Mary being known for their practicality rather than frivolity, but the people didn't care. It would still be an all-day celebration, with pubs and taverns overflowing with humanity, and every able-bodied person out in the streets to watch the royal procession to Westminster Abbey. This was to be a double coronation for both William and Mary, the first of its kind, in the seventeenth century at least.

The buoyant mood of the people had been palpable this afternoon when we'd arrived, and I could only imagine what it would be like tomorrow once spectators began to line the streets, eager for a glimpse of the monarchs. I imagined it would be something like Prince Charles and Diana's wedding, which I had seen footage of on television when I was a child. At the time, it had seemed like a fairy tale, with Charles dashing in his uniform and Diana dreamy in her princess gown. I was no longer the innocent child of those days, but I still longed to be part of this historic moment, a moment I had only learned about in school.

I smiled at Frances as she continued to pout. "I am sure it will be long and dull," I said in the hopes of making her feel better.

"I still would have liked to see it," she replied as she took the dress off its hanger, held it against her body and twirled around. There were times when Frances seemed much older than her eighteen years, but there were those rare moments when she was nothing more than a child; her natural innocence and exuberance shining through for brief seconds before being eclipsed by her reserve born of years of subjugation. I was glad to see that since marrying Archie, she had not withdrawn deeper into herself, but had blossomed in a subtle, but notice-able way, which reassured me that all was well between them.

"I will tell you all about it; I promise."

"I want to hear all the details of the reception at the palace,"

Frances said dreamily. "The gowns, the food, the music. Oh, I am sure it will be glorious."

"I wish I could smuggle you in," I replied, knowing that Frances would probably enjoy the occasion a lot more than I would. I was terribly nervous, especially after my awkward experiences at Versailles. I suppose that after having survived the Court of Louis XIV I had nothing to worry about, but I still dreaded being put in a position where people would be judging and speculating about me. I wasn't one of them; I was an outsider with no impressive family tree or a sizeable fortune which tended to pave the way for even the most unaristocratic of creatures. I was simply Hugo Everly's wife, a woman who had snagged a lord with nothing more than fading good looks and a fertile uterus, according to some.

Frances sat down on the bed and stifled a yawn. "I am tired," she complained. "Perhaps I should go to bed. I doubt Archie will be up any time soon. They are having a game of cards in the parlor."

"I think Archie would eagerly lose the game in order to join you," I joked, making her blush. "Come to think of it, I think I'd like Hugo to join me as well. Let's go put the idea into their heads," I suggested.

Frances and I were halfway down the stairs when a loud banging sounded at the front door. It was nearly ten o'clock at night, and my heart leaped into my throat with sudden fear. No one brought good news at night. Ever. I froze, my hand gripping the banister until my knuckles turned white. I heard Frances's sharp intake of breath behind me; she was just as scared. The flame of the candle she held wavered, casting shifting shadows onto the wall.

Hugo appeared in the doorway of the parlor with Archie behind him, his hand going to his hip for his sword, but it wasn't there. Both men had taken off their swords upon arrival and left them upstairs. Billingsley, the old family servant, had retired an hour ago with our blessing, so Archie stepped around Hugo to answer the door. The thick wood of the door practically vibrated with the relentless banging, the person on the other side determined to gain entrance.

Archie unbolted and opened the door and was instantly pushed aside and pinned to the wall by a member of the Royal Guard. Three more men trooped into the foyer, going straight for Hugo, who stood still despite the obvious hostility of the men. Any show of resistance would be futile.

"Lord Hugo Everly, by order of His Majesty King William III, you are under arrest. You will accompany us to the Tower of London where you will await trial." The man was clearly in charge, and he motioned for one of the other soldiers to clap Hugo in irons.

"That won't be necessary. I will come willingly," Hugo replied, his tone even. "What is the charge?"

"Treason," the man replied with a smirk. "You just can't keep your nose clean, can you, *Your Lordship*?" he sniggered as he shoved Hugo toward the door.

Archie made a move toward Hugo, but the man who'd pushed him against the wall punched him hard in the stomach, making Archie double over in pain.

"Stay out of the way," he growled, driving his knee into Archie's middle for good measure.

Hugo turned around, his eyes searching out mine in the dim light of the foyer. "It will be all right, Neve. Don't worry. I love you."

I opened my mouth to reply, but the men had already forced Hugo outside and slammed the door shut behind them. I felt as if my knees turned to water as I slid down onto the step beneath me. I was shaking with shock and terror, unable to comprehend what had just happened. Why had Hugo been arrested? What did they have on him? And what was I to do?

Frances was torn between supporting me and going to

Archie, who slid down to the floor and was still gasping for air, his hand on his stomach. "Go to him," I murmured to Frances. There was nothing she could do for me.

* * *

Eventually, Archie and Frances talked me into going to bed, but sleep was impossible. I lay in the empty bed, staring at the canopy as my mind went absolutely haywire. It was me. I had done this. I had talked to Hugo about changing history with the proof being our attendance at the coronation. Well, history was at it again. There was no proof that we could change anything since we would not be at the coronation after all. Something had happened at the eleventh hour, changing everything— possibly forever. Archie, Frances, and I had sat up for hours, trying to brainstorm a way to help Hugo, but we couldn't think of anything. If Hugo had been arrested, there was some evidence against him, some accusation, and since we all knew what Hugo was involved in, we also knew that it was probably not fabricated. Hugo had cheated death several times in the past few years. What if his destiny had finally caught up with him?

Hot tears slid down my cheeks as I sat up, wrapped my arms about my knees, and rocked back and forth. I had lost my baby, and now I might lose my husband. What if Valentine and Michael were next? What if this was the final reckoning?

SIXTY-FOUR

William of Orange stood patiently as his manservant went about undressing his person. He was tired and ill-tempered tonight, his nerves thrumming with tension at the thought of tomorrow's coronation. A myriad of little details had been seen to; last-minute preparations finally complete. He could have left all the planning to others, but he was a man who liked to be in control, and he needed to be sure that everything would be done to his satisfaction. The palace kitchens would be going all night with numerous cooks and maids preparing for tomorrow's celebration, but the royal apartments were quiet at last, the hissing of the fire in the grate the only sound in the vast bedchamber.

William closed his eyes and lowered his head as his faithful servant began to knead his shoulders skillfully. William sighed with contentment as the tension began to ease and a languid drowsiness stole over him, making him wish that he could just retire. But there was one more thing he had to do. Mary had asked to see him before he went to bed; she had some urgent matter to discuss. William didn't feel like visiting her bedchamber tonight, but his wife was his loyal companion and advisor. He wouldn't join her in bed, but he would go and talk to her, as courtesy demanded.

"Thank you, Wilf. That will be all," William said as he flexed his shoulders, threw on a dressing gown, and headed to the adjoining door between the chambers.

Mary was still fully dressed, her face tense as she sat staring into the fire. Her maid hovered in the background, waiting for the order to help her mistress prepare for bed, but Mary paid her no mind, her eyes alert and full of anxiety. Mary was a woman who rarely allowed herself to relax; she was always in control, at least when in front of others. She'd had a few episodes of utter despair, but those occasions were preceded by the loss of their unborn children. William had held her and allowed her to cry as he'd smoothed back her hair and told her over and over again that it wasn't her fault, and their childless state was the will of God.

Could Mary be with child again? William briefly wondered. Her anxiety could be caused by fear of another miscarriage, but he didn't think that was the case. He hadn't been around her much lately, not in the intimate sense, so the likelihood of pregnancy was slight. It would be a blessing, though. He must try harder to get Mary with child. Perhaps the good Lord would be kinder to them this time and allow them the joy of welcoming a live child into their life.

William took a seat across from his wife and reached for her hands. They were cold despite the roaring fire in the grate. "What is it, my dear? You look upset."

Mary sighed as her gaze slid to her husband, a look of relief passing over her features. Talking things over always helped her put things in perspective, and now that William was there, they'd put the matter to rest.

"I'm better now that you are here," Mary said with a gentle smile. "I've been fretting all evening, but you were too busy to see me, so I had to take measures into my own hands."

"Regarding what?" William felt the blissful relaxation of only a few moments ago slipping away, the tension stealing back in, his neck and shoulders stiffening. Mary was a strong and intelligent woman who made her own decisions without consulting him on every detail. If she felt this anxious about something, it had to be rather serious. "What troubles you, my love?" William asked patiently. "Tell me."

"I've issued an arrest warrant for Lord Everly in your name. He's been apprehended and taken to the Tower," Mary said, her words coming out in an uncharacteristic rush.

"What? Why?" William gasped. "I've just issued a royal pardon for the man. What possible reason could you have to have him arrested?"

"I've applied a little pressure to my cousin Henry. You know how wily he is, and I was sure that he was passing information to my father in France. I needed to frighten him into declaring his loyalty, and to find out who else is working on behalf of James II. I took a gamble, William, and blackmailed Henry into giving me a name of a traitor as proof of his loyalty."

"Have you any proof?"

Mary pulled out a folded piece of paper from the pocket of her gown. She held it out to William, who unfolded the letter and looked at lines and lines of indecipherable gibberish.

"What is this?"

"It's written in code. Henry helped me translate it. It's most incriminating, William."

"But it's not signed, so there's no proof that this was written by Hugo Everly. Henry could have written this himself, for all you know, to deflect attention from his own activities. You can't put a man on trial based on one piece of coded correspondence that isn't signed, Mary. I think you might have blundered on this one."

"William, I believe Henry when he says that Everly is a traitor. I didn't want him to be at the coronation, honored by our invitation and then arrested for treason later. It would make us look weak and foolish." Mary was becoming agitated, her cheeks stained with two patches of bright color.

"Mary, my love, Hugo Everly worked with the Duke of Monmouth to bring about a Protestant monarchy. What reason would he now have to spy for a Catholic king? This makes no sense. We can't arrest a man simply on hearsay from your cousin, who would do anything to save his own skin, I might add. This should have been handled delicately. I could have put one of my best men on Everly: watched him, intercepted his correspondence, and questioned his contacts. Now that he's in the Tower, we can do nothing to prove his guilt unless we can get someone to testify against him or produce actual proof of treason."

"I am sorry, William. I thought I was doing the right thing. What are we to do?"

William pulled Mary to her feet and wrapped his arms about her waist, resting his cheek against her stomacher. "We do nothing for the moment. To arrest Everly and then to release him will make us look even more foolish. Perhaps we can find evidence to support our claim that he is a traitor."

"You mean fabricate evidence?" Mary asked, her voice filled with hope.

William nodded silently against her as she stroked his hair, a faraway look in her eyes. They needed to assert themselves and make a show of strength. Sacrificing one for the benefit of many was a sound strategy, if it worked.

SIXTY-FIVE

"Archie, what is going to happen?" Frances asked as she gazed at Archie in the cold light of a merciless dawn. She hadn't slept at all, and although Archie had drifted off sometime in the small hours, she could feel the tension coursing through his body even in sleep. The room was cold, the fire having burned down to ashes, their acrid smell filling the air. Frances snuggled closer to Archie, desperate for warmth and reassurance.

"I don't know, Franny. I keep trying to think of what his lordship would do, but nothing comes to mind. There are only two things that can save him: proof that the evidence against him is false or a royal pardon—neither of which is very likely to happen, given the circumstances. I didn't want to say so in front of her ladyship, but I believe Hugo's luck has run out."

"Shall we send a messenger to Master Bradford?"

"And what can he do? He has no influence at Court, and even if he did, nothing he can say or do could make a difference in a case of treason. He'd helped Maximillian escape the death penalty by engaging Gideon Warburton, but this time, there will be no escape. To show mercy to a man who'd been charged with treason twice would look like a sign of weakness in our new monarchs. Everyone will be watching and waiting, eager to see what others can expect for supporting Old King James. There will be many who will be accused of treason in days to come, and if William and Mary set a precedent of being lenient, there will be that many more."

Frances began to cry quietly, unable to believe that things had changed so quickly. Less than twenty-four hours ago, she was pouting about not being able to attend the coronation, and now she had to accept that Hugo would likely die very soon, leaving Neve and the children to fend for themselves in a world where they would be disgraced and ostracized for their connection to a traitor. Little Michael might even be stripped of his title and estate, leaving Neve destitute.

"We'll look after her, Franny," Archie promised as he planted a kiss on top of Frances's head. "We will remain loyal."

SIXTY-SIX

Hugo stood before the narrow window, his hands braced on the stone walls. He hadn't slept a wink last night, unable to still his brain long enough to rest. He'd been betrayed, he knew that, but at this point, it didn't really matter by whom. If there was proof of his treachery, he was done for. He'd played a game and lost. Checkmate. The worst part was that the only person he could blame was himself. He'd been living on borrowed time since the spring of 1685. He should have faced the consequences of his actions and spared Neve the horror he'd put her through. He should have let her go when he had the chance, but he'd been weak. He couldn't say no to love, couldn't say no to the promise of a family. He'd craved those things so desperately that he allowed his need to cloud his judgment.

And now Neve would be left a widow so soon after losing Elena. How would she cope? How would she survive in this world that wasn't her own? Would she take the children to the future? He hoped so. They were young enough to forget he ever existed, to forget that their father was a source of shame and disappointment. Neve would meet someone eventually, and the man would raise Hugo's children, never knowing that the man who sired them was right there in the history books, his name synonymous with treason, just like Benedict Arnold whom Hugo had read about while in the twenty-first century.

Hugo moved away from the window and smashed his fist into the stone wall, gasping as the pain shot up his arm. He knew he should stop, but he hit the wall again, smearing blood on the stone that had seen many a prisoner's fear and frustration. The physical pain momentarily eclipsed the emotional pain, but no amount of blood could wash away the sense of guilt.

Hugo lay flat as a plank on the cot. He was suddenly exhausted, emotionally and physically, and he sank into a deep sleep while cradling his injured hand.

SIXTY-SEVEN

Max looked around in wonder, amazed to see so many people lining the streets. The buoyancy of the crowds was amazing to behold; the people of London united for one brief moment in a show of unity and support. Everyone was happy and excited, people chatting loudly over the roar of the crowds and exchanging opinions and bits of gossip. The royal procession would begin in about an hour, but already the streets were impassable; the throngs of onlookers impenetrable as they waited for a glimpse of the royal couple.

Max suddenly wished he could just get away. This was all too much. Being pushed and shoved by strangers made him feel angry and anxious, so he carefully made his way through the crowd toward a tavern he'd seen earlier. It was probably closed, but at least he would no longer be in the thick of it. Being surrounded by such happy people united by a sense of camaraderie left him feeling lonelier than ever—a man apart.

The tavern proved to be open, and packed, spectators getting tankards of ale and beer while waiting for the show to begin. Some weren't as interested in a glimpse of the royals as they were in simply enjoying the day and basking in the feeling of well-being, which permeated every corner of the city on a day like today.

Max ordered some beer and sat in the corner, relieved to be in a place where he could have some personal space. He took a sip and leaned back in his chair, watching the comings and goings. He had nowhere to be and no reason to rush. Getting out of the city today would be impossible anyway.

Max stiffened as two men walked into the tavern. One was a stranger, but one he recognized as a guard from the Tower. He was the man who'd escorted him to the trial and clapped him in chains. Max withdrew into the shadows, not wanting to draw attention to himself, but the men were oblivious, happy to have a little time off. They were talking loudly in order to be heard over the crowds outside as they gulped their ale. Max paid no attention to the conversation. It was all "shop talk" about the prisoners at the Tower of London and something about a lion dying at the menagerie. Max ordered some bread and cheese and tucked in, feeling suddenly ravenously hungry. He hadn't eaten since lunchtime yesterday, but lately his appetite came and went, and he often forgot to eat altogether.

"Have you heard about our latest arrival?" one of the guards asked the other with a look of glee. "A friend of yours, I believe, Cecil."

"And who might that be?"

"Hugo Everly. Accused of treason. Again."

"Really?" Cecil asked in astonishment. "Last I heard, he'd been sent down to Barbados. What's he doing back in London? And up to his old tricks already? I tell you, some people just have a death wish, they do. God's wounds, if I were a wealthy lord, I'd enjoy my estates, collect rents, and chase all the pretty village girls. Do they still have that custom where the lord of the manor can sample the girls before the marriage?"

"That was during the feudal days, you fool. It was called 'Droit du seigneur,'" the man replied with a laugh.

"Well, aren't you well informed," Cecil guffawed. "In that case, I'd like to be a feudal lord. Just give me the money and send in the women. I wouldn't care a jot about who is on the throne or of what faith they are. I'd be lord and master of my own little kingdom."

"If you're quite finished fantasizing, oh lord and master, it's time for us to return. The Constable of the Tower reckons today might be a good day for an escape attempt since attention will be on the coronation, so we need to return to our posts. Wouldn't do to have someone break out; there'd be hell to pay."

"Right you are, Rich. Right you are. Let's go then." Cecil threw a coin on the table and followed his companion out into the bright April morning.

Max stared at their retreating backs, his mind still trying to absorb the news he'd just heard. Hugo had been arrested for treason, which meant several things: Neve was alone and vulnerable; Hugo would most likely be executed; and Clarence would inherit the estate as he was meant to, unless Hugo and Neve had a son. Still, the child might lose the title thanks to his father's propensity for getting caught red-handed. Was it possible that everything would still turn out as it was supposed to? Max wondered as he took a slow pull of beer.

* * *

The sounds of jubilation had long died down, but Max sat immobile, his bread and cheese forgotten. The tavern wench had refilled his tankard twice, but Max had covered it with his hand the last time she came round in the universal gesture of "thanks, but no more." He had no wish to be drunk.

Max was lost in thought, his eyes focused on some faraway point only he could see. He'd felt aimless and depressed for the past few months, but suddenly everything had changed with one random conversation. Or perhaps it hadn't been random at all; perhaps he was meant to overhear it and act on the information. Years ago, he had scoffed at the idea of fate or destiny, but not anymore. Things had a way of happening, as if they were all part of some grand design, invented by a celestial architect who probably had a wicked sense of humor at best, or a cruel streak at the very worst.

The news changed everything. Max now had a purpose, a destiny to fulfill. He finally rose to his feet, paid for his food and drink, and made his way out of the tavern onto the less crowded street. People were still celebrating, the inns and public houses overflowing with patrons, and drunken masses of humanity moving in slow motion from place to place. Sounds of song could be heard erupting from various establishments, and the city's commerce seemed to have come to a standstill, people of every social class taking a few hours out of their mundane lives to celebrate a new chapter in their country's turbulent history.

Max walked toward the inn where he'd taken a room the day before. He had a few hours in which to come up with a plan since now he knew exactly what he had to do.

SIXTY-EIGHT

I paced the parlor like a caged lioness, unable to settle down for even a moment. I had planned to go see Hugo first thing in the morning, but Archie had dissuaded me, rightfully pointing out that the Tower might be locked down for the coronation and that even if it wasn't, we'd need money to bribe a guard, and to approach Hugo with no plan was pointless. We needed another day at least, since between the three of us we still had no clue how to proceed. Even in the clear light of day, we had no ideas. There was no one to bribe, no one to appeal to, and no one to ask for guidance. The only way to free Hugo was to break him out, and that was the equivalent of Mission Impossible.

My tired brain suddenly conjured up an image of Alice in Wonderland at the Queen's croquet match. "Off with his head!" the Queen of Hearts yelled in my mind, making me shake with terror. All I wanted was to wake up from this night-mare and find myself safe and sound in my own world. But this was my world now. There was no going back, no undoing what Hugo and I had done. It wasn't just us anymore; we had chil-dren and people who depended on us.

I finally sat down and accepted a cup of tea from Frances.

She'd learned to like tea, and knew that it was my go-to remedy in times of crisis or indecision. Archie refused a cup. He remained by the window, looking out over the street as if he were expecting the answer to just present itself somewhere out there.

"We need a plan," I said yet again, but got no answer from either Archie or Frances. They remained mute, lost in their own helplessness.

"Your Ladyship, I think you and Frances should return to Surrey," Archie suddenly suggested.

"Why?"

"The children need you, and there's nothing you can do here. I will remain in London and try to find out what evidence the Crown has against Hugo. Only then can I attempt to find means to discredit it, or the person who's provided it."

I gaped at Archie, reading between the lines. "Archie, are you suggesting that you will kill the person who might testify against Hugo?"

"If I must," Archie replied, his voice laced with tension. "They can't send a man to his death without proof, and if the proof is unavailable, they might reconsider."

"But what if the proof is already in their hands? What if it's a document of some sort?"

"Hugo would never put anything in writing or sign his name," Archie replied stubbornly. "Whatever they have is not enough to convict."

"It is if they want to make an example of him," Frances said quietly, voicing what we were all thinking. "They don't need solid proof, just enough to raise suspicion. Besides, as we know from the last trial, witnesses are not always truthful."

"I'm not leaving London until I see Hugo," I said, my tone brooking no argument.

"Tomorrow then," Archie conceded as he stepped away from the window. "Then you go home."

"All right," I replied through clenched teeth. How could I go home when Hugo was in the Tower, awaiting a trial which would most likely send him to his death? I needed to find a way to help him; I had before.

We all started with surprise as a loud banging announced a visitor. I yelped in shock as hot tea spilled over my hand, and hastily put the cup down, following Archie into the foyer. He shooed Billingsley out of the way and carefully unlocked the door to admit Bradford Nash, who looked as if he'd ridden hell-for-leather for the past few hours.

"Brad, you heard?" I asked as I went to him, taking his gloved hands in mine.

"Heard what?" Brad asked, his confusion evident. His gaze flew from me to Archie and Frances, clearly looking for Hugo.

"About Hugo's arrest."

Brad froze, his eyes opening wide with shock. "Hugo's been arrested? On what charge?"

"Treason," Archie spat out.

Brad didn't say anything, simply walked into the parlor and sat heavily on the settee. "Get me a drink," he said to Billingsley, who was hovering in the doorway, waiting to see if refreshments would be required. "I didn't know about Hugo," Brad said at last. "That wasn't why I came."

I sank into a chair, suddenly cold all over. Brad had ridden to London on the day of the coronation because something was wrong at home. I tried to retain some semblance of control, but my hands were shaking in my lap as the implications of Brad's arrival began to sink in.

"The children..." I mumbled, unable to form a sentence.

"The children are fine, Neve," Brad assured me immediately. "Harriet and Ruby are looking after them."

"What is it then?" I screamed, unable to contain my agitation any longer. "What's happened?"

"Neve, you mustn't return to Cranley. An accusation of

witchcraft has been made against you. An ecclesiastical committee has arrived at the behest of Reverend Snow. They will arrest you and force you to stand trial as soon as you return to Everly Manor."

"Oh, dear God," I moaned, unable to believe what I was hearing. "Who accused me? And why?"

"I don't know. Ruby's brother works at the inn and told her that three witch-hunters had taken rooms yesterday. Ruby came to tell me, thinking I might be able to do something to help."

I don't know what Brad expected, but it wasn't the hysterical laughter which bubbled inside me, making me laugh like someone who'd lost their mind. I couldn't stop, laughing until tears ran down my cheeks. Then they became real as sobs shook my whole body.

Brad looked taken aback, but Archie walked over, pulled me into his arms, and held me until the fit subsided and I slumped against him, feeling helpless and weak.

"We will work this out," he said to me as he looked into my eyes. "Do you hear me?"

I nodded, unable to speak, my eyes drawn to the door of the parlor. I thought I must be hallucinating, but Frances jumped to her feet with a squeal.

Jem stood in the doorway, his face pale at the sight of my tears. A smile that had been on his face only a moment ago was replaced by a look of fear as he inched into the room, no longer sure of his welcome.

I stepped out of Archie's embrace and went to Jem, pulling him against me with all the fierceness of a mother who was reunited with her child. Jem's arms went around my waist, his face pressed against my chest as he held me tight.

"I had to come," he mumbled. "I needed to be with you all. Please don't make me go back."

"Oh, Jemmy," was all I could muster before dissolving in tears again.

SIXTY-NINE

Night had fallen on London, ending a day of celebration and returning the jubilant masses to everyday reality. Hugo could see a few lights from his window, but, for the most part, the city was shrouded in darkness, the sky strewn with countless stars, which paled next to the crescent moon that shone like a beacon in the night sky. The prison was quiet, most people going to sleep to preserve their candles. Hugo had no candles. No one had brought him anything, and he had no money on him to pay for supplies. He'd been given a plate of cold mutton and bread, and a cup of ale for supper, but the food remained untouched, the smell of the meat turning his stomach.

Neve hadn't come. He couldn't blame her. She was probably too angry to even talk to him, and she had every right to be. His only wish was that she wouldn't come to the execution. He could face death with dignity if he were on his own, but if Neve were there, watching him with eyes full of love and pain, he would break down and cry like a child, unable to pull himself together and behave like a man. He'd always thought that he wasn't afraid of death, but he was. Not the moment itself, but the knowing what he would lose. He would never see his children grow up, or hold Neve in his arms again, smelling her sweet hair and hearing her intake of breath as he kissed her neck or slid his hand between her thighs. He would cease to exist, cease to matter to those he loved. They would forget him in time and move on, leaving him to burn in the Hell of his own making.

Hugo turned away from the window when he heard the scrape of a key in the lock. Surely it was too late for visitors. He strained to see in the dark, but with no candle, all he saw was a hooded figure entering his cell. The guard's lantern cast a pool of golden light onto his visitor, but the man's face—and it was definitely a man, judging by his height and the breadth of the shoulders—remained in shadow, hidden by the deep cowl.

"Ten minutes, ye hear?" the guard called as he locked the door, leaving the two men alone in the darkness.

"Archie is that you?" Hugo enquired calmly as he peered into the gloom. He was fairly certain that the person standing in front of him wasn't Archie; Archie wasn't given to such theatrics and would have revealed himself right away. But Hugo hoped to identify his visitor from the sound of his voice, if that's all he had to go on.

The man remained silent as he continued forward until he stood by the window. Hugo waited patiently; arms crossed, head cocked to the side, all senses on full alert. He couldn't begin to fathom the purpose of this nocturnal visit, but wasn't fool enough to believe it bode well for him. Friends didn't come cloaked under cover of darkness.

The man finally pushed back the hood of his cloak, the moonlight revealing the unexpectedly familiar features of his visitor. Hugo stared in astonishment, not bothering to hide his surprise.

"Hello, Hugo," Max said. A small smile played about his

moonlit face and his eyes glowed with amusement at having caught Hugo off-guard. "It seems we were destined to meet again."

A LETTER FROM THE AUTHOR

Huge thanks for reading *The Queen's Gambit*, I hope you were hooked on Neve and Hugo's epic journey. It concludes in book five, *Comes the Dawn*. If you want to join other readers in hearing all about my new releases and bonus content, you can sign up for my newsletter!

www.stormpublishing.co/irina-shapiro

If you enjoyed this book and could spare a few moments to leave a review that would be hugely appreciated. Even a short review can make all the difference in encouraging a reader to discover my books for the first time. Thank you so much!

Although I write several different genres, time travel was my first love. As a student of history, I often wonder if I have what it takes to survive in the past in the dangerous, life-altering situations my characters have to deal with. Neve and Hugo are two of my favorite characters, not only because they're intelligent and brave but because they're fallible, sensitive, and ultimately human. I hope you enjoy their adventures, both in the past and the present, and come to see them as real people rather than characters on a page.

Thanks again for being part of this amazing journey with me and I hope you'll stay in touch – I have so many more stories and ideas to entertain you with!

Irina

Printed in Great Britain
by Amazon